*The Alchemy of Desire*

# TARUN J TEJPAL

# The Alchemy
# of Desire

HarperCollins *Publishers* India
*a joint venture with*

New Delhi

HarperCollins *Publishers* India
*a joint venture with*
The India Today Group

Published by arrangement with
Macmillan Publishers Ltd UK

First published in India in 2005 by
HarperCollins *Publishers* India

**Second impression 2005**

**HarperCollins *Publishers***
1A Hamilton House, Connaught Place, New Delhi 110 001, India
77-85 Fulham Palace Road, London W6 8JB, United Kingdom
Hazelton Lanes, 55 Avenue Road, Suite 2900, Toronto, Ontario M5R 3L2
*and* 1995 Markham Road, Scarborough, Ontario M1B 5M8, Canada
25 Ryde Road, Pymble, Sydney, NSW 2073, Australia
31 View Road, Glenfield, Auckland 10, New Zealand
10 East 53rd Street, New York NY 10022, USA

Printed and bound at
Thomson Press (India) Ltd.

*For*
*my mother, Shakuntala;*
*my father, Inderjit;*
*and, always, Geetan*

BOOK ONE

*Prema: Love*

# A Morning Chill

Love is not the greatest glue between two people. Sex is.

The laws of school physics will tell you it is more difficult to prise apart two bodies joined at the middle than those connected anywhere near the top or the bottom.

I was still madly in love with her when I left her but the desire had died, and not all the years of sharing and caring and discovering and journeying could keep me from fleeing.

Perhaps I recall it wrong.

Strictly speaking I did not leave. Fizz did.

But the truth is she did – as always – what I wanted her to, what I willed her to. And I did what I did because by then my body had turned against hers; and anyone who has stretched and plumbed both mind and body will tell you the body, with its many nagging needs, is the true engine of life. The mind merely steers a path for it, or consoles it with high-sounding homilies when there is no path to be found.

The ravings of the puritans and the moralists are the anguished cries of those whose bodies have failed to find the road to bliss. When I see clergy – Hindu, Muslim, Christian – rail against the instincts of the body, I see men who are lost and angry and frustrated. Unable to locate the glories of the body, unable to locate the path to surpassing joy, they are resolved to confuse all other journeymen. Those who fail to find their sexual synapse set our mind and body at war against each other.

I agree there are the truly spiritual, just as there is the one-horned rhino, but they are few and far between and easily identifiable. For the rest of us, the body is the temple.

The truth is godhead is tangible.

Smellable. Tasteable. Penetrable.

The morning I woke up and felt no urge to slide down her body and inhale her musk I knew I was in trouble.

As always, we were sleeping in the small room overlooking the Jeolikote valley, on the pinewood beds hammered into being in a day by Bideshi Lal's scrawny young boys. Fading yellow chir planks. Straight lines. Not one flourish. Hard, fundamental, with absolutely no give. After years of sleeping on beds of string and plywood, we loved the sense of solidity these beds exuded. Lying on them, we felt less like urban flakes. Our bed was a single piece – what the carpenters called a kuveen bed, a bed-and-a-half. We would have preferred a king bed, with more space for roll, but the room was tiny and since we always slept close, bodies touching, anything more than a bed was redundant.

As every morning, the yellow curtains were drawn and the evenness of first light sat gently over the room. Only in the mountains, with all the windows open in the morning's first hour of sunless light, can you get this condition where the light within and without is exactly the same, and there is the perfect tranquillity of a fish-bowl when the fish do not move.

The world is cast in one colour. It is both fluid and frozen.

On the discolouring gnarled oak outside the window, the crested white-cheeked bulbuls were starting to dart about, still low on chatter. I sat half-propped on a broken pillow against the rough stone wall and looked out the bank of big windows at the wavy mountain opposite. A fresh skin of light green was beginning to grow where a landslide had raked an ugly gash two years before. When you looked at it through the heavy Minolta binoculars – focusing tediously with slow turns of the fingers – it had the ugliness of the new.

Ferns, grass, saplings were pushing out their first shallow claims. No layers, no depth. Like new buildings and new furniture and new clothes and new lovers; waiting for time, history, travail to etch them with worth. But the new skin allowed you to look at the mountain without flinching. Last year the open gash had drawn and repelled the gaze like the exposed wound on a beggar. Two seasons of drumming rain had worked their ministrations.

Without shifting my eyes I could take in the strings of grey woodsmoke curling from the floor of the valley like wiggly lines in a child's drawing of a mountainscape. And by shifting my head only slightly I could see Fizz asleep in her usual foetal position, curled away from me.

She wore only a round-necked T-shirt with a green slogan about saving trees etched in a sharp Helvetica typeface at the back. The image under the type was of a jagged designer tree morphing into a skull. One of those clever graphic things. The slogan declared: Kill a Tree, Kill a Man. Sometimes, when I rode her in slow frenzy and the shirt collapsed around her dipped shoulders, the words would begin to blur until all I could read was Kill Kill. It was an exhortation to run amok, and it added something to the moment.

The shirt was now scrunched up under her breasts, and by raising the thick blue quilt we shared, I could see the generous curve of her body. The wide flaring from the narrow waist, the fullest part of her, always capable of arousing me in an instant.

I looked at it for a long time, tenting up the quilt with my left hand. She did not wake. She was accustomed to me voyeuring on her all hours of the day and night. Like a dog that ceases to hear the footfalls of familiar servants, her skin had ceased to prickle at my staring. In fact there were occasions when I had in the pit of the night engaged with her body in all kinds of ways and she had not woken, not known of it the next morning. It spooked her each time I told her, the knowledge that she had been a participant in something she had no awareness of.

Her curly hair lay in roiled black masses over the white sheet – she never used a pillow, something to do with the angle of the neck and the threat of a double chin. She had beautiful hair and there was a time when just burying my face in it could make me heady. Many years ago, before she was eighteen, minutes after we had made love for the first time, she had stood in my tiny bathroom in Chandigarh looking into the grimy mirror above the sink, contemplating an irrevocable rite of passage, and coming up behind her I had buried my face in her rich hair and the novel smell of perfumed shampoo and the damp skin beneath had got me going again and in no time at all we were back on the mattress, amid the flotilla of books adrift on the terrazzo floor.

The second time had lasted one full stroke.

The first time had only been an entry.

Much later, when we could talk of these things, she had labelled it the double-dribble. It happened while I was watching a basketball game on television, and explaining to her the rules. She plucked the phrase out of my commentary and hung on to it. She said, Remember your first great double-dribble?

Ever after she used it to toy with me. And sometimes, after I lay finished and she was still frisky, she would cup herself in her hands and say, Don't you want to double-dribble?

And of course I always wanted to, and did.

But now I looked at her and felt nothing. Most mornings of my life with her I had woken nudging myself into a hardness against her softness. The memory of her smells filled me all hours of the day, and in those first moments of waking I would go in search of them. I would travel up and down her body, inhaling, inhaling, inhaling, hunting the secret source, the throbbing in the blood growing till it burst in a crescendo; then there would be the peace of slow panting, and the day ahead.

Today I felt nothing. Nothing but a vague affection as I looked at the two dimples on her lower back, which now lay ironed flat by the stretch of her curled pose. Small depressions on either side of her spine, a beckoning doorway into the deep line of her fullness.

I had never been able to look at Fizz dispassionately. In the beginning, for very long, there had been an aching, formless love. The love that does not look.

And then after the double-dribble afternoon on the floor of my room in Sector 9 there had been a relentless craving, a mounting need. The desire that does not see.

Like her I was naked beneath the T-shirt, the lungi unwound by the night. I tested myself with light fingers but there was nothing there. The night had again taken its toll of me. I was sated, drained of energy and desire. In all my life I had known this feeling only in the minutes after epic loving. After I had been consumed and consumed till there was nothing left.

Fizz had a phrase for those manic occasions when you scaled every final peak, fell off the other side, and passed out. Mightysatiety. The oblivion of maximum pleasure.

Last night it had happened unprovoked and in a vacuum again. And I had no idea when I had passed out.

Fizz turned in her sleep and threw an arm around my waist. I had an urge to push her away. Instead I put my hand on her hair and ruffled it slowly, lifting the bunched black curls and dropping them. Like her flawless skin, her hair was alive. It moved in the hand, as if caressing you back.

Nothing about Fizz was dull. Everything glowed. When I first met her I thought her smile could light up the world.

Ruffling her hair sent out the wrong message. It was the kind of gesture that always got her going. She sent her hand lower, looking for me. I wasn't there. She tried to create me. Something she had never failed to do. But I had been consumed too completely during the night and there was nothing left to create.

I love you, she mumbled in her sleep.

It was the first thing we said each morning.

I love you too, I said.

Her hand became more urgent. But there was nothing there. I

could read the growing puzzlement in her fingers, as they rolled, pulled, peeled, tugged. Familiar moves that called for a familiar response.

But he doesn't love me, she said.

He does, I said, caressing her hair.

My other hand lay on the notebook lying by my pillow. The tan leather felt smooth and warm. I had to fight the urge to crack the cover and dive into it.

Some respectable minutes later, I kissed her cheek and swung my naked legs out of the bed. I extricated my lungi from under the quilt and knotted it around my waist.

Come back here, she mumbled. Let me show it its true place in the world.

I need to pee, I said, and I was out of the room and onto the wooden floorboards, creaking my way to the upper terrace. I stood at the edge of the flower-bed in which no flowers grew and pissed into the roots of my favourite silver oak – it was higher than me now – and looked down at the waking valley.

🌿

Buses and trucks were beginning to move the mountains with their shifting gears. A deep grating, a high-pitched whine, and you knew another bend had been conquered by an ageing Tata carrier. In Jeolikote market, way below, across the span of the valley, you could dimly sense the first stirrings of the shops as men began to move and fires started to smoke. Traffic at Number One – the Y of the valley where one arm of the road went off to Nainital and the other came to us on its way to Almora – traffic at Number One was still lazy, the occasional Maruti creeping up from Jeolikote, pausing briefly at the sprawled Y, then swinging away to Nainital or sliding smoothly towards us.

The mist had not yet begun to move. At this time of the year it was always the slowest to awake. Another two hours and it would start to rouse itself from the valley floor. It would begin as a few tight white cotton balls, impossibly pure, and rapidly inflate to its full size till it filled the entire valley. At nine o'clock it would visit Beerbhatti and then begin the ascent to our house. By nine-thirty it would cut us off from the world, hiding from us even our own gate. By then we would be eating honey and toast in the unfinished study, debating between Scrabble and reading.

I suddenly felt the chill. I had come out without a shawl. And I had wet my feet in the heavy dew. The light was beginning to brighten and the world was getting its first shadings of the day. When I turned around, the other valley, the Bhumiadhar valley, its slopes fur-thick with pine and oak, lay in a greyer, more motionless zone.

This was one of the virtues of the house. It sat on a spur that divided two very different valleys. Two different worlds. One green and wild and silent and cold and dark; the other civilized and hum-drummy and green-brown and warm and bright.

You could match the valley to your mood, but mostly we sat at the edge of the Jeolikote valley, the warmer, brighter, more hum-drummy scape. Here, when you sat on the terrace, the mountain fell away at your feet, opening up the entire valley expansively: the wind-ing roads, the old red-roofed bungalows, the sprouting concrete constructions, the faraway roadside shops, the neatly painted govern-ment installations, the crawling cars, the pear and peach groves, the sweeps of pine and oak and silver fir, gifting us company but at a distance, gifting us movement but at a distance.

On the other side, the Almora road – running just below the boundary wall of the house – separated us from the Bhumiadhar valley, damaging both the view and the intimacy. The vista here was closed, dark, loaded with secrets. Thick oak and pine forests ran all the way to an unseen bottom; the few habitations and terraces that were there were tucked in tightly under the road, almost invisible from the house. It was from the heart of this valley that the wild ani-mals padded up, especially the panthers.

This view dragged you down with the irresistible melancholy of a Mohammad Rafi song. It would have had great charm, were it not marred by a terrible scratching of the soundtrack – for each time you began to be drawn in by the valley's seductive darkness, a moaning-grinding truck bisected the view and shattered the mood. Some days – the rain just over, the mist in separate fluffs, the late-afternoon sun catching everything at an angle – some days the Bhumiadhar valley became more beautiful than the other. But that was rare.

I took the stone ramp down from the terrace to the kitchen, feeling quite cold now. I rattled the warped pine door till the inside latch loosened, went in, turned on the gas and put water to boil in a pan. Bagheera padded behind me, up and down. Not expecting us to wake so early, Rakshas had not yet come up from the outhouse. I was glad of it. I was in no mood for banter or to listen to him singing his bhajans.

Entering the boarded-up interior of the house, I stopped at the dining room to adjust my eyes, and paused again in the decrepit living room, which was even darker. Then I found my way to the stairs, stepping gingerly over the gravel on the unfinished floor. I creaked up the third, fourth, fifth steps, stepped over the broken sixth, and tip-toed across the upper lobby and the veranda, then softly pushed open the door into our small room.

The old deodar chest – womb of chaos – sat by the far wall, dark and immovable, the rich wood lashed in brass strappings, a shiny lock hanging open-mouthed on its face.

She was still sleeping, the big quilt pulled in close. Only her nose and forehead were visible – the rest was a tangle of hair and cloth. The floor here was concrete – unfinished, unpolished – and we had chosen it so we could do what we wished, day and night, without worrying about floorboards creaking and sounds carrying.

I moved around the room noiselessly, untying the strings to open the curtains, smoothing over the chinks.

She woke just as I was pulling on a jacket and, putting out a hand, said, Where are you going? Come here please.

I went across and kissed her outstretched hand.

I'll be back in a minute, I said, The tea is on the gas.

But I did not come back up. I poured myself a large mug of strong, sweet tea, picked up a packet of glucose biscuits and went out the back door up the stone path onto the terrace. I desperately needed to clear my head. What was happening to me was surreal. If I did not make sense of it quickly, it would rip my life apart. One more night like the last and I was gone.

I suddenly felt the need to put even more distance between Fizz and me. I walked up to the next terrace, the house's highest point, where the water tank had been laid eighty years ago and from where you could see the upper reaches of Nainital, the sprawl of unplanned construction that led to the dominant spires and red roofs of St Joseph's School. We had put in a bench of red Kota stone after we acquired the place. It was broad enough for two people to lie on and scan the open sky. The bench was damp with the night's dew, so I squatted on it on my haunches, hugging my knees.

In fifteen years I had never felt so distant from Fizz. Even during our worst spats, our near break-up, the passion and need had survived. The maddening edge had never left us; it had kept us live crackers around each other. Even when we fell into a resentful silence our bodies would speak to each other, and the slightest touch would spark a frenzy that washed away all the canker.

Once at her aunt's, two days into a silent stand-off – the reasons were always vague and trivial – we had bumped into each other in the bathroom, washing hands at the sink before lunch. The smell of her skin, a glance in the mirror, and we fell to kissing. In an instant I had her up against the door, one hand reaching for the latch, the other for the zip of her jeans, while she chewed on my lips with her particular mad hunger. As always we fitted like a puzzle, wetness and hardness, flesh and hair, love and lust.

When we sat down to lunch the edge was back, hard and sharp as the knife in her aunt's hand slicing the mangoes. We rushed home wordlessly. This time the puzzle was figured and configured, fitted and refitted many times; and every last peak was climbed till we fell off the other side. Mightysatiety.

But now there was something afoot that was rocking me back on my heels.

I had made this trip with trepidation – a journey which, for the last two years, had been my favourite journey in the world. There had been both fear and longing when we set off from Delhi. The last two visits had been strange, so strange I could not even articulate to myself what was happening, leave alone tell anyone else. Since the last trip I had been torn between the urge to come right back up and to stay away forever. So I had left it to Fizz to make the call.

I had been preoccupied during the drive, and when we sat eating breakfast at Sher-e-Punjab dhaba at Bilaspur Fizz had asked, Is something worrying you?

I had replayed an old quip: I think it's dying.

I'll talk to it, she said.

In Hindi, I said, You have to talk to it in Hindi. This is the Hindi belt.

She said, But it doesn't understand Hindi – it's too full of old Ezra.

We had laughed.

But I had felt no sense of assurance at all. Yesterday, as night approached, that mix of dread and desire had begun to grow. Fizz, busy tending to her saplings, had not noticed anything, not even when we got into bed, two warm whiskies in each of us.

We were tired. There had been a tedious traffic jam in Moradabad, and we had been stranded at both the railway crossings. Fizz curled into me, her head over my left arm, her face in the crook of my chin.

When I did not run my hands over her body, she said, Do you want me to talk to it? I can talk to it in Hindi, you know!

I said nothing, grunting noncommittally, and she was asleep before another breath could be drawn. I lay awake, watching the last lights blink off across the mountains. Soon only the observatory's arc of illumination remained, and the squares of sky through the windows, jammed with pulsing stars. At intervals came the toc toc toc of the resident nightjar from the lantana bushes stuffed into the armpit of the terrace below the house. I had once spent many hours wandering around the bushes trying to spot it, but it seemed to nestle somewhere really deep.

At some point I disengaged my arm from under Fizz's head, and as always she rolled onto her other side and curled up into a ball.

I sat up against the wall, opened the tan notebook and fell head-long into it. Soon my eyes were straining against the rolling writing – the rushing wordwheels – in the dim yellow glow of the hurricane lantern. But I persevered, convinced if I could stay awake I would be able to fend it all off, outlast it. The chimera would shatter and fade, and it would be all over. I must have fallen asleep half-sitting because when it finally happened I was still in that position. It lasted deep into the night, and by the time it was over, hours later, I had fallen off so many peaks that I did not know how to put myself together again.

My legs began to hurt and I had to get off the bench to stretch them. I flung the last dregs of the tea down the slope – they vanished without trace – and stared at a vista I had fallen in love with from the moment I set eyes on it.

This house was meant to be our salvation, the final seal on our love and life. But now the intimations were bad. For the first time in my life with Fizz I had woken up without desire. Cold to her body stretched out beside me.

Something terrible was brewing. I could feel it in my bones. In the air.

The morning was cool and crisp, but no matter how much I shook my head I could not clear it.

My big back tooth began to ache. At least some things had not changed. I closed my eyes, waiting for the pulse of pain to settle into a steady throb.

I had no idea how my life was about to be torn apart, the only life that had ever mattered to me.

The sun was still just a warning glow beyond the observatory on the further peaks.

# Squalls

It had been raining heavily all day, and was still pouring when – six months after that cold morning – I stood at the lower gate with her, waiting for the bus from Bhowali that would take her down to Kathgodam, and perhaps away forever.

It was ironic. The broken stone berm beside which we stood was precisely where we had sat the very first time we had set eyes on the house. It was in a bend in the road, a little past the sanatorium when you came up from Jeolikote, poised at the first moment the house opened itself up to view. The berm lay below the house and caught it at an angle, giving it a particularly romantic mood.

It was not good to sit on any more. It was full of jagged edges and unsteady. It had been hammered by a runaway truck a year before. The masonry had shattered and the stones had come loose. The truck had hung, one wheel over the abyss, for days before a crane came up from Haldwani and yanked it back. The owner, a Sikh, after roundly slapping the driver and helper, had distributed laddoos and said, God is kind. It could easily have been at the bottom of the valley.

We were standing close together, shoulders barely touching, under the big green J & B umbrella we had once been gifted at the only polo match we had ever attended in Delhi. When we unfurled it for use we put on airs and said things like, Wonderful chukker, what? And, Dafedar iss pony ka gaand mein thoda jaldi daalo!

But today we had walked down from the house wordlessly. She had turned down all my offers to take her to the railway station. It was a dangerous signal, without precedent. It told me I had pushed things so far that I no longer held the prerogative of making or breaking the relationship. The dam had burst. The water would find its own level. My control of the sluice gates had no meaning now.

In fifteen years of being with Fizz I had never ever failed to pick up and drop her at bus-stands, railway stations, cinemas, offices, hospitals, every every where, each each time. It went beyond concern. It was closer to paranoia. I lived in dread of something happening to her, and in a self-preservatory way knew my life would fall apart if she ever went out of it.

Once, in our first year together when we were still in college, she had to go to Nahan for a family wedding. It was three hours by road from Chandigarh. I wouldn't let her go alone. We took a rickety Himachal State Roadways bus, sat close together and talked without pause all the way, unperturbed by the endless halts, the early monsoon mugginess, the flies, the dust, the inquisitive stares.

At one point the route ran through the state's sleepy backroads. Narrow trafficless country lanes, just below the foothills, shaded by kikars and neems and banyans, winding through glistening green paddy fields, patrolled by officious naval-white egrets. Immediately we ran under a thick grey cloud fighting to hold in its swollen belly; a cool breeze rich with rain struck up and swept through the broken windows of the creaking bus.

Like sand under a shower, the trauma inside the packed carrier washed off in an instant, and sweat turned minty on agitated skins. All conversation ceased. Even the engine sounds of the bus seemed to fade. As if on a director's cue everyone lifted their faces and closed their eyes, offering themselves up for deliverance.

For a godless man it was a religious moment. I held her hand in mine – camouflaged by her leather handbag – looked at her shining half-smile, her thick hair blown back from the perfect cheekbones, and was happy beyond any singing of it.

Of course when we reached Nahan – up the Himalayan foothills – I wanted to walk her as close to her destination as possible. Deliver her unto her doorstep. We set off up the slope to her aunt's government bungalow, and so sunk were we in conversation that her aunt was literally upon us before Fizz spotted her.

Oh, hello, massi! Fizz burst out.

And without breaking step I turned on my heels and walked back down the slope to the bus-stand, not daring to turn and look back even once. Those were early days; she was barely seventeen and I didn't want her in trouble with her family. The three-hour ride home lasted a lifetime, and when I got back to my room it was late and in the evening light the piles of books on the floor were like fingers of rebuke. That night I was consumed by an unfinished air, as if pulled away from a half-seen film.

Next morning I was at the Sector 17 bus-stand before dawn, checking my bicycle into the parking lot. I dreamed of her and writing all the way up – all I did in those days. Without her by my side the winding country lanes lacked magic. I walked up the slope and at the top, where the hill opened out into rows of houses, I sat at the corner tea shop, ordered up an omelette and asked the gnarled hillman bubbling endless tea in a stunningly black pan the whereabouts of her uncle's house.

Tiny as a sparrow he was chanting, Har Govinda Har Gopal! Har Govinda Har Gopal!

The fat water engineer? he said, between chants, Well, if you want to meet the fat engineer and his fat wife you will have to wait because they have both just gone down to the mandi to buy the cheapest vegetables possible. You know the government sorts who want everything for free. But to do anything they first levy a charge.

I said, I have to deliver something.

He looked at me. I held up the copy of *A Farewell to Arms* I was reading.

He said, There is a sign on the gate with a fierce dog painted on it. Just go in. The dog is like them – fat and lazy – and will bite only if he is paid to.

I put three rupees on the cracked wooden table and said, You don't like fat people?

He said, No, sahib, everything should be fitting. Your house should not be bigger than your heart; your bed not bigger than your sleep; and your food not a grain more than your stomach.

He hopped off his perch next to the hissing stove – so birdlike – scooped up the money and continued, Men should not put an ounce of extra weight on mother earth. The earth is already overburdened. Overburdened by flesh, overburdened by greed and overburdened by sorrow. When the balance tips over we will have apocalypse. The world is what it is because men have forgotten the difference between right and wrong.

He did not look at me while saying all this, but kept working: rinsing the small lined glasses and the scratched plastic plates, and throwing in more water and sugar and milk into the continually brewing pan.

So walk lightly, my friend, he said, And listen to your heart and not your mind. The world has been ruined because it listens too much to the mind. Har Govinda Har Gopal!

I found the house easily and boldly swung open the gate with its ugly tin-plate warning of an Alsatian, and went right in. The old tea-man was right. There was a fat golden Labrador sleeping under a wicker table on the veranda, its head stretched out on its paws. It looked at me with one inquisitive eye and didn't move a muscle.

I rang the bell. It played out 'Jingle Bells' at length. A bratty-looking boy opened the door. He was wearing tight red nylon shorts and a faded Bruce Lee sweatshirt, with King of Kung Fu printed on it.

What do you want? he said, pulling out gum from his mouth with his right hand and stretching it past his fat nose.

I want to meet Fiza.

Why? he said, through clenched teeth, pulling the gum out further.

I have to give her a book.

I showed it to him. It had Catherine Barkley on its front cover, dressed in her nurse's uniform. And there was a small ambulance in the background.

Is it a storybook?

I pointed to the ambulance.

What is it?

It is about small boys who swallow the gum they are chewing and what doctors have to do to them.

He was eyeing me now, motionless.

Show me your navel, I said.

He lifted his Bruce Lee sweatshirt with his left hand and man-oeuvred the gum back into his mouth with the right. It was an ugly, protuberant navel.

Another six months, I said, And they will have to cut your buttocks open and scrape out the gum.

His face crumpled.

Go call her quickly and I'll teach you a trick that might save you.

Fizz walked in, looking luminous.

I've brought your book, I said, holding up Hemingway.

Her face broke into a smile that lit up the world. Her smile was always artless, a straight response to some stimulus. Never a carrier of hidden meanings, silent conspiracies, secret instructions. When something made her happy she smiled, and the world lit up.

You are crazy, she said.

Good crazy? Bad crazy? I asked.

Really good crazy! she replied, grinning.

It was the second time I was seeing her like this: wearing the crisp white kurta-pyjama she slept in, her hair worn loose to her shoulders, her skin glowing. She could have walked out of those lavishly illustrated fairy-tale books we read as children – the white flowing gown replaced by the kurta-pyjama. She was beautiful beyond any singing of her.

Where? I said.

The house is full of people, she said, They'll all start waking up and coming down now.

She was unusually calm. This was another thing I was to learn about her over the years. While she was no radical, no natural breaker of rules, no seeker of the bold statement, she was in her own serene way uncaring of convention and others' opinions.

There must be an empty room, I said. And added, with an eye on the boy, Where I can explain the book to you.

And him? she said.

Bruce Lee, come here, I said.

I took him into a corner of the room.

OK, here's the trick. You go right now, sit on the pot, stick a finger tightly into each ear, and say Leeeeeeee loudly. Repeat it one hundred and one times. Then check. If the gum isn't out, repeat it one hundred and one times again.

He went off, putting the gum ball back in his mouth.

Where have you sent him? she said.

To practise Kung Fu.

I looked around. The room was full of the bric-a-brac of every Indian middle-class drawing room: plastic flowers, ceramic figurines of gods, sandalwood elephants marching in a line, shabby dressed-up furniture, family pictures in crude frames. I looked around for exits. There were way too many doors. It was the central well of the house. We needed to get out of here. I was dying to hold her, smell her under the ear.

Where's your aunt's bedroom? I said.

Her face was flushed. The moment of derangement was close. That is how it was with us when we were near each other. Mostly we could barely talk. The need to make contact choked everything else.

Right there, she said, nodding towards the far wall.

The moment we were in I had bolted the door and pulled her into my arms. The room was dark and my mouth was everywhere and the white cotton she was wearing was crisp and thin and I was firm and insanely in love and she was wet and impossibly beautiful and our hands were potters and our flesh was clay; and then there were voices outside the door and she was on the edge of the bed and I could smell her love and I could taste her love and I could hear her love and my love was straining for her love and then I was where I belonged and where I wanted to live and where I wanted to die and the world was a slip of skin and the world was two slips of skin and the world was only slips of skin and the world was liquid and the world was tight and the world was a furnace and the world was moving and the world was slipping and the world was exploding and the world was ending and the world was ending and the world had ended.

When we could hear again, there was someone calling for Fiza from the living room. Only a few minutes had passed.

Get out this way, she said, flinging open a mesh window with a wide ledge.

I jumped out and landed in a flower-bed of scraggly red roses. With a confident step, without looking back, I walked towards the gate. As I unlatched it, from a corner of the house out floated a determined Leeeeeeee . . .

On my way down I passed the fat water engineer and his fat wife struggling up the slope. They were carrying baskets full of vegetables whose green ears flapped about. They did not notice me as I floated down the road, riding the thermals of profound happiness.

Nearly an hour had passed and there was no sign of a bus from Bhowali. The rain was gusting now and the J & B umbrella was inadequate protection. Below the knees our trousers were soaked, and one shirtsleeve each was drenched. The bus service was tardy because it was a Sunday evening; the ceaseless downpour had perhaps added to the delay. Of course there was no fear of missing the overnight train to Delhi because it left Kathgodam at nine p.m. And though it was prematurely dark due to the thick curtain of rain, it was only six. She had insisted on leaving with time to spare.

There was no electricity – it always blew in the first minutes of a squall – and the house was a dark silhouette across the road. The trunk of Trishul, our huge deodar towering over everything, seemed blacker than ever. The Bhumiadhar valley at our feet was sinister, resonant with the footfalls of running rain; looking down at it you expected some giant prehistoric animal to come ambling up its forested paths.

Yet in the peculiar soothing way pouring rain works in the mountains – amid the slopes and greenery – there prevailed an air of motionless calm and deep silence.

We hadn't exchanged a word all this while. I wanted to say something, something conciliatory, something commonplace, anything, but no word came unstuck. The fact is my head, having reeled for so long with such a jumble of feelings and thoughts as could never come together in a coherent word, had finally frozen over.

Her face was set. The fine wedge of chin, the fine nose, the perfect wide mouth, all still as a sheet of glass. The eyes told a story. They were red-rimmed and puffy from a lack of sleep and an excess of crying.

It was ironic. For years I had jibed at her – because she had developed a penchant for doing it often – that her crying was only genuine when it led to rain. And now it had been pouring since the previous evening, platoons of rain marching in a military clamour up and down the iron roof and shooting in through the glassless windows. And she had sobbed through it all.

I think, standing there amid the weeping skies, she had finally run dry.

Twenty-four hours is a long time.

Six months is a long time.

It was six months since the morning when I woke in our room overlooking the Jeolikote valley and felt no desire. It was six months since I had stood looking down at the valley, sated and frightened by the night that had passed, fearing for our future.

The six months had gone very badly. We had put distances between us we had never imagined possible.

Our private mythology after every spat had been that we were like a snugly zipped-up jacket: occasionally we scrapped and came half unzipped; on specially awful days the zip opened all the way down. But it was always held together by the clasp at the bottom, and then it took only a moment to zip it back all the way up. Warm and tight. But in the last six months we had not just opened wide the jacket of our relationship, we had taken scissors and cut it into two distinct parts.

Let it be said, it was entirely my fault.

With each day I found myself becoming a different man; with each day my olfactory senses turned tail on me. For fifteen years the smells of her body had defined my life. The whiff of a fold of her skin would get me started and derail me from anything I was doing. Reading, working, watching television, talking on the phone.

But when we returned from the mountains after that morning six months before, my nostrils had begun to jam. I tried smelling her skin, behind her ears, in her bristled armpit, in the moist undercurve of her breasts, in the dip of her navel, in the fern of her abdomen, in the gullies between her legs, in the dark ravine of her hips, in the back of her knees, in the tight loopholes between her toes. I tried smelling everywhere, but it was no good.

And it was not only my nostrils. A switch seemed to have been thrown on all my senses. Sucking on her flesh, any part of her flesh, could work me into a frenzy. There had been occasions when I had fallen over the edge just sucking her calves. But now her skin had no taste. Like chewing on gum hours after it has lost its flavour. My eyes were failing me too. All my adult life, morning and night, watching her change had been a favourite pastime. A mere glimpse of her naked waist or thigh would arouse me. But now I kept my head buried scrupulously in the notebooks while she peeled off her clothes in our bedroom and extricating the panty from her jeans smelled it for unwanted odours, before flinging it into the washing basket.

It's not as if we stopped making love immediately. Like a swing that keeps moving long after the last child has dismounted, the momentum of the years ensured I kept reaching for her. But it was passionless coupling. Some hand, some mouth, some of the old in–out in–out.

We fell off no peaks. In fact, we failed to climb any.

In a few weeks Fizz began to worry. Soon she found she was taking the initiative and I was just going along with it. We had played these games in the past, alternating the aggressor, but this was different. I had never been able to play cool once she would begin to travel her mouth on me. Now she had to struggle to make me ready. Finally one night she fell back exhausted as I lay propped against the bed watching her strive. In the lamplight her mouth glistened wetly, but it was her eyes that held me. They were confused and resentful.

I am sorry, I said, not looking at her.

What's happening? she said, not looking at me either.

Just let it be. It'll be OK. We'll be OK, I said.

I don't think she slept that night. She was shaken. This was alien to her. My ceaseless desire for her was one of the grand verities of our life. It was the fact that anchored everything else for her – her work, her friendships, her relationship with her family. When anything jarred her or failed her, she could return safely to the cocoon of my endless desire. I knew my keening need of her made her strong.

But desire is an unknowable thing.

I don't think she slept that night, but I did. I was turning dangerously cold. I felt less and less passion, and I was less and less perturbed by the anguish I was causing her. I was too busy wrestling with the strange demons that were swirling inside my head.

Soon after Fizz decided we should go up for a few days to First Things and all would fall into place. I wanted to go and did not want to go. Her taking the decision made it easy for me. So we left before dawn on Saturday morning and drove up almost wordlessly, Shammi Kapoor songs playing cheerfully on the car stereo all the way up. I cannot say what thoughts raked her, but the truth is I hardly once thought of her or us. I was focused totally on what was waiting at the top of the hill.

The trip was a disaster. We could not find the misplaced key to our bodies, and along with that we seemed to have lost the key to our conversation. Fizz made many attempts, launching fresh sorties with the things we loved – trees, birds, books, sex, films, relationships, music. I tried to respond, but my mind was elsewhere. On Saturday night it happened again – with a preternatural force – and when I woke on Sunday morning I was even more detached.

I fell into my monosyllabic worst, sounding like our nightjar, toc toc toc; and Fizz became sullen – the continuing rejection now bringing on anger.

Inevitably, after breakfast, in the goat shed, we got into a screaming rage about the quality of the wood used for the doors. Young pine that was already beginning to warp. I blamed her for bad detailing; she told me I was a lazy woolly-headed asshole. I called her too cavalier; she said I was the worst kind of self-centred carper.

In embarrassment the carpenters took an early lunch break and moved out of earshot. Silence fell. The only sound was Rakshas chanting his hymns as he worked near the waterpoint.

Instead of Monday morning, we came back on Sunday evening itself. Which was just as well because who knows what wreckage another night would have yielded. We drove back even more silently than we had driven up, playing Rafi's weepy numbers now, and reached Delhi late at night, having negotiated homicidal drivers, treacherous roads, and screeching trucks and buses. Once or twice I was seized by the temptation to let go and sail with a sweet smack into a pair of blaring headlights.

That would end everything gloriously, not with the dereliction that was beginning to creep up on us.

Things just kept worsening after that trip. She would come back from her interviews in the afternoon and I would be sprawled on the broken sofa in our tiny study, buried in the notebooks, struggling to decipher the wordwheels, making notes. She would go into the kitchen, brew tea for both of us, leave mine on my worktable and go out on the terrace with hers to check the plants.

How did the interview go?

OK.

Lunch?

Had it at Maharani Bagh.

What's happening with ms meanqueen?

Nothing.

Toc toc toc. Enough to destroy any relationship.

Of course she couldn't ask me about my work. That was forbidden. She always had to wait for me to talk about it. It was an old unchanging rule of the game. At no time was it to be flouted: not atop the peaks of passion, not in the caves of intimacy.

But I knew she knew I was doing no work any more. One morning, emerging from the bathroom, I had glimpsed her checking my table for any signs of fresh writing. I had said nothing. It hadn't mattered. I felt nothing. Earlier it would have driven me into a rage.

The days were just about manageable, but the evenings and nights were tricky. We tried to get past the evenings by never being in – we would catch a film or meet up with friends for dinner. We were both drinking a lot. She would put down three-four whiskies most nights, and I was doing five-six. Conversation would be perfunctory; we would literally stagger around brushing our teeth and shedding our clothes.

I was glad for that. There was no way I could handle a serious conversation or, worse still, an inquisition. It had always been the case when I was trying to work something through – I would wait till everything was catalogued and indexed in my head before opening the subject with her. Then I would take her input to fine-tune it all. But this time it was pure detachment. Her shadow hardly ever passed through everything that was filling my head.

It was a strange and sad time. And I behaved badly through it all. She tried her best. After a few forays into sulking and withdrawal and anger – all of which yielded nothing from me: I had turned cold as fish – she began to try. Try to reconnect with me, try to humour me, try to seduce me, try to understand what was really happening. But if I didn't know it myself, how could she?

In fact it made things worse. Her desperation, her naked need, for the first time in my life, made me recoil from her. After a few months of leaving me alone and waiting for me to crawl back (in the past I had done so within days), her resolve began to crack. I was, of course, grateful to be left alone. I could hear her moving about the house. Cooking, dusting, cleaning the bathroom, mopping the floor, watering her plants, listening to sixties music.

Most often the television would be on, and I could hear the mock-grave tone of news being intoned. As the conversations in our life petered out, she had rapidly become a news addict. It seemed she was filling up the sudden gaps in her life with all the unfurling garbage of the universe. The news channel has to be the strangest way of making yourself feel relevant in the modern world. There is an earthquake in Puerto Rico, it gives my life meaning. Some standard-issue American lunatic guns down children in a town in Texas, it gives my life context. Some sad politicians slag off each other for the benefit of the camera, I feel involved. The faux urgency of the news voice irritated me no end. And Fizz tried to use the newscasts like a quiver of arrows to breach my armour.

She would burst in through the narrow study door and say, They are talking about a possible war with Pakistan.

India has won by a run.

The prime minister has been charged in a bribery scam.

Lady Di's having it off with her bodyguard.

Superman's flying past your window.

Demi Moore called for you.

Toc toc toc.

Toc toc toc.

There wasn't an arrow in the world that could pierce my carapace. Sometimes while walking out to the terrace to catch a breath of fresh air I would pass her slumped in the love seat in the sitting room listening to music and staring vacantly, and something in me would catch. And then she would look at me with her mourning eyes, and the moment would be gone and I would carry on.

As she sank into despair, she scrabbled for all the old keys, desperate for the one that would unlock the door.

She played the music: Beatles, Doors, Dylan, Louis Armstrong, Ella Fitzgerald, Neil Diamond, Simon and Garfunkel, K. L. Saigal, S. D. Burman, Geeta Dutt, Kishore Kumar, Mukesh, Rafi, Asha Bhonsle. Ragtime, qawwalis, the Brandenburg Concertos, Beethoven's Ninth, Mozart's Fortieth.

She pulled out the books and piled them on our bedside: Kafka, Joyce, Greene, Steinbeck, Miller, Naipaul, Pound, Eliot, Larkin, Auden. *Catch-22, Slaughterhouse-Five, The Great Gatsby, All About H. Hatterr, The Ginger Man, Zorba the Greek.*

She went and rented the films and, as I walked in and out of the room, played them on our video player: *Roman Holiday, Bicycle Thieves, The Sting, Chinatown, Amarcord, Ran, Spellbound, Goopy Gyne Bagha Byne, Aparajito, Pyaasa, Half Ticket, Jaagte Raho, Abhimaan, Jaane Bhi Do Yaaron.*

She pulled out her white kurta-pyjama, got into it and loosened her hair.

She wore only a T-shirt and bent in front of me.

She knelt on the edge of the bed naked.

She squatted on her heels in front of her cupboard naked.

She read Nancy Friday in bed and put her hands between her legs.

She left the day's panties hanging on the hook behind the bedroom door.

She made her sheet rub and rustle once the lights were off.

She trimmed her hair in front of the mirror where I could see.

She left the bathroom door ajar so I could hear the sound of her piss raining in the bowl.

No key turned in the door.

Perhaps none existed any more.

I would be unfair to myself if I said I did not try. I did, even if desultorily. But desire is a curious thing. If it does not exist it does not exist and there is nothing you can do to conjure it up. Worse still, as I discovered, when desire begins to sink, like a capsizing ship it takes down a lot else with it.

In our case it took down the conversation, the laughter, the sharing, the concern, the dreams and nearly – the most important thing,
the most important thing – and nearly the affection too. Soon my
sinking desire had taken everything else down with it to the floor
of the sea, and only affection remained like the bobbing hand of a
drowning man, poised perilously between life and death.

More than once she tried to seize the moment and open up the
issue. She did it with a hard face and a soft face; she did it when I was
idling on the terrace and when I was in the thick of my work; first
thing in the morning and last thing at night.

We need to talk.

Yes.

Do you want to talk?

Sure.

What's happening?

I don't know.

Is there someone else?

No.

Is it something I did?

Oh no.

Then what the hell's happening?

I don't know.

Is there anything you want to talk to me about?

I don't know.

What do you mean you don't know?

I don't know.

What do you mean you don't know?

I don't know. That's what I mean – I don't know.

Toc toc toc.

All the while I tried to save that bobbing hand – of affection –
from vanishing. I felt somehow that if it drowned there would not be
a single pointer on the wide stormy surface to show me where our
great love had once stood. That bobbing hand of affection was a
marker, a buoy, holding out the hope that one day we could salvage

the sunken ship. If it drowned, our coordinates would be completely lost and we would not know where to even begin looking.

Even in my weird state, it was an image of such desolation that it made my heart lurch wildly.

For a long time, with her immense pride in herself – in us – she did not turn to anyone for help. Not friends, not family. For simply too long she imagined this was a passing phase, but then, as the weeks rolled by, through slow accretion the awful truth began to settle on her. By then she had run through all the plays of a relationship: withdrawal, sulking, anger, seduction, inquisition, affection, threat.

Logic, love, lust.

Now the epitaph was beginning to creep up on her. Acceptance.

Strangely I had not even bothered to think through what was happening. I knew things were a terrible mess, but I don't think I recognized they had assumed a terminal drift. With the stupid fixity that had marked my life, only one thing preoccupied me now. At some level, perhaps, I thought she would leave me alone and reorganize her life around me and my new concerns. More likely I did not even think about her and what was happening to her, so fixated was I on my new obsession.

Then one night she didn't come back. I was working in the study, reading the notebooks, making notes, and I fell asleep on the broken sofa – it was more comfortable for being broken because it provided more angles to sprawl. When she came in next morning, into the study, I said nothing. I was not even aware she had been away.

She did not go out at all that day. She shut herself in the bedroom and cried. Through the thin, single-brick walls of our barsati on the second floor, her sobs echoed around the house. Perfunctorily I called out to her a couple of times.

Don't do this.

Open the door.

This is really stupid. It's not going to help anything.

Fizz.

Fizz!

Fizz?

Having made the formal noises, I went back to the study. After some time her sobbing became a toc toc toc and I ceased to register it. Only when I went to the kitchen to get myself some lunch did I hear it again. I made more clinical appeals, but she refused to answer.

Much later, when night had fallen, I heard the bedroom door creak open. I did not venture out. There were sounds of activity in the bathroom: bristles on enamel, nose-blowing, gargling, flushing, water running, lathering, splashing, scrubbing, and then the hot whistle of the hairdryer. When two people in a house fall into a deep silence of disconnect, it is amazing how amplified every trivial sound becomes.

I heard the bathroom door open and the bedroom door shut; and when I went out a little later, seemingly to take a breath of fresh air on the terrace but mainly out of some last lingering curiosity, I saw her emerge looking wonderfully glamorous in black trousers and a stylish white cotton shirt. Her hair was blown full and she had – unusually for her – touched up her face. Only months before it would have reduced me to slavering and I would have been backing her up against the door, nuzzling under her ear. Now there was nothing.

I went in from the terrace, offering her an opportunity to say something to me. But through her kohl, through her mascara, she was sullen and sore-eyed, and she swept past me in a whiff of Madame Rochas, out the door and down the stairs, flicking on successive lights as she descended.

It was nine-thirty at night. In fifteen years she had never once left at this hour without me. When I went back to the study and slumped into the broken sofa, I could hear myself breathe.

I don't know what time she came back, but when I woke next morning her breath on the pillow next to me was heavy with stale whisky and her crushed clothes were scattered all over, the lacy bra climbing down the side of the chair like a creeper.

I asked her nothing. She said nothing. And the following night she again dressed up, and was gone. Next morning again there was the sour whisky smell on the pillow and a bra trained up the chair. Two days later I woke up to find her asleep with her clothes on.

Later I said to her, Fizz please be careful about drinking and driving.

She looked at me with so much hurt in her eyes that I turned away and went back into the study. I did not know what she was going about, and I didn't really care, but I did not want her to be unhappy. At the same time I could summon up nothing in me to make her happy. I hoped in a vague way that she would find her resources for happiness somewhere outside of me and removed from me. (The flawed nature of selfish love: to be charitable only when your needs are over.) But I really could do nothing.

About two weeks later her night-time excursions stopped, and just as I was getting used to them, the morning whisky vapours vanished. The clothes were back where they belonged, behind the bathroom door and in the bin.

Suddenly her friends began to show up at the house, all hours of the day. Her friends, not ours. Jaya, Mini, Chaya. Confident, tough women with aggressively independent lives, for whom Fizz was a lovable curio, something of an enigma. They saw her independence and they saw her need, and unable to understand how she harmonized them, they both mocked and envied her. Now their emphatic presences filled our small barsati. The air acquired a certain militancy – a kind of declaration-of-rights mood – that had always been alien to our living spaces.

I tried to keep to the study, avoiding confrontation. They would meet me accusingly, then huddle in the living room talking softly and relentlessly.

Sometimes they would pull the cane chairs out onto the terrace and sit there sipping Old Monk rum with Coke and arguing late into the balmy Delhi night. I never felt the need to eavesdrop but resented their occupation of the terrace. It took away my only airing option, as in the evenings after a day in the study I liked to walk up and down the terrace for an hour, clearing my head.

Always it seemed Fizz spoke the least. But her decision to open up the battle and enlist outside support was again a first. For fifteen years we had considered it sacrilegious that our love should ever be up for examination, correction or discussion by anyone else. No spat, no heartache, no misery had ever spilled out from our tight embrace to be scrutinized by friends or family.

But then we had never lived without desire either.

Sometimes when I walked through the living room and saw the statuesque Jaya leaning forward and speaking urgently to Fizz, and Fizz holding her chin in her cupped palms, her eyes following me, I felt this was another production aimed at wringing me. It was intended to highlight her injury and her need; and my obvious cruelty.

Jaya in fact in her brassy way – her big nose ring waving in my face – tried cornering me, demanding answers. But I snubbed her politely. I was not yet ready to bring the world into my life – mainly because I did not even know what I wanted from it. It didn't matter. Soon enough the Jaya–Mini–Chaya presence in our life began to dwindle, and then vanished altogether. So did the air of militancy and the declaration-of-rights mood.

Once again it was just the two of us.

Eventually Fizz swallowed her pride, her grief, and made fresh overtures. She asked one evening if we could go out for dinner, and I said yes. She suggested Daitchi in South Ex, but I didn't want to go anywhere that was littered with our memories. So we went to a toney new pizza place that had opened in the Defence Colony market, and took chairs opposite each other near the big plate-glass window.

She looked small and lost and vulnerable.

Had I just reached across and put my hand on her arm, she would have collapsed in relief and everything would have been instantly washed away. But I couldn't bring myself to do it. The shiny cold interiors – impersonal chrome and glass and ceramic tiles – helped me stay aloof. Passionate love does not play itself out in places like this. On the other hand Daitchi, with its musty interiors, fraying fabrics, slant-eyed waiters, wafting food smells and encrypted memories, might have fleetingly undone me.

We ate the crusty pizzas in silence, listening to the chatter of families around us.

Finally she said, What do you want to do?

I don't know.

Are you saying it's all over?

I don't know.

You want me to move out for a while?

I don't know.

I don't know. I don't know. I don't know.

Toc toc toc.

I couldn't even look at her.

When we went home and got into bed, without looking at me she said, Please come here.

I turned off all the lights, and in the glow of the street lamp flowing in through the ventilator I unwound my lungi and rolled on top of her.

She began to kiss me, using her tongue and teeth, trying to ignite an old magic. I turned my mouth away, offering my face. Her hands were all over, as she groped for the lessons of history. I moved aside onto one hip and put my hand between her legs. It skid in her readiness. I rubbed the slippery flesh. Her hips moved. She pulled me back on top of her. I had nothing to offer. Her hips moved again. I tried to push, closing my eyes, concentrating. But no amount of concentration can help hammer a noodle through a wall. She suddenly went stone still. Neither of us stirred. I was dead weight on her. She was almost not breathing. I rolled off. She did not move. I could see her eyes open, staring up as the mock galaxy stuck to the ceiling slowly lost its acquired glow.

I am sorry, I said.

She kept quiet.

It's got nothing to do with you, I said. The problem is me.

She didn't stir or say a word.

I lay politely for a few minutes, then got up and went into the

bathroom. I picked up the Dettol soap and washed her smells off my
hands.

When I went back she hadn't moved. She lay there, T-shirt around
her waist, hands laced under her head, staring at the ceiling, the half-
light of the street travelling over the slope of her belly and vanishing
into her hair. She was fighting back the deluge; she was not going to
abase herself in my presence any more.

I could think of nothing to say. I picked up my lungi, knotted it
around my waist and went into the study.

At the end of that week I packed a duffel bag, took a three-wheeler
to Old Delhi railway station and came up to First Things. Rakshas
was shocked to see me. Early in the morning, emerging from a
Maruti cab, and alone. It was the first time I had come up without
Fizz and it was perhaps a mistake for her to have let me.

By the time she called a week later at the thakur's shop, I had
moved even further away. In fact I must have sounded like a complete
stranger because when I took the phone she had nothing to say
except to ask after Bagheera and his anti-rabies shots.

She came four days later, driving up slowly in the Gypsy.

Rakshas was more courteous to her than ever. He sensed her
injury.

I think it took her very little time to discover that I not only
sounded like a stranger on the phone but had actually become one.
By then I had laid off Bideshi Lal and his gaggle of young boy-
carpenters, and the house had fallen eerily silent, amplifying our
chasm even more.

We did not touch; we barely talked. I spent my day in the
unfinished study with the notebooks, sitting on the Jaisalmer stone
ledge, staring for long stretches into the valley. She spent it wandering around the grounds in her grey tracksuit bottoms, brandishing
her orange-grip clippers, snipping and shaping her plants, Rakshas
trailing her with a look of concern and a sackful of manure.

The silver oaks – finger-small when we had bought them the year before from a derelict nursery on the Ramgarh road – had caught with the aggression of the native and were shooting up. Most of the other saplings were still struggling.

The semul near the lower gate, after an inspiring summer flourish, had turned black in the winter frost and died. The six gulmohar and amaltas saplings, bought from the Jor Bagh nursery in Delhi, had not even declared themselves in earnest, announcing their loyalty to the heat of the plains by wilting swiftly.

The peepul near the front gate, transplanted from a flowerpot on our Delhi terrace, was hanging in by a thread, a tightly curled bright green shoot heralding its intent. The banyan, the length of a small hand, again transplanted from Fizz's Delhi pots, hung in limbo. Too tough to die; too proud for haste. The Chinese bamboo – picked from a Hapur nursery – was gaining no height, instead spreading like a bush. But the jacaranda and kachnar – bought from the Haldwani foothills and planted along the pathway that led up to the house – were green with sap and hope.

The shisham – another Fizz–Delhi child – was leafy too and running tall, but its trunk was so slender that we worried for it. We wondered if it would hold once we took away the bamboo stick holding it in place. Surprisingly, a rash of mango saplings, from Jeolikote, had caught on the lower slope in a burst of dark-green leaves; then there was the increasing promise of a casually planted tun and, surprisingly, a jamun on the path behind the house.

The tree to watch was a weeping willow near the tap. Fizz had plucked a sprig from Naukuchiyatal and jammed it in, and it had begun to immediately assert itself.

We stayed out of each other's way and left Rakshas, now cook-caretaker-mediator, to engineer the bridges of food and tea that allowed us to sit together. Rakshas was in his sixties and had only one arm. When he was a child, gathering firewood with his siblings in the forest, a panther had jumped him and taken his left arm in its jaws. His two older sisters had immediately grabbed the seven-year-old's right arm and right leg and refused to let go.

Just as the panther was planning to mop up the rest of him, his oldest sister, fifteen-year-old Rampiari, had with a blood-curdling scream jumped the panther and stuck her wood-cutting machete into its head. The panther's eyes had apparently popped out in surprise and pain, and it had leapt back in fright. Plucking the little boy's arm out in the process. But it wasn't over for the terrified animal, for Rampiari then charged it with another shriek. The shocked panther dropped the dripping arm and shot off like an arrow, Rampiari's machete stuck in its head like the flowing crest of a Khaleej pheasant.

The young Rakshak – defender: that was his name then – survived, left with a pointy six-inch stump of tight, glistening skin that he could wiggle and rotate with great energy. When he spoke animatedly or sang aloud he held his right hand still by his side and waved his stump like a conductor's baton. The locals giggled that the stump had over the years provided great pleasure to the village women.

It was plausible, for he was rangy with a classically handsome peasant's face. Strong jaw, strong nose, unexpectedly fair skin and a bushy moustache. Even in his sixties his skin had not collapsed, and he walked like an army man. There was nothing he could not do, from chopping, cleaning and cooking to fixing taps and fuses, and hammering in doors and windows. He had a spectacular native gift for construction and geometry: masonry, tin, wood, plinths, beams, angle, plumbing, piping, wiring. Each time the workers hit a road-block they instinctively turned to him.

He would say, Maaderchod! Are you the artisan or am I?

It seems he had been terrific at sports in school, playing centre-forward in the football and hockey teams, and bowling and batting on the cricket field with great ferocity. Even in his sixties his arm was packed with power. I could not hand-wrestle him down with both my hands. He did not study beyond class eight, but the school kept him on for many years to milk his athleticism. He was strong enough to out-punch everyone else, becoming a literal dervish once inflamed. At some time in school, in tribute to the phantom limbs he appeared to have working for him, he was named Rakshas, a many-armed demon.

He even developed the temperament of one. Rage broke in him like a flash-flood and then he would roundly abuse – even assault – those around him. One moment he would be squatting calmly, supervising the work, the next he would have leapt to his feet, caught the errant worker by his neck and sent him flying with a clip to his ear and a volley of abuse, Maaderchod! Gaandu! Big as a motherfucking camel and you can't pull a straight line!

Everyone took it because of his age, his reputation and the fact that he was almost always right. Also, he had his tender moments in the evening, when he would put his arm around the workers, give them a drag from his chillum and a cup of chai and impart the wisdom of his years.

Fizz and I were not spared his scorn.

To our faces he would only say, Arre, you won't find this in any book in the world!

But just out of sight and within earshot he would say, They wipe their asses with paper, they try and understand the world through paper. How can they ever know the language of the earth? How can they know the secrets of soil? Tell me, would you ever wipe your ass with paper? Better to die than be such a fool!

He always trashed us through our toiletry failings.

Tell me, he would say to the congregated workers, If you sit on a chair and shit, can you ever void yourself completely? Arre, you sit on a chair to meet your friends and your father-in-law. To eat in a hotel. To give an exam. Can you crap sitting on a chair? You do that for a lifetime and you're bound to be left full of shit! You've seen how constipated city people look? The trash the white man left behind!

If he was upset with a worker he would say, What's wrong with you? You wiped your ass with paper today?

Rakshas lived in the crumbling outhouse near the gate, all by himself, fiercely independent. His wife had died many years ago, and though his daughters-in-law were scattered in the villages around, he could not bear to live with any of them. All four of his sons were in the army, strapping men who seemed to fear their father more than any enemy.

A resolutely optimistic man, Rakshas too got infected by the maudlin mood created by Fizz and me. He began to hum sad songs even during the day. Rakshas had a pattern: religious and sad songs at daybreak and twilight, and happy Hindi film numbers from the fifties and sixties the rest of the time. He did not have a particularly sweet voice, but now I was glad for his constant humming. It broke the melancholy of the house.

When he was not following Fizz around he took to sitting at the waterpoint, both valleys stretched beneath him, and full-throatedly singing the Ramdhun that Gandhi had made famous during the freedom struggle.

> Raghupati Raghav Raja Ram, patit pawan Sita Ram;
> Ishwar-Allah tero naam, sabko sanmati de bhagwan.

He intoned the secular hymn in different registers, filling the valley, sending us a message, his stump rotating slowly. But a chant that had once moved millions failed to move me; and Fizz hardly needed anything to deepen her anguish.

Five difficult days after she arrived, one evening a violent squall hit the mountain. The sun had set when a brisk breeze struck up. Soon it began to rattle and buzz the pines and oaks. I was up the spur, absently sitting on an old deodar stump. I don't know where Fizz was, but I could see Rakshas below me on the bench by the waterpoint. Snatches of his chanting had been floating up to me for the last hour.

Now suddenly the only sound was the wind running on countless feet among the branches, the leaves, the grass, spreading the word on what was coming. The undergrowth began to babble in a dozen tongues. No Hitchcockian music can create the tension of a presaging wind in the mountains.

Instinctively I stood up and when I looked down Rakshas was standing on the bench and, holding his right hand above his eyes in a telescopic shield, scanning the mountain peaks. And as I followed his gaze I saw the muscular grey-black clouds heaping up, layer upon towering layer, down the entire length of the valley. They were apocalyptic in their menace and size. Soon they would press down hard on the peaks and on us. The hills darkened rapidly as I watched. He turned to me and shouted. The forcing wind carried the words away in the other direction, but his one waving arm spoke clearly.

I hurried down the steep pine-needle covered path, and by the time I bent through the slack in the barbed wire the wind had become wet – the warning spray on the beach before the wave strikes.

Rakshas had vanished, presumably to drag in the chairs and clothes, and to lock and latch windows and doors. Bagheera was tearing around the kitchen quadrangle in paroxysms of fear and defiance, barking at the screaming wind and lowering clouds. A window was banging steadily on the other side of the house. Someone got to it and the noise stopped. The sheet-iron roof was waking, stretching itself with creaks and groans. Soon it would be moving at a gentle trot; and then as the raging winds crept under its skin it would begin to gallop in every direction. Bideshi Lal and his gaggle of pimply boys and all their hammering and banging would soon be on test.

The lubricated wind, moist and relentless, was beginning to buffet me, filling out my shirt and making it difficult to keep my balance. I hurried down from the waterpoint to the upper terrace, to the concrete slab we had laid when we had bought the house, and sought shelter in the lee of our unfinished bathroom.

To look down the valley from here was to see a landscape of terrible beauty and terror. An ominous greyness had descended, as the massing black clouds killed the day. Summer and late summer squalls were not unusual in Gethia, but mostly they struck at midday and without rain. Just tearing screeching winds that knocked things off their perches and pushed you around. In the clear light of day a dry squall is only a briskly chaotic thing; in fading light, accompanied by thunderous rain clouds and howling winds, it is a fearsome and other-worldly affair.

As I watched, every tree and every blade of grass on every visible slope was in anarchic motion. Swaying, rustling, tossing, turning. Without seeing it you knew every living thing in that sprawling valley was in a frenzy, ushering itself and everything it valued indoors, and into nooks and crannies where a reasonable stand could be made against the marauding wind.

Goats, dogs, horses, cows would bed tonight with their masters and mistresses. The thick lantana bushes beneath the house would cocoon a thousand birds – the nightjar sleeping feather-to-feather with the bulbul and the thrush. A million moths would flatten themselves inside hollow tree trunks, and prepare for a hungry night. Many hundred families would move their lips in practised prayer as they hunkered down under their musty quilts and hoped their roofs would not abandon them in the dead of the night, departing with the screaming winds.

Having given sufficient warning, the rain struck with the fury of a boxer in the first round. Fist-sized drops landed like a flurry of blows, banging on the tin roof, splattering on the concrete terrace and stinging where they hit me. In the ten seconds it took to cross the terrace to the bedroom, I was soaked to my underwear.

Rakshas was downstairs in the kitchen, squatting on his haunches, lighting up the hurricane lanterns. The lights had blown with the first powerful gust, well before the rain had come. The men at the power station always took this pre-emptive action to avoid tempting the nature gods. Tomorrow morning they would try and switch it on, fail to do so, then trudge around the hills making repairs.

Rakshas was boiling ginger tea, its pungent aroma cut by the stench of the kerosene being poured into the lanterns. After several days he was singing a different if equally popular hymn – clearly brought on by the raging elements. It spoke of the age of decay as prophesied by Lord Rama, the age we were living through now. A time when the venal would feast on the earth's bounties, while the good scrabbled for survival.

> Ram Chandra keh gaye Sia se, aisa Kaljug aayega;
> Hans chugega dana-tinka, kauwa moti khaayega.

I pulled up the canvas folding chair and sat down to wait for the tea. It was always fascinating to watch Rakshas work. Deftly with one hand he unscrewed the lantern tank, stuck in the funnel, poured the kerosene from a plastic can, screwed it back tight – all the while gripping the lantern tightly between his feet – popped open the glass, yanked up the wick, picked up the candle, fired the wick, readjusted the glass tightly, wiped it clear with a dirty rag, then put the live lantern aside and dragged another dead one between his feet. Through it all the phantom arm waved magisterially keeping beat with the hymn.

Will Bideshi Lal's roof hold? I said.

Of course it will, sahib, he said with typical optimism, This is hardly the worst storm this house has seen or will see.

Has this house's roof ever been blown off?

He put the third lit lantern next to the other two, took out a big plug of green-black dope from his shirt pocket, bit off a chunk, massaged it in his fingers, stuffed it into his small chillum and lit it with the candle. A deep drag and the sweet heady aroma began to waft in the room, snuffing out the kerosene and ginger smells. He leaned back against the wall, the yellow glow highlighting his strong features, pulled smoke through his cupped hand, and said, Sahib, when its time comes nothing will be able to hold it down. Not the greatest carpenters, not the longest nails, not the strongest steel belts.

So has it ever been blown off? I asked again.

Without giving a reply, he got up, finished boiling the tea, strained two glassfuls, gave me one, and then came back and sat down in the same posture in the same place against the wall. Taking a long audible suck on the chillum, he said with the grave air of a village storyteller, Listen, sahib, I will tell you about the first time the roof of this house was blown clear off.

Yes, I said.

He said, Hindustan was not yet free. The white man still had many years to go, and the road to Nainital was a mere horse track. The guldaar ruled the hills and the water in the tals was as pure as nectar. I was six years old and we lived near Ramgarh with my mother. My father was mostly away – he worked in Gethia. We had come to visit my uncle's family in Beerbhatti. My uncle had a job in the distillery and every weekend he brought home a container of beer, which we all drank. His son in fact was named Bir Bahadur Singh. Everyone thinks he was named 'veer', to be brave, – the truth is he was named for the angrez's beer that we were all guzzling.

I laughed. But he stayed sombre. The wind and rain were a howling tumult outside, assaulting the windows and doors and machine-gunning the glass panes. The unpainted window frames were beginning to spring small drips.

Savouring the calm of the weed, he closed his eyes and continued, It was a late summer evening like this and my uncle had just come home with the beer container and we were all sitting outside our hut drinking, when my uncle suddenly raised his head, looked all the way down the length of the valley, where the stream runs down to Kathgodam, and jumping up shouted, Get up, all of you! Hurry! Put everything inside! We looked where he was looking and in the distance monstrous black clouds were chugging towards us like a billowing steam engine from Delhi.

My aunt let out a loud lament and then we were all scampering about, dragging and carrying things inside. In a minute the entire village was running around, everyone shouting at each other. That night who knows what seized the One Above, but he decided his subjects needed to be taught a lesson. That night was then and this night is now, and I will tell you, sahib, that in all these more than fifty years I have seen very many things, but I have not seen anything like that. And let me tell you I have never felt more fear – not even when the guldaar had my arm in his jaws.

I took a sip of the tea. Wonderful. It was what we called surrrchai: very sugary, piping hot, and to be drunk with a loud slurp. Surrr . . .

Rakshas responded with his own surrr, and continued, I clung to my mother as the storm hammered us from every side. The wind was screaming so loud that even standing next to each other we had to shout to be heard. And the rain, the maaderchod rain! Those were not drops. It was as if someone was pouring an endless river down our heads. Then in the night the roofs began to blow.

Bagheera padded in and lay down at my feet. I leaned forward and began to stroke his thick fur. He was blacker than a moonless night, a pedigree Bhutia with a folded left ear that never cocked up. Bagheera had the equable temperament of the mountains: he never begged for food, nor ever barked without reason. Yet he was universally feared in the area. For in the mountains they know of the ferocity of the Bhutia, and it is acknowledged that on a good day a pair of Bhutias can take on even a panther.

Rakshas said, When the roofs began to blow, there was a banging on our door and my uncle ran out to help. The winds were so strong that we couldn't close the door once we had opened it. Ten of us, including my mother and aunt and cousins, were pulling together, but by then the wind had filled the house and everything was airborne, and then the pine rafters began to shake, and then the nails, the rope lashings, the steel belt fastenings were coming loose, and the shivering roof began to jump, and then there was a tearing sound and then we were looking up at a dark, stormy, rain-filled sky, senselessly holding on to a door that had no meaning any more.

I got up and fetched a Marie biscuit for Bagheera. He took it gently in his mouth, without greed.

Rakshas said, With old sarees my mother lashed me at the waist to my cousin Bir, and my sister Chhutki she lashed to Rampiari. Because a wind that could lift a roof could also lift a child. All around it was dark as death, and there was so much noise – of the demonic wind, the pouring rain, the claps of thunder, of tin roofs rattling, of rafters being ripped, of people shouting, animals yelping, children crying – there was so much noise that you did not know what was happening. It was like the end of the world. Suddenly a cry rose that the mountain above us was beginning to slip. Everyone began running down the slope lickety-split, not knowing which way lay salvation. The soil was already gruel and rivulets had sprung alive, and Bir and I fell and stumbled and ran and fell and stumbled and ran, and we didn't know whether the roar in our ears was the stream below us, or the slipping mountain above us, or the blood pounding in our head. Finally we found an overhang of rock and huddled under it, clinging to each other.

Just the two of you? I asked.

Yes, we didn't know where everyone else was and were too gone to care. We fell asleep and when we woke the day was bright, the sky was blue, the sun was shining and our clothes had dried on us in creases of mud. That day, if you looked up the world was perfect, but if you looked down it was as if Changez Khan had run through the valley and the village. Forests of pine and oak had been uprooted. There were more trees lying on the ground than reaching for the skies. The ground had slipped in a hundred places, and every path was blocked with mud and rock. In our village not a roof remained, and everything of everyone's was littered over the mountain slopes – clothes, utensils, roofs, furniture.

And this house? I asked.

Like a giant cap, the roof of this house was lying in the valley. This magnificent roof, the biggest around here at the time. The wood was intact, the tin was intact, nothing was broken. It was as if a demon had taken the cap off the house and placed it gently fifteen hundred feet below. We all went to see it and climb it and run under and over it. Then in the afternoon the memsahib arrived, carrying her rifle in her hand. We all moved away. She made a slow circle of the whole cap, then gestured to Gaj Singh and trotted away. In the evening Gaj arrived with a hundred men who lifted the cap and through the night carried it up the hill back to the house. Next morning the cap was back on the house and a dozen carpenters were busy hammering and nailing and belting it down. Of course it took the rest of us weeks to put our roofs back. After that the villagers took to saying, What can you say of her? What is a roof for us is a mere hat for her. While we await our destiny, she makes hers.

And this roof has not been off since?

Not as far as my memory serves me. Not till you took it off and laid a new one.

What we removed was the original roof?

Arre, didn't you see the thickness of that tin? That was sheer steel. Why do you think everyone in the village was begging you for a mere sheet. And you were handing it out like you were the nawab of Jagdevpur!

I put my mug down and went out onto the front veranda. I was a little lightheaded with the dope. Rakshas was now sucking on his chillum peacefully.

The rain was tearing up the ground. And the gale was slapping the trees about remorselessly like a schoolmaster raging in a classroom. Only our deodar, Trishul, seemed to be unmoving in its solidity.

Through the fury of the wind and rain could be dimly spotted the glow of a few lights on the Nainital slope below St Joseph's. The mountain opposite the house was a dark brooding shape, darker than the rain, darker than the night. There was not even a pinprick of light in the temple that perched at its tip. On the veranda, two storeys below the roof, the clatter of rain on tin was muffled – down here was the less tinselly, more solid, sound of hard water hammering soft soil.

I had been standing there for a long time when I suddenly realized I was not alone. On the first and only step of the veranda, hugging the square stone pillar on the extreme right, the rain pouring through her body, soaking skin and soul, sat Fizz.

She was so motionless, so darkly close to the thick pillar, that I had failed to sense her presence. She was like the statue of a dwarpal, an ancient gatekeeper in a derelict palace. A voluptuous shadow guarding against all intrusions, of man and spirit – her wavy hair now straight, her classic profile etched on to the liquid night, her forearms on her knees, her hands clasped together.

My heart lurched. All this while it hadn't occurred to me to wonder where she was. Instinctively I wanted to reach out. But something held me back. I knew that one gesture would lead to other things.

I just said, Fizz, get out of the rain. You'll fall ill.

She did not reply.

I said it again. More firmly. Fizz, don't be stupid – come inside.

She said nothing. She did not even acknowledge my presence with the slightest movement. I stood there, empty of all feeling, wondering what I should do.

Meaninglessly, I repeated, Fizz!

Unable to leave, unable to extend myself, I went and slumped on the heavy cast-iron dragon chair lying by the inner door.

You go and sleep, I said to Rakshas when he came for dinner.

The downpour did not abate, and we did not move. I kept nodding off and each time I came to, her silhouette was exactly as before. At some point in the night her shoulders began to heave – with shivers or sobs I could not tell. Nor could I bring myself to go to her. I watched and I slept. And when I woke, I watched again.

First light came grey, bleak, fighting the rain and the clouds for space. It was a battle it would not fully win through the entire godforsaken day. But moment by moment the contours of the world re-emerged – the trees, the hills, the faraway houses, everything soaked and dull and dripping. Bagheera padded in from outside, stood in the middle of the veranda and shook himself vigorously, sending a million cold drops into orbit.

Caught out by the creeping light, unwilling any more to be the object of my scrutiny, surely soaked to her soul, surely at the end of some kind of a night's journey, Fizz finally stirred. With a hand on the pillar she stood up – her trousers and shirt lumping on her in wet patches – and after a moment of flexing her knees slowly, she walked out in the pouring rain towards the gate.

I watched her back recede down the gentle incline. She walked like a peasant, with a solid tread, a strong sense of connection to the earth.

On the old broken gate she laid out her forearms, put her chin on them and gazed down the dark Bhumiadhar valley. At that distance, through the moving curtain of rain, it wasn't possible to see her expression, but I could imagine her lower lip quivering as she wandered the twilight zone between abject weeping and proud despair.

She stood there staring out, a lonely, ghostly figure. The occasional truck drove past, groaning at the bend, battling gentle slope and driving rain.

After what seemed a long time she broke her pose, bent down and checked the peepul and gulmohar saplings that flanked the gate, and then began to walk slowly along the stone wall, checking every single sapling she had ever planted. Walnut, pear, silver oak, kadam, bamboo, bottlebrush, weeping willow, kachnar, jacaranda, kail, soapnut, variegated bottlebrush – she vanished from eyeshot behind the house – deodar, tun, shisham, chir, banj, lime, jamun, bougainvillea, guava, tejpatta, morpankhi, surai, mango. She knelt and felt each plant, caressing their leaves, smelling some, touching others to her face. I held myself still, frozen between detachment and memory.

Many minutes passed. Then she emerged from around the other side of the house. She had several different leaves in her cupped palms and she walked in past me without a look in my direction. I sat there, not knowing where to go, not knowing where my life lay.

She spent the rest of the day in the unfinished study, sitting on the Jaisalmer windowsill, looking down at the Jeolikote valley, the rain gusting within an arm's length of her. In the harsh light of day I did not have the courage to be in the same space. I sat on the upper veranda – the wraparound – listening to the falling rain and staring at nothing. I felt drained of all words, all feelings.

In the late afternoon I heard the floorboards creak. It was her step, firm, heavy. She went into our room, and when I half-turned to look some minutes later, she was stuffing her clothes into her leather bag.

When we went downstairs, Rakshas and Bagheera were waiting on the veranda. She rubbed Bagheera under the chin a few times and repeated the vet's instructions on the tick wounds under his shoulder.

Rakshas said, Come back soon, didi.

I had opened up the big green J & B umbrella and was waiting at the edge of the rain. She stepped under it without touching me and wordlessly we began to walk in perfect rhythm. Steps perfected over a thousand walks in the last fifteen years. We went down the old stone steps, turned right under our old dripping deodar, and walked down to the old broken lower gate that we had walked through the first time we came to see the house.

There was no gate now and I had to pick aside the two barbed-wire coils to let us through. Instinctively she took the handle of the umbrella while I unhooked the wire from the bent nails in the pillar. When I looked back I could see Rakshas's one-armed silhouette standing under the eaves on the open terrace, looking down at us.

We crossed the road and positioned ourselves by the broken stone berm. Here it was we had sat the first time – in glorious sunshine and light blue skies – peering up at the house, convinced that this was what we had been looking for all our lives, that this was where the rest of our lives lay.

The crisp sun and air making her skin glow, Fizz had said, It's as if we have a karmic connection with this place.

Now we stood in the pouring rain waiting for the bus from Bhowali that would take her down to Kathgodam, and away. There was virtually no traffic moving up or down, and in the canopy of ceaseless rain and the gathering darkness we could as easily have been standing on the mountain edge a hundred years ago – before electricity, before motorcars, before Gandhi, before Independence. Before love.

My parents, and my parents' parents, and her parents and her parents' parents, and so on and on, did not understand the concept of romantic or sexual love. They understood marriage, money, duty, copulation, children. We thought we understood nothing except love. But now we stood in a place before electricity, before motorcars, before Independence, before love; and I at least no longer knew if I understood anything, and if she did, there was no way for me to know.

We stood there for so long that the umbrella's protection began to fail. The water gusted in, wetting our sides. Rakshas came down at one point in a heavy green army macintosh, and suggested Fizz leave next morning. It was a formality. He knew her temperament. He went back up and positioned himself once again on the terrace under the eaves.

It was well past seven o'clock before we saw the wide-set eyes of a bus sweeping the mountain face above us. Slowly, moaning through the falling rain, it took the last bend and entered the straight stretch towards us. There was a moment of total blindness as it closed in, losing speed all the time. It rolled past us and stopped with its front door at our very feet, and the glare went out of our eyes. Like most hill buses it was old and its engine had a sickly thrum, a rattling as if someone had thrown a handful of marbles into the machinery.

The door was flung open with some wrenching by a slim young conductor. He was dressed in tight blue jeans beneath his wide-open khaki rain cape, and had a jaunty, old-fashioned, upturned moustache. She passed him her bag, and in a fluid movement he swung it onto the seat next to the door. She put her hand on the steel handrail; he moved aside; with a single heave she was on the bus.

I put my head in and looked. There were barely a dozen passengers and they were all huddled under ragged capes. She had gone across to the other side and was sitting behind the driver. The young boy waited for me to clamber on, but I just folded the green umbrella and handed it to him. He waited, puzzled.

I withdrew and, hand held straight up, palm open, quickly walked across the front of the bus. Strings of rain punctured the yellow headlights. The rattling engine was pulsing out smoky heat that cut through the rain. When I banged on the driver's side, an old sardarji cracked open the door. He was wearing a weathered green army parka.

I said, Sardar sahib, please take care.

Have no fear, son, he said and clanged shut the door.

I stepped back as he revved the engine, puffing grey exhaust, and with a loud grating put the bus into gear.

It jerked, and she was by the window, the hair pulled back

tightly, the classic profile looking straight ahead, and I could not tell if her face was wet with the rain or something else.

Then I was looking at a pair of dimly glowing red tail-lights.

In no time at all the bus leaned into the next bend and was gone.

I stood in the middle of the road for a long time, open to the skies, letting the water run deep into my skin till its initial chill had become warm and comfortable.

When I went back to the house and climbed up to our room and took off all my clothes, I felt as naked and empty as the day I was born.

# The Inheritors

Few cities in the world are older than Delhi. For millennia adventurers, seekers, marauders, wayfarers, kings, scholars, sufis and mendicants have arrived at its gates in melodramatic fashion, pursuing different things.

A new Delhi is continually overlaying an older Delhi.

The derangement of power is the only constant.

We moved to Delhi in the winter of 1987. That is, baggage and all. To live in, to put our roots down. We had made a preliminary foray, living out of two suitcases, casting for anchorage. Then soon there was a home, a barsati, and we went off to collect our stuff and come back for good. We had first come when the last monsoon showers were over, and in our two months of living out of suitcases we had seen the leaves fall, the autumn pass, the days shrink. Traffic had become thin, and now after midnight there was only the occasional grind of a car engine or the flash of a headlight. Fingers of mist were beginning to clutch at the mornings and nights, and soon there would be the full embrace of the wakening fog.

We were moving to the epicentre of India, and India was no longer innocent. Terrorism in the eighties had ripped out our complacencies, and the three-decade-old grand glow of having kicked the British out with fine dignity was fading fast.

In the coming years it would all go: cups and saucers and tea cosies, mother superior in convents of mary and john and hark the herald angels sing, Oxbridge assistant editors in newspapers,

Gandhians in white doily caps in public places, ethical dacoits who stole only from the rich, underworld dons who smuggled but did not kill, honour in cricket and tonic in gin, proprieties of caste and Constitution, moral and material accountability, karma and dharma.

The man in power would soon pull up his dhoti and show us his bum; the man in the street would pull down his pyjama and show us his bum; and we the middle class would bend in front of the mirror, pull down our readymade trousers and show ourselves our bums. There would be fine scholastic talk and media analysis of subaltern forces, post-colonial reconstructions, rural stasis, Third World entropy, the Dalit dawn, cultural nationalism, and so on. But in the end it would only be all of us showing one another our bums.

In the end it would all only be a confederacy of bums.

As my mother's father used to say about his wastrel sons, who squandered everything pursuing chimerical 'iskeems', from selling packaged six-inch datuns that would supplant toothbrushes, to trousers with a back fly so you could crap without needing to pull them off, to force-feeding hens with steroids so they would lay eggs every eight hours (till they bloated like balloons and began to burst), as he would say examining the wreckage of another iskeem, making his big wood-and-brass hookah bubble in anger, In the dark even a bum can look like a face.

In the winter of 1987 India was full of iskeems that had gone awry. Agricultural iskeems, political iskeems, economic iskeems, educational iskeems, religious iskeems, stop black money iskeems, attract white tourist iskeems, drinkable water iskeems, animal protection iskeems, women's welfare iskeems, nurture children iskeems, don't scan female foetus iskeems, quickly snip male vas deferens iskeems, nationalization iskeems, privatization iskeems, medical iskeems, entertainment iskeems, science iskeems, sports iskeems, clean India iskeems, old India iskeems and new India iskeems.

We had mastered the art of nomenclature from the white man.

Grand labels could disguise unforgivable things.

Across the country stern-looking men and women in floppy-style clothes sat in committees and offices pulling out iskeem after iskeem from their flaccid imaginations. They all had meaningful names. These were then fed into the perpetually masticating teeth of government, like sugar-cane sticks through the turning grinders at roadside stalls. The juice was then set aside; the husk put into play.

The people looked at the juice, and ate the husk.

As a friend often said, India is a gymkhana club, where the people have the votes, but the politicians and bureaucrats have the membership.

My grandfather only said, In the dark even a bum can look like a face.

In the winter of 1987 Indira Gandhi was dead. In fact had been dead three years. My father had wept when she was riddled with bullets. I had looked at him with contempt. She had a lot to answer for and hopefully someone was holding her to account now.

Rajiv Gandhi was alive, but rapidly unravelling. He had told us he had a dream. But at the moment it was being methodically disembowelled in the abattoirs of his innocence. In his mother, arrogance was the poison. In him, innocence. It would all end badly, tragically. When it was over, he would have questions to ask and hopefully someone up there would answer them.

The Hindu Right had not yet arrived at their loony genius. It takes a people time to climb down from lofty heights. 1947 had left us in a lonely, difficult place. The loony Right's time would come as we steadily lost the grand ideas of modernism and democracy we had been fed by those splendid warriors against colonialism and reverted to our smallnesses of caste and community and religion.

The loony Right's genius would be to understand that in the dark a bum can look like a face, but it is still only a bum. To address a bum as a bum is to spark a dialogue of recognition. It can be such a relief to stop pretending to be a face. Like dropping the fork and knife and attacking the food with your hands.

It can be such a relief to drop your pants and show your bum.

Such a relief to be a confederacy of bums.

Indira Gandhi's poison was arrogance.

Rajiv Gandhi's, innocence.

And the loony Right's, pettiness.

In the winter of 1987 Indira Gandhi was dead, Rajiv Gandhi alive and the loony Right embryonic. But coming to Delhi – for good, with Fizz by my side – none of them, dead, alive or embryonic, detained me. Making the move to the capital had been a sudden decision, but had been a long time in the coming. That was typical of us. We would talk and talk and talk about something, and not do a thing to make it happen. Then suddenly one day a penny would drop, a mood would seize hold of us, and before we knew it, we would be up and doing.

In this case the penny had dropped first about my job, then about moving.

In March of that year, a day after I had turned twenty-six, I came home late in the afternoon, stood in the kidney-shaped kitchen the size of a bathtub, while Fizz brewed tea, and said, I want to quit.

With her trademark equanimity about big things, she turned and said, So do it.

And then with an arch of the eyebrows: In any case, my dear, I need some time with you. I have things to show you.

Immediately – before drinking the tea – I put my red-coloured Brother typewriter on the dining table, popped open the black moulded cover, fed in a foolscap sheet, adjusted the margins and without hesitation or error banged out a resignation letter to my editor.

It was not elaborate. It just said I needed six months off and would be grateful to be given leave without pay. If that was not possible, then this letter should be treated as my resignation. I ascribed no reasons for wanting leave. I pulled the crisp sheet out with a flourish and gave it to Fizz. When she had finished reading it, she hugged me, her face flushed with excitement. Then she kissed me. I instantly picked her up and laid her out on the table and sat on the chair and worshipped her with my mouth till I could hear her voice no more.

Fizz. Crazy Fizz.

Always turned on by random acts of integrity and generosity and artistic madness. Just as some women are turned on by cars and clothes and muscles and money.

From the dining table we went straight to the bed and only got out of it at night, and then we took out the bike and went for a long drive, cruising up and down Chandigarh's wide avenues, from the lake to the university and down the link road that ran to Mohali, open green fields flanking its sides. The traffic was scarce, the night was cool, the bike smoothly zipped open the silence behind us, the wind was in my face, and she held me tight, her soft hands inside my shirt.

Few things match the high of quitting a job. To reclaim your life, howsoever briefly. To be – if only for a time – your own master. We rode up and down, letting our hands do what they could, and only when there was nothing more our hands could do, and we needed our home to finish what our hands had started, did we turn back.

We woke very happy next morning, stayed happy all day and were very very happy for the many days that followed. But I was determined not to dawdle. And my determination seemed to galvanize Fizz.

Next morning while I was left at home to draw up my plans, Fizz picked up the Brother and went off to the Sector 21 market to get it serviced. It came back in the evening, its red body shining, the keys lubricated for speedy assault, and a new ribbon installed for indelible prose. She also brought in a ream of quality foolscap, a box of hard-lead pencils, a spiral diary for keeping notes, a big green-and-white eraser, a small bottle of Eraz-Ex whitener, and a plastic pencil sharpener shaped like a book. Typically, she also took the micky out of me with a wooden plaque on a lean-to stand: it featured a shock-haired girl clapping her hands together in adoration and the legend, My Hero!

For my part I prepared to yoke myself to a timetable and a code of conduct. I wrote it out in a notebook, edited it, revised it and finally typed it out and taped it to the mirror in the bathroom. Facetiously – perhaps not entirely – I headed it: The Manual of the Artist as a Young Man. Circa 1987.

Breakfast, sex, newspapers, ablutions by 9.00.
Start work at 9.30.
Break at 1.00.
Light lunch and siesta 1.00 to 4.00.
Resume at 4.00 and work through till 7.00.
A cup of tea at 5.30, at the table, without breaking work.
Write a minimum of 800 words every day.
Allow for two off-days every week. That is, 4,000 words a week.
Remember: writing is as much discipline as inspiration.
No films during the week.
No reading Kafka, Joyce, Faulkner.
Read poetry at bedtime: Hardy, Larkin, Stevens, Whitman,
    Yeats, Eliot.
Read a page of Shakespeare every evening.
No alcohol on working days.
No sex while working.
Jog every evening to keep the blood circulating.

Then there were injunctions about the actual writing, which were separated from the rest of the Manual by a black rule:

Be ambitious – keep the canvas expansive.
Remember: great books don't worry about plot.
Ideas and characters – focus on those.
Form matters as much as content. Innovate.
Write in the third person – with authorial omniscience.
Make the prose memorable – provide stylistic joy.
Steer clear of displays of emotion.
Keep the writing hard-nosed: the world is a hard place.
Don't struggle to be plausible – India is implausible.

Avoid writing about sex – difficult to pull off, easy to trash.
Don't talk the writing away.
The world is full of unread garbage – do not add to it.
Writing is not life. Fizz is.

Fizz had taken a felt pen and in the last injunction crossed out the 'not'; and then added Fizz at the end of the second sentence. So it read: Writing is life. Fizz is Fizz.

I could agree with that, without saying it to her.

Each morning I would read the list while brushing my teeth, and count the injunctions I was managing to stand by. In the beginning it mostly went well. The working day would begin at nine-thirty and close at seven in the evening, with appropriate breaks thrown in. Afterwards there would be Fizz and the rewards of the day's work. But the one unpencilled hazard was that there was Fizz during the day too. It was with her that no rules of mine ever seemed to apply.

The mornings continued to begin with the smelling of her body; and by the time I settled down at the dining table I was usually content. I tried to stay that way till lunchtime and the siesta. The siesta was always part sleep part love, the sleep following the love. But there also ended up being many uncharted interludes when the impulse suddenly grabbed me and it was impossible to keep sitting at the table.

It could be sparked by anything. The afterglow of great love-making; or the nagging dissatisfaction of lousy. Her lingering musk on my face; or its unsettling lack. The work going well and setting the adrenalin pumping; or going badly and creating a vacuum that demanded a charge.

Her teasing presence, or her teasing absence.

When it happened I sought her out urgently – in the bedroom, in the kitchen, in the living room – and we were brutal and swift with each other, as if punishing ourselves for breaking the discipline. It would be over in minutes and I would be back on my straight-backed chair, fingers lightly poised on the keys, a pianist in search of the perfect composition.

Like the earlier one, this manuscript too began well. The opening sentence had floated serenely like a drifting kite into my mind the night of my resignation as we drove up and down Chandigarh's roads, her hands moving inside my shirt: Each time Abhay rode his throbbing motorcycle through Chandni Chowk's rustling-bustling streets he felt the entire weight of Indian history riding pillion behind him. He felt everyone from Shahjahan to Queen Victoria to Gandhi–Nehru–Patel–Azad clinging to him and choking him and demanding of him, and no matter how much he zigged and zagged and swerved and sped he just could not shake them off.

That first morning of work I woke, loved her with commemorative zeal, bathed, ate an omelette with toast, waited as she swiftly cleared the table, then hoicked the Brother onto it, popped it open, set aside the cover, rustled a sheet in a loosening gesture, slipped it in, gave a slow twist to the smooth roller, set the margins, held down the upper-case key, and with deliberate loud clacks wrote: Working Draft One. 15 March 1987. Then shunted it down two lines, and: Chapter One. Two more ringing shunts, and then in a flurry of rhythmic clacking: Each time Abhay rode his throbbing motorcycle . . .

The house acquired an air of gravitas. At the altar of art the clacking of a typewriter is a religious chant. Fizz moved through the rooms with a feathery tread and spoke to the part-time help in whispers. She pulled the wire of the phone into the kitchen, and answered it on the first ring, passing no calls on to me.

I wrote strongly and well, roasting the sentences slowly in my head, turning them over and over, before banging them out on the machine. For the first few weeks writing eight hundred words a day was no problem. With the back of a lead pencil I would count the wordage painstakingly, and at the end of each day note it down precisely in the spiral diary. 15 March: 887 words. 16 March: 902 words. 17 March: 845 words. Soon it became a tic and I began to take a count after virtually every paragraph, tallying and totalling the words – as the curved paper flapped on the platen – for large, and wasted, tranches of time.

Fizz kept the faith and asked no questions about the writing, waiting for me to broach the subject. There were days when I wanted her to read what I had written, to give me some feedback, to be dazzled, but I held my hand, playing a game with myself, seeing how long I could last, how long I could retain confidence in my own judgement, how much I could put down before I brought her in.

Also, increasingly: how long I could keep her in a teased state of expectation.

Locking her out had created a nice erotic tension, a mystery about the processes unspooling on the shining Brother. And I was part of that mystery. It heightened her ardour for me and conjured up unexpected magic. She tiptoed around this obelisk of writing I had planted in our lives and seized on me from whichever direction she could approach.

I was never more special for her than when I was writing.

Breaking with the run of our lives, she began to take the initiative. This would always happen at the end of day, once the work was done, the dues paid. I would be sitting on the love seat or on our bed, listening to Beethoven, whom I was training myself to read, and she would lean forward and start kissing me under the ear, or start to run her fingers lightly over my face, or put the tip of her wet tongue against my chest, or put her head on my lap and start chewing me softly through my clothes.

Once she made contact, I was a goner.

She would then take me out, ready me for the sacrifice with her bodily oils, straddle me expertly, trap me in excruciating places and then proceed methodically to kill me with her powerful haunches. I would scream, she would scream, Beethoven's Choral would crescendo; when it was over she would lie with her beautiful face on my damp thigh, the moonlight streaming in through the open windows shining on the wetness everywhere.

Sometimes I would reach out to the old Philips cassette player – with hard buttons that worked with a loud schtick! sound – I would reach out and noisily rewind the Ninth, and play it again; and by the time the chorus came on, she would have begun afresh.

Every single night I took to lying back and waiting. It was wonderful to be taken.

During those months we made some of the most intense love of our lives. Soon it became the greatest reward of the writing; all day as I worked I was acutely aware of what the night would bring.

The writing went well for the first six weeks, but then I began to lose my way. In my mind I had etched a grand narrative. At the time I was sure I did not want to write small books about small things. The trivial social, emotional, material and relationship concerns writers labour on about. Mothers and sons, sons and fathers, family intrigues, lovers' tiffs, teachers and disciples, crime and punishment, peasant emotions, nature's lessons, friendships and bonding.

I wanted to write the capacious stuff. The grand drama of life, the sweeps of history and ideas and civilizations, the arching movements that make and unmake the world.

The book I was trying to write was to begin before Partition, span three generations and serve as a metaphor for the predicament of India – the canker at the heart of liberty. Abhay, the young man thrumming through the streets of Chandni Chowk on his motorbike, was to be generation three – the inheritor of the mythologies of the freedom struggle through the endlessly repeated narratives of the state and his parents, but condemned to live in the venalities of the present.

His father, Mahendar Pratap, was generation two. He was a mild-mannered youth when India was struggling to come unto freedom and, defying his father's wishes, he had participated in the satya-grahas, hartals and andolans launched by Gandhi and the Congress against the colonial British.

Generation one was Pratap's father, Pandit Har Dayal, a large, flamboyant, violent man who in the 1930s rode a Rolls with running boards and thought nothing of caning his serfs to within an inch of their lives. He genuflected only to Tim Anderson, the ruddy-faced district commissioner, did relentless business with the cantonment, kept a portrait of George VI in his sitting room, and actually thought the white man was good for India. In Pandit Har Dayal's house the women never opened the massive front door or answered a call from the streets. If there was no male at home, the visitor had to simply turn away, unwelcome, unanswered.

The story was to start with Abhay and then be rapidly intercut with the lives of Mahendar Pratap and Pandit Har Dayal. I was excited about the stylized narrative I had worked out. The book would progress in clusters of three chapters: Abhay's story; Pratap's story; the Pandit's story. Each cluster would end with a coda: an Elizabethan sonnet that captured the sweet sadness of their lives and married it with the unfurling chaos of India. I felt verse could provide the philosophic summations it is so difficult to pull off lightly in prose. I was also drawn to the novelty of the form.

The first two clusters proved easy. I managed to establish the three main characters with strong flourishes.

Sick of being served inspirational Gandhi–Nehru lectures by his father, Abhay is a trendy if confused young man, who wants to join the National School of Drama and become a film actor in Bombay. He wears blue jeans, smokes Charms, drinks beer, and at twenty-one has a girlfriend he pets with feverishly in cinemas. He understands the power of money; and he wants the fame of an actor. He thinks his father is a crank and an anachronism.

The father, Pratap, in the 1930s in the Punjab, was an inspired young man. At sixteen he had heard Gandhi speak in Amritsar, exhorting the young to sacrifice. Pratap had gone home, shed his drainpipes and silver-cuffed shirts for khadi pyjama-kurtas, quit his college and joined the local branch of the Congress. All this in the face of his tyrannical father, whom he had never dared cross till the afternoon he heard Gandhi. He detested his father's opulent ways, his ass-licking the white officials, and his treatment of women and servants.

Pandit Har Dayal was a tough, self-made man. He was big, over

six feet, with a handlebar moustache and a strong belief that men
were what they made of themselves, and the world belonged to those
who seized it to their advantage. Early in his youth he turned his back
on his father's niggardly village sweet shop, went to the Lahore
cantonment, seduced the white sahib with his self-assurance, and
earned a contract to supply poultry to the barracks.

In a few years the entire supply line ran through his hands, from
milk to grain to meat to clothes, shoes, kitting. He had havelis in
three cities – Lahore, Amritsar, Delhi – and a sprawling farm at the
village. He rode Arabian thoroughbreds, wore Savile Row suits,
smoked a meerschaum pipe, ate on a table with a fork and knife, and
bought the first motorized car in the district. Women came from as
far as Karachi, Lucknow and Bombay to amuse him. His three wives,
fifteen daughters and one son watched through the fretwork marble
walls as swirling dancers, by the moving light of torches, ducked and
weaved in front of the Pandit, who stroked his moustache with first
his left hand then his right.

I ended the first cluster with an ironic coda, a sonnet on the
dubious and circular nature of freedom. On how we struggle to free
ourselves from one prison, only to submit ourselves to another. It
took two days to construct.

The day I finished it, I spent the afternoon tallying up the numbers. Two days short of three weeks. Fourteen working days. Eleven
thousand seven hundred and eighty-two words. Thirty-four foolscap
sheets; and one for the coda. Then I counted the stars and skulls at
the bottom of every page of the spiral diary in which I kept my notes
and the daily wordage. They had been drawn neatly in a line – the
five-pronged stars easily; the skulls with more labour, but boasting
eyeholes, grinning teeth and all.

The stars were for Fizz and me making out together.

The skulls for me going at myself alone.

I counted fifty-four stars, and fourteen skulls.

Fizz had not yet read any of it, but that afternoon I showed her
the arithmetic of the first cluster. We were sitting on the bed, and she
was wearing a yellow sleeveless vest and a flared skirt – the kind of

clothes she never went out in. She looked at the sheet of paper, her eyes smiling.

Days: 19

Working Days: 14

Words: 11,782

Typed Pages: 35

Stars: 54

Skulls: 14

She took a pencil and did some calculations.

Two hundred and eighteen words per star, she said, looking at me in mock interrogation.

Is that good or bad? I asked.

Very good-bad, she said.

It was our phrase for bad things done well.

You'd better watch out, she said sternly, sucking the end of the pencil, At this rate you are going to run into trouble with your Hemingway limit.

I said, I still have years of catching up to do.

She waved the pencil at me, and I leaned forward and stuck my face in her armpit, where the stubble was just beginning, and the smell of her clean sweat filled my head.

In fact I need to work on it right away, I asked.

Get away, you animal, she said stabbing me with the pencil, Snuffling pigs make no literature.

Life over literature! I mumbled, and buried my face wherever the musk grew.

Later, naked, she picked up the paper again – crushed now – and continued her calculations.

Eight hundred and forty-one words per skull, she said, twirling the pencil, Now that's not bad. That's acceptable.

Actually it's worse, silly woman, I said.

Why?

To check the Hemingway limit you have to add the fourteen skulls to the stars and then divide from the words.

She did it.

54 stars + 14 skulls = 68

Words: 11,782

Divide.

Oh my god! she said, That's an orgasm every one hundred and seventy-three words.

Yes?

She said, At this rate, by the time you write three books you will have exhausted your life's quota.

Shall I stop writing? I said.

She gave me the look.

Or shall I . . . ? I said, with a raised eyebrow.

Yes, she said, Immediately.

That's it then, I said, No more.

My hero, she said.

We had read somewhere that Hemingway believed every person in their lifetime had a finite number of orgasms given unto them – therefore they needed to be rationed. Each time things were going fast and furiously between us we joked about our quota. But this time we needn't have worried. By the time I finished the second cluster and began to struggle with its coda, the writing started to falter. Curiously, as the writing began to fail me, the sexual intensity – the heightened urge – too began to weaken. After day fifty-two, as I commenced work on the cluster, the stars and skulls at the bottom of the spiral notebook became fewer, and fewer.

Soon my special status began to diminish; soon she was no longer taking the lead; soon the threat of the Hemingway limit faded.

But all that came later. The first six weeks were perfect and the second cluster went well. In this I tried to expand on the relationship between the fathers and sons.

The domineering Pandit thinks his son, Pratap, bred in the midst of fifteen sisters, is a wimp – a near-girl who lacks the masculine virtues of ambition and aggression. I placed Pratap close to his petite mother, Kamla, and gave the Pandit a withering line against his wife: The good god should have made it sixteen! Why has he given us this illusion of a son?

For his part Pratap thinks his father is a weak man, full of the hollowness that is born of avarice. Pratap learns gentleness and strength from the women – sisters and mothers – who fill his life. From them too he learns fortitude – an ability to crouch close to the ground so that nothing can blow you away. The Pandit tries very hard to enthuse his son with his sprawling trade. But Pratap has no interest in selling or buying chickens and shoes, and showing up every week at the starchy cantonment to walk on eggshells and kiss the white man's ass. But he fears his father, his fiery temper and his swinging paw, which lands on his ears like a clap of thunder. So he goes where his father orders, leaving his heart at home, in the milling keep of the locked-in women.

One fateful afternoon Pratap joins a flowing tide of the ordinary going to listen to the Mahatma. In that sea of people he feels Gandhiji is speaking to him alone: the pure soul knows no fear; it is only the weak who turn to violence; the one and only truth resides within us; we are what we do, and what we do has worth when it benefits the least fortunate amongst us; India must be governed by Indians; true courage has only a moral dimension; in material things, less is always more.

Before he returns to his college Pratap has shed his fancy clothes; by the time he returns to his father's house he has shed all fear. His father is now only another rich man seduced by the white sahib's crumbs.

The cluster closed in the mid-1930s, with the Pandit and Pratap poised at opposite ends of the Indian spectrum. One shoring up the scaffolding of empire; the other working to dismantle it.

In many ways the other father–son relationship between Pratap and Abhay proved more dodgy to handle. It did not allow for easy polarities. Pratap as a liberator and inheritor – of the great Indian dream – no longer possessed the purity of his freedom struggle days. His left ear was gone with lathi blows, he had spent years in prison, and in 1947 when Nehru had spoken just before the midnight hour as 15 August and a new country were born he had listened on the radio and wept for his youth.

His father, the tyrannical Pandit, had died in 1942, an increasingly isolated and reviled figure among his own people, as history and the Mahatma's inspired millions swept past, dumping him and his white gods in time's bin. Pratap could not attend his father's cremation because he was preoccupied being a jail statistic in response to the Mahatma's Quit India call. And when he came out of jail he did not hesitate – in the spirit of the time – to apportion his father's vast wealth into two parts: one part he divided into eighteen sub-parts and gave to his sisters and mothers; the other he donated to the Congress's struggle. He kept nothing for himself, precisely as the Mahatma would have wished.

With the dignity of labour he has now acquired, he reverts to his grandfather's vocation, and opens a mithai shop in bustling Chandni Chowk. He remembers the big brass karahis bubbling with milk and oil, stoked by dark sweating men; the open-mouthed sacks of sugar stacked in the corner; the smeared glass cases enclosing white burfi and saffron laddoo; the sickening sweet smells jamming the nostrils; his grandfather sitting on a raised cushion; and flies every everywhere, dotting the confections, dotting the glass, dotting the people. Pratap finds he has a gene for the business, and even the faux affability of the businessman comes easily to him.

But as independent India's decades roll by – and Gandhi dies, and Patel dies, and Nehru dies, and Azad dies, and Radhakrishnan dies – and Pratap's shop does better and better, he finds his flesh weakening. Pratap is idealism's orphan, idealism's debris. And idealism's debris contains the most tragic of lives.

Idealism's orphans inevitably discover that the grand highway of history they proudly rode, with the wind in their faces, song on their lips, surge in their hearts – the grand highway of history, all grand highways of history, end in the bazaar. And to work the bazaar, to move, sit and stand in the bazaar, to buy and sell in the bazaar, to manoeuvre lightly and nimbly through the bazaar, you have to leave the clunky armour of high ideals, the heavy helmet of lofty ideas, at the gate, where the bazaar begins and the grand highway of history ends.

When India's grand highway of history ends at that midnight hour in 1947, and the redoubtable travellers begin to array themselves into a bazaar, Pratap fails to spot the opportunity. He wanders in still wearing his helmet and armour and finds himself – as the years roll by – colliding irascibly with all and sundry, most unhappily with his old comrades. Men who had been felled by lathi blows as they walked by his side, men who had inspired him and exhorted him.

By the late 1960s the greatest warriors are dead or dying, and the rest of the army have become artists of the floating world, anchored by nothing, wafted by greed, petty businessmen negotiating the cramped bylanes of minor politics and minor commerce. Noble men driven to smallness by keening spouses, demanding children and grubbing relatives.

Once valued for their principles, now measuring themselves by their possessions.

Kings of ideals become kings of deals.

Slowly, inexorably, Pratap too sheds his weight and learns to float.

He gets his toehold back in the party.

Nominations to market committees begin.

He gets the gas agency his wife has been hollering for.

Party stalwarts begin to send for him.

Party aspirants start showing up at his door.

He becomes a negotiator of disputes.

A connector of needs.

A fixer of desires.

He prepares to become a municipal corporator.

The government schools begin to order Independence Day sweets from his shop.

Yet he continues to think of himself as the young man who helped

India win its freedom. He continues to be a follower of Gandhi. He believes his life is devoted to the service of the nation. His self-image remains more or less intact.

I was satisfied with Pratap, but Abhay created problems. It was difficult to pose him against his father in a way that lent itself to large readings. I didn't want Abhay to be a complete wastrel, an obvious and clumsy counterpoise to his father.

Pre-Independence India allowed for black and white characters, but 1970s India – of human rights violations, nuclear detonations, lightning wars, hilltop summits, student movements, forced sterilizations, money-laundering scandals, demonic acronyms like Misa, Cofeposa, Fera and crumbling values – 1970s India had so mixed up its dreams and desires that you couldn't pick out a clean man with a telescope the size of a tree.

So I made Abhay a man of his times. Not too good; not too bad; and not concerned with any of it either.

Abhay is a strapping, handsome man, like his grandfather, the Pandit. Like him, he is quick of temper, hot-blooded – petting ceaselessly in the cinema – and violently ambitious. His only values are friendship and success. He defends every misdemeanour of his friends and brawls fiercely for them when required. After each skirmish he feels exalted. A profound sense of duty discharged fills his spirit.

His friends call him yaaron ka yaar. The friend of friends.

A similar exaltation grips him when he comes in touch with someone hugely successful. A rich businessman, a powerful politician, a famous actor. Like his grandfather in the presence of Tim Anderson, Abhay then becomes deferential, attentive, a curious seeker of the secrets of success. Abhay believes men are what they make of themselves, and the world belongs to those who seize it to their advantage.

Friendship is his religion. Success is his god.

Abhay abhors the mithai shop, as well as the gas agency. The smallness of their ambition is distressing. He wants no part of either. He hates his father's low-key business style, and hates his dress code. The same white kurta-pyjama repeated endlessly, day after day. But what galls him most is the white cloth cap – the Gandhi cap – his father pulls on each time he steps out of the house.

Why must he wear that stupid cap? Abhay screams at his mother, Even Gandhiji was embarrassed to wear it!

Abhay, of course, wears blue jeans, tight T-shirts, and calf-leather boots. His father drives a pot-bellied, puttering green Bajaj scooter; Abhay a heavy black Royal Enfield motorcycle, whose throb can be heard three lanes away. In his room Abhay has a faded brown photograph of his grandfather posed next to his long car, elbow planted on the bonnet. Each time he sees it he wants to rush out and clobber his father with his big leather boots.

Abhay wants to be a famous actor in Bombay. He wants the big stage, the big play, the big world that lies just beyond the confines of the mithai shop and the gas agency. He has self-belief; and he has a portfolio of his photographs. Abhay has sent his portfolio to several directors in Bombay. Each day he waits for the phone to ring, for the postman to arrive. Each day he stands in front of the full-length mirror in his room in his calf-leather boots, wears his Stetson, bends his knees in a slight slouch and practises his draw. When he fires the bullet, he says, Tishoooon!

Then he blows away the curling smoke from the barrel.

Pratap thinks his son is a layabout and a fantasist. He knows his son smokes and drinks and rides young girls pillion on his motor-cycle. He disapproves of Abhay's dress sense, his friends, his ambitions for himself. But what he hates most is the khaki Stetson his son wanders around in.

Who wears a stupid hat like that? he shouts at his wife, Does the fool think he's living in London?

The father aches to see an echo of his own youthful idealism in the son. A reaching for larger things, some serious endeavour. He tries to talk to him about the splendour of India's history, of the humane vision of Gandhi and Nehru. But Abhay is a man of his time. He has no demons to slay outside of himself. All he wants to exorcize are his father's nagging stories of sacrifice and goodness, and how the young should be continually grateful for what they have been given.

Abhay looks at the giant posters pasted on Filmistan and Regal and Golcha – garish pictures of Amitabh Bachchan and Dharmendra firing guns, hugging women, long hair flying, blood streaming down their faces – and he just wants to be up there.

He wants his father to shut up.

He wants his father to be a minister.

He wants his father to close the mithai shop and open a department store.

He wants his father to sell the gas agency and get a petrol pump.

He wants his father to buy a white Fiat car.

But most of all he wants his father to take off that damn Gandhi cap.

Abhay continually rants to his mother about her husband's stupidities. Yet he dare not accost his father. Not because he fears him. But more out of a kindness, a sort of piety. Abhay knows his father has been an abject failure in the worldly sense. He is basically a follower, a meek follower, who has failed to leverage his struggles into any greater success. He knows those youthful years of sacrifice and that one initial act of rebellion against the Pandit are the twine that holds his father's life together. If he slashes it, his father will fall apart.

I closed the cluster with Abhay increasingly identifying with his grandfather and increasingly contemptuous of his father. The traitor of a generation ago is now an inspiration, the hero a disgrace. When the cluster ends Pratap is beginning to float lighter and lighter, manipulating his ticket for the municipal elections, stepping out of his meekness into a new world of corruption.

Abhay awaits his call from Bombay, perfecting his draw. Tishoooon!

The Pandit's ghost grows steadily more muscular, feeding on the venalities of a new age.

The coda took several days. I finally constructed a sonnet about heroes and villains, declaring that a day would come when Gandhi and Nehru would be blamed for India's flawed freedom and scorned for being weak. And those who had been weak and bigoted would be hailed by a new and petty age as heroes.

Despite all my attempts, despite my ear for metre, it remained arhythmic, and I finally gave up on it and committed it to the Brother.

That evening we went out to Suzie Wong in Sector 22 and had a Chinese dinner. I was abstracted, irritable. The chopsuey was too tart, and I got into a spat with the slant-eyed waiter. He came back with a slant-eyed head waiter. It's the Punjabi idea of a Chinese restaurant – staff from the north-east and thick noodles, and the rest of the food of no consequence. It's the two things slant-eyes monopolize in India, Chinese restaurants and kung-fu psychosis. You don't eat in a Chinese restaurant that is not serviced by them and ever since *Enter the Dragon* you avoid getting into a brawl with any of them. But I didn't care. I was looking to vent. I screamed at the head waiter. He came back with the owner. Turned out to be a fat, bluff Punjabi called Jollyji.

What is the problem? said Jollyji, smiling dangerously.

The chopsuey is fucking awful! I said.

Jollyji turned to the waiter and said in a caress, What's wrong, son?

It's fine, said the waiter, eyes darting all over.

Who's eating it, son? asked Jollyji, still silken.

He is, said the waiter.

Who is paying for it, son?

He is, said the waiter. He was beginning to shuffle.

Then who should know, son? whispered Jollyji.

He should, said the waiter, beginning to inch back.

Then take this motherfucking garbage away and get a fresh one! roared Jollyji, landing a clip on the waiter's ear and sending him scurrying.

Jollyji had obviously not seen *Enter the Dragon*.

Send it back again if it's not OK! he said, turning to us, smiling broadly, rubbing his fat hands together, In my restaurant Customer is King!

Thanks, I said.

I asked him where he had got the name of his restaurant. He smiled coyly and said it was from a film he once saw. He said he fancied the woman in it. We both laughed and he slapped my back.

Fizz was silent through it all.

When we left she said, What happened to you?

I kept quiet.

Next time you want to bond with Jollyji and beat up poor waiters leave me at home, she said.

I said nothing, and she didn't push it. We drove home silently and made love. It was like nothing; just rubbing off. Next day I didn't get down to the dining table in the morning, lingering in bed. Fizz said nothing.

In the afternoon I said, Let's go to a film.

She cracked a smile, Why? You feel like beating up some ushers today?

We went to KC, absurdly shaped like an aeroplane hangar, and caught the Hindi matinee. The film was noisy, but the clamour couldn't drown out my worry.

Later we sauntered through the Sector 17 plaza, winding up at the New Variety Book Store. It had so few books that they were all displayed like posters on the walls. The man who ran it was a queer fellow. He did not seem like a reader of English books, but he stocked the best collection of English literary titles in Chandigarh. There were titles there – including paperback editions over fifteen years old – that no one else had.

The shop was musty, but he kept each book preserved neatly in cellophane. When you removed the cellophane and opened the books the edges would be yellowed, but the spine was always uncracked and the paper crisp. He stocked only literary titles – no textbooks, no guidebooks, no primers, no stationery. The shelves were like magazine racks, running up the walls, and each book was placed face up. Standing in the centre of the shop you could read the title of a book all the way near the roof.

We called the man Sirji, and he was pleased with that. Sirji had an aluminium ladder, he ran the shop alone, and he spoke no English. The strange thing was Sirji was no old crank. He was not one of those Anglophone leftovers of the Raj who, having witnessed first-hand the splendour of the white sahibs, imagine there is virtue in everything to do with the English language and English books. Sirji was probably in his early thirties, and sometimes when we walked into his empty shop quietly I would spy him reading a garish-jacketed Hindi novel behind the counter. He would hide it quickly, jump up, shake my hand and start pulling out outré titles that he thought would interest us.

I had first visited his shop seven years before as a student, with a few rupees in my pocket, and had been instantly hooked. Over the years a major part of our teeming library began its journey into our lives from Sirji's shop. European masters, American heavyweights, new-wave Latin American writers – the most unlikely books appeared on his shelves: Frank Harris's erotic memoirs; Cortázar's *Hopscotch*; Desani's *All About H. Hatterr*; Wallace Stevens's collected poems – books nobody had heard of or seen in the city.

Fizz and I bought and bought, and the miracle was Sirji never charged a penny more than the original listed price. It was the done thing in the city's shops to paste a fresh price on a book the moment a more expensive edition appeared. But Sirji sold at the original price, and there were days when we walked in with fifty rupees and walked out with three or four priceless books.

Wrapped in dirty cellophane, but mint fresh inside.

We went home, took off the cellophane and caressed the skin gently. Cool and smooth outside; rough and warm within. If you did it for long enough you could almost hear the books purr.

Never – almost never – were there any other customers in the shop. When I first left the city to come to Delhi to work, I used to worry how Sirji would get by. We seemed to be his raison d'être.

I asked Fizz to swing by occasionally. She took it up with the metronomic regularity of a nursemaid, going there every week to pick up a book and provide an inoculation of enthusiasm and money.

That day's letter would have a standard postscript: Sirji saved by Camus. Fizzji in need of saving.

Curiously the quiet of Sirji's shop distracted me more effectively than the clamour of the film. For more than an hour I mastered my own anxieties as I felt my way through dozens of books. I would open the taped cellophane carefully, riffle through the pages, then pass it on to Sirji to tape back neatly. I found myself contrasting my own writing to everything I was riffling through. I worked through the first few pages of master storytellers, trying to compare turns of phrase, character, mood, dialogue. For a time it took me away from the trauma of the unwritten that had been growing in me for the last week.

By the time we left Sirji's shop we had bought two books, but the inspiration I had been out seeking – the road map I needed to find – was still as elusive.

The simple fact is I had not started on the third cluster because I didn't know how to continue.

I dawdled for a few more days – with Fizz looking on quizzically – and then decided to force myself back to the table. After three wasted days, one morning I stood in front of the mirror and read the Manual aloud. Orating it as in an elocution contest. Making it echo in the small bathroom.

One injunction in particular stung me: The world is full of unread garbage – not do add to it.

When I came out, Fizz said, Much better than your singing.

I hit the Brother that morning and began to hammer. It was not writing; it was typing. There was no inspiration, no excitement. I had no idea where I was going.

That night I let Fizz read the manuscript for the first time. I needed reassurance. She was thrilled with it, stopping to read out sentences dramatically. When she finished each, in her childlike way she would throw me a hug.

Later she ladled out the compensations of art. She turned me on my stomach, draped her T-shirt over my face and, leading with the point of her tongue, did things to me that made me forget the Pandit, Pratap, Abhay, India, writing and everything else I had ever known.

I moaned like a baby. Then slept like one.

But next morning there was again the mirror with its stern commandments and the waiting red Brother. Gamely I continued banging on the shining black keys, but there was just no juice, in the prose or the story.

That evening I suggested we take a break. I said I felt empty, like a drum drained of water. I needed to fill up again, let the material drip back into me drop by drop. Early next morning, in the dark, we packed a haversack, locked the house and rode the bike up to Kasauli. We crossed Pinjore with dawn licking greyly across the horizon, and when we went through the congested central artery of Kalka – flowing now but beginning to coagulate – and hit the slopes of the lower Himalayas, and began to climb, and the pines began to crowd around us, our spirits soared. We did not rush. We puttered along, with Fizz pulling my head around every few kilometres to give me her mouth.

At the bend before Timber Trail, as always, I stopped. Eight years earlier, when we were in college, I had lost two of my friends here. Driving down in gently falling rain from Shimla, high on youth and beer, their Yezdi had skidded, sending them sprawling into the middle of the road. Billa, the pillion, had held on to Timmy, the sardar, as they went rolling on the tarmac, and a speeding truck had driven clean over their middles. When the double wheels went over them Billa had been on top of Timmy, and below the waist they had been fused together in an indistinguishable soup of bone, flesh and blood. When the rest of us reached the spot minutes later they were both still talking, heads inches apart, unaware they no longer existed below their navels.

Green-eyed Billa was saying, I told this stupid sird we are going to skid.

Timmy, his turban gone, his long hair flowing on the road, said, I told this fucker: don't hold me so tight, I won't be able to steer.

Billa said, Next time, you bastard, just let me drive.

And Timmy said, Shit! My pop's going to kill me! Is the bike screwed?

No, said Miler, kneeling, in his quiet, authoritative way, It's fine. Everything's just fine.

Timmy said, Make sure no one tells him – man, he'll freak out!

They were dead within minutes. It was strange. They were talking one moment and the next they were gone. They were so badly mashed together they had to be removed on a single stretcher and, later, even cremated on a common pyre. For all of us it was our first major rite of passage. We had been touched by mortality. We now knew it was not the preserve of only the old.

For weeks after we saw life as a miracle. Then the sorrow passed, the memories became beautiful and we only grieved when we were drunk.

At the bend, on a big kadam below the road, we carved out a legend: Timmy and Billa, 26 July 1979, Himachal Hostel, Room 102, Great Friends and Wristy Masters, Now Room-mates Forever, and Fuck Any Warden Who Tries to Separate Them. We made a covenant we would put a notch on the tree each time one of us drove past. When I shuffled down the leafy, slippery path to the kadam I counted the notches on the trunk. There were twenty-seven. Four were mine and I picked up a stone and rubbed in a fifth. Billa and Timmy were getting enough company.

By the time we took the next bend the moment of memory had passed and Fizz was talking about breakfast. We stopped at a shack and ate greasy double-egg omelettes with bread slices toasted directly on the fire, and knocked back several tiny glasses of tea. The sun was out, but hadn't worked its way down the slopes to touch the road yet.

When we turned off the main road at Dharampur and entered the last lovely stretch to Kasauli, we were light with fresh air and happiness. In those last thirteen kilometres the road narrowed – a ribbon undulating in the air – and the traffic died away, and the trees came closer, and the magnificent red-billed blue magpies appeared carelessly on the culverts, playing tag in noisy pairs, and magical glades appeared just off the road, and we stopped the bike to go into one, and we used the broad, scaly trunk of an old pine tree and the down of a million pine needles to drink afresh the crazy cocktail of urgency and love.

She was wearing a loose red pullover. I lifted it – and everything underneath it – and bunched it under her neck. She arched her back and she was more beautiful than all the trees and birds and mountains. Little bumps appeared on her skin and her pink tips asked questions I was born to answer. I answered one with an open mouth, the other with an open palm. Her face became the colour of sunrise, and she held my head and guided it everywhere till my face shone like the first dew of morning. And when I poured my love into her, moaning her name, the wind in the glade whispered it with me.

Fizzzzzz.

We checked into a government rest house on the Lower Mall, and the room was musty with damp green carpets and mouldering curtains. The mattresses were thick, but the bed creaked and the bathroom door, once closed from inside, jammed and had to be kicked open from the outside. For the next four days we would call out to each other, Kick, babe! And the reply would come, OK! Stand clear! And bam! we would hammer it with the soles of our feet. It was like being an action hero in a film. Typically, the bathroom had modern fittings but they did not work. The gleaming white cistern and the gleaming white geyser were both defunct. One gave a dry gurgle when approached; the other never opened its red eye. In time-honoured Indian style cold water went into the pot via the bucket, and hot water for bathing arrived from the hamam via the bucket, the scrawny caretaker swaying perilously under the weight.

But we were on a high. Nothing was going to get us down. Within minutes Fizz threw open the doors and windows and, summoning the caretaker and his wife, had the room dusted and aired. Two hours later she sat us down on easy chairs on the veranda, overlooking the thickly forested hills, and sent for bun-samosas from the market.

She ordered extra for the caretaker, his wife and their three children. They immediately became her followers, and when the tea came with the samosas, it was well brewed, scalding hot and soaked in sugar. Surrrchai. You slurped it when you sipped it.

It was just past ten. The sun had enough light, but no heat yet. The morning nip however was gone and it felt nice to sit on the veranda in just shirtsleeves. There were absolutely no traffic sounds here – only the constant chirring in the undergrowth and differently pitched birdcalls. A cheerful gang of white-cheeked bulbuls had taken over the lawn and several made friendly forays onto the veranda, flaunting their crests with jaunty nods. They were speaking in a variety of notes. It was definitely a party.

I could live here forever, she said.

She looked like a sentimental hill painting – wavy black hair loose, feet on the old wooden table, skin glowing, holding her white enamel cup in both hands, staring off into the distance.

I could too, I said.

She said, You could write, and I could run a poultry, or do something with mountain herbs.

I said, You know anything about them?

She said, It's not so difficult to figure out. You just need a terrace or two. And who knows the Pandit and his descendants might make us some money.

Yes, we'll tell the publisher: take the book and give us two hill terraces. Maybe three – one each for the Pandit, Pratap and Abhay.

That's it! We'll build a two-room cottage on one, with a study and a fireplace. And on the other two I'll grow exotic herbs.

And I will write *The Herbivores*, a dark study of a lonely couple living on a farm, using erotic herbs for sinister practices.

I said exotic herbs, not erotic.

Literary licence.

I will not let my herbs be exploited for base purposes.

For literature, for literature.

It's not about sex?

Absolutely not. *The Herbivores* is a compelling tale of plants, passion and purpose. In moving prose it explores the timeless dilemmas of flesh and chlorophyll, through the strange story of a stranded couple struggling with melancholic plants and untimely erections.

In that case I will let you use my herbs.

I said, Literature owes you a debt forever.

After breakfast we went for a walk to the Upper Mall, ambling past the sprawling old bungalows hidden behind trees and foliage, only chimneys and red roofs showing. Kasauli was special for us. I had been coming here for eight years and we had been coming here together for six. I had never heard of Kasauli till I met Sobers in my first week in college. He was one of my three room-mates, and a joy of generosity. His father worked in the Kasauli veterinary research institute and he had grown up there.

Sobers's real name was Arnab Dasgupta. But in college he had been named after the great cricketer Gary Sobers.

In our freshers' cricket match he had announced himself as an all-rounder. He was short and stocky and distressingly confident. He said he was a leg-spinner and after ten overs of medium pace our captain threw him the ball.

The over went down in hostel history. It lasted seventeen deliveries, as Arnab failed to drop the ball anywhere on the matting. The first ball actually flew off his hand to hit the square-leg umpire. Finally he was encouraged to bowl underarm and finish the over. Later he went in to bat wearing one leg-guard. He turned his back to the first ball he faced and the ball got lodged in his fat buttocks. For a moment no one knew where the ball had gone. Then it fell out with a plop.

Outside the boundary our captain looked at me and said, Chutiya, where did you find this Gary Sobers?

When composure returned to the field, the next ball was delivered. It struck him on his unprotected leg and clean bowled him. Collapsing in a heap, he screamed aloud in Bengali, summoning the bowler's mother for instant sex.

Fortunately the bowler was a Jat who understood nothing.

After that he was universally known as Sobers. When his father visited the hostel six months later, no one was willing to tell him where – or who – Arnab Dasgupta was.

I had first come to Sobers's house in Kasauli in a group of five, all of us barely eighteen, and as a plains boy from the frenzied towns in the heart of India, I had been overwhelmed by the mood of the mountains. The lack of crush, the trees, the air raspingly cool in the lungs. It had felt incredible. Immediately the old cantonment town had become my first choice of retreat. I came back with Sobers whenever the opportunity arose, and in time his wonderful parents opened their house to me as if they had known me all my life.

Later when I first took Fizz there they adopted her with the same unquestioning generosity. They knew we were not married, but they gave us a bedroom together – no mean leap in the great Indian middle class – and in the morning aunty would knock on the door before bringing in the tea. It was how people reacted to Fizz. It was easy to trust her, easy to love her. It was the smile, the open body language, the eagerness to roll up her sleeves and do the dishes or chop the vegetables. While I would be tongue-tied, Fizz would chatter on, enquiring into aunty's family history, the story of her marriage, the antics of her children, complimenting the liver curry she had cooked, the silk saree she was wearing, the scraggly money plant she had growing in an old Vat 69 bottle.

The house given to them by the institute sat at the tip of the Upper Mall and provided a panoramic view of the plains. It was old and in a state of disrepair – the glass panes held together with brown packing tape, the wooden frames of doors and windows rotting, the rafters termite-tunnelled – but it had a rare warmth and intimacy. Once Sobers's parents left – he for the institute and she to teach at the local missionary school – I spent the day launching campaigns on Fizz's body.

I insisted she pad around the house only in a short shirt, and when she cooked our breakfast I held her from the back and trapped my hand between her legs. We were so wired, we fed each other food with our mouths, while we fed our hands each other's bodies. Ever so often I leaned her out of the dining-room window and, falling to the floor behind her, I put my lips on the ball of her ankle and began a familiar journey.

I took the hard little ball of her ankle in my mouth and sucked it so fully that it acquired a deeply erotic dimension. I then journeyed to the promise of her fleshy calves and sucked them so fully that they became sexual organs. And then I slowly curved around the shin and ascended the dome of her knees, resting at the peak, mouth open and lips moving. Descending on the other side I banked to the back, and drove my tongue flatly down the smooth highway of her inner thighs, eyes firmly set on the dark line of the final ranges. And so I journeyed slowly, seeking the source of the musk; and as I came closer and closer and the flesh grew and grew and the musk grew and grew, my control began to waver. From my mouth I became my nose. From handing out pleasure I began to hunger for it. Window by window, my thinking mind shut down. Reason, intellect, analysis, perception, speech – everything went, one by one.

I was now an ancient beast, on all fours, prowling in pursuit of a spoor and a secret place.

Outside the pale of civilization.

An animal no longer to be denied.

And when I had drunk at the source, deep and long, I was nothing but a tumescence. I rose behind her and seeking traction held her at the waist, and as she looked down the rolling green slopes all the way to the sweltering north Indian plains, I began to move in the oldest dance of all. The wind carried her moans to all corners of the subcontinent.

We moved from room to room, savouring how the body changes

as the surroundings change. We became different people in different settings.

Aristocrats in the bathroom.

Plebeians in the kitchen.

Students on the veranda.

Adulterers in the living room.

Lovers on the dining table.

And in the bedroom partners and soulmates.

And in doing so we discovered that the greatest lovers are not those who are blessed with constancy and sameness, but those who never stop changing. Those with the gift of being different people at different times.

Each time peace came to our bodies, I read aloud from my anthology: Louis MacNeice and the world is crazier and more of it than we think; Eliot and because I do not hope to turn again, because I do not hope, because I do not hope to turn, desiring this man's gift and that man's scope; Conrad Aiken and order in all things, logic in the dark, arrangement in the atom and the spark, time in the heart and sequence in the brain, such as destroyed Rimbaud and fooled Verlaine – and I read and read while she lay with her beautiful head on my thigh, her warm breath moving in my matted hair. And as I read I felt connected to larger things. I felt my life, our life, had a design, a purpose different, more significant, than that of others.

Occasionally, without moving, she said, Do that again.

And I went back and reread the lines.

Again and again.

I read and read till the rhythm of the poems began to move in our blood, and the peace passed, and her breath began to stir me at the root. She opened her mouth then, and we were soon moving to a music more urgent and eloquent than anything in the anthology.

We bathed at one o'clock – filling three buckets with hot water from the geyser, and pouring it in slow mugfuls over each other: aristocrats in the bathroom – and when Sobers's parents returned for lunch at two, the table was laid, the vegetables heated, the chapattis made; and Fizz was bubbling with conversation, and I was content.

In the afternoons we set out to wander the town, taking forest tracks, going down to the cobble-stoned bazaar for tea and bun-samosas, hanging by the bus-stop to watch the crowds mill, wandering through the graveyard with its heartbreaking epitaphs, exchanging pleasantries at the local missionary school with the brisk nuns cheerfully marshalling the ruddy children in noisy sport, spotting thrushes and barbets and bulbuls, sitting out on the stone benches at the edge of the Upper Mall to see the sun fall.

I told Fizz the stories of the bungalows as I had heard them from Sobers. There were only two roads in Kasauli, the Upper and the Lower Mall; they were lined with majestic trees and old colonial bungalows, many owned by famous names. Not that any of it meant anything to us then. We were young and, like the young, unimpressed and indestructible. We looked at the old couples walking slowly up and down the Malls, and had absolutely no sense of their lives. How did they end up here? How did they live? What was the worth of their lives? Most of them were grey and bent, but with the ruddiness the mountains bestow. Curiously you never heard them talk, and they sailed by in slo-mo like characters in a silent film.

It was on those visits that our passion – and plans – for the mountains began to crystallize. Sobers's crumbling government house, the languorous walks of Kasauli, the talking wind in the old trees, the chill air that came upon you at all hours and pricked the skin alive, the hint of mystery as you sauntered past the brooding bungalows with exotic, anglicized names, the flaming sunsets, the unbelievably tranquil nights with the silence strung out on the bows of cicadas, and the pulsing stars, sharp and immediate and more in number than anywhere else in the world – all of this became completely intertwined with the rituals and discoveries of our love.

Before we had ever said it both of us knew that eventually we would end up in the mountains. It was the destination of our love. Not even in our most macabre imaginings could we have foreseen what lay in store for us.

It was on this trip that we first discussed owning a house in the hills, her teaching in a school while I wrote. We were sitting on a stone bench, on a pretty outcrop on the Upper Mall. At this point the mountain was like a fat man's belly, and like a thick belt a walkway ran around it. At the tip of the swollen belly, at the very navel, just off the walkway, were some benches.

There was no one around and we sat close, the last two people in the universe. At this time of night, with clear skies, we could see all the way to Chandigarh's shimmering lights – prosaically geometrical even from this distance.

Fizz said, We must have a house in the mountains – one day. You could write and I could teach.

Yes, I said, We must.

She was holding my hand and her blue padded jacket shone in the moonlight.

You don't sound convinced, she said.

No, I said, You know I love the mountains. I was thinking of you. You've always said you prefer the sea.

Yes, I did. But I've thought about it. Now I think I'd rather just visit the sea, but live in the mountains.

Why?

You know I prefer the sea because it's forever alive and restless, while mountains are stolid and unchanging, and a little boring. But now I don't think I can handle two restlessnesses in my life.

I gripped her hand tightly.

She turned to me, cracked a smile and said, So, for the moment at least, I have decided to pick you over the sea.

I looked at her in complete adoration.

She said, And I would love to teach in a hill school full of apple-cheeked children.

I said, They will all fall in love with you.

She said, So win me back with deathless prose.

I said, I think we'll just go to the sea.

Leaning forward, she kissed me and said, No, I think *The Herbivores* will make a better book than *The Beach Bums*.

I took her face in my hands and kissed it for a long time as the moon tracked its way across the sky, and the faraway lights of Chandigarh dwindled.

Our four days went by in a happy daze. Or mostly happy daze. Because between the passion and the play, I couldn't stop wrestling with the problems I was having with the manuscript. If there was anything dripping into my creative drum, it was way too slow. At this rate I would have to stay in Kasauli for a lifetime before it filled up.

※

As we drove back to Chandigarh the panic began to mount again; by the time I docked the bike in the narrow driveway at home it had peaked and I was ready to run right back. It was evening when we arrived and I slept badly that night.

Fizz sensed my unease. She knew I was in trouble with the writing. She said, most casually, Do you want to try an early-morning start? Just for a change.

It was an idea. I knew H. G. Wells had recommended this strategy for writer's block. Attack the work when it's not expecting you – take it by surprise.

So I went to bed early and set the alarm for five, but I was in a state of half-wakefulness hours before that, tossing and turning, and working the pillow around from under my head to between my legs and back.

I had a weird dream. I was standing in the witness box in a courtroom – of the kind you see in Hindi films, a waist-high cage of wooden slats – and reading aloud the Manual. After each statement the porcine, wig-wearing judge banged his gavel and a gaunt policeman with haunted eyes stepped forward and smacked me hard with a cane on my ass.

Read a page of Shakespeare every evening.

Whack!

No sex while working.

Whack!

Steer clear of displays of emotion.

Whack!

Each time I was whacked the packed courtroom rose to the last and clapped.

And each time I screamed, Oh, Shaakessspeeeare!

I noticed after some time that most of the people in the packed courtroom were wearing funny party hats, clutching bunches of balloons and blowing on tooters. One young man in the front row had yellow cellophane glasses on, and was throwing up his arms and jigging each time I was whacked. The bunny-rabbit ears on his cap jumped up and down with him.

After each bout of jigging he would lead the parody on me, shouting, Oooh, Shaakessspeeeare!

In unison the partying mob would scream, Oooooh, Shaaaakeeespeeaaare!

As the reading and whacking progressed the atmosphere got increasingly festive. Laughter, hoots, high-fives, anarchic backslapping. It was like a New Year's Eve party. There were couples whirling and dancing. Then I began to recognize faces.

I could see old school friends, college mates, teachers, my hostel warden, Father in a dark suit, Mother in a maroon saree, Bibi Lahori with short-cropped hair and tied breasts, uncles, aunts, cousins.

Hell, the guy in yellow cellophane glasses jigging away, rabbit ears flopping, was Miler. And there was Sobers dancing on a chair at the back wearing a big false nose like Inspector Clouseau. And the college fruit-shop owner! Fat Govindji! What was he doing here? Tossing up apples and oranges and bananas and catching them in the whirring steel jar of his mixer-grinder!

In all the din Fizz was sitting quietly in the clerk's chair under the judge's table, wearing a lawyer's collar and studiously taking down notes. She appeared grim.

I looked up and the judge had put on a conical red party hat with a silver papier-mâché bell on top. He was blowing loudly on a curling tooter, puffing his fat cheeks out, and instead of his gavel he now had a big pineapple in his hand.

I looked at him with pleading eyes and said, Milord, your most gracious honour, may I please go home now and finish my writing?

Milord said, Whaaat?

I said, Milord, *Troilus and Cressida*.

The crowd shouted, Milord, glycodin and paracetamol!

And milord picked up the big pineapple, held it aloft like a trophy for the raucous crowd to applaud and then banged it on the table.

It exploded like a bomb, sending neat pineapple slices scything through the courtroom.

The mad crowd screamed, Ooooh, Shaaakeeesspeeeare!

And reached out and grabbed the slices like frisbees.

The judge looked at the hollow-eyed policeman and barked, Franz!

Franz leaned forward and gave me another resounding whack.

I shouted, Oooh, Shaakeeesspeeare!

Everyone cheered, threw up their arms and broke into a jig.

Fizz looked up sternly, took the tooter out of her mouth and detonated the adjournment bell.

And I woke with a start, reached for the alarm clock and jammed it dead.

Without waking Fizz, I made myself a cup of tea and drank it standing out on the balcony. It was still pitch dark. No lights were on in any of the neighbouring houses. Come six o'clock, in a flurry of fifteen minutes, they would all spring alive with children, newspapers, tea and morning walkers. It was the hour of final stillness, and even the street-lights seemed a little wan after a long night.

The tea drained, I went in and popped open the Brother, and reread everything I had written so far. There were some satisfying moments. But when I finished I found myself exactly where I was when we had left for Suzie Wong a week earlier.

I was determined, however, not to dither any more: remember, writing is as much discipline as inspiration. I began to bang on the keys. The third cluster was on its way.

I stayed with it the entire week, writing joylessly. Fizz read my lack of animation and tried to make it easy for me by staying off the subject of the writing. But other problems were also brewing in our lives. While I was running thin with the story, we were also running thin with our money.

I had hoped my provident fund would be released within two months of quitting my job, gifting us another three months' survival. But now it seemed it might take years to process. We had no savings, and my last salary had long been spent. Fizz had managed to sell our small grey Akai television for three thousand rupees, which is what we were surviving on.

But sticking to our original covenant we refused to fret about money.

Refused to even talk about it.

Fizz said simply, I will take a job.

For some reason I was reluctant to have her work while I wrote. I think it took away somewhat the sheen from the writing.

She said, That stupid St Caesar's – I can teach English and geography. That Mr Sharma is always asking me to join.

I said, It's an idiot place. The guy's a crook. His main business is selling motor parts. He must be a champ at counting, but I doubt he even knows the alphabet.

She said, How does it matter? It's just the mornings, and just for a couple of months.

We were sitting on the love seat. She took my hand, beamed her smile and continued, Then in any case the Pandit will take us away.

Next morning she went across and sure enough, after the manner of these garage schools, was appointed a junior teacher immediately and asked to begin work the next day. It's the mystery of India's burgeoning garage schools – they are always named after imagined Christian saints and they always seem desperately in need of teachers. There is always a place for one more student, one more teacher. Classrooms sprout on balconies, verandas, under the stairs. Yes, ma'am, put his chair right there, next to the teacher. No, he's not too close. He'll get special attention. It's too crowded? Not at all. We have strict rules about how many children we take in a class.

Her salary was set at twelve hundred rupees.

With some desperate budgeting we could get by. We still had five hundred rupees left from the television sale.

When she started going to the school, I reverted to my old working hours. Basically I wanted to spend the morning with her because without the peace of satiety it was difficult to focus on the work.

Nothing gave on the Brother, though.

Simply put I had made theoretical sense of Abhay, his father, his grandfather and the story of their lives. But that, I now realized, meant nothing. I needed to make narrative sense of them all. The problem was I knew nothing about the minutiae of their lives. What did they eat? What soap did they use? What oil? How did they travel? What paper did they read? How much money did they spend? I also had no way of entering their heads and their hearts. What did they think about? Did they have impulses of love? How did they play them out? Did they talk to their wives about their feelings? What form did their conversations take? Did they ever chatter idly with their children?

I had a rudimentary knowledge of all these things, thanks to my conversations with my father and other elders who had lived in the period. The vague historical details were an amalgam of loose reading. But it was only enough, I now painfully understood, to write perhaps a five-thousand-word essay; certainly not a hundred-thousand-word novel.

With my initial bravura waning, I had begun to feel, with growing dread, that I was conjuring up a castle of sand. Grains of ignorance, falsity and pure conjecture stacked up smartly – which the first wave of critical reading would wash out of existence.

I tried to pretend plot was my problem. Not the absence of knowledge or lived experience. So I went into contortions in cluster three. I told myself, Real life is contrived, and there is no reason for me to be self-conscious.

I set up dramatic clashes between fathers and sons. They handed

out prolix lectures to each other on philosophy, values and material-
ism – shouting and banging doors and windows. The action got
hectic. The Pandit bribed the jailers to give his son better food and
bedding; Pratap got to know and ran amok. Abhay got a call from a
Bombay producer, but had to pay a large fee to facilitate his debut.
He convinced his father to accept a bribe to make it possible. Abhay's
girlfriend got pregnant. Abhay dumped her. She went to his father.
Pratap organized a job for her. And an abortion. She soon began a
deep relationship with him. In the other narrative strand the Pandit
was caught adulterating the food supplies to the cantonment. He had
an emergency meeting with Anderson. The despotic Pandit fell at the
white man's feet. A truce was struck. The Pandit began to supply the
best catamites from the region to the district office. Meanwhile, in a
tacky touch of irony, Abhay was forced to service his producer to
secure his foothold.

In short, the book fell apart totally.

In short, the book fell apart totally.

Two months after we returned from Kasauli I was still clinging to the
rituals – the strict timings, the Manual, the word counts – but it was
empty ceremony like the foot-stomping of decorative guards outside
palaces.

In Miler's parlance, I was fishing for prawns in piss.

I let Fizz read my progress every few days, and I could sense she
was in a quandary. I think she could see the book was slipping away,
but she wanted to keep faith. So we kept the charade going. The
typed foolscap sheets – in double spacing – kept piling up on the
cabinet, weighted down by the shock-haired girl on the wooden
plaque. My Hero.

On the top sheet could be read: The Inheritors.

And beneath it, the subtitle: An Indian Century.

And right below: Working Draft One.

Soon after the narrative had begun to flounder the stars and skulls
had begun to dwindle. Curiously now they began to proliferate

again. The more uncertain I got about the writing, the more I looked for solace in Fizz's body. In the beginning the writing had made me feel calm, calm and whole. Now the calmness was gone; the wholeness was gone. I felt splintered, panicky. I tried to fill myself up with her flesh; I pursued the peace of the post-coital moment. The stars multiplied.

Desire is a truly unknowable thing.

For with her it was the other way around. While I was writing strongly and well her need for me had spiralled. She had sought me out. Wanting to test my wholeness; wanting a piece of it. Her body lubricating all the time. Now it waned. She ceased to play aggressor. I could no longer lie back and wait for her to master me. The old order reasserted itself. I had to step forward and ask for what I wanted.

Then one by one the injunctions of the Manual began to fall by the wayside. I started talking away the writing; I began to drink every evening; I stopped reading the daily page of *Troilus and Cressida*; we began to go out to the movies every other night; I became a desperate plotmeister.

Pratap was about to become a corrupt chief minister. Abhay was about to become Indian cinema's King of Romance. The Pandit was about to be revealed as a do-gooder, who secretly aided the freedom fighters.

A blind man could have seen I was trawling for prawns in piss.

But worst of all I began to read fiction with a vengeance again. I dragged Fizz to Sirji's shop and picked up several new cellophaned books. I dived into other people's stories and got lost in them; I slowly forgot my own.

Fizz didn't blow the whistle on me.

I did it myself one day.

About five months after I had sat down at the dining table to bang out my resignation on the gleaming red Brother, I cornered her in the evening in the kitchen where she was cooking and declared, I am going to dump it.

She was wearing only a blue denim shirt and was chopping a tight faded-green cabbage into wavy flakes. So lightweight a cabbage looks once you take a knife to it. At the moment it reminded me of *The Inheritors*.

Without stopping she said, Stop worrying! Just take a break.

We had been going through a trying time the last two months. We still refused to talk about the money, but tackling it had become a neurosis. I was aware Fizz had created envelopes for different expenses – newspaper, milk, groceries, petrol, maid, rent, electricity, gas – and was calculating each one down to the last rupee.

While pretending we were doing nothing of the sort, we had started spending hours each day working out permutations to square it all up.

Stop the newspaper – borrow it from the folks downstairs. That saved about thirty rupees.

Lay off the maid. I do the dishes; Fizz the sweeping and mopping. Seventy-five rupees.

Walk to Bijwara Chowk every other day and shop at the whole-sale vegetable market. Buy Amul butter in hundred-gram packs, instead of five hundred, and make it last.

Avoid the bike and walk (that was easy – we had so much experience of that).

No more balcony seats. Sit in the upper stalls.

Every coin that came our way Fizz would put aside in an old Bournvita tin and upturn at the end of every week to see how much she had squirrelled away.

To my utter disgust, negotiating the money had become a more central concern than the writing.

This was a greater failure than the writing. Many years ago it was the only covenant I had sought of Fizz. That no matter what happened money would never be an issue in our lives. If we had it we would spend it. If we didn't we would not fret about it. Despite her worst moments of anxiety, she had stuck to the promise. I knew it was tough for her. Wrestling an enemy she could never name.

But it was an enemy I feared more than anything else. I had seen it corrode the entrails of my family and clan and friends. It consumed the middle class. Like a female anopheles mosquito it delivered a double whammy. It sucked out the sap of decency and left its victims in shivering fits of avarice. It was an enemy whose every embrace, I was convinced, made us less than who we were.

Money had made more big men small than anything else I knew.

My concern had spiralled when Fizz suggested taking on the after-school InstaEnglish classes, which promised young aspirants, Speak Like a Gentleman in Sixty Days! From Hello to Bye-Bye! Fullum-full Guarantee! Become a First Class Yankee!

The classes were held on the school premises in the evenings, lasted an hour each and were patronized by an odd mix of people: young boys from the small towns of Punjab, Haryana and Himachal Pradesh, girls improving their marriage prospects, and mid-career oddballs who thought a smattering of English phrases would change their lives. Mr Sharma made a killing running six packed classes every evening. If Fizz agreed to take a class through sixty days she would be paid two thousand rupees.

That was a real alarm bell. The small town – small city – was beginning to infect us.

The kitchen was tiny, so I was standing in the doorway, hands braced against the frame.

I said, I must abandon it.

She said, Finish it, you'll know better then.

I said, It's over. There is nothing there.

She said, That's not true.

I said, It is.

She said, You are being too harsh.

I said, Fizz, remember: the world is full of unread garbage – don't add to it.

She put the knife down and came and put her arms around me. I bent my head low to kiss her. The edge of her hairline was damp and there was the thinnest film of sweat on her upper lip. The smell of her skin aroused me and I closed my eyes and began to eat into her slowly opening mouth. When her hands held my face I could smell the green juice on her fingers.

That evening we went to Sukhna Lake, where tourists and revellers were winding down. The noisy families had left, and the golgappa and ice-cream carts were canvassing the last stragglers – mostly romancing couples or college boys leering at them. We found a boat that rowed us out into the steadily shrinking lake – like most artificial things the lake had come up against the illogic of its existence. Big cranes brought in to dredge the choking silt could be seen in the faded light squatting on the sandy bed, like giant insects sipping at the water.

When I could sense the water ran deep, I gave her the packet and said, OK do it.

Why me? she said, So you can blame me for it later?

Yes, I said.

She was quiet, holding on to it.

A couple of red-wattled lapwings went flapping just above us. I could feel the beat of their wings. They demanded shrilly, Did-you-do-it? Did-you-do-it?

I said, Writing is not life. Fizz is.

She said, Writing is life. Fizz is Fizz.

Just do it, I said, We need to move on.

The dark wiry boatman – from eastern Uttar Pradesh or Bihar – looked at us curiously, trying to intuit the drift of our conversation. Were we scrapping? Were we conspiring? What was the meaning of the bundle that had been handed over from one to the other?

Just do it, I said again, There is nothing there. In time there will be the right one.

Without looking at the water, looking me in the eye, she put out her left arm and dipped the packet into the lake. She didn't drop it, there was no splash, no sound; she kept her hand under the surface, letting the pores in the papers fill, silently drowning its lungs so it would never bob back up. Her trailing hand created a small wake in the darkening water, and when she finally pulled it out it was empty, and her arm was wet to her elbow. She put it against her smooth cheeks and closed her eyes.

The Pandit, Pratap and Abhay could disintegrate slowly.

The boatman looked back once to see the point in the water where Fizz's hand had gone in with the package. If the police came with an enquiry tomorrow, he would know the coordinates.

When we reached the shore the lapwings came wheeling past again, Did-you-do-it? Did-you-do-it?

Yes-we-did.

Yes-we-did.

We drove back slowly, in third gear, and hardly spoke the rest of the evening. When I got home I put the black lid on the Brother and stood it once again next to the bookshelf in the living room. Its red underbelly shone like an admonition. The dining table – after five months of harbouring the machine – looked strangely bereft. Like a bathroom without a sink. The Webster's two-volume dictionary went back onto the shelves in our bedroom. The thick bundle of pristine foolscap sheets, still partly in packaging, was stowed away at the top of the clothes cupboard. The small bits of stationery – pencils, clips, Scotch tape, pins – went into various drawers. The Manual was peeled off the mirror, rolled into a tight cylinder and jammed into the back of the bookshelves. My Hero! went on the windowsill in the bathroom. In a few days it would be hidden behind the shampoo and oil bottles.

We did it all wordlessly.

When we had finished there was not a trace that a manuscript, or a page, or even a word had ever been written in that house.

At night Fizz said, The first went into fire, this one's gone into water, what do you want to do with the next?

We were sitting up against the bedrest. The lights were off. The tip of her cigarette glowed like a nagging idea. Several years after college she had recently resumed smoking – one cigarette every night before sleep. Three years earlier I had got her to consign another sheaf of typed papers into the fireplace at Sobers's house in Kasauli. That time it had been a finished manuscript, but so much worse. I had felt relief seeing it go. It was so bad even the fire had protested. It had stuttered and choked, then belched smoke, and the room had filled up with sooty flakes floating up to the rafters. In the dead of night we had to fling open the doors and windows of the bedroom, and let all the smoke and soot out – and do it noiselessly. For more than an hour we stood outside shivering in the cold Kasauli night while the smoke and soot settled. We had laughed and Fizz had warned me about writing any more sooty books.

The mood was quite different now.

Garbaging a first book can be a glorious act. Dumping the second is less honourable, and more fraught with uncomfortable questions. We were both putting a brave face to it, but I think we were both wondering about the fish that were nibbling at *The Inheritors* and the message they were sending us.

The air, I said, The next one belongs to the air. Out of a plane. Or maybe from the edge of that house on the hill.

Yes, she said sucking the cigarette into a hot glow, Fire. Water. Air. And maybe then we can go to a publisher.

The next day when I woke I had nothing to do.

Fizz left for her school and I tried to read, but was too scattered to stay with it. I found myself rereading every page because each time I reached the last line I realized I had not registered a word. Listening to music was no good either. I called Amresh and drove across to his annexe in Sector 34 for a cup of tea. He was a strange guy and I avoided him most of the time. I only reached for him when I was in a weird place myself. His screwballness never failed to comfort me in my own sense of displacement.

His annexe – in Chandigarh parlance the room above a garage –

was an experience. Every square inch of wall was covered with strips of paper written over with famous quotations and passages. The sources ranged from Hindu and Western philosophy to literary texts and poems. From very short ones like tat tvam asi – thou art that – and Descartes's I think therefore I am, to long passages from Marcus Aurelius and the Upanishads. Each was written out in his bold cursive hand with a thick, coloured felt pen – various shades of red, green, yellow, purple, orange, blue, black, brown.

On the ceiling he had painted an entire poem in large black letters, Stopping by Woods on a Snowy Evening. He had obviously meticulously measured out the space, for the poem filled the ceiling to precision. The last stanza – the woods are lovely, dark and deep – the last stanza was done contrastingly in deep red. The effect was psychedelic. All that surrounding text buzzed you, and there was always a deep sense of relief when you exited the room.

By any standard he was a crank.

Amresh worked as a reporter for an obscure south-based newspaper and had a dire sense of morality. At press conferences while everyone attacked the food he refused to even take a sip of water. He carried a fattish steel canteen with him – an army issue, slung across his back along with his black satchel – and he took a glug from it if he felt the need. Within the city he used no motorized form of transport. He had a superbly maintained Atlas bicycle, with a small lockable steel box welded to the carrier, on which he could zip across town in minutes. Tall, well built, he was a familiar sight in Chandigarh, pedalling furiously down its wide tree-lined roads. He wore a black hairband around his right ankle, into which he tucked his trouser leg each time he got on to his bicycle. His grey socks had black grease streaks from the chain.

To appearance he was utterly conventional. He dressed formally – creased trousers, ironed crumpleless shirts, grey socks, black leather shoes. His hair was trimmed military short, and he was always freshly bathed and shaven close. He did what no Punjabi middle-class boy does: he cooked and cleaned for himself. He was from

Amritsar, the border town famed for its machismo, but was quietly deferential.

I covered many breaking stories of terrorist attacks with him, and while the rest of us ran about urgently demanding information he was always extremely considerate, making polite enquiries and taking down detailed notes. We would arrive at a rural link road with the morning dew still not killed by the sun, and the spreading fields gently stirring under the assault of the early birds. There would be the reassuring thrum of tube-wells in the distance. Village dogs would be barking in relay. The ramshackle Punjab Roadways bus would be parked just off the road, at a broken angle. There would be a small crowd of villagers standing at a distance. Unwashed men in unruly turbans, women with fading dupattas over their heads, and snotty children, holding on to adult fingers while trying to edge closer.

If it was winter – which it mostly was because it made it easier for the killers to conceal their AK-47s under their wraparound blankets – if it was winter, the mist would be still rising off the ground. In particular the water ditches by the roadside would be steaming. At a remove there would be a couple of grey police jeeps, and either a discoloured ambulance or a police truck. Also, always, there would be at least two white Ambassador cars with dark film over the windows, one belonging to the senior superintendent of police and the other to some senior district official. We would bring our cabs – announcing Press in bold handwritten stickers on the windshield – close to the official vehicles and, jumping out, stride towards the scene of the crime.

The photographers would dart ahead, bending, kneeling, leaning, clicking. The bodies would be lined up in an adjoining field, neatly, and three deep. Sometimes they would be covered with white sheets, which the photographers would peel back to make their pictures. Mostly they would be laid out as they died and as they were pulled out.

It was always an eclectic mix. Men, but also some women and sometimes children. The early honour codes of terrorism were long gone. The AK-47 rapid-fire bullets would have hammered the dead in arbitrary ways. Shattered and ripped arms, legs, skulls and guts hinted at the manic moment when testy fingers would have squeezed the trigger. Occasionally you saw the ooze of brain or an intestine.

In the dead of night the bus would have been seized by three young boys parting their wraparound blankets and revealing their guns. One by the front door, one by the rear and one navigating the driver to a lonely country road. The comforting smelly air in the bus – of stale food, pickles, bad breath and hot eructations – would suddenly be charged with menace. Without being woken, passengers huddled in coarse blankets would begin to stir, their hearts clutching. Soon there would be no eye shut on the bus, no bowel not loosened.

A passenger in the front seat, a smart-talking salesman from Ludhiana, known among his friends and family for his wit, trusting in his persuasive ability, would begin to beg and cajole. He would talk of the innocence of the passengers, their ordinariness, their hardships. He would admire the cause of the boys, their bravery, the unfairness of the government hunting them down. He might even ask them which militant group they were from – Khalistan Commando Force? Babbar Khalsa? Khalistan Liberation Force? Perhaps even which town, which school, college. All the while the cheery-faced clean-shaven salesman would smile, trying to make light of the moment.

The hawk-eyed leader standing by the driver, with a nose and a chin sharp as an arrow, with a beard still too sparse to trim or tie, high on the opium he was chewing and the sensuous AK-47 he was cradling, would at some point place the short barrel on the man's pounding chest and detonate a round. It would make a quiet, muffled sound, no indication of the inferno to come. The salesman would die with his eyes wide open, the mouth still smiling, the last pitch still unfinished. Like a good soldier, in battle finally only for his life. At close range the snug bullet would have exploded his heart all over his body. It would also have silenced the other sharp strategists on the bus.

The driver would have been solicitous. Showing no resistance. Trying to switch sides. Politely asking for instructions. Do you want me to turn left from here? Towards Khakkar village? You want me to slow down? Park here? Right here? By the roadside? Just say the word, my lords. Just say the word.

We all believe in our ability to dodge death.

In our ability to touch the pulse of goodness in the killer.

Every last person on the bus would have believed they would somehow survive even if death was visited inside the bus.

But the boys would be disciplined soldiers with hearts of polished steel. They would work to plan. The Sikhs would be first removed from the bus and laid face down under the kikar tree. The women and children would follow and be similarly spread on the ground. One boy, scrawny and gap-toothed, would range over them with his wooden-handled AK-47, the pride and meaning of his life.

The hawk-eyed leader would cast a last lingering look over the cowering bodies and, stepping down from the bus, signal with his sharp chin. The new convert's heart would fill with excitement and dread. He would order all the remaining men into the middle seats of the bus. Shuffling, shrinking, wrapping their brown coarse blankets closer, they would comply. Each man would be riven on the final dilemma of his life: should he make a last desperate appeal for mercy, or make himself so insignificant that the boy, and fate, missed seeing him and passed him by?

In a loud and misguided invocation to the almighty, the young convert, with angry acne peeping through his thin hair, would shout, Jo bole so nihal . . . and levelling the beautiful gun at his waist, in a moment of pure intoxication, squeeze the smooth trigger. The rest of his rousing cry would be drowned out, as he began to rock in a gentle arc, while the gun spat and spat and spat.

A medley of sounds would erupt: the sharp spitting of the gun; the soft thud of the bullets spanking the blankets; the crack of skull and bone being chipped and shattered; the ting of bullets ricocheting off aluminium seat handles and steel walls; the screams of the dying and the hiding; and the flowing abuse of the young convert as he revved himself up for the power that pulsed through his hand.

Moments later, aeons later, he would fill a sudden silence with the sound of a fresh magazine clicking home. Those not yet dead would have only a moment of hope as the young warrior walked the wetting aisle systematically picking out anything that stirred. The driver would be there too, his heart now open like a flower, leaning on the man from the village near Gurdaspur, whose wife and daughter lay face down under the sky.

When the last moan had melted into the night, the boy would open the rear door, step down and turn to his hawk-eyed chief, who stood unmoving in the moonlight, the blanket falling from his shoulders like Batman's cape, the AK-47 slack by his side, barrel pointing down. The chief would lift his gun aloft in a timeless gesture of victory and declare, Jo bole . . . and in a voice the recruit would join in . . . So nihal . . . and in a voice, from under the kikar tree, the third boy would enter the chorus . . . Sat sri akal.

They were religious warriors. Not thugs, not mercenaries. Like all soldiers of dogma, they marched out from barracks of morality to practise great immorality.

I remember walking through those buses. The aisle was always slippery with thick blood even though the bodies had been removed. The feel of catastrophe was complete, with bundles and blankets strewn all over, streaks of dark-black blood on the seats, bullet pocks everywhere, chips of white bone which you learnt to spot and point out to each other, and the seat stuffings pouring out like the innards of the dead – and once I recall a harmonium on a seat like a surreal painting, its lid wide open, the lungs exposed, shot clean through its heart of burnished wood.

The sweet-acrid stench of fresh-stale blood would fill my nostrils, and I was unable to get rid of it for days.

At the site, while I and the other young reporters worked the bus, the villagers and the pot-bellied policemen, the senior reporters, with a smoothly oiled manner and masses of confidence, went straight to the senior superintendent of police and the district officials, pumped their hands, backslapped them and began to mine them for information. While we hunted for atmosphere and drama, colour and quote, they dug for the inside story, the exclusive take – normally an official plant, part of the propaganda war between the various sides. But it was not a journalism of partisanship. In another setting, in a room of the Golden Temple, the militants would give the inside story, the exclusive take, and it would be dispatched into the world with equal fervour.

I liked Amresh when he reported because he was serious, hard-working, methodical. More than any of the rest of us. He took his time, spoke to every source, tried hard to reconstruct things as they might have happened and was completely sceptical of the official line. He was also the only one among us who was not brusque with the information givers, the innocents unwittingly marched onto the stage of history. He did not demand rudely and move on. He was gentle, sympathetic, willing to wait for the mauled emotions to untangle and articulate themselves, as the wretched peasant squatted on his haunches, his head between his hands, absorbing the latest blow to his life.

Looking at him work, I often thought he seemed more like a social activist practising therapy than a hard-bitten reporter chasing a dead-line.

He was also immensely helpful. Selflessly he shared his informa-tion and often pointed out our errors. In Chandigarh and Amritsar we were a large, and growing, band of reporters from all over the country, chasing the big, unending story that had made many journalistic careers and continued to do so. Sikh terrorism had exploded in the Punjab in 1983 and grabbed the imagination of Indians. For a country forever in search of a cause and a focus, this was good stuff. We had gained a sense of self only fifty years ago with the extravagant symbolisms of the freedom struggle. We still needed an enemy in order to understand who we were.

In India's march to adulthood, if the Emergency was the loss of virginity then Punjab was the first full-bodied affair. Psyches and bodies were exhaustively explored, promises were made, scars inflicted, intense and dangerous emotions played out. At one level the whole bloody thing was a macabre joke. Like a Kurosawa battle sequence where the master forgot to call cut and suddenly went home to his wife. No one else had the balls to speak up, step in. The horses kept galloping, the armies kept clashing, the samurai kept slaughtering with their broad swords and sibilant cries. Hosho! HoshoKoshoPoshoWosho! Hosho! By the time the master returned – having then gone off to solicit beady-eyed producers for more money – the set, the armour, the horses, the actors, everything, had been run into the ground.

After some time the illusion of battle had given way to real battle. It is not unusual. Men have emotions, and too many hits even with a wooden sword can ignite volatile feelings.

When the political masters in Delhi and Punjab went to sleep the bit actors took over. The games the masters played were contrived, artificial. Their reasons were false; their sufferings make-believe. The agonies of the bit players, on the other hand, were real. The three boys who walked through the bus were not playing a game. They were putting their lives on the line for real things. They were acting on real wounds. They had been hurt badly by the wooden swords.

They would kill real people.

They would die real deaths.

Soon.

The masters meantime, old and new, had lost all control of the script and were struggling to intuit its original intent. The action had been taken out of their hands. In the August of 1987 when I went to meet Amresh in his lunatic room – *The Inheritors* disintegrating at the bottom of Sukhna Lake – the bit players had taken over completely and were dragging the scenes all over the place. A megaphone was not enough any more to bring them to heel. Someone needed to go after each of them systematically and beat them into sanity.

Of course it was never better for Indian journalists and the news-reading public. The high drama was riveting. There were assaults, assassinations, mass killings – the entire spectacle of the Sikhs, traditionally India's bravest and most patriotic grouping, locked in battle with the Indian state in pursuit of a cuckoo idea of a separate country, was just too irresistible a mix of entertainment and morality tale.

And with our blockbuster myths and our hell-for-leather Bollywood films, we love nothing better.

News as high entertainment began with Punjab and many many years later, when my life and my love had run their course, and the curtain had been pulled down on a tumultuous century, and I had long ceased to be a journalist, news would be a national obsession, and around the clock half a dozen television channels would drag us collectively from one manic incident to another, making each of us relevant by making us part of some large unfurling drama some-where. By then the bit players of the Punjab drama would have long been hammered into line or eliminated from the screenplay. The rest would be back to what they loved best – profit and loss and the celebrations therein. Punjab would have reverted to the boring issues of free electricity, bankruptcy, wheat prices, water-sharing and the minor corruptions of sex and liquor.

But back then, in 1987, Punjab looked unsolvable.

Everyone talked of it as Ireland. Chronic, ceaseless. But worse because the Sikh was crazier, and less afraid, than the Irish.

As Sikh lovers, Amresh and I often spent hours discussing the great Indian screw-up that had turned India's most ballsy defenders into its most tireless foes. But we were young then and tended to read the alleyways of history in which we found ourselves as the auto-bahns; and with the knowingness of the young we thought we could see where the autobahn went. But today I know it is not possible to foretell the future of even two people, leave alone that of millions.

No one can say what will be, for no one knows what men will do.

Today I know I did not even know what I would do.

As for the autobahns of history, there are no autobahns of history while history is happening. As DNA tests nail the real father later, history's autobahns are identified and established much after. Only after the dust has settled can the journey of the killer sperm be tracked. The seed with the phoney moustache that squiggled forth from Linz. The one with the flowing robes that raged forth from the Arabian palace. The bearer of the uncut beard that came out barracking from a religious seminary near Amritsar. The one in voluminous short pants that marched timidly out of a middle-class home in sprawling Hindustan.

Sperm singing the song of universal homicide.

Each scorching a fiery autobahn into which history collapsed, choking for air.

But back then in the alleyway, incapable of reading history, we scrabbled for tools to navigate. In this Amresh, as a rooted Punjabi, was an invaluable guide. He had a solid knowledge of the land, the language, the people. As we moved in the dark, bombarded by contradictory information, he saved many of us from death by propaganda. He was unlike any reporter I had seen then or since. He worked the hardest, yet was the least competitive. If he had a lead he was prompt to share it and then help you the rest of the way. In fact everything about his reporting process was different.

While the rest of us scribbled haphazardly in tiny notepads he carried a big spiral-bound book in which he wrote neatly and long. In his room the spiral-bound books were catalogued and kept stacked in a row like long-playing records.

When we hit the post office in the evening, while the rest of us rushed to grab the teleprinters and bang out our stories – if the damn lines held – he would settle down at a rickety wooden table in a cobwebby anteroom in the old colonial buildings with high roofs, distant jammed ventilators and long-limbed ceiling fans, away from the cranking of the machines, and begin to draft his piece. After we had all left to gather and gossip or hit the hotel bar, he would settle down at the teleprinter and carefully type out his dispatch. Most of ours would be five to seven hundred words long; his were never less than fifteen hundred. And they were full of elaborate atmosphere and moral positions. Lines like: The lone child sat huddled under a tree, her pretty face stained with timeless tears, wondering what she had ever done to have her only father so cruelly snatched away from her.

He was the kind of bleeding heart seasoned reporters find appalling. But nobody mocked him – even behind his back – because everyone had been helped by him at some point, and he exuded the kind of innocence you can only shake your head at and steer clear of: there is little pleasure in running it down.

Most of us took him in small doses. I certainly did. I would meet him when I was in turmoil and needed to play myself against the reassuring solidities of his rigid moral order.

When I sat down on the only chair in his room, he said, You will have lunch with me. I am learning to cook Chinese – fried rice and vege-table sweet and sour.

There was no point arguing. He was a desperate host.

Who's teaching you? I said.

It's easy, he said, waving a paperback from the airless kitchen attached to his room. There was no door in between – it would have made it a tomb.

He was chopping green French beans meticulously on the marble slab. Next to his slowly working hands lay a small pile of sliced onions and potatoes, both cut lengthwise. A small Hawkins pressure cooker was whistling softly on the gas. The room was heavy with the smells of cooking. A Shiv Kumar Batalvi cassette was playing on the Sanyo recorder. It sang of the pleasures of love and how they all end in pain.

I looked around the room to see if he had pasted up anything new. There was so much of it that I couldn't tell, though it did seem more crowded than before. I wanted to pick up the thick black felt pen lying on his work-table and scrawl FUCK in big letters all over the walls.

He poked his head out of the kitchen – heat beads decking his forehead, small knife in hand – and said, nodding at the Sanyo, He understood what true love was! No one understands it these days.

He smiled, eyes twinkling, as if we – he and I – knew better.

I said, But he drank himself to death.

Boss, that is the mistake he made. That is the mistake everyone makes. They think there can't be poetry or love without drinking. You must be high on life, boss, high on love.

His eyes twinkled, as if he knew something no one else did.

I knew he neither smoked nor drank. I was also convinced he was a virgin. He had the anxious romantic and sexual certitudes of one. For some time I had wondered if he even masturbated. Till I unearthed a copy of *The Sensuous Woman* by 'J' while picking up his pillow to prop against the wall. With a twinkle he had said, It's a wonderful study of the sexual revolution.

I didn't want to talk about love or writing. The first time he had visited our house he had looked at the books – on the shelves, on the tables, on the chairs – and said, You like reading Penguins, do you?

He came out of the kitchen. I could hear the low sizzle of a pan. He had a stirring ladle in his hand now. He walked to the table, wiped his left hand on the seat of his jeans, and picked up a thick hardbound register – the kind used for attendance rosters. He riffled through it, stopped somewhere midway, and handed it to me.

Read from here, he said, Many new ones. You can skip the Punjabi and Hindi.

Like cooking, he had learnt his poetry from a primer. It was all in blank verse. Each poem neatly filled a full page. Some lines were only a word long. Punctuation appeared only at the end of each poem – a full stop, a question mark or an exclamation. He had written about fifty new ones since I was last here a few months before. Fortunately many were in Hindi and Punjabi and I could skip those. The rest I could rush through in a single scan. The busiest word in there was love; followed by heart, moon, blood, twilight, flowers, dewdrops and the golden sun. There were some with long titles, like the Frost poem on the ceiling. One was: The Heart of the Lover Resides in the Swaying Fields by the Flowing Canal.

When an adequate time had passed, I closed the register. The cover label read: Amresh Sharma: Poems and Musings: Volume VI. I said, You've been busy. I like that one in which you compare your lover to an AK-47 that spits fire into your body and wounds your heart.

He came out of the kitchen, eyes twinkling, but before he could start a discussion on the poems, I said, I am planning to move to Delhi.

He said, Why? You've got a job?

No, I haven't, I said, But I am going to look for one.

Why do you want to go to Delhi? he said.

There was no twinkle in his eyes now. He looked concerned.

I said, I need a job. I need to get back to work. I need the money.

But why Delhi? Why do you want to leave Chandigarh for Delhi?

I said, Just like that. Get a move on.

But, boss, you can do all that here. This city has everything.

I suddenly looked up and saw tat tvam asi: thou art that, written in black block letters above his kitchen doorway, and I was tired. I wanted to go home. I didn't want to talk to him any more. I didn't know why I had come over in the first place. He was a good guy but full of half-assed notions. His wide-eyed goodness was a kind of poison. It was blind to the complexity of the world.

But that morning, killing time, looking for my own locus, I could never have imagined how strangely it would end for him. Ten years later I would learn, through a chance meeting with a common acquaintance, that he was dead, found hanging by the fan in the same scrawled-wall room. There was no suicide note; no one knew the reason.

The unbearable burden of morality.

I said, I have to go; I need to finish some work Fizz gave me.

Of course he detained me till I had eaten the fried rice, but I ensured the conversation stayed focused on Punjab. We talked of police friends who had died, about the militant groups that would become dominant. I thought it would be the Khalistan Commando Force; he thought the Babbar Khalsa. They had the bomb expertise which gave them the edge, he reckoned. I left the moment I had finished. The fried rice was not bad at all, and we ate it with large dollops of Kissan sauce, washing it down with fizzy Thums Up.

He packed a plastic lunch box for me to take along.

I need Fiza's approval, not yours, he said, his eyes twinkling.

In the night I was crumpled into the love seat reading, when Amresh called.

I said, Fizz loved the rice. Let me give the phone to her.

He said, No, I've called you about your job in Delhi.

The do-gooder had gone to the press club in the evening and worked the tables for gossip. He had a couple of hot leads. One with an old newspaper expanding its features pages, and another with a new modern paper, blazing new paths. Amresh had gone as far as acquiring contact names and numbers. If I really wanted to leave serene Chandigarh and go to the big bad metropolis, he was going to set me up. All I had to do now was to pick up the phone and call.

I said, By the way, I liked that other one too, the one in which the lover's body is like moonlight – forever to be basked in but never to be touched.

I gave the phone to Fizz before he could reply.

The next morning I went to the market and called Delhi. I had to go back several times to call before I managed to speak to the relevant assistant editors. They were desultory. Send in your papers. Come and see us.

Two days later, on a Saturday morning, I took a pre-dawn bus to Delhi. Fizz came along. It was like that with us. We hated to be parted. It was dark and cold and we had seats at the back and a big brown shawl and the excitement of a new journey and our hands in each other's laps walking us up and down dizzy peaks and the hours sped by like the manic Punjab Roadways bus.

Travelling did it for us. Being together did it for us. We could string out life and the world at the end of our moving fingers. With love I walked her slippery body and each time I arrived at a joyous place she closed her eyes and convulsed. Then we held hands. Then she held my desire and let it bloom and bloom. And we were never more happy.

We spent the day in Delhi like backpackers, moving around in local buses, snacking at roadside eateries, waiting outside offices. The meetings went OK. Between them we managed to catch a film at the Regal in Connaught Place. It was a bad Hindi film. The hall was empty. But we didn't care. We were striking out to do new things. We were together. We were happy.

My résumé looked good. But my seeming lack of ambition confused the editors.

I was a reporter who was not looking for a reporter's job. It was most unusual. At the time, in the eighties, becoming a reporter was every young journalist's only aim. To be a reporter was to be a journalist – with it came the bylines, the travel, the contacts, the glamour, the career mobility, the money. But I was looking for an editing job. That too of a lowly subeditor, at the bottom of the pile. I didn't want anything with responsibility. I didn't want anything that ate up my mental and physical time.

I had thought it through – in those long days after the sinking of *The Inheritors*, when Fizz was away at school and my life was again a blank. I was certain I did not want to report any more. I did not want to speak to any more boring politicians, feckless bureaucrats, trigger-happy policemen. I did not want to write any more news reports declaring who said what about whom. Anyone could do that and everyone was doing that. I did not want to write any more 'mood' stories, conjuring up the atmosphere and colour of the world in spurious ways. I did not want to think up new names of rickshaw-pullers and shopkeepers into whose mouths I could put words I had thought up.

I did not want to propound new theories.

I did not want to pretend I knew what was happening.

I did not want to pretend I did not know what was happening.

I did not want to simplify complex things.

I did not want to make simple things seem complex.

I did not want to play the looking-finding game any more.

Anyone could do that and everyone was doing that.

I wanted to sink into least-deception journalism.

I wanted to conserve myself for other things.

At the bottom of the heap I wanted to be responsible only for the full stops and commas, for language and tenses and datelines and headlines.

For the unbending niceties of form. Not the sleight-of-hand of content.

For this I wanted a little money and a lot of time. Abhay and Pratap and the Pandit were so much fish food now, but there was a story out there waiting for me and I needed all my resources to look for it.

And I did not want to be away from Fizz any more.

That had been one of the hardest things about reporting. The constant going away.

I wanted to be the foot soldier of the business, the GI, the legionary, the sepoy, the man at the bottom who keeps the armies moving but who sleeps peacefully without the worries of loss and gain, and the weight of deaths and disasters.

Least-deception journalism.

Subeditor.

Haven of the timid, the neurotic, the book reader, the stutterer. The boy in the class who knows everything but can never speak. The man in the office who analyses the world but can never fashion it.

Like Herodotus of Halicarnassus who wrote, I wanted to be the subeditor who wrote. And finally be counted for more than emperors.

My stance puzzled the editors, but it made their job easier. By the time Fizz and I returned to the bus terminus in the evening, I think I had both jobs. If you were good with the English language and did not want much money you were the kind of cheap body newspaper offices were always looking for. Journalism's engines thrum on the oil of the eager young.

We got home past midnight and when we had finished loving and the lights were off, Fizz smoking her first and last cigarette of the day pulled at the hot tip and said, We are never ever going to come back to Chandigarh. I know it in my bones.

I knew she was right.

We were never coming back.

What I did not know was how far away we would end up going. So far that it would be difficult to tell who we once were.

BOOK TWO

*Karma: Action*

# In King Cupola's Court

The packing was easy.

I took the job with the modern new paper, and they gave me two weeks to join. Fizz resigned from the school and the InstaEnglish course. Her students gave her a card saying: We will miss you, beautiful madam. One of them had drawn her with a dark lead pencil, with sharp nose and masses of hair and bow lips. She looked quite glamorous.

We collected some cardboard cartons from friends and some we got from Sirji. We carefully lined them with polythene sheets, threw in heaps of roasted neem leaves to ward off insects, and stacked our books in tightly, ensuring not a page was creased. By the time we finished there were fourteen cartons, of varying sizes and so heavy you couldn't move them without bracing your feet.

There was little else. The kitchen stuff went into a big steel trunk. Bed linen and curtains – with more crispy neem leaves – went into a small steel trunk. The music system went into its own packaging. The television was already gone. The beds belonged to the landlord. The dining table and chairs we sold. The only piece of furniture we were left with was the one we had started out with – the love seat. We placed the red-bellied Brother on it, and we were done.

The landlord – a wonderfully bluff retired army colonel who wore a starched turban and suit first thing every morning, and tightly netted in his beard so that not a hair escaped – the landlord generously gave us some space in his garage where we could stack our things. We promised him we'd be back in a fortnight to pick it all up. The moment we had found ourselves a place.

In a ho-ho voice he said, Make sure, son, you are back before the Chinese get here.

He had been in the disastrous Indo–China war of 1962 and there was some persisting neurosis.

I said we would make sure.

Back in Delhi, we stayed with an old friend who had a flat in Vasant Kunj. It was a triumph of bareness. The flat was large – three bed-rooms and a living-dining. Philip, my friend, had let it real cheap. It's possible he wasn't even paying anything for it. It belonged to a Member of Parliament from his home town in Kerala and had no value on the rental market.

At the time Vasant Kunj was pretty much the end of the world. You peeled away from the city and drove through scrub country – rock and thorny kikar, the phallic Qutub Minar rising to your left – and you hit a nightmare forest of concrete blocks. They were clearly the spawn of a brain-dead government official. Meant to pack in the bodies; square up the stats; line some fatcat contractor's safe. If you didn't carry your life inside you, soullessness was guaranteed.

Philip's flat was on the second floor of one such concrete box – the boxes were so indistinguishable it took some time before you could find the one you wanted. It had one creaky bed with a lumpy mattress and a greying bedsheet. It also had two cane chairs, a wooden table and a coil heater to cook on. The coil heater was the central dynamo of the flat. It sat splendidly alone in the kitchen dis-pensing hot water, tea and food. Its ceramic plate and coils were layered with brown-black flecks of boiled tea leaves, and some yellow residue of dal. It had no plug and the naked wires were jammed into the socket and held in place with matchsticks. The whole contraption looked like a completely burnt-out affair. But when you threw the switch the naked connections sparked and sizzled – dangerously –

and then, slowly, the coils began to glow. First – with smoke, sounds and smells – they burnt off the last spillings, then settled down to a strong pulsing heat.

The only other personal item in the flat was a big iron trunk in the room in which Philip slept. All his belongings were stuffed into it. Every cupboard in the flat was bare. From socks to toothpaste to books to condoms, he pulled everything out from the trunk. The trunk had a fat golden lock. You could crack a skull with it. The trunk also had his name and address in Kerala, right down to the full pin code, stencilled on its lid. You could drop it in the letterbox and it would reach his home.

When I first looked at the flat I thought he could vacate it in five minutes flat, and no one would know anyone had ever been there. Maybe that was the politician's brief to him.

Philip gave us a choice of the remaining two bedrooms and we took the one with the bathroom. We bought a cheap coir mattress, a broom, a mop and a bottle of phenyl. In the evening I picked up dal-roti from a cheap dhaba nearby, and when we had eaten Philip wanted to linger and talk. We made excuses – of exhaustion – and stole away. I had been stroking Fizz's forearm and I could see the colour rising on her slowly.

We had reached the point in the evening when we were no longer talking to each other. We needed to go through our bodies to find conversation again. Desire had pushed all the words out of us. We needed to burn in it, to burn it off, before space could be made for them to find their way back in.

We had some sense of what was happening. We were in a strange city and we needed the solace of what we knew best in the world. We had made a big move and we wanted the only reward we ever craved. I had been here before. Each time our lives walked an edge the pleasure of holding on to each other spiralled. The mattress on the floor was perfect. It made madness possible. I was straining by the time I had closed the door and taken off my clothes. Fizz was waiting. The magic moment. At the starting line of all possibility, all pleasure.

The room was in half-light. Fizz had thrown a towel over the weak bulb. She was on the mattress, sitting up against the wall, her legs naked beneath the T-shirt, a hint of dampness in the dark shadows. Her hair was loose. She looked unbelievably beautiful.

When I lay down, she unzipped her moist flesh and fed all of me into it. My nose, my mouth, my fingers, my ache. The musk of her love swamped my senses and my entire life was instantly refined to one word. Fizz.

Leaving everything else for later, I went looking for where her hair began and worked my way through its musky trails to where there was none. And having found her burning core, and having drunk of it, I left it, and wandered her body, only to keep circling back to it for sustenance.

We began to climb peaks and fall off them. We did old things in new ways. And new things in old ways. At times like this we were the work of surrealist masters. Any body part could be joined to any body part. And it would result in a masterpiece. Toe and tongue. Nipple and penis. Finger and the bud. Armpit and mouth. Nose and clitoris. Clavicle and gluteus maximus. Mons veneris and phallus indica.

The Last Tango of Labia Minora. Circa 1987. Vasant Kunj. By Salvador Dalí.

Draughtsmen: Fizznme.

Fizz screamed silently through it all – through gritted teeth, through wide-open mouth – and only those who have known a woman screaming silently in orgasm know how loud it is. It ripped through the room and set me to pounding frenzies.

Every now and then she climbed up such high peaks that she went out of sight, and I had to wait patiently for her to climb back down before I could touch her again.

Sometimes she returned raring to climb another. At other times she seemed to be flagging and I had to prepare her afresh. And there was no way of knowing how high she would go the next time. I tried to follow her, to keep track of her, but it was not always possible. There is no doubt that in sex men are only base-camp creatures: they can enjoy the many pleasures available halfway up the mountain, but the dizzy peaks are not for them. They lack the air, the imagination, the abandon, the anatomy. Their task is to prepare the true summiteers, the women, the artists of the high peaks. Ghorals who can spring from coign to coign, peak to peak, till there is nothing ahead but the spread of eternity.

Men have struggled with this knowledge for millennia. The knowledge of where they cannot go. It is not easy to be inferior.

It is not easy to live among gazelles and be a boar.

Cunning men wait and are vicarious. They create pornography and surrogate joys. They abet the climbers, gaze from a distance and are pleasured.

Stupid men clap the ghorals in irons. They close ranks, create religion, create morality, create laws, erect palisades and shut out the mountains. None will go where they cannot. The high grounds are lost forever.

We were at love for hours and soon the small room began to smell of sex. And then her skin began to smell of it; and taste of it. Wherever I kissed her – from her face to her breasts to her back – it was the same maddening musk. Like a passionate preacher, it seems, I had travelled everywhere and spread her molten core.

Eventually, deep into the night, I knew she was finally gone and was on her last ascent. I scrambled after her, desperately keeping pace, and we went higher and higher and higher, till my blood swelled beyond containment and my lungs burst and my knees buckled and the base of my spine melted and I lost sight of her as I exploded into nothingness.

When I came to the next morning we had an encore. It was not a command expedition like the night before, but was as full of love and desire.

I went to work and it was strangely satisfying. There is something to the puritan ethic of working the day through and earning your keep. Being an art man for six months had been great, but coming back to the solidities of the daily grind was unexpectedly pleasurable. That evening I had the satisfaction of the manual worker. I had taken bad materials, bad furniture, bad words – other people's bad constructions – and hammered them into things of functional beauty. These things would go out into the world and be devoured by avid readers. They would serve a purpose. I had been part of a manufac- turing chain that had produced something of immediate and real value.

I had earned my dinner.

The problem with art is dealing with the fluff of art when no art is happening. It can be nauseating. Fatuous men holding forth on aesthetics. Maudlin men waiting for the big idea. By the time I had gone to Amresh's quotecoated room, I had been in the throes of acute nausea.

The fluff of art when no art is happening.

I didn't tell Fizz all this. Some illusions must never be destroyed. They sustain rock-solid realities. We were going to do other things. This had to be suffered.

Fizz had made our room cosy. She had bought two cane murras – so there was a seating alternative to the bed. She had put out a fluorescent green jute rug. She had hung up the black-and-white framed poster of Ezra Pound someone had once brought us from England; and a smaller print, in golden inks, of Rabindranath Tagore. And she had neatly piled up the stack of books, which always travelled with us, next to our mattress, to keep us warm. In the dull bathroom she had nailed a cheerful calendar showing Goan beaches in winter – with a hint of white women sunbathing naked – and had put out some colourful plastic glasses and soapdishes to break the monotony.

But the moment you stepped out the bedroom door you were in a wasteland. Balls of dirt rolled about, meeting in the corners. There was a half-inch-thick patina of grey-brown dust over everything from floors to windowsills. Cobwebs were strung up all over the house like festoons – between the iron grilles, on the walls, in the cupboards and in the unused bathroom over the pot and the taps. The flat was new, but the paint was already flaking. It caught in the cobwebs, creating a mess and taking away from them even a semblance of sinister beauty. Curiously I never saw a spider. The cobwebs, like the dust, seemed to be self-propagating. You had to be careful as you wandered through the rooms to not stir up anything, else a paroxysm of asthmatic coughing was at hand.

The first day Fizz, predictably, made some noises about rolling up her sleeves and cleaning the flat. I put my foot down. I could see it was a futile endeavour. I was reminded of the parables where the bush always, in the end, reclaims the white man's clearings. Between Philip, the dust and the unseen spiders, Fizz had no chance. The old order would reassert itself the first day Fizz flagged. She was better off tending her own little yard and shutting the door on the creeping wasteland.

Philip was an even more hopeless case. When I had known him before – in my first job – I had liked his mind, and we would spend days talking writers, politics, cinema and sports. Like me he was an Ali lover, and like me he had spent his school years hunting down material on Cassius Clay/Muhammad Ali, and following his fights in tiny reports on the sports pages of the daily newspapers. Unlike me he swore by the communist manifesto.

Then Philip was slim, almost thin. But now – at twenty-six – he had already put on a soft belly and his face was going to fat. He had given up journalism and turned to television. One of his uncles back in Kerala was a famous film-maker known for his art-house films, which explored social iniquities and identity stresses. The films were never commercially released outside Kerala, but were avidly tracked by students of serious cinema. Philip had a cultivated air of dismissal about most things – illustrated always with a sharp wave of his right hand – and he dismissed his uncle, too, as irrelevant. But secretly I knew the intense film-maker was Philip's lodestar and Philip felt he had cinema in him only because of his uncle. Yet, unwilling to admit it, he had to take another route. He had chosen television, whose tentacles were just beginning to creep into Indian lives.

When we came to live with him in Vasant Kunj he said he was drafting the script of a mega-serial. Since we last worked together, he had gone back to his home in Bombay and then come back here to write. In Bombay he had worked for a year with a television production company and picked up the vocabulary of the medium. He said television was going to change India – it was going to change the way we thought, lived, ate, fucked. He said it was going to change our politics and our society. He said a day would come when we would have a hundred television channels talking to us every hour of the day.

He said we would lie back and let television take us.

In the missionary position. Our legs around our ears. Our brains between our balls.

We would hear nothing but television.

We would see nothing but television.

We would amuse ourselves to death.

Fizz and I had no interest in any of it. We thought it all improbable and wild; we heard him out with incredulous noises, waiting all the while to get back to our room and flatten the mattress.

Our need to flee infuriated him.

Each night he said, You buggers came to Delhi to sleep or what?

Philip himself appeared to live by no rules – of sleep or dress or work. He would wear trousers and a shirt – and his chunky black cardigan that came down to mid-thigh – and not take them off for days. He would sleep in them, wake in them, wear them outside the house. If he did not have to go out he would slouch around like a bear, dishevelled, his long hair in clumpy disarray. If he had to go out he would pat his hair down with water, using wet fingers to train it. Then he would check his profile in the small misty mirror above the washbasin in the dining room, tease more hair down, shove his hands into his pockets and slouch off.

One evening I saw him stand in front of the basin and pull up all his clothes – shirt, vest, cardigan – around his neck. Then he ran the tap, leaned over the basin and began to wash his armpits. He soaped the sticky-stuck hair, then rinsed it off with splashes of water. First one armpit, then the other. The water spilled all over. The floor, his feet, his clothes. When he was done he cocked his head and sniffed his armpits. Then he walked to his room like that – arms up, clothes bunched under his chin, a fat man being led to his execution. He picked up a dirty towel and vigorously rubbed the hair dry. Then he pulled out a pink tin of Cuticura powder from his trunk and shook it aggressively into his armpits. The powder spilled everywhere. The floor, his feet, his clothes. He flexed his arms a couple of times like a wrestler to settle it. Then in one move he pulled down all his clothes and was ready to go. Philip obviously had a love life he was not talking about.

There was no pattern to when he would finally bathe and change his clothes. Many days would pass, then one evening we would see him painstakingly heating pans of water on the pulsing coil. He would vanish into the bathroom for a long time and emerge steaming in a towel. New clothes and a neat shave would herald the makeover. He would smile sheepishly and look embarrassed. Bathing was so bourgeois. In his own reckoning, a succumbing to the brahminical order.

For half a day he would smell of Old Spice cologne and it would be possible to sit near him. Then the process of decay would set in again, and very often it would be so bad that there would be flecks of dal crusted on his cardigan, and when he spoke vapours of trapped food would come wafting out.

He ate like a dog. You felt he never used his hands, just stuck his mouth into the food. But then you looked at his nails. And they were yellow with unwashed curries and had grains stuck under them.

But food etiquette was not his problem. His problem was rum.

I have never seen anyone drink like Philip. He drank a bottle a day. Squat Old Monk bottles lined the walls of his bedroom, crouching there like soldiers defending a troublesome border. All day the amber level in his glass fluctuated as he poured, mixed water, drank; poured, mixed water, drank. He worked through it all: sitting on his bed, back against the wall, writing on white foolscap sheets, stacking them face down. He would drink deep into the night, and last thing before sleeping he would mix a dark glassful and place it under his bed. When he woke, before putting on his thick glasses, he would reach for the glass and drain it in one go. Like therapy, like lime water or tea. Then he would get off the bed, go to the bathroom, brush his teeth, take a piss.

It was remarkable. So counter-bourgeois.

Like a chant he would say, Rum in the tum is better than shit in the bum.

I don't know what it meant.

The mega-serial Philip was working on began at the turn of the twentieth century, came up to the present, and was the story of three generations and the making of India. It was an epic, a saga. A sweep of history and its ironies. He was writing the first draft.

*The Inheritors* disintegrated slowly at the bottom of Sukhna Lake.

I wondered how he would respond when the lapwings came demanding, Did-you-do-it? Did-you-do-it?

Fizz, in a curious way, liked him. She liked his amoral madness. Far more than, say, the pious lunacy of Amresh. She found Philip's opinions interesting and they would spar about all kinds of things. He, of course, went soft around her and tried to rein in some of his grossness. He was forever offering to run her errands; even to help with the dishes. Considerations I had never seen in him before. Soon he went as far as to offer us an indefinite co-tenancy of the flat. But Fizz just couldn't stand the filth, of his body and the house. Revulsion and fondness battled in her, and we would discuss him late into the night, while relaxing at base camp before the next ascent.

We finally decided against staying on. His filth was only part of the reason. More important was that I wanted to stay in town. I was keeping long hours at work and I didn't want Fizz to be stranded at the outer end of the world. In Vasant Kunj then the bus service was skeletal and the three-wheelers dodgy. There was another reason. We wanted to be by ourselves. Our need to mess with each other was continual and urgent. And I wanted to hear her voice ring out loud when she scaled those final peaks.

We contacted some property dealers. Most of them cut the phone after being told our budget. We worked our way down till we were finally in conversation with two down-at-heel blokes. They both turned out to be Punjabi, paunchy, balding and bumblingly smooth. Smooth talkers, but bumbling agents. Over the years we would recognize this as a Delhi prototype. Fizz christened them Noproblemmadam and Verygoodmadam. It was how they spoke, rubbing their hands and smiling, bowing and scraping, and addressing only her.

We want a first- or second-floor place. But independent.

Noproblemmadam.

No landlord trouble. Separate entrance.

Verygoodmadam.

Must have a terrace, or at least a balcony.

Noproblemmadam.

Ideally with some trees around the house.

Verygoodmadam.

In the first few days they showed us some two dozen houses, and not one came close to pulling us in. They began to seem increasingly like freelance tricksters winging their way as estate agents. We would end up at houses comprehensively locked, and they would fall to quarrelling with each other in snappy Punjabi.

I told you to speak to him and organize the keys.

If I did everything what would you do? Be the tour guide of the Taj Mahal!

No, I would warm your mother's bed!

Finish warming your own mother's first!

Then they would both turn to Fizz and begin to rub and smile and bow and scrape.

Noproblemmadam, we will show you much better house.

The next one would be a servant's quarter; the next a huge flat four times our budget; and the next would have neither terrace nor balcony; and the next would have a shrieking harridan for a land-lady. Each time they would round on each other in high-pitched Punjabi.

Dickhead, did you find out anything at all or not?

And if I do everything what will you do? Come like King George to attend the durbar!

We would wait while they argued, levelling sexual charges against each other's sisters, mothers, wives, daughters; accusing each other of oral sex, buggery, bestiality. When they were done they would turn to Fizz, beaming, rubbing their hands.

Noproblemmadam. Verygoodmadam. We will show you much better place.

Soon we began to discover the neuroses of Delhi. It was not enough for us to like a place and be willing to pay for it. We were up against a check-list. Owners interrogated us and asked personal ques-tions. About our jobs, our background, our friends, our marriage, our religion, our working and partying hours. We failed on so many counts.

We were not south Indians, but aggressive north Indians. Delhi house-owners always imagine they can scare off a south Indian tenant. Most of them have obviously not heard of Velupillai Pira-bhakaran.

We didn't have children. They seem to provide a degree of respectability and comfort to landlords. Philip told me of friends who used to borrow other people's children when they went house-hunting.

We were a mixed couple. At least two owners commented to our property dealers about Fizz being Muslim. They wanted to know if we had eloped. One even said he would like to see our marriage certificate.

To the eternal credit of Vgm and Npm, they said, These are the dickheads who screw up this country! Are you letting out your house or getting your daughter married? Soon they will start asking for horoscopes!

And, of course, we did not work for a foreign bank or a multi-national corporation and so could not provide a company lease. A company lease. A phrase I had not heard till I started looking for a house in Delhi.

They wanted deposits. Guarantees. Wanted to nail down the laws of life.

The questioning angered me. I was not used to offering explanations. So I began to step back and let Fizz handle the inquisitions. I was also sick of the slapstick routine of Abbott and Costello. But Fizz was not. She was cheerfully tolerant. And like everyone else they were enamoured of her. They spoke only to her and did not even look at me, afraid I might in a moment of irritation snap off the relationship. They wore shiny brown second-hand suits, and drove an antiquated lime-green Lambretta that was so heavy they both needed to pull on it together to put it on its stand. Each time they had to do this and were pulling, Vgm, who drove the scooter wearing a tin-can helmet, would say, Dickhead, you didn't eat breakfast again?

And each time Npm, the perennial fall guy, would say, You want my Bata shoe to open up your asshole like the Buland Darwaza?

Their shoes were not in good shape either. They were held together by the Band-Aiding of leather and rubber. Some of it I think had to do with the Lambretta's brakes. The brakes caught insufficiently, for I noticed each time they had to stop they would both put their feet down and scrape them along the ground till the beast came to a lumbering halt. A couple of times they even banged into cars and walls, sending the tin helmet clattering and Npm crashing into Vgm.

Vgm would say promptly, Now what? You want to bugger me?

And Npm, disentangling, would shout, Maaderchod, is this a fucking scooter or a runaway horse? Why can't you get the brakes fixed?

We followed them around in a three-wheeler, burning a hole in our pockets. Twice during those wanderings – coming from the office, wanting her – I shook off my irritation by taking Fizz against a wall, after sending the lunatics off with a series of questions for the landlord. Once I pulled down her jeans on the stairs of a duplex and kissed deep into her core. It ended with her sitting on the topmost stair, her legs around my shoulders. At that angle she almost broke my neck. We discovered it is true that empty houses have an erotic charge – an eerie vacuum that demands to be filled.

But neither the furtive sex nor the antics of the duo could hold me indefinitely and I began to tire of the hunt. Fizz held her faith. Not only did she find them amusing, she actually approved of their cottage-industry approach, their bumbling spirit of enterprise. It's the slicksuits, fancydegrees and smoothstyles that she had problems with. But my tolerances were soon completely exhausted; I told Fizz that we either got ourselves new dealers or I was getting out of it and she was on her own. In any case I had just started work and could not be missing for hours on end every day.

Fizz looked at me with her big eyes wide open and said, But, you will come and live in it with me when I find it, won't you?

I said, I will ravish you on the threshold.

I also told Mutt and Jeff to behave themselves since I wouldn't be there the next time.

In unison they said, Noproblemsir, verygoodsir. We will show madam everything. We will find her best house in Delhi. She will never want to leave it. And every day she will remember us.

I looked at Fizz. She smiled back sweetly. She looked in charge.

A week later I was struggling to edit a mass of gibberish on the gathering crisis in the Congress party when my extension rang. Fizz said, I have something to show you.

I met her near the All India Institute of Medical Sciences, and we went to Green Park, where she showed me a barsati overlooking the Deer Park. The stairs were narrow and winding, but once you were on the second floor it all opened up. There was a sizeable terrace, one big room and two small ones, a bathroom with a pink pot, and a kitchen both of us could stand in simultaneously if we didn't move our arms. In the evening light the park opposite was in moving shadows and the ground under the trees was covered with leaves, both old and mulchy and fresh and crisp. Walkers were weaving their way along winding paths. Some were couples holding hands.

There was a gulmohar tree outside the house, and its arms had been chopped and chopped – to allow light and sun into the lower floors – so continually that it had violated its genetics and gone straight up, and like a palm tree opened its canopy high, on the second floor. The branches dangled onto the terrace. In the summer we would be bathed in a blaze of orange and red. The gulmohar must have clinched it for Fizz and it clinched it for me too. As much as its bloom, I loved the gulmohar's dewdrop leaves, strung out serenely on feathery branches. It was nice to pluck a fan and run it soothingly on the skin. As children we would do the opposite. We would strip a branch to its spine and use it to whiplash each other.

Philip was disappointed when we told him about the barsati.

He drained his amber glass and said, Rum in the tum is better than shit in the bum. And then retreated into a sulk for the next few days. We had brought definition to his life. He had been able to play out his radical lifestyle for an audience. But without us around it would have no meaning. It would simply revert to sloth and dirt.

I think there were other reasons too. The fact is bodies are addictive. You get used to them quickly. Their shape, their movement, their warmth. With Fizz it was doubly true. In that dank flat she was a luminous presence. Philip knew when she walked out the door it would be like switching off the lights.

The morning we left the flat – loading our mattress and suitcases into a cab – we both felt lousy. Philip was sitting on the edge of his bed, nursing his second drink of the day. He was in the middle of his unwashed cycle and spectacularly dishevelled. Fizz had left the little green rug and the cane murras for him and bought him a biography of Orson Welles and a Jamini Roy print.

When she half-hugged him, he said in a gruff voice, If he ever misbehaves with you, you know where to call.

Fizz smiled sweetly and said, I know where to call even if he behaves.

Philip's walrus moustache split in a grin and he scratched his chaotic hair.

I embraced him roundly and said, See you soon.

He said, Bastard, you don't deserve her.

Even with nothing in it the house became home in two days flat. Fizz went to a nearby nursery and bought some potted plants. A leafy palm, a rubber plant, a bamboo and two ficus trees. With four plants, twenty books, one framed picture of Pound, one of Tagore and a mattress, she made the barsati seem full. I knew how that illusion worked. I had been a happy victim of it in the past. Basically she filled up spaces in a way that you never noticed anything but her. She could be alone in an empty hall, and you'd never realize it was empty because you'd only be focusing on her. There are people like that, apart from glamorous stars and great men. Fizz was the finest exemplar of it I had ever known.

When I came home I saw only her, and it was great.

Every night as the time for me to leave office approached my mind would begin to wander. Memories of pleasure would start to tease me. The copy I was editing would blur. I'd find myself rereading paragraphs again and again. My head would fill with what I was going to do when I got home. I would begin to make packing-up noises, and would be looked at with total puzzlement.

Very quickly I had realized the office was neurotic. No one ever wanted to go home. It was organized around a single principle, the Doctrine of Eternal Insecurity. If you left early you left with the burden of knowing that someone was climbing steadily past you, logging in more hours, more words, more stories, more brownie points. If you were not on your chair – turning around words, dashing off headlines, barking instructions – when the bosses walked by, you had slid down the pole and now had the boots of your colleagues in your face.

And, as I soon discovered, the colleagues had been psychologically manufactured to grind their boots in once they had them on your face.

It was not how I had worked before. In my earlier jobs everyone had vied to be louche and lazy. It was crass to be competitive. That was for the swish MBAs and the studious Civil Service blokes – that is, till they cleared their exams and inherited India. In the journalism I had so far known everyone was a variation on Philip. Cynical, knowing, unkempt, contemptuous of everything to do with money and starched suits. Each one was engaged in his mind in some project much larger than the job he held. Everyone was writing bad fiction, bad poetry, or taking bad pictures. The rest were waiting for inspiration and talking it up with Old Monk while they did.

Rum in the tum is better than shit in the bum.

In contrast, this office was a well-greased malkhamb pole, with everyone slithering up and down the shiny wooden pillar. Right at the top, as in a ship, was a crow's nest, a comfortable cupola where one man sat. The idea, I gathered, was to get as close as you could to the cupola and the one man. What happened then I had still not figured out. Quite clearly the man was not going to pull you into the cupola. You stayed on the greased pole. But, going by the ceaseless frenzy, something did change.

Matters were not helped by the cupola man's conduct. Every now and then he leaned out and slopped some more grease onto the pole. It had the immediate effect of sending the ones nearest him into a panic of slipping and sliding. Boot-on-face, boot-on-face, boot-on-face. All the way down the pole the climbers went grinding boot-on-face.

Then the frantic climbing began again.

There were some very smart people slipsliding away on that pole.

Their clothes were dirty, their hands stained, their faces shone with grease, but in their eyes was a fervour. Their sights were set firmly on the man in the cupola, and the more grease he slopped on the pole, the more boot-on-face he unleashed, the more they became convinced that up there – in the cupola – lay the answers to the riddles of their life and career.

Some very very smart people. Faces shining with grease. Slipsliding away.

There was this young guy, no older than me, who was burning up the grease as he rabbited over clusters of bodies. Even in those early days I could sense the consternation he was triggering among the other polemeisters. This guy was my immediate boss, the copy chief. He was testosteronic in his hunger, charm and abilities. He had read the right books, seen the right films, he seemed to know something about everything that was happening in the world, and he could write sentences of such sibilant alliteration that the mind reeled in musical rhapsody.

Dull events, prosaically written, would land on his table, and by the time they left his scurrying fingers they would have acquired an epic grandeur. His copy was full of lofty echoes: Greek tragedy; Damocles's sword; manna from heaven; the myth of Sisyphus; the last of the Mohicans; hydra-headed and Circe-voiced; experiments with truth; discovery of India; biblical resonance; the lessons of Vedanta; the centre does not hold; the road not taken; the mimic men; for whom the bell tolls; a hundred visions and revisions; the power and the glory; the heart of the matter; the heart of darkness; the agony and the ecstasy; sands of time; riddle of the Sphinx; test of Tantalus; murmurs of mortality; Falstaffian figure; Dickensian darkness; Homeric herpes; Chaucerian cunt.

He was called Shulteri, which in Punjabi means nimble, speedy, uncatchable. He had been named by Gogia sahib, the general manager of the company – a joke-cracking, slimy Punjabi – because Gogia sahib had been outwitted casually by him during the salary negotiations. The nickname obviously had more to do with the kind of man he really was and less to do with his body language. For in appearance Shulteri was laid-back, with an easy laugh.

A leopard in a lion's skin.

I marvelled at his efficiency and aplomb as his lightning fingers spun current affairs garbage into singing gold. But what was killing the other pole warriors clearly was Shulteri's amiability and charm. Unwittingly, many of them found themselves taking their boots out of his friendly face, only to find he had scurried up the pole ahead of them. They made way for the lion; the leopard went bounding up. Then they tried desperately to grab for his ankles. But a hand on the ankle can do little compared to a boot in the face.

I could see the man in the cupola was pleased with him. He had brought new drama to the pole. I could see King Cupola wanted him to reach the upper echelons, where the big boys were slithering away. The arena of the greatest prizefights, the heavyweight stuff. He took care not to slop any grease in Shulteri's direction. This benevolent eye confused the others. They wanted to kick Shulteri even harder now, but they didn't want King Cupola to see them doing it.

When I saw Shulteri talking amiably to someone – senior, junior – I saw a small, rodent-faced man smiling expansively as he held your balls. It would be a reassuring caress, till he decided to squeeze. For someone who had been there only a year, he seemed to have a lot of balls in his hands.

Subs like me were so far down the hierarchy that we were not even at the base of the pole. We were mere onlookers. Bemused students of the Doctrine of Eternal Insecurity. The good thing was we caught little grease, except for the occasional flecks that flew in our direction from the scrabbling on the pole. We were also saved from getting too much boot-on-face. But then we could give none either. The real downside was that for King Cupola we did not exist. Whatever goodies were being dished out at those greasy heights would never ever come our way.

Very quickly Shulteri took a shine to me. It perhaps had to do with the mix I presented of good language skills and lack of office ambition. Immediately he began to offload the messiest copy onto my desk. Most of it was the pastiche of political reporters – half-assed quotes, banal colour, cliché'd analyses and, of course, rank grammar, spelling, syntax. There would be sentences on end where you had to just guess at the meaning. Some of them compounded matters by trying to inject a flourish – stuff like Damocles's sword and the myth of Sisyphus.

Shulteri would look over my shoulder at the pulsing screen and say, This is fucking junk! Just throw it back at them. Screw them!

But I was not interested in screwing anybody. I was only interested in going home swiftly. To Fizz and my books. This puzzled and pleased Shulteri. Our covenant was sealed. He could take all the credit for the copy work; I could leave the office the moment night settled over the city and the main bazaars began to down their shutters.

He knelt at the altar of King Cupola. I at the haunches of Fizz.

He for the little life. I, the little death.

There were other very very smart people too. Faces shining with grease. Just under the cupola. Slipsliding away.

Some had been to universities like Harvard and Oxford and they crushed the lowly subeditors – from Bhopal and Cochin – with their casual accounts of Brodsky lectures and West End plays.

Some spoke of glamorous names – film stars and writers – with an intimacy that was difficult to believe.

There were those who could dial a number and drag powerful government ministers out of their beds in the middle of the night. And not even apologize for it.

There were those who travelled the globe at such velocity that their passports were thicker than the *Oxford English Dictionary*.

There was one who knew everything about everything. From the origins of buzkashi in Afghanistan to the politics of the Ku Klux Klan to the British fascination with smelly underpants. He also fancied himself a funny guy. He would gather the staff and make them laugh.

But you could not make a crack back. If you did his eyes would glaze over. The smile would freeze. You would be in danger of being kicked down the pole a little.

He was called Haile Selassie. He was an aggressive Bihari from Patna with big chips on his shoulder, the rolling walk of a boxer, and a lot to prove to Delhi's stylish aboriginals. Many years ago at an office party it seems he had delivered an oration on Ethiopia and so been named.

Each time he walked out of the copy room after a monologue, everyone would rise, hold out their right arm, bend at the waist and declare, Hail Selassie!

A trainee once actually let his byline go through as Haile Selassie. In complete innocence. She lost her job the next day.

Haile Selassie was a comedian with no humour about anything to do with himself.

Every word he spoke, every step he took, was designed to make him the master of the universe. He was a journalist of immense gifts – far greater than Shulteri's – but his inner anxieties, his need to rush it, were making him slipslide frantically.

Haile Selassie was one of the key climbers who had King Cupola's benediction. Humour was not the only weapon Selassie used in his struggles on the pole. He was very very smart. He held his cards close to his chest while he encouraged you to spill your guts. His lips smiled while his eyes calculated. He married superficial humour with serious menace. He knew between one or the other you could always get some purchase on the slippery grease.

With Shulteri you felt a friendship could grow. But with Haile Selassie you knew intuitively you could never be friends. Everyone for him was competition. And friendship can get in the way of self-interest.

I could see Shulteri and Haile Selassie were headed for some serious boot-on-face.

Humour and menace and knowing everything versus charm and wordiness and leopard in lion's skin.

It was quite extraordinary. The Greased Pole of Eternal Insecurity. And very very smart people slipsliding away.

The best formula for survival had been worked out by this guy from Varanasi – Mishraji. He was a runt who wore white churidar-kurtas and chewed paan all day. He was the nodal person between accounts-administration and editorial. The office fixer – phones, tick-ets, cabs. Unlike others in the organization he had no respect for the journalists because he dealt with them all day and knew their money-grubbing ways. He wandered the office, bantering with everyone. Each time he made a crack he would sign it off with a whistle. A low, sharp, loaded sound. Sswweeen.

Mishraji was genuinely funny. He had an uthao aur lagao formula. Lift and take. He would demonstrate it. He said each time you saw a senior you should lift your kurta from the back and bend over. Uthao aur lagao. Lift and take. Sswweeen. And each time you saw a junior you should lift your kurta from the front and go for it. Uthao aur lagao. Lift and take. Sswweeen.

In the night, afterwards, under the quilt, I would tell Fizz about it all. My hand would lie between her thighs, where I had just been, where the world is always the warmest and wettest. If the time came again, she would move against it. And in no time I would be sucked in under the quilt and out of the world.

Fizz marvelled at my accounts, laughing all the while. At the mad-ness. The desperation. But there was method in it. I explained it to her. King Cupola was a military despot in the guise of a liberal master. He was a businessman who employed the simple, time-tested principles of the army.

Insulation. Illusion. Hype. Activity.

Seal the borders so no agents provocateurs can creep in.

Establish the pretence of a larger cause so none may complain about the infested barracks.

Create the notion of elitism – we are the Marines – so everyone lives in a bubble.

Create a mountain of tasks so high that no one can see past it.

Army men salute everything that moves and paint everything that is stationary. In our case we rewrote everything that appeared in our vicinity. Rewritten stories would go out from our machines, bounce off some other machine in the office and come back and be rewritten again. Some stories would bounce around being rewritten and re-rewritten so many times that they would read worse and worse. Others would end up declaring precisely the opposite of what they started out saying. But that was a small price to pay to keep the army humming.

I felt I was in a journalistic cantonment. Its hold on reality was tenuous. But its mastery of gloss was complete. The brass shone; the uniforms were starched; the troops kept marching up and down. It was here I learnt that corporate principles and military principles are basically the same. Insulation. Illusion. Hype. Activity.

In the case of the army it results in discipline and victory.

In the case of the corporation it results in insecurity and profit.

Liberty and truth are dodgy values in both.

Before two months were over I knew I could not work here for any great length of time. Just looking at the pole was making me dizzy. I realized my best bet lay in ensuring King Cupola's eyes never fell on me. Keep a low profile, tread soundlessly, say nothing smart, merge into the thicket of humming computers, seek no credit, deal only through Shulteri, and wonder not at all about the rewritten copy you send out from your machine. Somehow I knew that once King Cupola dragged you to the pole you were lost. It was clearly magnetic. The grease, the climbing, the boot-on-face. Joys I could not see at this distance obviously propelled the frenzy of the scramblers.

A hand on the pole and I was sure I could bid goodbye to my writing and perhaps much of my real life.

🌿

The day I collected my second month's salary I took three days leave, and Fizz and I went back to Chandigarh to pick up our stuff. By now she was desperate to fill the barsati. The in-transit feel was getting to her.

It didn't matter to me. When I came home I only wanted Fizz and I could have done without the one mattress too.

The journey back was strange. This we knew was truly the last one. Now when we returned we would have removed every vestige of ourselves from that strange inorganic city created by geometry not need. A city built with protractors, rulers, set squares and dividers rather than passion, emotion, hunger, creativity. The Frenchman who had built it had bleached it of both the practised sensuality of the French and the earthy lustiness of the Indian.

He had left geometric dwellings. Only time would make it a city. A great deal of time.

But for us it was singular. It was where we had found each other, found us. Our cynicism was forever scored out by sentimentality.

The Sikh colonel opened the door and said, You took very long, son. Lucky the Chinese haven't got here yet.

Because both the colonel and his wife adored Fizz we had their guest room to sleep in. I called a friend of mine, a bureaucrat in the state education department, a reader of books and a forever helpful guy. He said he would organize transport so we could move our stuff. I said I just wanted trustworthy guys who wouldn't rook me. Like a true Punjabi, he said, Your problems are over, brother! Prepare to leave!

The next afternoon – a lovely winter sun bathing the city – we got onto a cycle rickshaw and had ourselves pedalled through Sectors 9, 10, 11; and then around the university campus and back through 15, 16 and into 17. We were riding nostalgia. The traffic was languid, the sky high and blue, and enough trees in green to make you feel splendid. Sensing we were in no hurry, the puller – from Jaunpur in Uttar Pradesh: I asked – sensing our languor the puller settled into a gentle rhythmic gait. Creak-pause, creak-pause, creak-pause. His ass rising off the saddle each time a foot pressed down.

We held hands and talked. It still excited me to do that. To hold her hand in public. The intense awareness of touching her never faded. It never became a casual act.

I dredged up memories. Of events, incidents, walks, eateries.

A kiss.

Many years ago. When the world of the body is still uncharted territory. Me and her in a rickshaw in pouring monsoon rain. Afternoon, but the day already dark, closed in by packed grey clouds. The skies rumble continually. Sometimes they flash. The rickshaw's roof up, but not holding a drop back. The puller hunched on the saddle, like a painting. Cloaked in a brown sack over which he has pulled a big transparent polythene packet, one side ripped open, the corner stuck onto his head. The indestructible cape of Povertyman. The water rushing in streams by the roadside. Just beyond, people massed under dark dripping trees. Traffic slow and minimal. Everyone, on scooters, mopeds, cycles, hunched against the driving rain. Everyone looking down to keep the eyes from being lashed.

We are huddled close. We are going to her house from the university. Our clothes are stuck to our skin. Her white bra is outlined against her blue cheesecloth top. My ribs ridge my T-shirt. We are cold. Madly in love. We suddenly look at each other and begin to kiss. It burns. Our lips burn. In the cold rain, our mouths are hot. The water drips off our hair, our faces. We suck on each other's lips. Test tongues. Our mouths are very hot. It is unlike anything ever.

Povertyman senses nothing. He works at steering the rickshaw and controlling his flapping cape.

We break for air. It is getting darker by the moment, and anyway no one cares. Everyone is a scurrying animal bolting for shelter. Our mouths cool. The rain runs into them. Then we look at each other, and we begin again. Our lips burn. Our mouths are hot. I am amazed mouths can be so hot. The water pelts us. Dimly I register Batra theatre looming blockish on our right, and then receding. We don't break for air. Can mouths be so hot?

We pay Povertyman with soaked notes that are difficult to separate with soggy fingers. He stays inside his cape, takes the money and leaves. The front door is open. Her great-aunt is in the living room shelling peas. On a plastic plate the green skins are heaped like comatose grasshoppers. Her glasses are thick. Just one yellow bulb casts light on her tray. She barely acknowledges our entry. I cannot see the maid. We go through Fizz's bedroom into the bathroom. It is made for encounters. It has two doors leading into different bedrooms, one hers, one her great-aunt's.

We peel our clothes like skin. They lie in wet clumps. The rain hammers away at the half-open ventilator window. A fine spray ricochets in. I bend her over the enamel sink. The smell of her desire fills my head. I hold her where her hips flare. She is on her toes. My love seeks her frantically. Misses, misses, then finds her in a slippery instant. I am in a place hotter than her mouth. It is unlike anything ever.

I move. She immediately bucks, throws her head and goes away. Our naked skin is damp and cold. All the heat of our bodies is only in one dark, unknowable place. Which we now share. I feel I am being massaged by countless oiled fingers. I move. She bucks and goes away again. A mad explosion is powering through me. I pull back a little, fighting. She is excruciatingly hot. My head is threatening to detonate. I close my eyes. It doesn't help. She bucks again and goes away again. My knees begin to tremble. I am shaking now. I am going away too. I fight to stay. I open my eyes. I can't see anything. I know my face is twisted in a held-in scream. I know if I look down it will all be over. I don't think I am breathing. I am not.

I pull back. The smells of her desire hit me.

I drive deep into her flowering-flowing-folding flesh. Pause for an instant of wet eternity. And explode.

The explosions last a long time, blowing away everything. I slowly sink to my knees on the white-tiled floor, my cheek now on her cool damp hip. I can hear her heavy breath. She is coming back. She puts a hand around and ruffles my wet hair. Climbs down from her toes. I am drifting. Letting the bits of me that have been blown apart come together gently. The rain hammers the ventilator. Once again I can feel the fine spray buffeting in through the wire mesh. I do not know how much time has passed. The room seems darker than when we entered it. Under god's curve, where my head rests, a thick slow trickle descends. Drowsily I put out the tip of my tongue, rest it against firm full flesh and catch our flowing love.

But now on the rickshaw, in the winter sun, Fizz was looking into the future.

She spoke of bringing our children to all these places. And telling them what we had done where.

The puller went creak-pause, creak-pause, creak-pause. Despite the cold his pinched face shone with sweat.

Fizz, practical as ever, said, But how will we all fit on a rickshaw?

I said, I will pedal while the three of you sit in the back.

She said, Oh, wonderful! You really have all the answers!

She squeezed my hand, then turned towards me, opened her eyes wide and said, But can you pedal and talk at the same time? It's not easy, you know.

I said, I'll practise – I'll take classes.

You promise you won't crash us? You told me you once crashed Miler and Sobers.

I said, The ride will be smoother than your thighs.

She said, That means it will be bumpy, right? You don't like my thighs, I know.

I love your thighs, I said.

You only love where they go.

Not true, I said, I love the way they go too.

She said sternly, This is not about my thighs. This is about our children.

We were creak-pausing through Sector 16. Amaltas trees flanked the road. In the summer they would be so dazzlingly golden it would be difficult to look at them in the midday sun. Behind them was more greenery. Gardens, shrubs, trees, hedges. Students bobbed past on cycles and mopeds and scooters, two and three abreast, chatting, jibing, laughing. Soon the colleges would close and the city would empty of its large and visible population of migrant students. We were them once, Fizz and I. But we were migrants who had found more than we had ever come looking for. We had moved on; and now were moving on for good.

The nip was making Fizz's lovely skin glow. Her right hand was in mine; the left tucked into the bright blue jacket she was wearing. She smelled heady as always, of fresh water, soaps, lotions, Madame Rochas, herself. Her mouth was parted in a happy smile, her eyes were alive. This is the kind of thing that worked for her. If I had taken her out in a cab she would have withered and died.

She suddenly looked at me and said, But do you need a licence?

I said, I'll get one. When I get a car licence I'll get rickshaw written in too.

Perfect, she said, And I'll make them wear dungarees and braid their hair.

We were always certain we would have girls.

I said, No, leave their hair loose.

Ok, she said, But when it gets badly knotted you brush it.

Anything. Baby, I'd do anything.

Anything?

Anything. For you, dear, anything.

Would you pull a rickshaw?

Anything.

Walk with me in a downpour?

Anything.

Never be a crashing bore?

Anything.

Take me to Udaipur?

Anything.

Ignore my every flaw?

Anything.

Write *The Herbivores*?

That too. And many many more.

She flashed me her smile.

I pitched my voice higher and sang, I'd do anything. For you, dear, anything. For you, dear, everything. For you . . . I'd go anywhere. For your smile everywhere. For your smile anywhere. For you . . .

It was an old routine – mildly changing each time – from one of our favourite films. The puller, without breaking rhythm, looked back, beaming rotten teeth.

Fizz gave him a smile, and said, Sahib thinks he can sing.

In the evening we went out for dinner to the first restaurant we had eaten in together all those years ago. It was a small subterranean eatery in Sector 17 called Golden Dragon. There was no one else there. It had the air of a failing enterprise and the sullenness which comes with it. We couldn't be bothered. We took our time over the food.

When we put our money in the folder, Fizz said, We won't bring our girls here.

No, I said, We won't.

In the morning we woke to a surprise. The vehicle my friend had deployed to transport us to Delhi was a second world war truck converted into a bus. It had been pulled in from an adjoining district, where it worked in a small town for the local school. It had a snout. Slightly open, as if it was having trouble breathing. A recent paint job – blue – that could not conceal its age. Fat round tyres with no tread on them. And two-by-two seats running its length along a narrow aisle.

The colonel examined it like a horse, walking all around it and feeling its flanks. He even tried the doors, opening and shutting them. As if lifting skin flaps to check gums.

He said, We used to have a couple of these in the regiment in the fifties. Solid fellows. They served Monty well at Alamein.

Should they be on the road? I asked hopefully.

In a museum, in a museum, he said, This should be in a museum.

But in India we know everything that should be in a museum is out on the roads being abused. From ideas to artefacts to buildings. People too, actually.

I said, Colonel sahib, will it make it to Delhi?

He patted its rump thoughtfully and said, It should, it should. It went all the way across the north African desert, didn't it?

The bus, as we would discover, was the lesser anachronism. The greater were the two blokes who came with it. To appearance they seemed regular enough. Middle-aged Sikhs with flowing beards. One, the driver, greyer and older than the other. They wore loose turbans and spoke in a guttural Punjabi. They were pleasant, offering to help with the loading.

When the driver picked up the first carton, he said, You are carrying stones to Delhi?

I laughed and said, No, books.

He said, Why? Delhi doesn't have enough?

I gestured at the cartons and said, These are our personal books.

He said, Books are a waste. My father used to say ploughing one field teaches you more about life than reading a hundred books. He pulled me out of school when I was in class five. He used to say if reading books gives you the answers then why is this country's ass in such a sling? All our leaders from Gandhi to Nehru have read thousands of books.

I said, That is true. Books are not all they are made out to be.

He said, Only one book matters. The Guru Granth Sahib. And you don't need to read it – you can just listen to it.

The younger one, the helper, said, Not a waste. They are an illness. Those who read books think they can understand life through them. Tell me, sahib, if you read a hundred books about tandoori chicken can you taste it?

The driver slapped him on the back and bellowed, That's it! You bring chicken into everything!

It was only an example, said the helper.

With their assistance we loaded our belongings. The book cartons we jammed under, on and in between the seats. The bike we pushed into the aisle, and tied it at various places to the seats so it wouldn't roll.

Fizz had bought Spike Milligan's second world war quartet for the colonel.

She said, This is military writing of a different kind, uncle. My kind.

The colonel looked at the wacky covers with a bewildered smile, turning them over and over. Then both he and his wife hugged her heartily. He took my hand in his firm grip, shook it hard and said, Boy, you don't deserve her, but you'd better look after her. Otherwise you'll have an old colonel coming after you.

I seemed to be forever getting this advice.

If they only knew how it would all end up.

The man who took no advice.

When the engine caught we had to hang on to the seat bars. It was shaking as if readying to fall apart. We were sitting in the second row behind the driver, while his partner sat on the single front seat next to him. Mercifully, after a few minutes the mad racket eased as the engine settled down to a tolerable jitter. We sat and waved to the colonel and his wife while the driver let the engine warm up. It was seven-thirty on a cold winter morning and the colonel was wearing his tie and suit. His beard was netted in flawlessly, and shining. Mrs Colonel was more real. She was in a flowery kaftan and shawl. The kaftan had wide armholes. When she lifted her hand to wave I could see her fleshy armpits.

The driver put the bus into gear and it jumped like a rabbit. We almost banged our faces into the front seat. Mr and Mrs Colonel leapt back too; and with a tremendous outpouring of black exhaust and an infernal rattling we were off. Both our transporters adjusted their turbans, which had slipped down around their eyes.

The journey did not turn out to be bone-shaking. Mostly because the bus travelled at about thirty kilometres an hour. The driver set the vehicle on the left verge and let it roll slowly. Everything overtook us. Trucks, buses, cars, bikes, scooters. Even mopeds and tractor trolleys. We were slow enough for young boys on bicycles to grab the rear mudguards and bum a quick ride. We were slow enough to need no braking at the police's zigzag barriers. We were truly worthy of the Grand Trunk Road, the subcontinent's greatest artery, through which courses five hundred years of history. Mostly pellmell and at break-neck speed.

The two sardars chatted away amiably, looking back once in a while to enquire if all was well with us. For the first hour we were on the edge of our seats, wondering how this journey was going to pan out. Then we began to relax a little as the morning mist faded and we hit a relatively clean stretch. But the relief was not to last. Suddenly, on a guttural command from the driver, the helper reached under his seat, picked up a dirty red brick and handed it across. The driver leaned down and in a practised move removed his right foot from the accelerator and replaced it with the brick. The bus barely jerked. The driver pulled both his legs up on the seat and crossed them. He then settled down to steering with one hand, while he massaged his feet with the other.

We almost passed out.

Fizz said, Sardar sahib, you really want to take us to god not to Delhi?

The driver said, Bibiji, you can only go to god when you are invited. No one can take you there.

Fizz said, But sardar sahib, you are trying hard to get an invitation, aren't you?

The helper said, Don't worry, bibiji. Nothing will happen. Singh sahib's growing old. His legs give him trouble now. A little rest and he'll have his foot back on the pedal. And it's a good brick. Bricks hold up massive houses. What's an old bus?

There was nothing we could say to that.

The driver, massaging his toes with his left hand, said, Bibiji, don't worry. If anything happens, it is we who'll die first.

We sat back and mulled the consolation.

Fizz said to me, Well, I suppose at this speed it is difficult to have a fatal accident.

True to their word nothing happened and fifteen minutes later the foot was back on the accelerator. The journey proved a long one. As the day wore on it acquired the air of a voyage. We stopped for water. For tea. To eat. To pee. We stopped to cool the engine. To pour water into the radiator. We stopped to fix punctures: the tyres were bursting like balloons every few dozen kilometres. We stopped to pray. At gurudwaras, roadside shrines. Once the driver said he had to go to Pakistan. He filled a can of water and disappeared into the fields. Near Panipat the engine copped it. The two of them pulled out heavy wrenches and disappeared under the bus. We took a walk amid the juicy green wheat stalks. When they emerged they were smudged with grease, but the engine was alive. They told us to guard the bus and went off to a pounding tube-well to bathe.

It was all worthy of the Grand Trunk Road.

We munched glucose biscuits and pondered our future.

Through it all the two of them stayed peaceful, bantering away with each other and dishing out philosophic calm to us.

The brick kept going on and off the accelerator. Each time it went on, Fizz closed her eyes and squeezed my hand.

The Chandigarh–Delhi trip, which normally takes five hours, ended up taking us nearly twelve. By the time we reached the outskirts of Delhi it was getting dark. The last stretch of double-laning after Panipat had made for a particularly merry ride, but now as we neared Delhi we saw a dramatic and dark change come over our transporters. As we chugged up the embankment to the circular road that opens up like a pincer around Delhi their voices began to die. The traffic was getting busy and headlights darted about. Trucks and buses were muscling for space. Every few minutes one of them would glance at us and say, Is this the way? Are we on the right road? How much further is it to your home?

With much confused stop–go driving we negotiated the bottleneck at the juncture of the pincer and turned left onto the circular road. Their panic levels eased a little as the traffic flow became one-way again. They kissed the verge once more, allowing the speedy cars, buses and trucks to hurtle past. They resumed talking. But no longer was it expansive philosophizing. Their voices had an anxious trip now. The talking tone that's fighting fear. They ribbed each other in hollow voices about the traffic. The steering hand seemed to have acquired a little jitter. Fizz and I sat on the edge of our seats.

We made it past Majnu ka Tila and the bustling interstate bus terminus without any real crisis. But inside the bus the tension was deepening. The brick had been put away for good. The driver was leaning into the glass, concentrating. His partner was doing the same, and shouting out instructions in a high-pitched whine, Watch that Maruti! Cut right! There's a bus coming in on your left! Oh, don't kill the fucking cyclist, sardarji!

The driver had gone utterly and dangerously silent.

One with his jerking animal, which he was struggling to steer.

Then we slipped behind the medieval bulk of the Red Fort and swam into a river of traffic. It was swollen with office disgorgements and fed by surging tributaries from Shahdara and Daryaganj. Hundreds of buses, cars, scooters and three-wheelers lapped around us, honking, screeching, shouting. Our man, the driver, finally lost his nerve. At the red light between Shahjahan's historic fort and Mahatma Gandhi's serene memorial he marooned the bus and would not move.

I don't know what happened, but when the red light changed to green the driver failed to budge. For some reason the floor gear-shift was stuck and he could not engage it. As he struggled with it, pulling and tugging, all hell broke loose around us. Behind us a hundred drivers detonated a medley of horns and the sound was deafening. As the seconds ticked away people began to hammer on the side of the bus and shout abuse. Faces showed up in our windows, snarling and screaming. We too exhorted the two to move, but the driver just couldn't work the gear. His face had gone pinched and pale, and in the flashing lights it shone with sweat.

We wanted to hide under the seats.

An urchin boy selling glistening coconut slices threw open our window, pushed his grinning head in and sang, Gaand phati toh har koi bola! Hajmola Hajmola!

Hands began to yank at the doors, rattling them.

Suddenly two distinct sounds cut through the cacophony. One a police whistle, shrill and clean, the other a police siren, rhythmic and cutting. I looked out and the policeman at the lights was running across from the other end blowing madly and waving his arms. To his left was a police jeep, threading through the traffic, red light blinking. A man was leaning out, gesturing with his fist.

The helper said, Singh sahib, get ready to be buggered!

The driver said not a word. He continued to struggle with the gear. He had turned on his side now and was using both his hands. The engine idled.

The light turned back to red.

All those trying to squeeze past our bus began to bang its sides harder in frustration.

The bus rocked gently.

The policeman flung open the driver's door and shouted, Maaderchod! Who allowed you to bring this breadbox into the city? Why don't you move?

Only his head was visible through the door, and behind him could be seen a host of angry muttering faces, several in shiny helmets with visors pushed up. The engine was idling and they couldn't understand why we were not moving.

Another grinning urchin boy selling tissue paper pushed his head in through our window and shouted, Chinchpokli! Chinchpokli! Hello, mr chinchpokli!

I could see the grinning coconut boy just behind him.

The driver did not have the courage even to turn around. His eyes were clouded and he was pulling with all his strength.

Fizz said, Do something, mr chinchpokli. He's going to die.

I looked at her. The urchin boy had killed me. Chinchpokli: suburb of fantasia. From whence rolled out film song requests that clogged the radio waves. She would nail me with that ludicrous epithet for the rest of my days.

I stood up and said, Arre, sahib, the gear's got stuck.

The policeman rounded on me, Maaderchod! You must be the owner of this fucking breadbox!

The cop from the jeep showed up behind him and said, Lock all these bastards up! And impound this fucking biscuit tin!

The first cop shouted, Pull the tin can over to the side and get down all you stupid dicks!

Just then the lights turned green and a chaos of horns erupted. A flurry of hands drummed on the bus. Abuse filled the air.

Suddenly the helper in a rush of manic desperation jumped up and yelled, Move back, sardarji! Let me do this!

He pushed the driver away and grabbed the gear-stick with both hands. Then he threw his head back like Tarzan and roared, Jo bole so nihal! Sat sri akal!

And with an almighty heave he pulled the gear-stick clean out of the floor.

Fizz said, Omigod! Omifuckingod!

Right in between the ostentatious seat of Shahjahan's power and the austere cremation ground of Mahatma Gandhi, in the middle of Delhi, lapped by vehicles from every side, the helper stood swaying, the iron gear-stick held aloft in his hand like a sword, the bus dead at his feet like a cheetah. A medieval warrior in a modern age, who had just killed the animal he had set out to save.

Puzzlement flooded his face. He said, What is this?

The rod had a smooth wooden knob at one end and dark dripping grease at the other.

The driver said, Theoneandtruegodbemerciful! Bemerciful!

And he closed his eyes.

Where the gear once grew, next to the driver's seat, now lay a dark oily hole.

The engine idled steadily.

Fizz said, Can you drive without a gear?

The helper looked as if he had gone to grab a sugar cane and caught a snake instead.

The cop who had clambered on said, Move this tin can! Move this tin can! How do you move it? Where is the bloody gear?

Without a word, with a deferential bow, the helper presented him the dripping rod.

The cop shouted, What is this maaderchod? Move this tin can! Where's the damn gear?

The driver chanted, Theoneandtruegodbemerciful! Bemerciful!

Shut up, you dickhead! said the cop. Then he looked around. Saw nothing resembling a gear. And went apoplectic. You sad bastards! he screamed, You brought a bus into Delhi without a gear! A bus without a gear! Maaderchod! Chutiyas! Brought a bus into Delhi without gears! A bus without gears! What do you have – mouths without assholes? Balls without pricks? Which gutter in Punjab have you all crawled out from!

Fizz said, The gear is in your hand, constable sahib.

This! he screeched, This is the fucking gear! Then what is it doing in my hand?

He looked like he had caught the snake now.

He threw it back at the helper.

The cop from the road said, Lock the whole bloody lot of pimps up! And impound the damn biscuit tin!

At that another manic fit swept the helper. He shouted, Teri maa di phudi maari! And holding the gear-stick in both hands like a javelin he slammed it into the hole in the floor. It didn't catch. He pulled it out and slammed it back in. And then, like an axe murderer in a low-budget film, he went berserk, stabbing at the hole in a frenzy, while invoking everyone's mothers' cunts.

I shove this into your mother's cunt! And this into your mother's cunt! And this into your mother's mother's cunt!

The cop leapt back in alarm; even the driver opened his eyes and edged away.

Fizz said, Mr chinchpokli, our mothers are in danger.

The helper hammered on, And your mother's cunt! And your mother's cunt! And your mother's cunt!

The cop from the road said, Oh, the bloody sardar has gone mad! Take him out of here!

The cop on the bus struck a sterner pose and shouted, Sardar! Get a grip on yourself!

The helper stopped mid-plunge and looked at the cop wildly.

The cop said warily, leaning back, Sardar, take it easy. Everything is OK.

The driver said, Theoneandtruegodbemerciful! Bemerciful!

The helper raised his javelin on high – the cop cowered – and plunged it down with all his strength, screaming like a banshee, You motherfucking hag I stick this gear into your dirty vulva so that you squeal like a virgin!

His face was twisted in a grimace, and his turban was askew and beginning to unwind.

Fizz said, He's raping the bus?

But when he tried to pull back this time, he could not. The gear had caught.

A demented smile broke on his face. It's caught, he said, It's caught! Bugger the whole damn world, it's caught! Glory to your mother's cunt, it's caught!

The driver joined his hands, closed his eyes, tilted his face up in prayer and shifted the gear. It engaged. The bus jumped like a rabbit. We all lurched uncontrollably.

Fizz said, The Gemini Circus hits the road.

Everyone around the bus scattered. The lights were red, but the cop on the road blew his whistle: Let them go! Let them go! Let the dickheads go screw someone else's happiness!

The cop on the bus shouted, O sardar, let me down! Your acquaintance is enough, I don't want your friendship! I promise I won't forget the two of you till I retire!

The driver said, Theoneandtruegodbemerciful! Bemerciful!

The two did not speak another word till we reached our barsati. After we had unloaded, I took them up and sat them on the terrace. I gave them a quarter of whisky and then went and got some food from the market. Their hands were still shaking and they were quiet. When they had eaten, and the whisky was warm in their veins, they told me they had never been to Delhi before. In fact they had never been south of Chandigarh; they had never driven the bus anywhere outside of their little town.

When asked to make this trip, they had figured it was a good opportunity to expand their horizons, see the world. See the Red Fort, the Qutub Minar, Chandni Chowk.

I said, Yes, you should see them tomorrow.

The helper said, We have seen enough to last us a lifetime. Now all we want to do is to show our ass to Delhi.

The driver said, We reckoned how big could Delhi be? It couldn't be much bigger than Chandigarh.

The helper said, Turned out to be an elephant's cunt!

Some of the bravura was returning. They went off to sleep in the bus. At about two in the morning Fizz and I were woken by the house bell shrilling hysterically. When I looked down from the terrace both of them were standing next to the gate looking up, wrapped in their grey blankets, tightening and tucking their turbans.

It turned out they couldn't sleep. They wanted to leave immediately. When Delhi lay dead. Its people dead, its policemen dead, its vehicles dead, its traffic lights dead. They wanted me to put them on one straight road that would lead them clean out of the city. Painstakingly I explained to them the way out of the colony; the road to AIIMS, the All India Institute of Medical Sciences; the right turn from there; and then the long looping ride around Delhi till they reached the crotch of the pincer, where they were to turn right. I also drew a bold diagram on a big sheet of paper. They shook my hand warmly, clasping it in both their hands, and said, Forgive us all our errors and lapses.

I said, You were both wonderful. Thank you for everything.

I meant it.

In unison they said, Give all our regards to bibiji too. Tell her she will be the mother of a hundred sons.

The bus engine rattled, juddered, then settled down. The open snout looked as if it was gulping in the cold night air. The driver prayed to the picture of Guru Nanak above his windshield and put the bus into gear. It jumped like a rabbit. They waved. Their faces were still white and drawn. The average age of the three of them, the driver, the helper and the bus, was more than that of modern India.

They were going back with the defining story of the rest of their lives. In seconds they were gone. In those days there were no iron gates locking in Delhi's colonies.

In a few minutes the sound of the engine died too. On our narrow lane it was cold and silent and, save for a yellow street-light ten houses down, it was also dark. The moon had already sunk. The stars could barely be seen through the cramped rows of houses and the stretching trees. There was the occasional hoot of an owl from the Deer Park. I stood in the middle of the street – in the middle of the silence and the cold and the dark – for a long time. I felt sad. Namelessly sad. I didn't remember the last time I had cried. It didn't come easily to me. But now I wanted to sit down in the street and cry.

It had to do with the thought of the two of them hurtling back home in the night, furtive and alone. The fineness of their spirit and the meanness of the world. I knew how large-hearted they were; and how easily they could be overwhelmed. It was the story of the rural and the tribal everywhere. The tale of all-who-will-be-swiftly-dispossessed. They approach the new world armed with a generosity of spirit – as can only be reaped from working the land. But the modern world has no value for it. They are stranded on the cross-roads of history; quickly overrun by the surging traffic of development and growth; stopped by the red light of new-fangled laws and economic theses; impounded by the gendarmes of corporate kings.

Those who try to grab the situation by the scruff of the neck find it upended altogether. They are left holding the gear-stick of their lives in their hands with the engine humming elsewhere and no way to go and nowhere to go.

They are left to play a game they did not choose. With rules they do not know.

The world survives by those who have generosity of spirit.

But is owned by those who have none.

By the time I walked up the stairs an idea was beginning to take hold of me.

Fizz was fast asleep on her side curled into a ball. I slipped under the quilt and cosied up to where she had made it snug. Her T-shirt was around her waist. Her skin felt warm and smooth; and if you went to places where it gathered and opened, hot and moist. I was unhappy. I wanted the solace of the incandescent moment, followed by the perfect oblivion. Fizz gifted me that, the ultimate paradox: she was for me the repository of total passion and total peace. I reached for her body for both things and always found what I sought. The same body that drove me into frenzies could, by its touch, becalm me like a swan on a rippleless lake. I would lie down, put my arm around her waist, my face next to the swell of her breast, and be drained of every anxiety, emptied of everything but an enduring peace.

It had given me my definition of love.

Passion and peace in the one person.

Now when I nudged into her from the back – a damp lip of accommodation – she turned over and I rolled on top, my weight on my elbows. I put a lick on two fingers and readied myself. The gentlest push; the perfect hot resistance. Because this was only about me I could focus on my every sensation. By moving only my hip I pulled back till I was held in only a delicate pout, and then I slowly sank back in all the way, letting the pleasure flood me.

Everything fell away.

Thoughts, ideas, sadness. Ego, ambition, art.

My face lay under her left ear, breathing her in. I closed my eyes and thought of things I had done with her. Then I moved without moving. The slow pleasure was excruciating, diffusing in me like a potent drug. Passion is a two-person game, but some days I liked this. Me driving my pleasure at my speed. The despotic glories of masturbation, with the body of a real woman. Soon a subterranean spasm coursed through my body, stretching it and stretching it in a languor that has no equal. Fizz had not moved at all. And I had done so barely.

Sometimes the rustle of a leaf is louder than the beating of a drum.

Through the tidal wave of sleep drowning me I was aware of a growing sense of relief. The shabby sadness of the two busmen had given me something to think about. Maybe I had found what I had been looking for.

Of course, I was wrong about this, as about so much else.

# The Nut Tightener

I had once read in school that poets let their poems mature in their head for a long time. Contrary to popular belief, poetry is not an instant inspirational process. Good poets, once lightning has struck, hunker down to wait. They allow all the ingredients to season and simmer to just the right taste and texture before taking them off the hotplate of their imagination and serving them up on paper.

Even after it is off the fire, the dish needs attention. Careful garnishing, decoration, tweaking. When you eat at a master's table, when you read a master's text, you do not partake of something sudden and speedy. Long hours and subtle spices – a lifetime of nuancing – lie behind it. There is no such thing as an instant master-piece.

I recalled this advice and took it.

Something had come to me.

Between vulgar and banal, there was a perfect moment to pounce on the material.

I decided to wait patiently for it.

My daily toil in the subeditorial trenches acquired a new meaning now. I could focus on it, secure in the knowledge that my real work was fermenting steadily inside of me. I began to enjoy the approval that came my way from Shulteri. I found myself invoking cornball words and phrases, essaying complicated rewrites, punning and alliterating. I also started getting proactive, venturing out of the trenches to discuss deployments with Shulteri – headlines, kickers, story spins. I began to befriend my fellow trenchmen. I was soon discussing the escalating tussle between Shulteri and Haile Selassie.

It was dangerous.

I was beginning to veer close to the greased pole.

I think once or twice King Cupola's gaze actually passed over me. I felt an unexpected frisson; and tremors were felt in the rest of the office.

It was easy to get sucked into the office's rhythms. The news environment was busy. People, issues, events, scandals were exploding on the Indian landscape like crackers on an endless string. At the heart of it was the strange and sublime saga of Rajiv Gandhi in Indian politics. He and his monstrous mandate – delivered on the dead bodies of a bigballed leader and the blackballed Sikhs – were both beginning to fray. Mr Nice Guy's very physiognomy was morphing. The hair was thinning; the easy smile hardening; the happy eyes tightening.

Innocence is a gift at fourteen. A disaster at forty.

In Indian public life, with its maddening weave of caste and class and religion and region; the gap between the said and meant; the play between piety and immorality; the illicit affair of the symbolic and the real; of medievalism and modernism: in Indian public life this – the danger of innocence – is doubly so. The young Rajiv had learnt nothing from his mother or his grandfather. He could not bend India to his noble will and vision like Jawaharlal; and he could not bend himself to India's feudal psychologies and cynical power-mongering as did Indira.

His virtue could have been to be himself: the decent man, with neither crippling baggage nor lofty vision. The lineage of a king, which Indians revere, and the steady hand of commonsense, which India could sorely do with.

But he was failing to intuit who he ought to be. He was falling between the stools. Followers demand clarity from their leaders, even if it be of a misguided kind. They need to know – amid their own fears and insecurities – that someone up there knows better. This is a perilous instinct. For stupid, desperate followers create half-assed, dangerous leaders. Indian followers had begun manufacturing these regularly in the seventies, and had stepped on the gas in the eighties. Optimum production, of course, was still some years away. Eventually every Indian who could do nothing else could at least claim to be an honourable worker in the country's Manufacture-an-Idiot-Leader industry.

Like brands of single-malt whisky, the MAIL industry was culled from distinct waters, imbued with distinct flavours and aimed at different palates. Idiot leaders could be manufactured in the high-lands or the lowlands, by the sea, or in the glen. They were created from different soils – the soil of dynasty and of caste and of religion. You could swear by Laphroaig or by Glenlivet, by smokiness or by smoothness, by caste or by community. But like all robust drinkers you drank what was available, no matter what you preferred.

We manufactured different idiot leaders and sipped of all of them.

MAIL was booming business.

It employed millions. It was easily the biggest employer in India.

The young Gandhi was from the highlands of dynasty, but was becoming uncertain of his flavour. He was looking too hard to blend. And having come up against the limits of the individual conscience in Indian public life, he was foundering. It was a hard, unforgiving place. Better men than him had gone aground here, and would do so in the future. With every passing month he would lose his clarity, and though I could not see it then, set in motion a process that would see the grand Indian party of Independence become a mere whisk, ade-quate only for brushing off irritants, while Indians began the hunt for a hard knife to carve out sharp identities.

Dangerous men would provide the hard knives.

Identities would be honed to lethal scythes.

By the time the millennium ended and my journalism and love and life were over, razor-sharp identities would be busy slashing each other open.

There would be too many bodies to count. Too much heartache to console.

But back then, 1988, all this chaos was good news for us. It provided more raw material to our factory. Each new disaster sent a ripple through the office: phones rang; meetings were held; people rushed about; King Cupola beamed and glowered; Haile Selassie bustled frantically; Shulteri smiled lazily; and the words flowed into and out of us.

On the greased pole the self-absorption and activity were so intense that I think everyone believed they created the news, not just reported it. Testosterone surged through the fluorescent corridors. Thinning the hair, thickening the intrigue. You could close your eyes and see naked men powering about with throbbing erections. The light glanced off their gleaming glans. The gnarled veins pulsed with dark intent. I had never seen anything like it.

The Brotherhood of Gleaming Glansmen.

Knights exemplar, with a code of polysyllabic words.

The trenchmen cowered at their footfalls. The women simpered from a distance, hid in corners or bolted out the door.

I noted another curious thing. Even those who had not yet acquired jutting erections had an inflated sense of themselves. A reporter would join, be at the bottom of the greased pole – boot-on-face, beginning to slipslide – but he would acquire the air of a savant. It was a self-esteem mirage. Each one thought his self-worth was directly proportional to the number of people who read him. It had little to do with how much you knew or how good you really were.

A bit like government. Positions, designations, flunkeys – things outside of yourself determining your sense of your self.

The universal law of men. You are not who you see reflected in the mirror. You are who you see shining in other men's eyes.

Hail Selassie!

Hail Hard-on!

Hail the Brotherhood of Gleaming Glansmen!

In all this excitement I lost track of time. Many months rolled by. One day when I walked out the tight corridor from the brightly lit backroom offices to the exit, I was shocked to see that not only were all the shops closed but even the parking lot was deserted. My bike, which I had squeezed in between a Maruti and an Ambassador at noon, amid a river of sloshing vehicles, now stood desolate. There was nothing else for yards around. Even the cripple who manned the lot – reversing the cars with one hand – had packed up, leaving behind the young boy, Pakora, who helped him. He was sitting in his dirty shorts on the kerb, shelling and popping peanuts into his mouth. He raised his hand in a salaam when I took the bike off the stand and I flicked him a one-rupee coin. The day stragglers were gone and the animals of the night – the pimps, the hustlers, the pushers, the catamites – were spreading out amid the colonnades and in the park.

I asked Pakora the time. It was eleven o'clock.

A nameless fear gripped me.

The roads were empty. When I puttered past Lodhi Gardens I became aware the winter had passed. That stretch always made me shiver and hunch up. But now the wind felt balmy. I pushed up the visor of the helmet and let it run into me. The night was clear. When I went over the Safdarjung flyover I could see the length of Delhi's original airport where only gutless gliders landed now. The AIIMS crossing had a red light but such an absence of traffic that I sailed through it without changing gear.

Fizz was sitting on the terrace. She had been reading, but now the light was off. The book lay on the stone bench next to a bowl of banana chips. She bought them regularly from the Madras Cafe in Green Park market. I hated them. The brittle chalkish taste. I brought out the Old Monk, and pulled out the other cane chair. We had bought two, along with a small glass-top table, from Panchkuin Road. The round glass sat unevenly on the cane and stayed dirty no matter how hard you scrubbed it. I poured two fingers, splashed in some water and sat back with my feet on the bench. The colony was quiet. The gulmohar leaves gave an occasional sweet rustle. She had a light shawl draped over her shoulders. It didn't cover her slender arms. Her glass was on the paved floor. Her fingers interlaced on her lap. Without saying a word we knew we were in a crisis.

I said, I am sorry.

She said, You like the work more and more, do you?

I said, It's idiot stuff. You just get caught up in seeing it through and so many of them are such halfwits that you just feel obliged to set things right.

She said, They like what you do?

I said, In their idiot way. But it means nothing. Listen, I am just a nut tightener for them. Maybe better than others. But only a nut tightener. If I dropped dead tomorrow, they'd push me off the chair and put in another. To be honest, no matter what they think of themselves, I think everyone there is only a nut tightener, and if any of them dropped dead they would be pushed off the chair and replaced in an instant. It's a good, efficient factory. I tighten nuts in it. We all tighten nuts in it. Yes, sure, they probably like the way I tighten them.

She said, You are a very good nut tightener. The best.

Her voice was slow and flat. She was looking directly at me. She had been thinking something through. For all her flip persona she had a native instinct for getting to the core of things.

I said, I am OK. I am good. But I am only a nut tightener.

The owl in the park was not hooting yet. We had christened it Master Ullukapillu. Every night we kept an ear cocked for it. We had a game, interpreting what it said. We could get Master Ullukapillu's hoot to mean anything we wished. From will you get me a glass of water to please turn off the light to the meaning of the scriptures.

She said, You are a very good nut tightener. You are the best.

I said, What's happened? What's bothering you? I said I am sorry I got late.

She said, You are such a good nut tightener you could probably do it in your sleep.

I stayed quiet, not knowing where it was going. The hoot finally came. Sharp and clear. Yet if you were not listening for it you missed it as a vague night sound.

She gestured with her head and said, Master Ukp agrees. You are the very best nut tightener.

I said, Master Ukp says, drop it. He knows nut tighteners are a dime a dozen.

She said, Not good ones. Not the best ones.

An irritation began to come over me. I wanted to snap. But I knew she was not angry. She was calm. She wanted to tell me something.

I said, OK, I am the best. I am the very best nut tightener in the world. So what do you want me to do?

She said, Worry about it then, mr chinchpokli. You'd better worry about it then.

Picking up her glass she drained it, stood up, walked to the edge of the terrace and plucking a branch of the gulmohar began to beat her left palm with its feathery leaves.

She said, Do you remember what you told me about the Pandit? Tell me.

She said, Petty success is a disaster.

Pandit Har Dayal. Decomposing at the bottom of Sukhna Lake. Along with his son and grandson. Even as his aphorisms bloomed.

She repeated slowly, Petty success is a disaster.

Then she took her glass, her book and the packet of banana chips and went inside.

I sat out for a long time, sipping the rum.

Master Ullukapillu hooted, once, twice. It was closer now, probably on the wires running the street. I tried to read what it was saying.

I think it said: The best nut tightener in the world.

I called in the next day and said I would not be coming in. Shulteri was dogged. Are you unwell? Can't you come for a few hours? He had begun to rely on me increasingly. In his clamber up the greased pole he needed good shoulders to stand on. Better still if they were unlikely to start climbing themselves. I was in no mood to explain, or to conjure a lie. I put the phone down. He called back a little later and I walked out the front door and down the stairs so Fizz could tell him I was not at home.

I went to the Deer Park, and winding past the dismal wire enclosures full of dead-eyed animals, wandered across the bridge into the District Park. It was nicer here. The sun more accessible. Green grass everywhere. Yellow-wattled lapwings inspecting the dry cracking pond under the Hauz Khas ruins. No cages with motionless deer and unlively rabbits. Under the papri trees the sudden flapping of a polished brown coucal. A hoopoe puncturing the earth with its needle nose. Drongos in gleaming black tuxedos casting around for a midday feast. Scrawny gardeners using supple hands to slowly turn over dung and soil in rose beds. In scattered clumps, ayahs with prams. Shelling peanuts, chatting. Baby's morning out, while double-income couple blazes a trail.

Fizz would always say, When we have our babies we will both stop working.

No-income couple. Two children.

On the mud paths pretty young mothers strolling. Absent expressions, dragged by prams, negotiating the narrow corridors life has entered. Single husband, single income, single child. Single soul.

I sat down on the green slope of the rise opposite the pond, but got up immediately. Walking was better. I had deceived myself into a calm. Pretended I was working – brewing and fermenting – while I circled closer and closer to the greased pole. Now Fizz had burst the dam of serenity. I was back in river restless. It was roaring through me and I had to start paddling fast.

Petty success is a disaster.

The best nut tightener in the world.

When we came back after dinner, having eaten uttapams at Madras Cafe, and got into bed, Master Ullukapillu hooted, the first tentative testing of the night.

Fizz said, Master Ukp says in the grand pursuits of their lives wise men heed their wives.

I waited in the dark, holding her hand. The next hoot came.

I said, He says you can't build a house without a plan.

When the next one came she said, He says good architects put their plans down on paper, they don't just keep them in their heads.

Some time passed while Master Ukp contemplated what to say next. We lay in silence. The only sounds were the ticking of the clock and an occasional rumble of dissatisfaction from the refrigerator. In the diffused blue nightlight I could see the framed picture of Ezra Pound on the wall opposite me. I liked his beard and sharp nose. He looked like a mad Russian count who rode his horses to death, drank a barrel a day and ravished every wench who crossed his path. His eyes were sunk in dark shadows. But I knew he was staring hard at me. Barely concealing his contempt of petty success. Yet he was no mean nut tightener himself. The superior craftsman. Tom would attest to that. Il miglior fabbro.

The hoot came. Sharp and clear, cutting a hole through the night.

Before Fizz could speak I said, Master Ukp says, talk is nothing; action is all.

And I rolled onto her, shutting out anything else the master might wish to add.

We bought a small study table from the second-hand market in Lajpat Nagar. It had two little drawers on its left side and a wooden foot bar. The drawers pulled open jerkily and had mock-antique knobs. The table had been polished to a shining dark tan and it looked rich and old. I actually thought it was. But when Fizz rapped it with her knuckles it gave off a faux sound; and when she scraped at it the putty used for filling up the fissures came off under her nails.

She laughed and said, It was probably hammered into existence yesterday.

It didn't matter to me. I just needed a work-table. We matched a cheap armless chair with it. The chair was a quarter-inch off in the back right leg. We asked the paunchy seller – who kept digging for flint in his navel while extolling the virtues of his products – to fix it, before carting it out.

As we wound our way out of the untidy sprawl of furniture sellers, we could hear furious conversations about original and fake ringing all around us. Everyone was going teak, teak, teak. Wanting teak, demanding teak, questioning teak. If you tried, in the din, you could also isolate the sound of fresh antiques – teak-thak teak-thak teak-thak – being hammered into existence at the back of the shacks.

The table and chair went into the small room. The room had a window, but it opened on to the service lane. The lane was in disuse, overgrown with grass, litter everywhere. The view was of the back of the tiny houses. Claustrophobic iron grilles shutting in tiny back-yards and choked verandas. The great Indian middle-class architec-ture of air and light and security. Mostly security, security, security.

Clothes-lines were strung everywhere, with colourful plastic pegs hung on them like buds on a branch. Around noon – past the wash-ing hour – they bloomed riotously with all manner of clothes. By looking at them you got an intimate map of the inhabitants. Some houses I noted had daringly skimpy panties.

The service lane itself had an untidy jumble of wires strung all down its length. Telephone wires and power lines. Their tentacles extended into the houses in the most unplanned way. The day we set up the table I noticed a fine grey-black crow hanging upside-down opposite our window. It was a fresh demise. The electrocution had no violence to it. The feathers shone. The face was unmarked and calm. It could have been a diving cormorant. The attritions of weather and insect had yet to set in.

Is that a bad omen? I asked Fizz.

She said, The crow always signals a visitor. In your case, the muse.

I said, This one is hanging upside-down and is dead.

She said, He waited too long. He probably died waiting.

Fizz got simple plywood planks put up on the walls. The carpen-ter said it was a new kind of ply, water and termite resistant, and would outlast the books. He said it a dozen times. Everyman's obsession with eternity. Looking at the books, I could have told him there were many I could see that were already dead.

The books had lain heaped on the upturned boxes for months, the stacks leaning precariously against each other. Now they got full and splendid play. Fizz arranged them by size. If you ran your fingertips along their colourful spines – dip-crest, dip-crest – you got a sensuous jitter as on a xylophone.

Fizz put up a custard yellow curtain at the window. It was of a light material. It billowed in the breeze and let the sun in generously. I could see the shadow of the hanging crow through it. It stayed there for weeks, giving itself up to the elements slowly. For a time it was like a tattered kite, fraying, with perforations. Then it was gone, and I would look out the window and feel the landscape had undergone a dramatic change.

The Brother was set on the table and unveiled like a dish. Its red body gleamed, and its black beautiful keys, floating in air, were an urgent invitation to the fingers. Pound was removed from the bedroom and hung opposite the desk. I had only to look up to catch his dark gaze. The golden-hued Tagore was strung up near the door. A wide-mouthed aluminium lamp was stationed on the table. It crouched over the typewriter like a zealous overseer. A cheap four-by-two brown rug was flung on the floor for warmth. All escape routes were blocked. When you shut the door the overpowering aroma of furniture polish swamped you. It took longer than the crow to disappear.

For many mornings I did not actually write. I pushed the Brother aside and tried to draw up a road map for the writing. I tried to make a tree of the characters and another of the plot. I would make many untidy squiggles, then cancel them out, shuffle the papers and make some more. Fizz began to retreat into a state of deference. I had to walk out frequently, both for the headiness of the wood varnish and the fallowness in my head. Each time I walked out Fizz would be curled up reading in the love seat in the small sitting room. She would look up knowingly and say nothing, except for asking me if I needed anything.

The temple to art had been established. Miracles were now awaited.

I asked Shulteri to put me permanently on the afternoon shift. It ensured I had the mornings for the temple. The temple worked its magic on my office life almost immediately. I lost all interest in the greased pole. Haile Selassie and Shulteri's boot-in-face antics suddenly seemed pathetic. And I couldn't care a camel's ass who had King Cupola's eye and how much grease he was slopping on whom. I scurried back deep into the subeditorial trenches. My language regained a sanity. The growing bombast began to seep out of my prose. The rewrites became functional again.

Was petty failure more honourable than petty success?

I don't think the Pandit had pronounced on that.

Curiously, Shulteri was almost relieved that I had retreated to my initial indifference. The greased pole was already too crowded. He happily accommodated my timings. He encouraged me to have a life outside the office. A healthy balance, he said. I began to leave every evening as the shop shutters were being pulled down. Shulteri left with the last sub, way past midnight, his arms firmly hooked around the pole, his eyes firmly fixed on the cupola.

For the first week I knew Fizz was puzzled. There was no music of clattering keys to be heard. But she asked nothing, holding herself in, waiting for me to speak. Then one morning a line came to me: The young Sikh had never been anywhere where he could not take his horse.

In clammy excitement I adjusted the already set sheet of paper and banged it out. The keys rang through the house like a loud temple bell and I could almost hear a huge sigh explode in the sitting room. I flexed my fingers nervously a few times and the next line came clattering out: For him the world had as much space for horses as for men.

That day when I emerged to go to the office I was floating. I had written only two paragraphs but that didn't matter. The engine had finally caught. The gear changes, the acceleration, could all come later.

In the night when Master Ullukapillu hooted, Fizz said, He wants to know if you want to tell us what's happening.

I put my arm under her head and hugged her close.

When the next hoot came I said, He's saying there is a time and place for everything.

She put her head under the sheet and a few minutes later mumbled wetly, Do you think this is what he meant?

Yes, I said. Yes, Yes, Yes.

I didn't go back to the old Manual, though several of its injunctions lingered with me. This time I decided discipline was an overrated virtue. I resolved to let the muse lead me, in whatever way she chose. I set down no work patterns. I kept no track of the wordage. The only thing I committed myself to was a minimum of two hours in the study every day. If the work flowed I would stay with it; if it didn't I would get up and leave without guilt.

The spontaneity of art.

In hindsight it is not a strategy I recommend. Perhaps it can produce poets, certainly not prose writers. To wait for a lyric impulse can sink you in a barrel of vague complacency. And non-doing. Poets' lives can be vindicated by six impulses, six poems. Prose writers with six pages – or even sixty – cannot even knock at posterity's door.

For the first week I wrote a few paragraphs every morning and it felt good. It was nearly a year since I had drowned *The Inheritors*; to be back in the writing made me feel alive and worthy. I also enjoyed the absence of the old regime. It made me feel less calculating and cynical. I now felt some nausea for my earlier methods. The rules, the word counting, the tics that became a substitute for the writing.

More than anything I loved the clatter of the typewriter keys. In the office – a modern place – I was using computers for the first time.

The soft-touch keyboard lacked the music of the typewriter. Also the sense of solidity. The pulsing words on the glowing screen seemed transient, watery; while the black type on white paper looked inerasable. When I worked in the office I felt I was creating tinsel. When I worked at home I felt I was hammering out something of enduring value.

It is peculiar. The hard realities of my office work appeared fake. The soft fictions on my typewriter seemed real.

As older Hindus never cease to tell you, the world is never what it seems.

Fizz in the meantime had been doing the rounds of the schools. She was bored, and we were again tight for money, though still refusing to talk about it. But there were no jobs to be had. A degree epidemic had swept India. Aptitude, talent, ability were good things, but they had to come riding the horses of degrees. And middle-class Indians were acquiring horses as if preparing for the charge of the Light Brigade. Double MA, MA-BEd, MA-LLB, MPhil-MEd – marriages, jobs, reputations, everything it seemed depended on these endless epithets. In most cases it was years before people discovered they were astride rocking horses and were not going anywhere.

A very large swathe of middle India was rocking on degrees, going nowhere.

Fizz was a plain graduate who had not even collected her degree. The arrogance of our college years. Her attempts were doomed. She would have been laughed out of the gates by the peons had she not appeared as if she had a full frisky stable at home.

I checked in the trenches for other leads. Of all the suggestions that came my way the most plausible seemed to be book editing. One rifleman in my trench had once worked in a well-known publishing house. He said it was a complete scandal. The house licensed some prestigious foreign titles for reprint, but mostly just pirated them. Even those licensed were never honestly accounted for. In recent times it had also begun to originate local books. These were shoddy biographies of businessmen and politicians who paid upfront for the printing and paper. Plus an occasional collection of research papers, pre-sold to some institution. It had also tried a few works of fiction. They had sunk without a trace. Novelists approaching the house were likely to be treated badly.

The imprint was called Dharma Books. Righteous books.

The man who owned it had a big moustache. It filled his cheeks like the whiskers of a Chambal valley dacoit. He smoked a cigar and drove a white Mercedes. His name was Dum Arora. He almost never read a book. His wealth came from dealerships of petrol pumps and gas agencies. My buddy in the trench said Dum Arora had once told him the name of his favourite book. It was *Jonathan Livingston Seagull*. Dum said he had learnt the meaning of life from it. And the pictures of the birds were extraordinary.

My rifleman said for these reasons Dum was a good man to work for. He paid you little but on time and he left you alone. He paid five rupees a page for editing, and three rupees a page for proofing. If he invited you home he offered you Johnnie Walker Black Label from a very big bottle. He was generous then. You were free to drink an entire bottle if you could do it. The rifleman said when you reached his home Dum Arora would bellow, Haanji, johnnie-shonnie ho jaye? Shall we to johnnie-shonnie then?

The barber came home to dye his big whiskers. For a few days after, said the rifleman, you could spot traces of black on his skin.

Fizz went to meet him. He was bluff and friendly. He spoke passionately about his love of books. He said he made no money from them, but they made him feel spiritual. And money, as we know, means nothing; only the divine matters. All will be left behind. Only god will travel with us. He said he would pay Fizz three rupees a page for editing. Fizz said she had been told the rate was five. He said OK. He would give her five because he could see she was a goodly and genuine person.

He gave her the life story of a bureaucrat to edit. It was a nicely typed, beautifully bound, thick manuscript. An autobiography. The man was long retired. This was an ode to himself. It was full of all the wonderful things he had done in the districts. How he had served the people of India. Whenever I peeped in at Fizz working I could see her rounded squiggle filling the pages, arrows pointing all over, directing the corrections.

She would say, He's just been felicitated for starting a community cowshed.

Or, He's just telling us how his speech on municipal reforms to the Rotary Club fetched a standing ovation.

At end of day she would stretch theatrically and say, Fifteen pages; seventy-five rupees.

My own work went well. I felt I had hit upon a great conceit, sparked by our lunatic journey into Delhi, and a report I had read in the newspapers. This book was going to be the exact opposite of *The Inheritors*. Not capacious, not sprawling, not spanning generations. I was going to build this around one incident. One incident, one journey, one character. I would carve not an elaborate choker, but a perfect diamond. I felt I had come to understand the power of the small to illustrate the big.

The young Sikh had never been anywhere where he could not take his horse.

So I had begun on the first day. My story was to be about a young Sikh orphan who grows up in a Sikh seminary in a small village in Punjab. Introverted, fixated on his religious and martial instruction – a warrior-saint – he never steps out of the boundaries of the seminary. He has only one passion outside of his Granth Sahib lessons and the chanting of the gurbani: riding the horses the school maintains.

They are his family. He spends long hours riding them, feeding them, rubbing them down. It is easier for him to be with them than with the other students, who talk about their families and friends. Sometimes he wakes at night with a deep loneliness haunting him. He then goes out to where the horses are tethered under the tamarind tree. Lying between them, hearing them snort and shuffle, feeling their warm silken flanks rise and fall, he feels calmed. Often he sleeps there.

The horses whisper to him. He loves to listen to them.

One day when he is twenty-one years old something happens – I hadn't decided what – that forces him to make a trip to the country's capital, to Delhi. He seeks the permission of the sant who heads the seminary, rolls his blanket, straps on his sword, picks up his spear, mounts his horse and sets forth. He goes to Amritsar, visits the Golden Temple, seeks directions and arrives at the railway station.

Now came the centrepiece of my story. At the station, he goes in, finds a train leaving for Delhi and boards it with his horse. No one dares stop him. He is clad in a blue religious tunic; he has his sword; he has his spear; and a look in his eye that brooks no argument. The journey through the plains of Punjab and Haryana is memorable not just for him, but for every person – traveller and official – who encounters him. Each is forced into new ways of seeing.

When the train slides into New Delhi railway station all hell breaks loose. The young warrior-saint dismounts with his horse. Passengers scatter. Vendors leap back. Coolies remove their turbans and scratch their heads. Railway officials are summoned. The police arrive. The media arrive. Medieval Hindoostan has appeared in the midst of modern India.

Innocence and bewilderment square off against cunning and bewilderment.

A strange dialogue commences.

I had read books like that. Morality tales. The cosmos in a kernel. One incident illuminating the universe. It was to be a small book. It would proceed slowly. But it would pose large questions. I could see it on the bookshelves: thick paper, large type, quiet resonance.

I hoped my reporting in Punjab and my stay in Delhi and my travels in trains would provide me with sufficient knowledge to navigate.

I did not rush anything this time. Some days my fingers did not even touch the Brother's keys. I would pace up and down the little room, waiting for a writable line, a workable thought. Or sit on the armless chair, pressing down on the table's foot bar, seeing how far I could bend the bad wood before it cracked. Surprisingly, like people, even bad wood has more resilience than you ever imagine.

All the while Pound looked down on me darkly and there was Tagore at my back.

I moved the narrative like a trickle of water across a bathroom floor. The tug of an unseen incline pulling it snail-like. I described every twirl of turban tying; every mug of chill water; every whisk of horse tail; every whetting of sword edge. Against my grain, I became a minimalist. I trawled the thoughts of my young hero, airing them with the leisure of a grandmother emptying old trunks.

I found it exciting, trying to enter the mind of someone simple and lonely. I discovered I had to pare away layer after layer of ordinary knowledge to arrive at that state. I also had to struggle to find a cadence in English that could echo that of the rural and the Punjabi. I used the two bumbling sardars who had brought us into Delhi as keys.

I took it a sentence at a time.

I did not show any of it to Fizz.

She heard the periodic clatter of the typewriter and was calmed.

❦

The months rolled by. The year turned. We made friends. She, me, us. They filled our barsati many evenings of the week. Designers, artists, actors, journalists, film-makers, activists – other marginalized seekers, looking for a door and a life. We went out drinking, eating, seeing films. Sometimes conversations would begin in the evening and go on past midnight. We argued about politics, literature, cinema, caste, community, cities. The churn in India was becoming dizzying as fault-lines were being opened every which way. Social, political, individual; region, religion, language, caste, community. Fault-lines that had been sealed and sutured fifty years ago to create a nation were being undone stitch by stitch.

Rajiv Gandhi's reign was about to end. A new beast, fatted on religious myths, was wakening. Preparing to stalk the land. To take on other beasts.

A million mutinies were afoot.

Fizz and I lived through it all with a sense of unreality. That old continuing sense that we were play-acting, doing our turn on stage while our real life lay elsewhere. Today, I realize that it is not such an unusual condition. Many people go through their days imagining their real lives lie somewhere else. In the end – like me – they have nothing.

Not the days they lived through.

Not those they thought were on their way.

Not that the days were all bad. They were fun. We discovered things, we learnt things. Two of the most gratifying were drinking whisky and watching birds. Some nights we did the one, and some mornings the other. We bought a pair of second-hand Minolta binoculars from Palika Bazaar. They were too heavy to hang around the neck and had to be held in the hand. But they were a miracle of magnification. So far away from the little plastic ones we had known as children. We played with the Minolta all the time, me often to just look at her across a room. To get even more of her somehow than I already had.

With great enthusiasm we would be out of the house before day-break. The district park, the ridge, the Yamuna barrage; and then later the sanctuaries at Sultanpur and Bharatpur. For the first time I began to see the birds I had seen all my life. The sight of a pied kingfisher or an elusive coppersmith became as much of a high as the whiskies, whose flavours we were beginning to distinguish on our palate, even as we slowly took water out of the equation in an attempt to get closer to the real burn of the taste.

One day in Connaught Place, waiting in a queue at my bank, I looked out and saw a grey hornbill alight on a neem tree. I almost shouted out in excitement as I rushed to the barred window. It was the first time I had seen one. I didn't even know you could spot them in the heart of concrete Delhi. I was subjected to curious looks, and the teller had to call out to me irritably when my turn came to hand over the brass token.

Yes, the days were not bad. Sometimes I could almost fool myself

I was leading a full life. But then suddenly the reel would end, the lights would come on and I would snap out of my reverie. This was not my life. It was a film. Enjoyable, but not real. This moment would come upon me at any time. Mostly it did when I was driving back from the office in the first flush of dark, the visor up, the wind in my face. Or when I was with friends but sitting outside of the conversation. At such times I felt everyone else around me was leading their true lives, but mine was a lie.

My life was a lie. And I could not suspend disbelief forever.

The only thing that always felt real was my ceaseless engagement with Fizz. The centre of my life continued to be her body. I made love to her several times a day. And at other times, in the office, at the Brother, I obsessed about her – what we had just done, what we would soon do. At times the ecstasy was beyond religious. I felt like a whirling dervish who has caught the thread to unravelling the universe and will not let go.

The whirling must go on till the entire universe is unravelled.

Till consciousness is lost.

Till the oblivion at the heart of the universe is tasted.

I drank of the oblivion day after day and could not imagine anything its equal. I understood why the ancients revered and feared sexual ecstasy. It allows each one access to their own god. You need neither priest nor king to show you the way. Love – without the rules of priest and king – is all you need. The key to the universe lies with no priest or king. The key to the universe lies in the body of the lover.

I had the key and I unlocked the universe every day.

How could I care about King Cupola or the greased pole or the money I did not have when I had Fizz? In those years we discovered and did things with each other we had never heard or read of. We kept stripping each other of all the shames that had been draped on us over the years. Beneath the shames we found an innocence of response we could barely have imagined. A rare joyousness that took away nothing from anyone and only gave. I discovered to make the earth move you need not just a nakedness of body but also a nakedness of soul.

When lovers bare their bodies they have sex.

When lovers bare their souls they taste godhead.

Each time I lay naked on Fizz I was aware we were naked in both body and soul.

We were also chronic adventurers.

We went to places where we felt – like all lovers – that we were the first.

We discovered the body of a lover has secrets that never end.

We discovered that at different times the same secrets reveal different truths.

I ranged over the crevices and folds of Fizz's body and was continually enchanted.

Sometimes the intensity was so great we would begin to visibly tremble before the first touch. We were like mine defusers, keyed up at what might happen in the first moment of contact. I would be hard, straining; wanting and postponing the moment. She would be flushed, her lips shivering. And then we would touch, and always there was the explosion, as we became both raw and sublime, animal and angel, flesh and light. Fizz and me.

Sometimes the pleasure was so excruciating I wanted to bite a chunk of her body and chew on it. At other times I just wanted to let out a wail that would fill the heavens.

I knew then that nothing two people in love do with each other is ever wrong.

I knew then that no one – no law, no parent, no friend – has any jurisdiction in the land of the lovers.

I knew then that those who have truly loved know that the key to the universe lies in the body of the lover.

I had the key and I unlocked the universe every day.

The universe I discovered was constructed solely from desire.

Things at the office started to go badly. Over time I had lost all interest in the breathless exertions of its people and prose. The Brotherhood of Gleaming Glansmen stalking the corridors had never terrorized me; slowly they even lost their curiosity value. An erection is exciting because it comes and goes. A 24/7 hard-on is a bore. The prose, of course, appalled me more and more. It was forever on cortisone, artificially pumped up. It said things in ways that made them other things.

Sometimes when I read it I actually expected it to sprout tumours.

In turn I had become an object of deep disappointment to the office satraps. Perhaps even derision. I was resolutely nestled in my trench, firing the mandatory rounds, but refusing full engagement. This was bad behaviour. Animals who behaved like this could undo the logic of the greased pole. The disease could spread. Given my initial promise, several attempts were made to involve me in more responsibilities. I avoided them all. I became paranoid. I worked hard to avoid any contact with the big dildos. I did not want to talk to them. I did not want to catch their eye.

When I finished a rewrite I actually went back over it carefully and excised every trace of flair from it. Made it completely flat. So neither eye nor sensibility would snag on its surface anywhere.

Shulteri took me out to lunch one day and said, I don't understand you.

I said, I am a wavering journalist.

He became melancholic and opened up his heart. He told me King Cupola might be god for everybody else in the office, but his gods were others and they were all dead and they were all literary. He said he had come to journalism twelve years ago because he knew of no other route to a writing career. He said he had expected to pass through journalism quickly into writing, but he had been trapped. Some success had come to him and some money. The years had passed. He had married. He had two sons. He had a nice flat. A red Maruti car. His elder boy went to an expensive school, where fancy tiffin was served in boxes with neatly folded serviettes. That was the word he used: serviettes.

He said some days he found it difficult to fall asleep as he thought about what he had set out to do and what he had become.

I was taken aback. The louche casualness I had come to associate with him was nowhere in evidence. Nor was there any trace of the boot-on-face climber. I looked hard to see if he was playing with me. But there were no signs of that either.

We were eating parathas at a cafe next to the Cottage Emporium. It had seen better days. It still had a reputation but clearly no future. The waiters were sullen and their uniforms showed lack of concern. They wore crumpled white tunics and had rubber slippers on their feet. The food – even simple parathas – took time to arrive. And when you asked for embellishments – pickles, onions, butter – they became footnotes, served up at the end of the meal.

Shulteri was eating badly. I had finished my paratha and he had barely dug a half moon into his. I felt for a moment that perhaps I was finally seeing the real man.

I said, It's never too late.

He said, That's what I tell myself.

It was strange to see him without the easy mocking smile. When had he acquired that? As a young boy fencing with competitive peers? Or later when he needed a camouflage to move in an alien world?

He said, Do you think I am fooling myself?

I said, Aren't we all?

He sat there, not eating, his rodent face set. The silence had congealed on the table like cold butter when he said slowly, I'll tell you what the problem is.

I waited. He was staring off in the distance.

He said, The problem is that people like me come from nowhere. We come from the margins of the earth. From nowhere. It takes a lot to arrive at the centre of the world. A lot more to carve a place in it. It is not easy to give it up, to cede it. It is not easy to cede the territory you have annexed at the centre of the world. It is not easy.

I said, Yes, it is not easy.

The flat, the red Maruti, the serviette.

When he kept quiet, I said, But it is not so difficult either. I think it's just a matter of reminding oneself of first things. If—

It matters not, he interrupted cheerily.

The mocking smile was back. The body had again slumped into laid-back mode. He was too proud to be patronized. He had let himself go briefly, to air himself. Not to be given instruction.

He said, In any case I think what we do has great worth. I think good journalism is a very valuable thing.

I said, I am sure you are right.

That was the first and last time I saw the mocking smile slip. Strangely, instead of making him more friendly, his confessional moment made him more ill-disposed towards me. Perhaps he worried he had revealed the anxiety beneath the composure. The vulnerable veins propping up the shining hard-on. I suppose in the warrior code of the Gleaming Glansmen the slightest hint of flaccidity was a disaster.

With Shulteri removing his benediction from my head, there was no one to watch out for me. I sensed I could plod on in the trenches for some time without inviting ejection. A small-time nut tightener. But I was on my own. Easy victim to any individual or collective vagary that might sweep the office.

As the decade turned, we felt increasingly splintered. In the office I had ceased to exist. Like a poltergeist I went in and out, turning a few inconsequential nuts. No one on the greased pole even threw a glance in my direction. The country was in the midst of a caste earthquake and the Glansmen were rushing about writing it up. Everyone was convinced one weepy man's misinspired sense of justice was going to turn India on its head. The arrowhead of the caste pyramid would soon be holding up the entire base. Elite India was in the grip of panic. It knew it could hold up nothing but its own indulgences.

The master, the mistress, and the frozen margarita.

But they need not have panicked. Weepy man was marching to his own drums; before long he would march clean out of the door. The man he had bested – Rajiv Gandhi – would soon be dead. The caste pyramid would be safely back, right side up. And weepy man himself would march past the horizon and fall off the edge of the earth.

He would demonstrate it is easy to best a redoubtable enemy, far more difficult to best a feckless self.

India's elite would be safe. It had survived five millennia of rude challenges and seen off the likes of Buddha, Mahavira, Kabir and Gandhi. Humoured them, coopted them and neatly slotted them on the mantelpiece. Weepy man, in time, in a very little time, would not even be a blip on its screen.

The master, the mistress, and the frozen margarita.

Defended by the Brotherhood of Gleaming Glansmen.

I had time to dwell on all this because I was making heavy weather on the Brother. Days would go by without a single key being hammered. I had become deeply riven about the worth of what I was writing. On some days I read the slow unfurling of the young warrior-saint's story and felt I was creating something of value. I entered his mind and marvelled at its simplistic wonderment of the world. I went with him to his horses and was touched by his love for them. I followed his daily ablutions and was moved by their rudimentary quality. I boarded the train with him and his horse and was intrigued by the way the other travellers responded to him.

Then, as swiftly, a day later I read what I was writing and was appalled by its phoneyness. I wrestled with the conundrum: why should fiction be good only if it's real? My story held together; it read well; wasn't that enough? How did I know *Tess of the D'Urbervilles* wasn't phoney?

The bravura never lasted.

Two days of certitude and banging, and I would fall silent on the Brother.

I had given Fizz some idea of the story, but had not yet let her read it. She was waiting patiently, not asking, though I could see a shadow of anxiety run over her face each time I emerged from the study without recording a single clack.

There was worse. We had begun to have frequent run-ins. Small things would spark off spats. The water left running. The newspaper folded badly. The door not latched. The light left on. The bread not bought. The milk not boiled. The tea not made. The curtain not drawn.

The book not written.

The road not taken.

Most times we would quickly forget what had kicked off the spat because it would spiral into any number of unrelated things. We would gouge at old wounds – of family, friends, losses, memories, things done for each other and things not done. She would lash out. I would slice. We would injure, we would hurt.

Once she threw a plate of sliced cucumbers at me.

I was sitting in my lungi on the love seat reading. She was angry at me for not having brought in the plumber to fix the leaking cistern in the toilet. It had been going on for days and I was irritated at being nagged. I didn't mind using the bucket to flush the pot. And anyway, why didn't she call him?

She said, Have you spoken to the plumber?

I said in a silly falsetto, Yes, yes, the plumber, the plumber. Spoken to the plumber.

She said, Are you going to get it fixed or not?

I said, Yes, yes, are you going to get it fixed or not. Are you going to get it fixed or not.

She said, Stop being an asshole!

I said, Yes, yes, stop being an asshole, stop being an asshole.

She picked up the melamine plate and flung it at me. It glanced off my shoulder, emptying its payload on my naked chest. The slices, drenched in lemon juice, chillies and salt, stuck to my body. Cool. And running water.

I sat there watching them drip. I could not believe it.

I said, Mad fucking bitch!

She said, The great writer chinchpokli!

And wrenching open the front door she walked out. Later she told me she laughed all the way down the stairs and around the park. By the time she came back I had had a bath and cleared up the debris.

These fights, breaking like flash-floods, went away as quickly, washing away with them the gathering frustrations of many days. They were good, cleansing scraps and we felt much better afterwards.

However there were others that started without fanfare, in a low key, but then settled to a slow burn. They would begin with some unspoken resentment, which in turn provoked another unspoken resentment. These would be concealed like the glow on a car lighter. But each time you pulled the lighter out it would be red hot; then hotter and hotter. These were the bad ones, strung out on long sulks. We would not talk, and the anger would calcify. Eventually we would have to shut down the engine so the burn on the lighter could cool off.

This always happened some days into the stand-off with some gut-wrenching lovemaking. At some point our bodies would begin to agitate, to crave. We would circle each other, looking for the perfect opening, the moment to wordlessly unlock the past. Some wiring between us told us when to make the move. It could come at night, in the dark, with a tentative touch. On the bike with a sudden squeeze. On the terrace with an urgent glance. We were good then. The mover was never rejected; there was always a passionate response waiting.

Our scraps ended in wonderful sex. We called it Spat Sex and looked forward to it even as we were in the middle of a grim fight.

I often wondered how many spats it would take for the passion to start fraying. For the edge to blunt. Miraculously, it didn't happen. But my anxieties did not die.

I was aware somewhere that the growing storminess of our relationship had less to do with us, more to do with the diminishing clacks on the Brother. That the stars and skulls, the peaks and troughs, mightysatiety and the key to the universe were all somehow tied up with my ability to summon up words on paper. When the sheets remained blank everything began to blank. Of course I could cheat. Clack on mindlessly. Let the sound be the story.

Let the illusion be the reality.

But I was not yet so far gone.

Fizz meanwhile had been having a mystifying time with Dharma Books. Several bad manuscripts had passed through her hands. We had no idea where they went once they were printed. They could not be found in any bookshop. We never heard anyone mention them. They seemed to vanish into some biblioblackhole that is the destination of most of the world's books. Few books can resist its gravitational pull. Over time even the biggest are sucked into it. It is wonderfully sanitary. If all the biblioblackholes ever began to spew back their gorgings, the world would be drowned in rubbishy paper.

Bad prose, bad ideas and rank bad descriptions.

Dum Arora was not fazed by the missingness of his books. We began to believe what we had been told. That Dum's books were a cosy arrangement with government departments. They went straight from the printing press to the government godowns, shrewdly bypassing bookshops and readers. Occasionally they were covered in the newspapers, in tortuous reviews that I could not believe anyone ever read.

If this were true, the biblioblackhole of the government was a very big one.

Fizz had no vanity about what she was doing so it did not bother her. Dum paid on time and was always polite.

Fizz's association with Dharma Books had one curious fallout. She met an unusual woman and got involved in an unusual project. It afforded us much conversation and amusement over many months.

This woman was a posh academic with a degree each from Harvard and Oxford. One in sociology and the other in psychology. She was married to an immensely rich man. He manufactured and sold parts for cars. We never quite figured out what parts. He smoked a pipe and talked about *The Economist*. He was distressingly gracious, littering his conversation with May I? Can I? Let me. My pleasure. I noticed he worked hard to make women comfortable.

In contrast, the woman had no time for niceties. She was handsome in a hatchety way – like Indira Gandhi, Margaret Thatcher. A sharp face that cuts through the crap. She wore her hair buoyant and short. It had lines of cool silver in it. Her voice worked like a tin opener – cold, measured, sharp. Slicing you open. We called her ms meanqueen. Between the two of us we never heard her drop a soft word about anyone or anything. Fizz said even her drivers and servants were cut open like soup cans. Whenever she spoke to them there was blood on the floor. You had to look away.

I think she had some notion of maintaining a hard and perfectionist view of the world. There are very intelligent people like that, who equate soft with weak, and are vehemently opposed to both. Empirical learning – and often wealth – give them contempt for sentimentality. The world is a hard place; it has evolved on Darwinian principles; it does not help to be woolly-headed about it. The vast vocabularies of articulation they acquire have no place for the ooze of ordinary niceness.

Ms meanqueen had everything – degrees, dollars, comforts, class, children, cerebration. But she made no allowances for herself or anyone. Her life was the product of her own endeavours. She owed no one anything. Those who had nothing had only themselves to question. She set her hatchet against the world and hacked her way through it.

The world is a hard place.

Dum Arora sent Fizz to meet her. Dum said she was looking for a smart research assistant. Dum said, She is very nice lady, very bold lady. Double degree, from Oxford and Harvard. But only she is a little angry always.

Fizz said, Angry? Angry with what?

Dum said, Angry with the world. Angry with the world. Some people are like that. Some people are angry with their mama–papa. Some are angry with their wife. Some with their boss. Some with their children. And some are angry with the world. Mrs Khurana is very angry with the world. But she is very nice lady. Very bold lady.

Fizz went to meet her. She lived in a big house in Maharani Bagh, with high doors, old colonial furniture and modern artworks. Fizz was first seated in a cavernous living room, given a glass of water, then taken into a carpeted study with teak bookshelves and angled lamps. A muted silence filled the house and the servants walked on the balls of their feet. I waited outside the big steel gate, leaning on my bike under a siris tree. It was shedding yellow fluff all over the road and I picked up undamaged puffs and blew them into the air. The guard in grey uniform and grey peaked cap with gold trim looked at me in disgust.

Ms meanqueen was not too angry with the world that day. Just very stern.

She carried out an interrogation. Her first question was, Do you have regular sex? Fizz said with a smile, How do you define regular?

The meeting went well. Even ms meanqueen was not impervious to Fizz's easy non-combative charm. She was carrying out a study on the masturbatory habits of the Indian male. It was an inadequately documented area, she said. She wanted someone to help with data collection. You had to do one-on-one interviews, write up the stuff and bring it in. No flourishes were required. No turns of phrase, no ordering. Just bring in the material. And collect the money. One hundred and fifty rupees per interview.

Remember, no fiction, no embellishment, no fluffing up of material.

Get it straight and true. Analysis can only be as good as the data.

Display empathy. Encourage confession.

Guarantee confidentiality. Appear scholarly.

Encourage graphic description.

Appear intimate. Don't get involved.

Hundred fifty rupees a man.

Cash on arrival.

Can you do it?

And yes. Nota bene. Discretion at all times. You can talk to your husband, but that's where it stops.

Only two people will know the real identities. You and me. OK, maybe your husband. If you want him to. I wouldn't advise it.

Fizz said she would call back in a day with her answer.

Ms meanqueen said, Remember, Fiza, this is a serious study. Don't get misled by the subject. Just think you are gathering data on the excretory habits of cicadas.

She stopped for a moment, pleased with that. Then gave a hard smile and said, Actually that's good, that's very good! That's it! Men are like cicadas – rubbing themselves, rubbing themselves, all the damn time. Their continual rubbing away is like a background hum to our lives. Sad little cicadas!

That night Fizz ran a pilot on me.

Do you do it?

Yes.

Even now?

Yes.

Yes!

Yes.

When did you start?

At eight.

It can happen at eight!

Yes.

How did it happen?

Pleasant accident.

No, how did it happen? Where were you?

Oh, in the loo. Sitting on the pot. The sun was shining outside. The window was open.

And?

And I rubbed. And rubbed.

Like a cicada?

Like a cicada.

And?

Never felt better. The earth moved. The birds sang. The mind opened like a flower.

Then?

I took it up with great self-discipline.

What does that mean?

At least twice a day. No matter how busy life was.

Did anyone know? Parents, servants, friends?

I am sure. All of the above.

Weren't you ashamed?

Not enough to stop.

Were you ever caught?

Yes. Once. In bed under the quilt. By my cousin. I said the doctor had prescribed it. I had just had jaundice.

He believed you?

I am not sure. He wanted to know if it would also prevent jaundice.

And?

I said, Yes, it would.

Does it?

I am not sure. But it is a universal antidote for torpor and overriding testicular itch.

Where all have you done it?

As in places?

Yes.

Bathrooms, bedrooms, trains, buses, libraries, classrooms, cinemas, planes, roadside.

Roadside?

Once. Was rudely provoked by fleeting exposure.

Of someone you knew?

No, someone fleeting.

Favourite place?

Bed.

Most unusual?

Riding pillion on a motorbike. Royal Enfield. At thirteen. With my cousin. It escaped my shorts, rubbed against the throbbing seat. Over before I knew it. Look, Ma, no hands!

Quit the comedy. We are talking about cicadas.

Sorry.

What do you think about when . . . when you are at it?

Women.

What about women?

Everything. Seeing, doing, getting . . .

All right, that's enough. What starts it off?

Book. Magazine. Film. Sight. Sound. Smell. But more and more memory, memory, memory.

Memory?

Of things done. Missed. Seen. Imagined.

You think of someone you know?

Sometimes.

And other times?

Someone glimpsed. Someone I want to know.

That's really random!

No more than life.

Do all men do it?

Yes.

Even when they can do the real thing?

Yes.

Do some men prefer it to the real thing?

It's possible.

Do you? Sometimes?

I refuse to answer that on the grounds it may be used against me.

This is about cicadas!

Sorry. Yes. No.

What?

No. I don't. Not really.

Are there different ways of doing it? I mean techniques.

I am sure.

What about you?

My approach is conservative.

What does that mean?

The writing hand. Sometimes a variation, the washing one. Apna haath jagannath.

What?

We are all blessed with the hand of god.

Anything else you would like to tell me?

I confess that unknown to you I have abused you thus on many an occasion. The mind is an immoral animal.

Just then Master Ullukapillu hooted.

Fizz said, That's it. Tell me no more. You are disgusting.

She called back ms meanqueen and said she would give it a shot. The academic gave her a questionnaire to structure the interviews – not so unlike Fizz's own pilot. And repeated her injunctions about empathy, confession, intimacy, distance, discretion, academic rigour. And excreting cicadas.

Fizz picked Philip as her first candidate. He came over to our home to become data. He was between baths, deeply immersed in sloth. He put on a show of inarticulate charm. He expressed himself with loose shrugs of his shoulders, scratching of his hair, and weak smiles. A nursery-school boy on his first interview.

Finally he stood up and said, Got some rum?

Rum in the tum is better than shit in the bum.

It was eleven-thirty in the morning.

She brought the Old Monk out.

He poured himself a big dark glass, drained it in a gulp, and began to speak. The trick, she said to me later that night as we lay in bed, is in the look and tone. I've got it figured out. You have to set your face steady. Never smile. If you have to, smile only with your mouth, never your eyes. Set your voice steady. Never stutter. Speak clearly and boldly. Make it all matter of fact. And you find you are talking about the excretory habits of cicadas.

Do you do it standing on your head?

Are figs the only fruit that make you want to do it immediately?

Does dipping it in hot custard change the taste of the custard?

Do you put it into the small power point or the big power point? And what do you do if it sparks?

Cool. And clinical.

The world is a hard place.

Treat everyone like cicadas.

Ms meanqueen was pleased with the effort. She handed over one hundred and fifty rupees immediately. Politely concealed in a white aerogram with blue and red borders and Fiza's name on it underlined with a slash. Two notes. One hundred. One fifty. Held together with a yellow clip. Fizz gave me the money and put the clip in her bag.

We went out that night, got drunk, came home and fell to loving. For the first time we felt the charge of another person's sex life run through ours. As I moved with her and in her, I began tentatively to ask her questions about her first interview and, as she slowly told me Philip's innermost secrets, we became so heady we could hardly breathe. She started disappearing for long moments, and I had to fight to stay where I was, in that exquisite spot between life and oblivion.

The point at which you are most alive before you are dead.

❦

The survey boosted our love life to new levels. Just when I had begun to think we were pretty much at the end of plumbing all there was between two people, and edge could now only be found through the dubious route of Spat Sex, we discovered the phantom ménage à trois. Five years earlier the mention of another man would have torn me with jealousy. Now it created excitement.

Before we were through with Philip, there was Ravi. And then there were Alok, and Anil, and Udayan. Each came into our bed for a few days, and each brought with him a distinctive menu. We would say virtually nothing as we got into bed, but would be bristling with anticipation, hard and loose, wet and hot, body and soul. And then in the very moment of sliding into her we would begin to talk. I would ask and she would tell. I would ask and she would tell. And we would talk and talk and talk. Deep into the night, moving slowly. Sheathed in her desire, I would say things that would have ripped my heart open at any other time. And often, later, as I sat at the Brother, or toiled in the subeditorial trenches, they did. I had to then hold my head hard to shut out my voice before it drowned out all reason. Before it turned a fun game into a fatal duel.

The phantom ménage à trois.

The problem was this was unlike any regular fantasy frolic. Unlike the anonymous teasing of lovers. This was built on real knowledge of real men. It was like having a real lover in your bed. Each time you finished and lay gasping for breath, holding damp hands, there was a nagging sense of being violated.

Of some special space that had been defiled.

But before we could begin to grapple with the dynamics of what we had chanced upon, not too far away fate was flexing itself to rewrite our lives.

To hand us the power to make our dreams real.

And, in the oldest parable of all, show us the worm at its core.

# Bibi Lahori

In a small village near Kurukshetra – where in antiquity the Pandavas and the Kauravas had fought the world to a standstill, and played out the Mahabharata to lay down the marvellous morally ambiguous template for the understanding of all of mankind – in a small village a resolutely optimistic woman was preparing to die.

The greatest book in the world, the Mahabharata, tells us we all have to live and die by our karmic cycle. Thus works the perfect reward-and-punishment, cause-and-effect code of the universe. We live out in our present life what we wrote out in our last. But the great moral thriller also orders us to rage against karma and its despotic dictates. It teaches us to subvert it. To change it. It tells us we also write out our next lives as we live out our present.

The Mahabharata is not a work of religious instruction.

It is much greater. It is a work of art.

It understands men will always fall in the shifting chasm between the tug of the moral and the lure of the immoral.

It is in this shifting space of uncertitude that men become men.

Not animals, not gods.

It understands truth is relative. That it is defined by context and motive. It encourages the noblest of men – Yudhishtra, Arjuna, Lord Krishna himself – to lie, so that a greater truth may be served.

It understands the world is powered by desire. And that desire is an unknowable thing. Desire conjures death, destruction, distress.

But also creates love, beauty, art. It is our greatest undoing. And the only reason for all doing.

And doing is life. Doing is karma.

Thus it forgives even those who desire intemperately. It forgives Duryodhana. The man who desires without pause. The man who precipitates the war to end all wars. It grants him paradise and the admiration of the gods. In the desiring and the doing this most reviled of men fulfils the mandate of man.

You must know the world before you are done with it. You must act on desire before you renounce it. There can be no merit in forgoing the not known.

The greatest book in the world rescues volition from religion and gives it back to man.

Religion is the disciplinarian fantasy of a schoolmaster.

The Mahabharata is the joyous song of life of a maestro.

In its tales within tales it takes religion for a spin and skins it inside out. Leaves it puzzling over its own poisoned follicles.

It gives men the chance to be splendid. Doubt-ridden architects of some small part of their lives. Duryodhanas who can win even as they lose.

In this, the ancient battlefield of the Mahabharata, the old lady lay dying. She had in many ways been true to the spirit of the land. She had raged against her karma, subverted it, changed it. She was a victim of the deranged schoolmasters and their disciplinarian fantasies, their haranguing religions.

In the dying days of 1947 a long-awaited midnight's evil had come visiting her farmlands. Late one evening her homestead outside Lahore had been ransacked by the schoolmasters' pupils. Her barrel-chested husband – whose crushing weight she had learnt early to avoid through some adroit manoeuvres – was dragged out into the front courtyard. His powerful arms were held akimbo and, as he roared and raged, he was systematically disembowelled with silvery daggers.

The pupils did their work quietly. They were doing a job. Not show-boating.

She was not surprised when he shouted her name as he died. Sheila!

It had the same intensity she was used to hearing at night.

Most of the farm-hands were dead or fleeing. She watched crouching on the floor, her beautiful blue eyes just above the windowsill. Fastidiously they cleaned their daggers on her husband's kurta once they were done. Then they rampaged through the house while she hid under the bed. They did not burn the homestead down because they knew one of them would be back to claim it soon.

They were only hunting for live bodies.

She came out hours later when the jackals began to call. First one let out a low long wail into the night. Then the chorus kicked in. She did not weep. If you did not look at the open stomach and the twist of red intestines, he seemed asleep. There was not a scratch on his face. She checked his kurta pockets. His camelskin pouch was there. She took that, and the Favre Leuba watch with roman numerals, the big gold ring on his finger, and the chain he wore around his neck with a picture of him and his father on Oxford Street in London. Both wearing bowler hats and overcoats. With difficulty she also pulled the bracelet off his right wrist. It came off smeared in blood. She had to wipe it on the kurta where the men had wiped their daggers. In cursive it had Sansar Chand engraved on it. The S and C had an extra whorl at the top.

The men clearly had not come to rob. They had come to cleanse.

The scavengers would follow.

She went back inside and removed every ornament she was wearing, including the tight bichchoos on her toes. She then opened the chests and sorted out her money and her jewellery. She set aside the small stuff with big value – the rings and nose studs. She made one exception. Heavy silver payals – four inches wide – that had been given to her by her mother, who had been given them by hers. She tied them all in a tight bundle of muslin no bigger than her two palms. The rest she threw into a small wooden chest with iron hinges and iron bolts.

She then opened the doors of the heavy Burma teak cupboard, propped the engraved mirror from Benares inside, placed a burning candle in front of it, took her cloth-cutting scissors and began to lop her long hair off. She had groomed it since she was a small girl. It fell below her hips and was rich in the body. It caught beautifully in the scissors and made a most gratifying sound when snipped. She cut it close, as neatly as possible.

In the flickering yellow light she saw herself become a fair, delicate-looking boy. Fine small nose, perfect small ears, perfect small mouth, and then that feature of resistance, the jutting chin with a shadow of a cleft passing through it. When she looked down she saw her hair massed on the floor like a shed salwar.

She took off her clothes. The night was silent but for the duetting jackals. The schoolmasters' pupils had perhaps retired for the night too. Like the rest of her, her breasts were small but firm. Despite two children the nipples were rosy not dark. But they were thick. Sansar Chand used to pull at them with his bulbous lips till she wanted to scream. She thumbed them for an instant. They were erect. The fear was moving in her. She tore a strip of cloth from the bed-sheet. Shaped it with the scissors and, drawing her breath in, strapped her breasts tightly. The nipples pushed out like milestones. She slowed her breathing, put her palms softly on them and waited. When she took them away the white band was a smooth highway girding her world.

She rolled the currency notes she had found into a tight cylinder and wrapping it in a scrap of fine white muslin she tied it with a small string. Putting her left foot on the bed she closed her eyes, opened herself gently with her left hand, and slipped the money in. It was no more difficult than easing in Sansar Chand every night.

She pulled out some clothes of her older son, Kewal, and began to try them on. Kewal and his younger brother, Kapil, had been sent away to Delhi when the Gandhi–Jinnah–Hindu–Muslim–India–

Pakistan trouble had begun to escalate. They had been there nearly six months. Sansar Chand had said he would get them back once everything settled down. What fitted her best were Kewal's khaki school trousers. He was only twelve, but he had his father's size. And his mother was so petite she could be lifted in one arm. In her entire long life she was never to cross forty kilos. She had to use a rope at the waist to hold the trousers up.

When she completed her ensemble with a shirt and coat she looked a pretty young boy ready for school.

A stern little schoolmaster's daily fantasy.

She buried the small chest with iron hinges in the hole dug in a corner of the puja room two weeks before. She flung mud over it, using hands and feet, poured a glass of water on it and tamped the soil down. Then she picked up armfuls of dirty and clean clothes and threw them into the corner. There was no other camouflage she could think of. She took a small cloth bag with her. It held the muslin bundle with her jewellery and more clothes of Kewal's. She also threw in a handful of crisp mathis. She wasn't terribly fond of them, but they wouldn't decay.

There was one thing left to do.

She went into the cookhouse and brought out armfuls of firewood and threw them on her spreadeagled husband. She had to make fourteen trips before she had enough to cover him. Each time she had to step over the slaughtered bodies of Kallu and Raka. The pupils had shown them less respect. Their faces had been slashed and their throats cut open. She could not bring herself to look, but what lay next to their open bleeding mouths appeared to be their chopped penises. Little pieces of bloody flesh.

Uncircumcised.

Peekaboo phalluses. Now-you-see-it-now-you-don't.

She knew the other ones were different. No Hindu hide-and-seek there.

She did not dare go to the farm-hands' shacks. She could see the low-slung quarters from the kitchen. The wooden beams, the thatch roof, the hurricane lamp dangling from the nail in the beam near the door. In the splash of the lamplight, across the threshold, lay sprawled the long body of Jarnail. His feet disappeared into the shadows. His topknot had been pulled loose and he lay face down, drowning in his thick hair. He had obviously gone down fighting. His back was mauled and there was blood everywhere, including patches on the mud walls. His kirpan was still clutched in his outstretched hand.

The two white hens – christened CollectorSahib and Collector-Memsahib – who lived in the shack with the farm-hands were walking around his body like naval officers on inspection.

The wood was thankfully bone dry and chopped small for the kitchen chullahs. It was easy to carry, easy to spread evenly over her husband. On it she poured, with difficulty, using a big brass lota, the two canisters of ghee lying in the store. Its soft sickly smell filled the night air.

She went back in, brought out her cloth bag and sat down near the husband-and-wood-and-ghee pile to gather her breath. She sat there for a long time, squatting on her haunches. Not a human being stirred on the sprawling homestead. For the last fifteen years she only had to raise her voice and a dozen feet would come pattering. She had come here at fourteen, Sansar Chand's pretty pint-sized wife. But she had taken no time in establishing herself as the bibiji.

She had listened carefully to her mother's instruction. Her mother had told her – again and again – that men are like snakes. Their myth is far greater than their reality. Most snakes are toothless. Some have fangs but no venom. And with the few who possess poison sacs you have to be an expert charmer. It is not difficult. Keep moving and make them look where you want them to. In time you will be able to defang most of them. In time you will learn to move in such masterful ways that they will never be able to look where you don't want them to.

Women who confront men, advised Sheila's mother, go nowhere

except out of heart and hearth. Women who treat men like slimy creatures of the dark, to be tricked into submission, rule the world.

Treat men like snakes. Their myth is far greater than their reality.

Sheila was enough of a woman at fourteen to understand her mother. From the beginning she treated Sansar Chand like a slimy creature of the dark. Very quickly she learnt to make him – twelve years older than her and an irascible man – whimper with pleasure. With instinct and calculation she used her body in ways her husband had never even imagined. She learnt to force him to moderate his flaming behaviour by withdrawing the whimpers at will. Very quickly she learnt, to her immense satisfaction, that a man who has loved a wriggling eel can never again be gratified by a lifeless fish.

She became eel and fish at will. Sansar Chand had no chance.

He learnt early to defer to his maddening wife. The rewards were too wonderful to forgo beyond a day or two.

Sheila gave Sansar Chand some of the most pleasurable moments of his life. But she fared poorly herself. Her constant calculations, her mother's practical advice, took away from her all capacity for pleasure. The engines of her desire were damaged beyond repair. The strategist in her head killed the celebrant in her body. Instead of the railhead of all journeys, instead of the resting place of all endeavour, instead of the happy end of all things, the act of love became for her an instrument for the achievement of other things.

Sheila's mother was a battered, bitter woman who cowered in the face of her husband, and could barely speak in his presence. She never knew a moment of tenderness from the man she married. Having known neither desire nor volition, she trained her daughter for survival. From a lifetime of observing and not doing, she knew what her daughter must do to retain the reins of her life. She never cared for the absence of a desire she had never known. She cared for the absence of control she had seen stunt her existence.

She gifted her young daughter the art of control.

Sheila became liberated from desire, and trapped by lesser things.

The dripping ghee had begun to mark the soil. Sheila could barely see her husband under the scattered wood. She looked around.

Just beyond the low mud walls of the homestead the fields began to run. At the moment they ran deep into the night with young wheat saplings. The only sound within the mud walls was the jangling from the cattle trough where the buffaloes were chained. Between champing cud, occasionally one snorted and shook noisily. The three family mongrels, one old and two young, who could holler the farm down most nights if they sensed an intruder, lay quietly by the door, not moving.

Mongrels survive because they can intuit the balance of strength.

Sheila had forgotten the taper. She went back in and brought it out. It gusted wildly in the wind but held. She picked up a ghee-soaked piece of wood and put the flame to it. The ghee-wood took a minute to warm and ignite. When it was crackling she walked around her husband and lit him up from all four corners. As she worked, she recited the Gayatri Mantra, the only religious hymn she knew.

Aum bhoor bhuwah swaha tat savitur varenyam bhargo devasaya dheemahi dhiyo yo naha prachodayat.

Over and over.

When the flames began to dance and jump with low singing noises, she threw the piece of wood in her hand into them, turned her back, picked up the cloth bag and the hurricane lamp, and walked away. The log gate was ajar. Unclosed after the departure of the pupils. She slipped out quietly, the lamp's wick very low, got off the mud track that led to the main road and melted into the green fields. Almost noiselessly, the three mongrels followed at her small, sure feet.

The sky was big with sharp-nosed stars.

The moon was swollen like a woman in her sixth month.

The last jackal was baiting the world with a voice out of hell.

She looked back once when she had crossed the boundary of her farm and was skirting her neighbour's mango grove. Her homestead seemed far away and inside it she could see a growing orange hole steadily eating up the night.

Sheila survived everything. Life just could not defeat her. It took her nearly five years to make a farm and home again, but not for a moment in those years did she doubt she would get back all she had once had. In the weeks and months after she had set fire to her husband's body and slipped out the open gate into the star-spangled night, she became a ceaselessly moving pawn among millions of ceaselessly moving pawns. This was one game the chess players had lost all control of. The Hindu, the Muslim and the white man. In fact they seemed to have fled the table, abandoning all pretence at control, logic or design. Now as the kings and knights cowered in the margins, the pawns were mindlessly crashing into each other, sparking Armageddon.

Sheila moved ceaselessly. And smartly. Avoiding banging into other pawns, threading her way across the heaving board. She walked and walked, alone and in groups. She rode buses, sitting and standing. She travelled by trains, on the roof and in the aisles. She saw more dead bodies than anyone should see in a lifetime. The schoolmasters on both sides had taught their pupils well.

Men and women, children and babies. Lying in heaps and singly. All their clothes coloured with the same muddy-bloody oneness. Throats cut open, guts pulled out, breasts sliced, heads crushed, phalluses chopped. Now-you-see-it-now-you-don't. She became familiar with the open-eyed vacant look, the untidy way people in a hurry die. Arms and legs twisted in different ways, necks turned awkwardly.

Some images burned themselves into her. They came back to her every day for the rest of her life. Huddling at a small station near Tarn Taran, stuck between many bodies cleaving together for warmth and security, with a red dawn breaking over the fields, she saw a long train roll past the platform slowly, scattering the morning birds. She opened her eyes and it was sliding by almost soundlessly. The bodies packed around her were all asleep. The slow train, she saw, was full of motionless people. A rich painting. Some had their foreheads open. Some their throats. Many were lying on others, in that untidy sort of way. All the doors were open, and the aisles choked with unmoving bodies. With slow clack-clack-clacks the compartments rolled by. Not a finger moved, not a whistle blew, not a vendor shouted. She watched it all unmoving, as in a dream. In the doorway of the last but one wagon lay a fair young boy with a moustache of first hair and curly locks, his head almost hanging out. He was looking straight at her. With deep quiet eyes. Then the iron wheels clattered over a joint, shaking the compartment, and the last connecting tendon gave. As she watched, the fair young head with a moustache of first hair and curly locks and the deep quiet eyes rolled onto the platform like a ball and bounced away. She screamed. Everyone stirred. She buried her head in her arms. The train rolled on and into the unfurling fantasy of the disciplinarian schoolmasters.

In those days she understood killing another human being is only a leap of faith.

Once you have made it, it is like slaughtering chickens.

You can kill one a day for the table. Or if required massacre a thousand for a party.

And at the moment India and Pakistan, newly born, were hosting a banquet for the ages.

Six hundred thousand chickens would be just fine.

Any shape or size will do.

Kosher or kaput. It really doesn't matter.

Home delivery assured. Within a thousand miles.

Thank you, sir.

Until the next time.

At the farm the night of the flashing daggers she had to steel herself to indifference, to calm. Now it came upon her with the weariness of terrible knowledge. After such knowing, what lament. She became even stronger than she was. She survived the distress and squalor of the refugee camps, she was reunited with her sons, she hacked through officialdom to obtain compensation for her husband's vast estate, and having got it – more than two hundred scrub and forest acres – she pulled the cylinder out from between her legs and the jewellery out of the muslin bag, and set to wrestling the land down.

Salimgarh had been abandoned by those fleeing in the other direction. On her new farm there was a homestead, badly pillaged. Some days Sheila stood in its yard trying to imagine if there had been a woman here who had fled it in the dead of night with her breasts tied and her vagina stuffed. If the men in her life had had their non-peekaboos sliced and set by their ears. If she was right now standing in Sheila's old yard in Chowdhury Kalan, six kilometres as the crow flies from the bustling bazaars of Lahore, next to the harsingar tree Sheila had planted, which filled up with sparkling white flowers and sweet perfume every night and was shed of it all in the morning. Sheila would spread sheets under its branches in the late autumn months, and every morning they would be covered with the beautiful tiny flowers with little golden stalks. She would then pile them in aromatic heaps all over the house.

Sansar Chand used to call Sheila his harsingar flower. Blooming at night, beautiful in the day.

Salimgarh had no tree like that. And Sheila held it against the fled woman that she had not left one behind.

Because no able-bodied man would come to clear her land, she went to the superintendent of police and convinced him to give her the lifers from the district jail. These were hard-bitten surly men – murderers and dacoits – and they arrived in chains. She rode her big brown horse as she oversaw their toil. Her hair was still short, tucked under a sola topi, and she had learnt to enjoy wearing Kewal's khaki pants. She had her own tailored now.

In the week they arrived, twenty of them with two policemen with clunky rifles guarding them, she shot one in the thigh when he caressed it leeringly, inviting her to sit on it. His name was Jagga. He had been a village wrestler and a contract killer for land disputes. The terror of the area. The superintendent commended her prompt action. The word spread in the district. The myth of Bibi Lahori was afoot. In time Sheila would be talked of as the Bibi who used to hunt on horseback with the white man, who had literally shot her way to

Salimgarh when the Partition riots began. The rest of the lifers learnt to behave. Because she fed them well and gave them an ounce of mustard oil every week to rub into their scalps and skin, they also learnt to respect her.

Many of them, after they had served their sentences, came back to the farm to work for her. As a child I heard their stories and saw some of them as old men. Bija the chuda, who had killed four brahmins with an axe because they had raped his sister. Dhuus the majhbi, who was seven feet tall and had once dropped a horse with a blow to its head. Gama the jat, who could drink a bucket of milk without breaking for breath. Bira the marasi, who grabbed snakes by their tails and smashed them against trees.

These were the men who swore her their allegiance.

Men will genuflect more readily to a strong woman than to a strong man. With a man they will do it with resentment and out of fear. With a woman they will do it out of unknowing and awe. Men understand the triggers of weak men, and of strong men, and of weak women. But they know nothing of the triggers of strong women. They know not what makes them tick; they know not how to unravel their DNA.

No man is ever the equal of a strong woman.

It took Indira Gandhi to die before the strong men of India found their balls.

History is full of such examples. Look around. Every family is full of such examples.

When the woods had been cleared – foxes killed, snakes battered, sambar, neelgai, spotted deer and wild pigs eaten – Bibi Lahori began to plough and plant.

As strong women do, Sheila became the pivot of everything around her: the villagers, the local administration, the kotwali, the traders, the middlemen of the mandi. The world around her was being shaped by tough men and women who in losing everything had learnt the value of the lived day. They were all unputdownable. She was the toughest of them all.

Uncompromised by desire. Cursed by its absence.

Set against her steel, her sons became puddings. She sent them to an expensive boarding school in Ajmer, and watched them grow up amid Rajput royalty and empty pomp. As they grew, she thought they were becoming coconuts. Floating far above the ground, under a rich canopy, imagining they belonged to another universe. One strong gust in life, she knew, and they would come crashing down. Neither of them, even in jest, learnt to work a plough, milk a buffalo or judge an ear of wheat.

Both the sons married girls their mother picked. Pretty, fair, moving early to plump, from their kshatriya caste. Bachelors of Arts. Able to cook up a vegetarian storm in three hours; able to knit a full-length sweater in three days. Both the sons took soft jobs in the city. Kewal became a chartered accountant and settled in Bombay, sparking a Manhattany lineage that would be removed not only from Salimgarh but almost from India. Kapil became a boxwallah, working with a corporation that made the selling of soaps and shampoos appear like an exemplary calling. It led Kapil into the small cities and towns of the Hindi heartland, giving him greater connectivity to India, even if it was from the safely luxurious cocoon of big bungalows, multi-servants, Grundig music systems, well-tuned cars, and rajresidual clubs run by paunchy retired colonels.

It was to Kapil that I was born. The doctor came home to make the delivery. Apparently I took my time. And after he slapped me to make me cry, I stopped in an instant and glowered at him.

In later years, as things soured, Mother took to saying that I had disapproved of my father's lifestyle from the very beginning.

I sometimes protested that I had not. But the truth is it bored me and out of the boredom rose a great disgust. I hated the rajresidual clubs with their shabby seasonal dances on wooden floorboards to the tune of 'These Boots Are Made for Walking'; the billiards rooms with sleek young boys and ageing markers betting on whisky pegs; the thin-legged men and fat-legged women in white sports shirts and tennis shoes swinging rackets and bustling around badminton courts; the musty bars with middle-aged men getting a phallic rush out of sitting on bar stools. I hated the puerile jokes they cracked and the familiarity with which they slapped my shoulderblades. I hated the peeling restrooms, always removed from the main bustle, where these shifty men – uncles – could corner me and put their sweaty hands up my shorts. Then take my hand and put it up theirs. I hated how big and fat and hot and moist and insistent frustrated men could be. I hated my helplessness in the face of the moment.

So it was with my father. He bored me and slowly out of the boredom grew a profound contempt. The world of selling soaps, building brands, understanding markets, did nothing for me. I could not bear his talk of management and marketing and profits. Whenever he came back from a tour and began to talk of the new consumer insights he had gleaned I wanted to scream. The idea of perpetually analysing people as purchasing units appalled me. The upwardly mobile soap. The status toothpaste. The film-star shampoo. I wanted to throw the dishes against the wall, upturn the dining table, do a shimsham dance.

In turn he thought I was a flake. He was always slagging off the books I was reading. Initially I would hide them under the mattress, among my school textbooks and between my clothes in the cupboard. Always taking great care to place them so they would not get scrunched. Then the years passed and the fear drained out of me and I would pile them all over my room, including on the cistern in the toilet. He would walk in, I would look at him over the book I was reading, he would give every stack in the room a withering look, mutter under his breath and leave.

He also passed up no opportunity to make mocking remarks about boys who were as weak as women. Boys who spent their time reading 'silly novels'. Boys who could not keep their trousers buttoned. Boys with no future.

We were just disconnected. It was one of those sorry facts of life that we were stuck with each other.

It was easier to be with Mother. She was not judgemental. In fact she had spent a life being the object of judgement. I could sit and talk to her for hours about her childhood, her college years. The kind of stuff that breaks the heart of all sons, if they only stop to listen. The passage of girlish fun, frolic, fantasies turning to soul-deadening routine as parents and tradition and clan conspire to make a cardboardbox out of a tree.

Pre-package and close every possibility of life.

I looked at the sepia pictures of her in pigtails, laughing with abandon, flashing new bangles on her arms, and I looked at her dull eyes now, and my heart was broken. The lost years. The tree cut into a cardboardbox even as it was beginning to grow. The lost life. There were days when I lay on my bed after a conversation with her and I thought if I had one wish in the world I would give her back all those years, all of them, with my father and every other man she had ever known taken out and placed far away.

Even now, as I write this with everything long over, I just have to think of her in pigtails, laughing, flashing her bangles, and a wilderness fills my heart. I have to get up from my desk and go for a walk. Climb up to the waterpoint, gaze at the valley, let the calm seep back into me.

I have trained myself to not think about her.

Sorrow must not be cultivated. It is a poor lifestyle choice.

In towns like Bareilly and Jhansi and Allahabad I was her companion. I accompanied her to the doctor, to the films, to the markets. What I enjoyed doing most with her was going to the vegetable bazaar three times a week. I don't think my father had done it once in his life. It was beneath his station. I carried the green plastic basket and helped her sift and pick. I liked the texture of vegetables and fruits. I would caress them, engage with them. Capsicum, tomato: fingertips. Cabbage, apple: full palms. Mangoes: nose. Coconuts: ear.

Above all I loved the singing sales pitch of the vendors: gobhi-alu putchee-putchee; alu-gobhi putchee-putchee. Ek rupaiya pyaaz – khaye mian nawab; khaye mian nawab – ek rupaiya pyaaz. Many of the criers were like Hindustani classical musicians, stoking up riveting patterns with the same words. Soft, low, high-pitched, extended, cantering, trotting, galloping. Bhindi-tori, bhindi-tori; le le bhindi, le le tori; tori le le, bhindi le le; le le bhindi, le le tori; tori-bhindi, bhindi-tori, thodi bhindi, thodi tori; tori-bhindi, bhindi-tori. They would go into a trance of chanting, and if you closed your eyes you could imagine you were in a music school with students flexing their cords.

The colours mattered too. In fact as I grew older the colour of the food mattered to me as much as the taste. I disliked vegetables that were cooked into a grey-brown mash. I liked shining green bhindi, sparkling yellow masur dal, burnished copper pumpkin, sliced red watermelons, diced orange papayas, unsliced red apples, leaf-green guavas, snow-white curd.

I liked to eat with my eyes as much as with my taste buds.

It was a gift from my time in Salimgarh, where everything came with mud and leaves sticking to it and was washed glistening clean in the tube-well before landing in the kitchen.

I loved going to Salimgarh. With its wide-open vistas, rolling fields of mustard and gram and cane and wheat, groves of guava and ber and mango, continual planting and growing and reaping of crops and vegetables, the herds of buffaloes and oxen and the one solitary horse; with its stringy peasantry, earthy flavours and the absence of any precious rules of etiquette, Bibi Lahori's farm was a wonderland. The precise opposite of our boxwallah home, with its calculations of soaps and its calibrations of consumer psychology.

As a child I went to Salimgarh every summer and winter, harsh times both. In the summer you could not step outside barefoot for most of the day, and you had to brace yourself with endless glasses of katchi lassi – half milk, half water, stirred up with plenty sugar and big shards of ice slashed from the slab that arrived in sack-and-sawdust every morning from the town. In the winter you could not touch the water without heating it, and it was in Salimgarh that I learnt to drink milky tea, as the kitchen brewed it ceaselessly for the endless visitors and labourers, who cupped it in their palms and held the brass tumblers against their faces, thawing their cheeks and breathing in the steamy vapours. It was there that I discovered surrrchai has a special flavour. Everybody in Salimgarh, including Bibi Lahori, went surrr.

I always went to Salimgarh with dozens of books, and for the many hours I was driven indoors I buried myself in paper. Since Father disliked visiting both the farm and his mother, this involved me in no grief.

When I could be out – early mornings and late evenings in the summer and midday in the winter – I just wandered through the fields. Walking the narrow bunds was fun. You could play games. Count the number of steps between corners, walk backwards, hop a field's length on one leg. In the mornings the farm-hands would bring datuns, and I would chew manfully on the stick till it was frayed, and then, spitting it all out, go and work the toothbrush. The Bibi would say, These are the sons my sons have produced! I am sure they also wipe their asses with paper after they've washed them with water!

Some days, just to feel macho, I would go out with the farm boys to defecate in the open. There was a patch near the dried riverbed, just out of our farm limits, that was earmarked for crapping. The riverbed itself was planted with melons. The crapland was arid and baked, with dips and rises and pockets of knife-edge rushes. You fanned out, found unsullied clumps, kept up the conversation and let go. Everyone carried a bottle of water; and on the way back the wet mud near the tube-well was used to wash hands. I complied with the ritual. But when I got home the first thing I did was to head for the bathroom and the hard red Lifebuoy soap.

Just beyond where we squatted was no-man's-land. It was on the other side of the riverbed. Here the scrub was dense and the tall knife-edge grass ran in a near-unbroken wall. This was the distaff defecation zone. Its sanctity was observed with more care than that of hotel bathrooms with bright queens drawn on their doors. But sometimes, from where I struggled with cramping legs, I glimpsed fair squatting haunches through a gap in the grass and felt a sudden rush.

Actually I hated those excursions, mainly for their physical discomfort. And as I slowly lost the need to conform to anything I stopped attempting them altogether. The other thing I hated was walking through the sugar-cane fields. The leaves slashed the skin. But at the time there was so much acreage under cane that you could not avoid tramping through the thickets every now and then.

The cane in Salimgarh marked me for good. As a child, I chewed sugar-cane sticks, drank sugar-cane juice, and endlessly ate the sticky gur being thickened in large boiling vats at the northern corner of the farm under two big mango trees. The rot in my teeth set in early, and never left me. If my life has three leitmotifs, they are books, Fizz and toothaches. Painkillers – aspirin, Combiflam, Brufen; home remedies – thorny cloves, soggy clove oil, ice packs, hot-brick compresses; very early in my life I ran through them all.

By the time I was in my teens I had learnt to ride toothache like a champion surfer rides ocean waves. Gentle pain I could live with most of the time. I'd suck on the aching tooth all day, pulling out the pain, tasting the brackish mix of blood and pus. At night I would jam my cheek into my fist and push down on the pillow. Life would carry on. In time the irritated tooth would settle. The passage from normality to pain and back would be the journey from smooth waves to rough and back.

But on days that a squall hit and a rotten nerve was exposed and the waves became stormy and the pain was brutal, I was put on my mettle. The throb would be so enormous it would be impossible to isolate in the mouth and it would take the roof off my head. Then I had to close in on myself, shut down my senses, and like all great sportsmen arrive slowly amid the frenetic activity at the centre of a zen calm. With motionless poise I would ride the big swells, and when they crashed I would cruise quietly till the next one came on me. I would retreat to a silent part of the house, close my eyes and surf. At such a time even the slightest noise, the least movement could upset the balance and send you crashing, the surging pain almost causing you to pass out.

Eventually I became a pain junkie. Sometimes when the waves

had died out – as I sat in a quiet corner surfing – I would tease the nerve with the tip of my tongue and as the throb hammered up my skull, I would begin to ride. Savouring the pain, savouring the peace. Pain, peace. Throb, ebb. Pain, peace. Throb, ebb.

Once you become a master you don't surf the nasty waters because you chance on them, you go out looking for them.

But even master surfers have a finite career. As the nineties began, I thought I was at the end of mine. My teeth were no longer just about ache and pain, riding and surfing. They were rotting into disuse, as in an old man. Several had shrapnelled, chips coming off them in the middle of meals. Some days when I kissed Fizz she complained they snagged on her lips, drawing blood. I was eating only from the left side of my mouth; the right had become a minefield of open nerves and treacherous ditches. I could not even think of biting into a hard chocolate or raw fruit.

I needed to get a major construction company in there.

While Salimgarh gave me enduring dental agony, it also taught me valuable lessons in forbearance.

Though we seldom had idle time with her, observing the Bibi gave me my first opportunity to learn that size and gender have nothing to do with strength. Wiry-tendoned peasants, big burly landlords, suit-wearing government officials, fat traders, uniformed policemen came to her for advice and help. They sat on the edge of their seats on the veranda, spoke deferentially, argued softly, and left with expansive salaams and deep bows. The Bibi always made her point without raising her voice. I saw her being sharp only with my father. She had so much contempt for his flabbiness, of spirit and body. She called him Pappu-Tappu, conjuring up images of a sulking fat boy. Father hated going to Salimgarh. He thought his mother was mad, stone-hearted, and a control freak.

Sometimes when he had been freshly insulted with a Pappu-Tappu remark, he would rage and say, I am sure she is the one who bumped off Bauji.

Now Bibi Lahori was dying herself. Rogue cells had taken over her body. The doctor's X-rays had shown the white shadows. He had held the film against the slim tube-light, taken off his glasses, put an arm around her great-nephew – her sister's grandson, Anil, my cousin, who had grown up on the farm with her after his father was killed in an accident – and told him to take her home and make her comfortable.

The doctor was old too. He had known Bibi Lahori all his life. The big steel board outside his clinic declared him an RMP, a registered medical practitioner. But he was not the kind of small-town RMP who thinks nothing of killing off a few people every week. He was not quite a doctor, yet he knew everything there was to know about medicine. There is nothing a hundred books can teach you that a thousand patients cannot. The doctor had tended to tens of thousands. Family trees had run through his hands. Births, deaths and the deaths of those he had helped birth. I had been to him for heat boils and fever; my father had been to him for dysentery, flu, wounds, ulcers. The doctor's son and daughter practised in American hospitals, in Los Angeles and Boston, with super-specializations in neurosurgery and orthopaedics. But neither of them could succour a patient with a word and a touch as their father could.

He had said to the older woman, Massiji, you are fine. A minor infection. I am giving you some medicines. Take it easy for some time.

The old woman was smaller than ever before. She weighed no more than thirty-five kilos. You could lift her with one arm like a baby. I knew. I had done it once, in jest. She was also very fair and her skin was like handmade paper. Crumpled but crisp. With her fine nose and mouth you could see she had been beautiful once. Now the filigree of fragile blue veins on the handmade paper skin made her an artwork. But she was saved from being uselessly delicate by a chin that had a resolute jut, and blue eyes that were unyielding. They had not the give of water, but the surety of sky.

Even in her infirmity, she was a matriarch. The centre of her world.

She looked the doctor straight in the eye. He had always been a calm one. She had seen him as a boy playing with her boys in the courtyard. His mother, who came to make the vegetable pickles in March and the mango pickles at the beginning of summer and chattered non-stop, always spoke of her Gattu's patient nature. She said, when he was a child, darting yellow chicks would eat rice droppings off his legs while he sat on the ground feeding himself. As a two-year-old, he had once stood patiently, sunk to his calves in a paddy field, for more than an hour, till a worker brought the news that there was a new sapling growing on the farm. Bibi Lahori had seen Gattu get polio and be left limping behind while all his peers flew the coop – to not just Kurukshetra, but big and bigger cities, Bombay, Delhi, Madras, and further to London and New York. He was much older than Kewal and Kapil and so much brighter. While her sons went to the elite school in Ajmer he had gone through the local municipal and government institutions.

He never showed any rancour about a life not got. He made his peace with – found his meaning in – wrestling with local disease. He was the kind of man who finds the world under his own tree and never needs to go wandering in a forest.

A stay-at-home Buddha.

He knew the Bibi was dead. He gave her six months.

She said, Gattu, am I dying?

He said, So am I. So are we all, Bibiji. Then he laughed and said, Can anything kill you? You will die after India and Pakistan are one again.

She said, I will kill myself before I see such a day.

When she came back a month later the lesions had multiplied. She was weaker too, but she did not admit to it. Gattu Chacha told me all this later. He said her resilience was daunting. He took two months off the first estimate when he saw the second set of X-rays. But she survived for another year and a half on nothing but resolve.

We came to know six months after the cancer was diagnosed. Mother called. But she did not encourage me to visit Salimgarh. My anger had cooled long ago and I was waiting for someone to prod me. I think Mother was not sure how the Bibi would take it; perhaps not even sure how I would respond. Also the Bibi had not been told, and my sudden appearance would have alarmed and alerted her.

Fizz kept saying I should trash the calculations and go. Life isn't arithmetic, it's chemistry. You have to trust in the alchemy of things.

I heard her out, but did not make a move.

Fiza! Bibi Lahori had said, when I had broken the news.

Fiza! Musalman! Are all the Hindu girls in the world dead!

Don't you know anything, you deranged fool?

Over my burning body!

We were in Salimgarh. In the open courtyard. I had come to tell her. I cared for her deeply and she was important to me. Mother and Father, unsure of confronting her, had asked me to go and break the news. As I had got off the local bus from Shahabad and walked up the dirt road leading to the farm, I had felt no trace of apprehension. It was evening. The sun had turned red and was plunging. It was the second most beautiful time of day at the farm. The most beautiful was dawn. Crisp refrigerated air, a wash of shivering dew on everything, clearest light of day, woodsmoke from the kitchens, birdsong everywhere. Now I could see fresh lines of hope in the newly ploughed fields and the last ploughmen unharnessing their oxen. Each of them saw me and waved. Paddybirds were walking the ploughlines, assessing the day's work. There was a great cawing of crows from the mango grove as they conferred before settling in for the night. The tube-wells were still throbbing water. Soon they would cease. Then, in the middle of the night, designated hands would wake and set them to throbbing again.

Mother and Father had ladled out their anxiety, but no trace of it clung to me. I was her favourite grandchild, and I knew of no argument in the face of love and passion.

I forgot I was dealing with someone who had known neither. Someone who had converted it all into a strategy for life. She was tough as nails, but she was also a cripple. She had the gift of success, but she did not have the gift of happiness.

She could vanquish the gods. But she could not touch them.

Fiza!

Don't you know anything, you deranged fool?

Are all the Hindu girls in the world dead!

It's true. She had always said to her sons and to us that we could do what we wished with our lives, except marry a Musalman. Even south Indians were fine, other castes were fine; if it got that grim perhaps Christians too. Everything in life and work was fine, but not that. Never a Musalman. Her breasts and cunt still ached with the baggage of that journey long ago. Her hatred had fuelled her survival.

Her hatred had stunted her life.

Fiza!

Over my burning body!

So be it.

I had left without argument. It was past nine and the last bus was gone. I had walked to Shahabad on the Grand Trunk Road, and then with cars and buses screaming past in manic fury. I had kept walking, and had walked all the twenty kilometres to Ambala, in the lee of rows of gawky, pale-skinned eucalyptus trees. I had arrived at the railway station before dawn. You could smell the parathas beginning to sizzle in the dhabas. By then my anger was cold and hard. Bibi Lahori was about to suffer one of the rare defeats of her life.

Later Father tried to reason with me; then I think he tried to reason with her, but was told he was a bigger fool for having begat a fool like me. She said, Oye, Pappu-Tappu, I sent you to a big school and you became a big fool. I should have kept you here. At least you would have been a small fool. I am glad your father did not live to see you, your brother and your surpassingly foolish sons.

Stung, Father's own buried prejudices leapt to the surface. He confronted me. I told him to fuck off. He repaid the compliment. It was just as well. A long painful charade was over. We were done with each other.

Mother swung like a pendulum in the background.

I did not meet Bibi Lahori after that day. And soon after we were married I stopped meeting Father too. Mother called occasionally and I would make enquiries after both, the Bibi and Father. But I knew the Bibi had not made one mention of me since. Mother would claim my exile had scored a deep scar into her soul. I had no evidence of it and I did not believe it to be true. Bibi Lahori had watched her husband being carved and immediately after, with unsentimental efficiency, had piled him with firewood and ghee and burned him. People like her negotiated life, not mulled over it.

Uncompromised by desire. Cursed by its absence.

I have to say memories of her eventually ceased to detain me too. My years of admiration for her slowly turned to a somewhat sour appraisal. I was not sure if it was wise to approve of a toughness – no matter how survivalist – that gives no quarter to any feeling.

How thick should a survivor's skin be before it results in coma?

When she did not die after Gattu Chacha's six months were over, and was still around when another six were over, I was convinced she was not going to. I began to believe she would lick the cancer just as she had everything else in her life. I stopped debating visiting her.

So I did not see her till she was dead. Despite the early warning, there was no one with her when she went. Her sons had taken to visiting her cyclically but were not prepared to stay there. Duty not concern drove them. She was, of course, too proud to ask for help. Even from young Anil, who stayed with her, and slept in the alcove outside her room. He told me at night he used to watch her painfully drag herself across the floor to the toilet. The cancer was now in her bowels, and her incontinence appalled her. She tried to hide it. She would struggle to make her passage noiseless. Anil had to pretend to be asleep. It would take here a long time to make the trip to the toilet and back, and sometimes when he would drop off then wake again she would be in the middle of another journey.

I took Fizz along when I went for her cremation. The whole

village and more was there, crowding the courtyard and the dirt track that led to the homestead. Men, women, children; old, young; peasants, traders, officials. Solemnly I hugged dozens of people I had known over the years. Of course everyone knew me. The prodigal grandson who had taken on the Bibi over a Musalman girl. Many men and women – some who had handled me as an infant – broke down and cried loudly when they met me. Fizz had covered her head with a chunni. Some of them instinctively embraced her too. Their clothes had the acrid smell of sweat and woodsmoke.

Bibi Lahori was laid out on the floor in the central courtyard. A steady wail filled the space. A group of old women were mourning professionally, rhythmically hammering their dugs. Mother hugged us. Her eyes were swollen. Father was in a black suit and seemed calm. He shook my hand, and then uncertainly shook Fizz's too. Though the men and women were sitting separately I kept Fizz close, by my side.

When Anil embraced me he said the Bibi had woken in the wee hours of the morning and, calling out to him, asked him to take her off the bed and lay her on the floor. She knew her time was done. He said he had barely straightened her legs when she was gone. The last thing she said was, O Sansar Chandya, I made you wait, didn't I?

Everyone said it was the biggest funeral procession in living memory. Along with her two sons, Anil, and my Manhattany cousins Kunwar and Tarun, I put my shoulder to her bier. She was light as a sheet. It was as if we were only carrying the bamboo sticks. The cremation ground, which lay just outside the village, was choked. Scores of people squatted on the half-made brick wall ringing the boundary. When the deputy commissioner arrived in a white Ambassador car a tremor went through the crowd. He was a youngish man in a cream bush shirt and gold-rimmed spectacles, and he walked through the parting mourners as a potentate through his people. Several came forward and touched his knees. He was carrying a bouquet of flowers – some tuberoses, gladioli, carnations. He went straight up to my father and Kewal Taya – both in impeccable black suits and ties – and shook their hands solemnly. I looked away when he cast around to see if there was anyone else he had to condole.

The priest began to chant the last rites.

After Kewal Taya had broken her skull through the flapping flames with a wooden stave, everyone washed their hands at the pump and picked up a twig each. Then in the dirt-track outside the boundary, phalanx on phalanx like Roman soldiers, we knelt in the dust, with our backs to the crackling fire, snapped the twigs when the priest gave the word, and threw the pieces over our shoulder. Our ties with the woman burning behind us were broken. The circle of life was closed.

When she was reborn she would be in new relationships with all of us. Settling old debts. Transactions from this life and the earlier. Giving and taking.

This is what the martyred Abhimanyu told his erstwhile father, the great Arjuna, who came seeking his dead son in the palace of Indra, the king of the gods. Young Abhimanyu, all of fourteen, killed doing glorious battle with a gaggle of the most powerful Kaurava warriors because he dared enter the chakravyuh – the circle of riddles – even though he did not know the way out. Young Abhimanyu, for-ever the role model for all splendid men, who will do what is right even though they do not know any of the escape routes. Young Abhimanyu, playing chess with the gods, who asked his heartbroken father, Arjuna, brought there by Lord Krishna: Why do you weep so copiously, man? And who are you? To which Arjuna said, I am your father, and I weep for your untimely death. To which, amid peals of laughter, Abhimanyu said, You were my father! And in many lives before that I have been yours! Do not behave foolishly. I have fulfilled my karma. I have done my duty as a warrior and died with honour in battle. You, man, go back and do yours!

In the new play we will have new roles.

Bibi Lahori and I. And we will again do the sums. Settle our scores.

I lingered back with Fizz as everyone melted away. We went and sat on the brick wall. Because it was low and unfinished it was easy to find a comfortable perch. It was the hour of last light and squadrons of screeching parakeets were streaking back to base. The trees ringing the ground – peepul, mango, neem, kikar, imli, banyan – were aflutter with activity. The untouchable who tended to the cremation ground had retired to his lean-to at the further corner and was helping his wife start a cooking fire. His two sons, barefoot and in loose shorts, were playing with marbles amid the cremation mounds. I sat there holding Fizz's hand, and after some time Bibi Lahori's grey ash began to swirl up and settle on our clothes.

When it was dark we rose wordlessly and began to walk back to the farm. The Bibi was still burning orange; and a smaller orange glow was the food fire in the corner of the cremation ground. Lines of black bats were moving overhead.

At the farm small clusters of friends and relatives sat about everywhere. The mood was relaxed and easy. Tea glasses were circulating. The two orphaned brothers were in the sitting room inside, sipping whisky. They had perhaps moved on to the logistical implications of the Bibi's demise. I went and sat with Gattu Chacha and he told me the story of the last year and a half. We then ate dinner and I told Mother we had to go. She understood. Anil drove us in Gattu Chacha's new blue Maruti car to the Pipli bus-stand. I hugged him hard. He was young and had goodness in him.

We sat on the cement bench plagued by buzzing clouds of mosquitoes. They formed spirals over our heads, and when we moved the spirals moved with us. Many tearaway buses later, one stopped. It was a Haryana Roadways boneshaker. We got seats at the back. I held her hand and did not say a word in the three hours it took to get to the Inter State Bus Terminus in Delhi. By the time we got to our barsati it was past midnight.

I was moving in her with a maddening love filling my head – drowning out the long day – when Master Ullukapillu called.

She put a restraining hand on my back and I stopped.

She said, He's saying this is as good as it gets.

I kissed her under her right ear, pulling her flesh into my mouth, forcing her to move her head slowly.

Yes, I said, the master is right, this is as good as it gets.

As the unfurling years would reveal, Master Ukp was an oracle out of hell.

BOOK THREE

*Artha: Money*

# The House on the Hill

By the time Mother called me to break the news more than a year had passed since the Bibi's death. In the meantime Rajiv Gandhi had been consumed by a monster of his own making; the Babri Masjid at Ayodhya, Lord Rama's mythic birthplace, had been ripped apart with bare hands in an engineering of wildly atavistic emotions – monsters of a new making; and my cosmos-in-a-kernel novel had meandered to a dead stop.

God had been cut to the size of bricks.

Our collective brains were slipping beneath our pricks.

And the MAIL – Manufacture-an-Idiot-Leader – industry was charging ahead lickety-split.

I was, of course, failing to juice anything more out of the innocent Sikh and his clash with the modern world. As with the earlier manuscripts, I had reached a stage where I had no more flesh to put on the bones of my ideas. I now felt the material of the young warrior-saint and his horse was more suited to a short story. But the genre did not attract me, and without announcing it to Fizz I had pretty much abandoned the project.

This time I was ashamed of my failure. I was convinced I was going to fall in Fizz's estimation. The worst kind of spielmeister. A starter of grand projects I could never finish. An empty talker. She had read some of the stuff and was unfailingly encouraging. But I had long ago been drowned out by my doubts. I had begun to wonder how anyone could write anything with certitude.

Some days when I sat at the table – its heady smell of polish long gone, the many black-and-white alphabetical eyes of the Brother scanning me for inspiration, my mind scrambling for some narrative purchase – some days I felt I would never be able to write anything of worth. I was convinced every word I banged out was headed straight for the biblioblackhole.

In desperation I would then reach for Fizz and fleetingly drown my desolation in her body; and when it came surging back I would go to her and drown it in her again. Her passion, her desire, made me whole. But there were days when my need for her was so continual and chronic that she could not cope. Then she just gave up her body to me and I found my peace in it.

Often ravaged by doubt, I would sleep badly. I would wake in despair and be seized by an urge to rush to the Brother to test if I had anything inside of me. I would lie in bed, trying hard to imagine what Fizz thought of me and fail to divine it at all. I would think of the past because for the first time I could not imagine the future. In the milky light of night I would listen to her gentle breathing; then I would begin to smell her skin, in the hope of blanking out everything – memory, doubt, existence.

For hours I would slowly kiss her body, smell its deep damp familiar secrets, and be reassured and obliterated.

Total passion and total peace. In the body of the one person.

At one point, many months after my return from Salimgarh, I was seized by the excitement of fictionalizing Bibi Lahori's life. It suddenly struck me that I had rich material in my own backyard. And now that she was dead, I reckoned, her story was fair game. But this time I proceeded with caution. I left my cosmos-in-a-kernel novel to stew on the Brother, and opening a big spiral notebook, I began to write down everything I knew about the Bibi. A fortnight later I had exhausted every dusty niche of my memory, and I had only sixteen pages to show for it. This included what she had told me over the years, what I had heard about her, and everything else I could conjure up. At best, another short story.

I put the spiral notebook in the table drawer and went back to staring at the Brother.

Fizz and her body kept me from sinking. I gorged myself on her to fill every empty day. But things were not so good between us. We were talking little; we were not doing too many things together. The fault lay entirely with me. Once my ardour was spent I was poor company. At home I was absented, fretting about the writing that was not happening, lingering between flicking through books and the idling Brother.

The rest of the time I was in the office, slumped in a trench, neither fighting nor dying. Long forgotten by the Gleaming Glansmen. My brain dissolving slowly in a cesspool of anxiety and dwindling confidence. I had withdrawn even from my fellow troopers. Some days I would not exchange a single word with anybody. When Fizz and I went out with friends, I was not really there. I knew this was a make-believe world that would soon cease. And then my life would begin.

Or be comprehensively over.

I was sullen, hostile. I would suddenly withdraw into myself in the middle of a meal in a restaurant, in the middle of a party. If someone made an attempt to breach the divide I would get up to go home. There were numberless occasions when Fizz and I did. Puttering back through the muggy Delhi night, carefully climbing the winding staircase to our barsati, sitting out on the terrace with the gulmohar branches swishing against the concrete, we were wordless. At such times even Master Ullukapillu could not prompt us into conversation.

At such times Fizz and I had moved onto different planets.

Amazingly Fizz did not make an issue of it, giving me the slack she thought I needed.

But – unsettled by my mood swings – she found herself a distraction. She discovered television. Philip's prophecy was coming to pass, and in the two years since the Gulf war, cable television had sprouted in Indian bedrooms like money plants had, out of old Scotch bottles, in the living rooms of our parents. We were limbering up to entertain ourselves to death.

Fizz, curiously, did not fall to watching the soaps and game shows. She got hooked on CNN. The global news shop lived in our bedroom. She would roll up its shutters first thing in the morning, and pull them down last thing at night. The blow-dried white men and women with their American accents, and their sombre-urgent tone telling us something critical to our well-being, were with us all the time, and they drove me mad. Even their sport was alien. Breathless scores of American football and baseball which meant not a word. When I could lay my hands on the remote I would try and catch some run of old Hindi film songs. But the moment I stepped out it would be back to CNN.

Fizz became an addict. Gathering senseless arcana about the world, ephemera that should never have entered our life, and was dead as soon as it was born. She followed whacko American stories about shoot-outs, kidnappings, bills, elections, concerts, spats, fires, rescues, summits, talk shows, Wall Street, Manhattan, Pentagon, Beverly Hills, Silicon Valley, dating trends, breast implants – and endless Mickey Mouse stuff that had as much relevance to our lives as the dietary habits of Emperor Bokassa. It was interesting to know that he ate his people for dinner, but beyond that what? So it was nice to know America existed and had its own dysfunctional interests just as we had ours, but beyond that what?

Often, when I was in bed reading, I protested with an irritated glance. She then threw the mute button and kept watching. I would look at her and she would say, How long do you think before I learn to lip-read?

Sometimes we would come back way past midnight, drunk, tired. We would collapse into bed, and as I was fading into sleep I would hear a click and the familiar blue glow of CNN would fill the room. Something urgent would be happening somewhere. America would be telling the world what it should know. At near-mute volume Fizz would hear a complete bulletin before turning in. It drove me mad. I became convinced that 24/7 news was a Western disease, threatening to swamp the Orient. It needed to be eradicated like smallpox. It created an itch that could scar sensibilities permanently.

My attempts at explaining this to Fizz failed.

Each time she would say, Are you telling me awareness is bad?

No, no, no, I wanted to shout. This is not awareness. These are third-rate stories. They are driving out the first-rate ones. If we only listen to the stories in front of our faces, we will cease to listen to the ones in our heads. It's a disaster!

But I never said it because I felt a fraud since I had myself in all these years failed to conjure up a single first-rate one.

In this limbo of CNN bulletins, subeditorial trenches, onanistic surveys, death on the Brother, general ennui, and intermittent hypersex, the phone rang late one night. For a change the line was clear. It was Mother.

She said, I have some news for you.

I said, Did you catch it on CNN?

She said, What?

When I put the phone down I was not sure how I should react. There was a clean-shaven white man with a jutting jaw speaking earnestly on the television. He wore thin-rimmed spectacles and a spotted tie. Then there were shots of many white men in black suits shaking each other's hands in controlled aggression. The volume was off so I could hear nothing. Another summit meeting, I supposed, to assert the rights of the rich.

Fizz was looking at me in enquiry. I said, What's happening?

She said, Shut up and tell me what's happened.

I swung my legs off the bed, walked to the door, put my hands in my pocket and turned around.

She said, Fresh trauma?

I said, I think we are rich.

To cut to the chase, the Bibi had left me a share of her property. There is obviously a limit to punishing unpalatable marriages, though in Indian lore of every language unacceptable liaisons are supposed to end in murder or suicide.

It was a small part of what she had. But it was more than Fizz and I had ever fantasized about. When the numbers were done, the taxes taken, the baksheesh given, fifty-seven lakh thirty-two thousand seven hundred and forty rupees were remitted into my account. It was the liquidation of the twenty acres that had fallen to my lot. At my current salary it was fifty years' wages. When I presented the cheque at the bank the Malayalee teller with a pencil moustache and richly oiled hair stood up and gave me his hand across the counter. It was the first time he had ever smiled at me.

Between Mother's phone call and the arrival of the cheque nearly two months went by. It was a strange, fraught time. We failed to locate a euphoria. We were embarrassed by our windfall – and the direction from which it had come. We felt rich, but also diminished. For the first few days we did not discuss the subject, each of us waiting for the other to set the tone.

One night, on the terrace, I finally said, Shall I say no?

She said, Of course, if it's worrying you.

I don't think I wanted to hear that. I wanted her to veer away from the honourable path and give me persuasive reasons for not saying no. I wanted to be the honourable one, guided into good sense by another.

I said irritably, It's not worrying me! It's just that I didn't agree with her and it doesn't belong to me. But then it doesn't belong to anybody! And not that any of the other jokers ever agreed with her about anything!

She said, If that's how you feel, then take it. But remember to forget about it once you do. Don't spend your life agonizing about it!

Maybe I shouldn't then, I said.

For weeks we went back and forth in the same vein. I think we knew there was no way we were not going to take it, it was just that we needed to work it out of us by debating it till the discomfort was spent. We needed to tell ourselves we had taken it reluctantly.

The truth is the discomfort was never spent. Not two months later, not two years later, not when everything was over. We learnt soon enough to not argue about it, but each time we ate the fruits of our windfall a bitter aftertaste lingered.

The first thing we bought was a Gypsy. A blue-grey one, with two doors, a hard top and a big door at the back for the boot. Fizz was the first to learn to drive, from one of those garage schools that make you crawl the kerbs and disrupt regular traffic. She taught me in turn. We sold the bike. It shamed us to say so, but the Gypsy felt good.

We stuck to our covenant not to talk money, but its abundance began to creep up on us. Walking past a swank showroom in the Vasant Vihar market we spotted a luxurious double bed with wings for stacking books, and ended up buying it. In the Gypsy we installed a fancy Sanyo stereo system with four speakers instead of the usual two. With poker faces we bought a sleek Panasonic vcr, with a multi-remote, so we could see all the classics we'd long wanted to. With alarm one day I found myself looking forward to a shopping expedition: a sad distraction from my non-writing life.

We realized we were in a peculiar quandary. If we did not spend the money then we were giving it undue importance. Hoarding it as something of value. And that was terrible. If we spent it, then we were becoming conspicuous materialists. Consuming units in my father's eternal algebra of profit and loss. And that was terrible.

So we lived in fear of it. Fear of it in the bank. Fear of it in our hands.

I think we were afraid it would change who we were, how we were. We tried to stay normal. Tried to pretend it did not exist. I did not give up my job. Fizz did not stop editing for Dharma Books, nor did she give up her research project for ms meanqueen. We did the old things in bed; and we did new things; and though we went to sleep clinging to each other as before, it always lay between us now, digging into our ribs, choking our hearts and our voices.

Fifty-seven lakh thirty-two thousand seven hundred and forty rupees.

If someone had suddenly taken all of it away I am sure we would have been swamped by relief.

As it was, someone did. It happened in as arbitrary a fashion as the arrival of the money.

Fizz came back one evening from the Green Park market with hot samosas and jalebis. We were almost into November and the weather was turning. It was Sunday and I was sitting out on the terrace, feet on the stone bench, struggling with Dante. All this frantic Christian handwringing about guilt and paradise made no sense to me. It was pretty crude stuff. If you had to buy any mumbo-jumbo about the hereafter, my money was on the Hindu karmic razzmatazz. So much class and room for manoeuvre there. Wrestling versus chess. Not about pinning down the conscience in a double Nelson, but about brilliantly plotting its evolution into higher planes. When she walked in, cheeks glowing with the nip in the air, curls alive and moving, I was relieved I could set the book aside. The book designer had put in a black cover: it even looked like bad news.

Fizz left the paper bags on the bench and went in to get a plate and the bottle of tomato sauce. I put my hand into the jalebi packet to pull one out and I saw the ad. It was above the waterline of the sticky jalebis and it said Hill Estate for Sale.

I stuck the train of jalebis I had picked up into my mouth, and carefully tore off the patch of paper, trying to steer clear of the leaky syrup. When Fizz came back out, the jalebis lay exposed and an irregular tear of paper was clinging to my forefinger. We spread it on the bench and studied it with care. It was brief. An old estate near Nainital. Didn't say where. At a height of five thousand five hundred feet. Going cheap. And a phone number. A Delhi phone number.

We emptied the jalebis onto the plate and tore open the entire packet, turning it over and around, to try and locate the date of the paper. There was no indication at all. It was from a section of the classifieds. No dateline. No news story anywhere that could have given us a hint. We weren't even sure which newspaper it was, since neither of us ever looked at the classified sections of any of the newspapers we bought.

We decided to make the call. We argued. It fell to Fizz.

The conversation was brief. It was a woman. The ad had appeared three weeks before. Yes, the estate had trees. The house was old. Of course, it was livable. There was another phone number, her uncle's. He would do the deal.

I made the call this time. After much yelling, the uncle came on the line. It was a bad connection. He spoke in an Anglo-Indian twang, with Hindi words thrown in. He said it was a fantastic place. Believe you me, sir, a historic house. Yes, it has trees. It is located beautifully. Right by the road. With valleys on both sides. Old stone walls. Old wood floors. Yes, of course, it has trees. Many, many kinds of birds. And monkeys and langurs. Believe you me, sir, leopards wander through the property all the time. Sometimes tigers too. Tigers? Tigers! Corbett Park is nearby, sir! Power connection is there. Spring water is there. Ekdum saaf. Ekdum meetha. Yes, yes, sir, there are many trees! You can come when you want. Come quick! Believe you me, sir, you won't leave once you come.

What are you expecting?

Believe you me, sir, it is worth thirty lakhs. I am expecting nothing less than twenty-five, but to you I will give for twenty.

We pinned the sticky paper and the numbers on the tack board. We did not talk of it the entire week. Once again we were waiting to take our cue from the other. On Friday night sitting out on the terrace, warming ourselves with whisky, discussing the weekend plans, we looked at each other and I said, Want to give it a shot?

I called the uncle again. Much yelling of names later he came on the line and he sounded like he'd been warming himself on his own terrace. He began baiting me immediately. Who are you, bloody murgichor? House? What house? I am not selling any house to any murgichodhu! You sell me your house, you fucking Dilliwalla!

I was about to abuse him back when the phone was snatched

away and a woman came on the line. I am sorry, she said, he's not well. I said, It's about the house. She said, yes, we could come tomorrow, he would be fine by then.

I could hear him ranting in the background. Wants to buy my house! I will buy his house and his father's house and his father's father's house! And his father's mother's father's house!

The woman on the line shouted, Shut up, Taphen! Then she gave me the directions. Fizz wrote them down as I repeated them aloud. Hapur, Garhmukteshwar, Gajraula, Moradabad, Rampur, Bilaspur, Rudrapur, Haldwani, Kathgodam, Jeolikote, Gethia.

It was to become, very soon, the mantra of our lives.

We left in the darkness before dawn and had reached Hapur before first light. It was cold and we kept the Gypsy windows rolled up. The small towns on the way were already awake and vegetable and fruit sellers were beginning to line the road. By the time we crossed the Ganges at Garhmukteshwar and went past odorous Gajraula the sun was up and our windows were down. The breeze was cool on our faces, we were chattering and we felt wonderful. We hadn't talked like this in a long time: lightly, happily. About the past, about the future. We spotted blue jays and pied kingfishers lining up on wires for early-morning forays; and in the fields man and animal were hard at toil.

The chaos of Moradabad gave us a reality check and we had to close our windows against the noise and fumes of the market with its autoshops, rickshaws, buses, cycles, vendors, dhabas, railway station, schoolchildren, tractors, all of them hurtling in every direction following rules made in a lunatic asylum. The market stretched like a child's sulk, dragging on and on, and when we were finally out of it we found ourselves stranded in an endless queue at a railway crossing. We were so far back we could not even see where the tracks crossed the road. We gained terror from the calm around us. Most drivers and passengers were out of their vehicles: stretching, soaking in the sun, squatting by the roadside, buying up Hindi newspapers and sliced green guavas and wet white radishes. Some had lain down in patches of sunlight and gone to sleep. Scores were pissing in the ditches, shaded by the pale smooth trunks of eucalyptus trees, throwing back glances to those talking to them from the road. Mongrels lay everywhere – parti-coloured, matt-haired, scabies-rabies seeming – totally disinterested in the din.

We received our first lesson in patience on our road to el dorado.

Soon we too got off the jeep. Bought radish, bought guava – peppered both brown-black with chat masala. Read the local Hindi paper. Fizz sat on the warm bonnet. I went off into the ditch to piss. The sun began to beat down. We bought a fake Pepsi. Wasn't bad. By turns we wandered up the queue to see how far it ran. It was like a python that had swallowed a clarinet, then a guitar, then a saxophone, and then a cello. And was now dozing in the sun. It bulged and shrank and narrowed and widened and had no sense of order at all. Countless trucks, cars, buses, two-wheelers, tractors, trolleys, three-wheelers, vans carrying buffaloes, lorries with squawking chickens, bullock carts full of hay, horse carts full of muscular sacks, and an old Willys jeep with its nose so high up in the air that I could not imagine the driver being able to see the road ahead – all these were jammed in any which way, wedged into each other in that last jostle for space before all movement died. The python appeared comatose, incapable of revival.

Then suddenly a shiver ran through the serpent. A rustle of movement. We could hear or see no train. But men, women, children began to clamber aboard their vehicles. Ignitions turned; engines gunned. Fizz and I settled in too. A warning whistle sounded far away, we felt a thrum under us, a faint clacking of iron wheels, and then without seeing anything we knew the train had come and gone. All was still. The last pissers were also out of the ditches and into their seats. The snake seemed to be holding its breath. And then with a sudden roar and a spitting it exploded into action. It began to heave and shake and undulate. As the snake from the other side began to move in our direction, ours began to straighten itself out. Amid shouts, horns, abuse, all the parts sticking out began to fall in line. The snake had to go through a narrow gateway and it streamlined itself and began to pour through. Many honking-braking-shaking-jostling minutes later we went over the bump of the double rails – the other snake slithering past slowly in the opposite direction – and were on the other side.

The industry that flourished at the crossing – the spice merchants of guava, sugar cane, radish, peanuts, aloo tikki, kulcha, golgappa, dal mixture – were now sitting back on the grassy verge watching their itinerant clientele jerk past.

With the next train the lines would grow.

With the next train they would break the bank.

Less than thirty kilometres later, just before Rampur, we almost yelped with dread when we saw another snake forming. But this time the train had run past and the snake was actually on the move, oozing its way through. We caught its tail and kept going.

Our luck at those two crossings, thirty kilometres apart, would forever determine the misery-scale of all our journeys.

We had been warned to watch out at Rampur for the Nainital turn-off, and we spied it on the left, right after the market, amid dozens of parked trucks. For another five kilometres the road ran past crowded markets, timber yards, auto-repair shacks, tyre dealers, animal enclosures. Then unexpectedly, splendidly, it opened out into a vista of green and golden fields scattered with trees. The road was gouged like a pockmarked face, and set the Gypsy at such a rattle we had to shut off the music system. But with the windows down and the roadside trees moderating the sun, the clear wind blowing in from the fields was a balm. The fumes and noise of the main highway were gone, traffic was down to a trickle, and the only sound was the unzipping of rubber on tar.

Fizz was grinning, her hair blown away from her face, her right hand clutched in my left.

We went past the dog-leg at Bilaspur, over the single-lane bridge where you had to wait for traffic to pass and on to Rudrapur, rattling on between more trees and more green-golden fields. Rudrapur had the roomy roads and roundabouts of Chandigarh, and we raced through it without pause. Minutes out of it we were among fields again and now had huge stately semuls lining the road.

Then we turned left, went over a derelict railway crossing, and were in a wide road in a forest, the cool wind whistling in our ears. The row immediately flanking the road was mostly semul and peepul and banyan and sal, but just beyond could be seen plantations of eucalyptus and poplar. It was a reserved forest, and for the first time since we left Delhi we could see no human dwellings. Traffic was minimal and the only thing you had to watch for were the troops of monkeys surveying the verge.

When we were almost out of the forest, and the first fields and houses had begun to appear, Fizz looked up and said, Wowhills!

And there they were, the lower Himalayan ranges, a dark silhouette that grew greener as we got into Haldwani. The passage through the twin towns of Haldwani and Kathgodam quickly wiped out the pleasures of the forest. Narrow roads, endless bottlenecks; the careening traffic of cycles, scooters, cars, buses; shops halfway into the street; vendors fully in the middle of the street; cattle everywhere. As we were despairing, it all ended abruptly, and the town was over and we were on the first winding road of the mountain. We hit the incline, and the hill signs appeared: sloping tin roofs painted red or green, grassy banks with bright bougainvillea bursts, dressed stone walls and stairways leading up from the road, lichen and moss in the cracks in the gutters and on the walls of the houses, wrinkled men squatting on verandas held up by old wooden rafters, gangs of chickens tracking grain, scrawny goats munching through the world.

We took the first curve and our spirits soared.

With every curve the world turned greener. The sal trees vanished. Above us soared tall pines, row on irregular row. Below us could be seen the rocky riverbed, with a slim silver chain of water threading through it. Just across it, the ranges rose again, largely uninhabited but for a few terraced fields, green with patches of brown where the land had slipped.

The air turned cooler and cooler and its just-minted freshness was heady. Fizz had a smile of such abandon it could have lifted the sorrows of the world. The song on the player was Mein Zindagi Ka Saath Nibhata Chala Gaya. Dev Anand, *Hum Dono*.

The road was wide and smooth, banking and climbing with easy grace.

Some bends had clear streams running across them. Occasionally there was barbed-wire fencing and iron gates, but few signs of habitation. Small wood and tin shacks showed up periodically, selling packaged snacks, chocolates, candy, cigarettes, bread pakoras, colas. There were wiry men sitting on their haunches everywhere, smoking bidis, sipping tea, watching the world go by.

We took a steep hairpin and a drizzle began to fall. It was fine, lacy, settling on my exposed right arm like gossamer. Fizz stuck her head out the window, eyes closed, and when she pulled it back in it was shining wet and she looked happier than I had ever seen her.

We crested another hairpin and there was a string of food shacks above the road. The first was a derelict dhaba with wooden benches and tables on an open veranda. Fizz said, Let's catch lunch.

The place was called Do Gaon. Two villages. It was not yet noon. We had been on the road for more than six hours.

The young owner was slumbering, but jumped up and began clattering his pots the moment we showed up. He got his tandoor going for the rotis and began to season some dal and gobhi on a gas stove. Just next to the dhaba was a fresh spring bursting through a lion face. We bent low and splashed our faces with the cold clear water, and it made our pores buzz. It was a slack time in the shops, and apart from us there were just some locals squatting around smoking. They looked at us incuriously. This was tourist trail.

We ate sitting opposite each other and watched the skies drizzle. There is nothing more beautiful than watching the rain fall in the mountains. Unlike in the plains, there is no fuzziness of shape. You can catch each line of moving water. When it moves faster you can go with the speed. When it slants you can shift with the angle. We were surrounded by green slopes with wild undergrowth and old but unintimidating trees. Big-leafed creepers sprang across the high treetops, harnessing them together. The scaly bark of the pines was dark with damp. A whistling thrush sat under the eaves, fluffing its feathers. It was plump, probably fattened on the dhaba's leftovers. Our skins were alive and prickling. The hair on my arms was moving. Fizz was in full bloom, face flushed, eyes shining. We knew we were in a special moment. Our lives together had been staked out around such moments, and it had been a long time since we had been in this zone. We were both living it, and filing it for future reference.

Fizz said, I feel I belong here.

I said, Yes, it's strange. It feels like coming home.

I did not say it simply to seal the moment. It was weird, it did feel as if I were returning to something I had known intimately. Some place I had lived, or somewhere I had been looking for all my life. My childhood towns on the great Gangetic plain had never felt like home: they were places to flee from at the first opportunity. Yes, once Salimgarh had seemed like home, but that feeling too had lapsed long ago. For too many years home just had been Fizz. Now I felt a curious sense of belonging begin to fill me. It was reassuring and disturbing. Sitting there in the falling rain, amid the tangled green slopes, nestled by a silence broken occasionally by a vehicle gear shifting the mountains and the sound of the water gushing from the lion's mouth, watching the fat thrush watch us, smelling the fresh rotis and woodsmoke in the tandoor, sensing the joy radiating from Fizz's body – sitting there I felt I might have found the locus on earth that we all seek. The one spot on the planet where our ankles are shackled and to which we have to return no matter how far and wide we wander.

Our bill came to just twenty-eight rupees.

Fizz said, I could live here forever.

I said, Without CNN?

I drove slowly, following hill etiquette, cleaving to the mountain, giving a spasm of horn at every curve. At no point did the road angle steeply, but we could sense we were climbing high and had already driven around several mountains. The dry riverbed had vanished long ago and the air was getting colder. Soon we were out of the drizzle and the skies were clear. The drizzle had already walked through here on its way down, for the air was washed and the foliage and road still glistened.

Fizz stopped me every now and then. She did not want to rush it. She was like the pilgrim who knows the fullness of the journey is the true devotion to the destination. She would spot an outcrop of road or a panoramic view, and snap, OK, here!

I would pull over. We would go to the edge – there were no precipitous drops, just mountainside gently falling away in waves of trees, undergrowth and terraces. These were friendly slopes. If you rolled yourself down you would snag every ten yards. Apart from pine there was a lot of oak – ugly in its gnarled asymmetry – and rashes of healthy bamboo, both yellow-limbed and green. Occasionally there was a ramrod-straight semul, magnificent in appearance, hollow in the wood.

I would hold her hand and we would breathe in deeply, filling our lungs with the giddy air. When I heard no sputter of engine I would stand behind her and fit my face into her neck and inhale her skin. Sometimes she would turn her face so I had access to all of her. At one point we stopped at an outcrop next to a huge boulder. A big peepul had cramped its roots around it like a leg spinner's fingers around a ball. The tree actually seemed to grow out of the huge piece of smooth rock, and you had to look hard to see where its single artery went into the soil.

Fizz said, I want this for my garden.

I said, Let's take it.

We both stood against the boulder, reaching less than halfway up its bulging curve, and bracing our feet, pushed with all our strength. Up close you could see the roots had fine tendrils that had invaded the invisible pores of the rock, stapling the tree firmly in place.

I said, One, two, three, haaishah!

Even a wall has give compared to a rock.

Fizz said, Love moves mountains.

I said, If you test love too often, it fails you.

She said, Do you think it knows it's being tested?

I said, I think so.

She said, Should we come back sneakily and do it?

I said, It's a possible tactic.

When the milestone said we were three kilometres from Jeolikote, a man stepped into the road and held up his hand. We stopped. He put his hand on the jeep and said, The time is ten minutes past one. Then he proffered his palm. Fizz put ten rupees into it. He gave profuse thanks and retreated to the kerb and sat down on an old sawn-off tar drum now filled with mud. He had close-cropped hair like an army recruit and was young, but was clad in old khaki trousers with turn-up bottoms. There was no watch on his arm. His eyelids were closed. He was sightless, but he held his head straight and not in the cocked manner of the blind.

Later Taphen the Juggler – Stephen – told us we had done well. On this road you ignored the blind youth at your peril. He was a guarantor of success and safety. Every truck and bus driver, each businessman going down to Haldwani to close a deal or coming up to Nainital to have a good time, paused and bought protection.

Believe you me, sir, said Stephen, if you had not given him some money I would not have sold you this house. Something would have happened. I don't know what. Something. I would not have liked your face. You would not have liked mine. Something.

Jeolikote began with a petrol pump and ran curving with the road till it suddenly became a packed market of food and provision stores. Above the shops could be seen haphazard dwellings climbing the slope. Most were modest hill houses, but some were two-storey buildings with freshly painted iron roofs. The area had an air of construction activity. A truck full of bricks was parked with its tailgate open; sand and gravel heaps could be seen on the kerb; and if you looked to your right below the road, iron rods stabbed the air waiting for buildings to grow out of them.

In the years to come I would get used to this. The hills were being continually built.

I stopped the jeep at the end of the market and got out. An old man sat on his haunches by the road in tight dirty pyjamas, pulling hard on a bidi. He had grey stubble several days old. I asked him.

Without getting up he said, Gethia? The big house? Taphen? There!

He pointed across the wide valley, and on the range opposite, higher than where we stood, cresting a spur, banked by trees, stood a solitary house. It had two chimneys and even at this distance you could see they had little hats pulled over their heads.

Minutes out of Jeolikote we peeled off to the right towards Almora and racing over a single-lane bridge spanning a shallow gorge climbed steeply for a few kilometres, the air getting cooler, the valley opening up expansively to our right, sporadic houses and an ugly ashram appearing by the roadside, and looping around the mountain arrived at the Gethia sanatorium and kept going, as we had been told, past a stately guard of twelve old silver oaks, till we came to a milestone that said Bhowali 10 km, and I leaned slowly into the bend, and when we emerged on the other side we were under the house on the hill.

The other face of the milestone read, Kathgodam, 24 km.

I had to reverse a little to find the path that wound up to the house. It was overgrown with weeds and grass and had clearly not seen the passage of a vehicle for a long time. The jeep took it easily. I parked under a big deodar tree next to an old white Ambassador car that had no wheels nor any seats. It was poised on stumps of bricks, and pointed towards the thick trunk of the deodar – a crouching climber preparing to scale the tree. A flight of old stone steps led up to the house.

By the time we had climbed them and walked around the thick brooding walls and up to the terraces at the back, Fizz had made up her mind.

The first thing she said was, I want this.

I had made my decision when I had seen the deodar.

There was a dog yapping in the distance. Every few minutes he would break for snarls and then go back to yapping. Soon another joined him.

The path up to the back terrace was overrun with weeds and big clumps of golden grass. There was shrapnelling stone underfoot, and we held hands to avoid slipping. The terrace held the ruins of an old building. Actually just a big room. There was nothing left of it except the last line of dressed stones, and one wall with a rotten window frame half out, rusted iron hinges still clinging to it. All that remained of the roof was a broken sliver of rafter, pointing to the sky like an accusing finger.

Weirdly, when you stood inside it, with nothing but open wind and sky around, you still felt you were inside a room.

From where we stood the roof of the main house lay parallel to us. If I took a running jump, and jumped like the devil was on my tail, I would land on its rusting tin, which was beginning to peel like wet cardboard left out in the sun. On either flank the valley fell away in a Dr Jekyll and Mr Hyde split. On one side I could see neat brown terraces and busy dottings of habitation – green and red roofs and whitewashed walls – and, just beyond, Jeolikote with its huddle of shops and the thread of grey road beading it to the mountainside. But when I looked the other way there was no trace of human life, just a sweeping glacier of green trees, dark and forbidding slopes of oak and pine running to a bottom I could not see.

We found a little path, cramped by the thorny branches of stunted lime trees, and I held them aside for Fizz as we picked our way to another smaller terrace. This was the highest point on the property. An old tank was embedded in it and you could hear the gargle of water. As we stood there, a pair of magnificent red-billed blue magpies appeared on the slope playing tag, their long tails floating in the wind. Around us were forested peaks. From where we stood the spur ran on, climbing a little through stands of tall pine and oak till it crested a few hundred feet away. The early afternoon sun beat down on us directly, but a strong breeze was blowing and it had a nip.

Above the wide bowl of the valley an eagle was gracefully cutting out widening circles of air.

From here the main house lay below us, the two chimneys like clenched fists. If I slung a stone with a lazy arm it would land with a clatter on the roof.

Leaning against me, Fizz said, I want this.

CNN? I said.

Even without CNN, she said.

A wild yapping of dogs began to grow closer. A voice from below shouted, May I know, sir, if you are there?

Stephen? I shouted.

Your man Stephen, sir! came the reply.

Stephen turned out to be in his sixties, a tubercular wreck of thinning hair, creaking joints, sallow skin and rotting teeth. He came dragged by four barking mongrels on leashes, of which two were mere lengths of rope. He tied them to the iron railing at the top of the stone steps, and the dogs pulled and clawed and yapped so much that we had to move all the way around the house to the other side to make ourselves heard.

Believe you me, sir, these are not dogs but the devil's hounds! They can take on a panther and make him run for his life!

We had to keep edging away from him as he talked. His breath stank of sour whisky. The maroon cardigan he was wearing was covered with dog hair of several shades, and even his grey trousers had long strands sticking to them.

He saw us eyeing the hair. Baring his rotting teeth in a deathly grin, he said, Believe you me, sir, finally only a dog is a man's friend. After a time the missus will not even let you come near her. Dogs don't care how you look or smell. They only see your heart.

Then he gave Fizz a wink and said, No offence meant, madam. But we men can never understand the ways of your race.

We stood outside the kitchen between the house and the Jeolikote valley. Below us the slope was cut in a series of irregular terraces. The first one lay fifteen feet below, a wedge of cake; but after that the terraces ran with just five to ten feet drops, steps a giant could take to walk all the way to the bottom. Lantana bushes were stuffed into the armpits of every terrace. Stephen took out a quarter bottle of Bagpiper from his trouser pocket. It had two fingers of whisky in it. He went to the basin nailed to the outer wall, stuck the bottle under the tap, ran some water into it, knocked it all back in one go, and with a wave of his arm said, Nothing like the Bagpiper to make a hill-man's heart sing! Come, sir, let me show you the most exciting house in all of Kumaon.

He opened the most exciting house in all of Kumaon by lifting the right half of the front door marginally and rattling it till the inside bolt fell. Inside, it was dark. We had to stand in the dining room for several minutes before we could see anything. The first thing I noticed was the thick rafters that held up the floor above our head and the wooden planks nailed on it. Wood floors were a fantasy from child-hood. We had always lived amid concrete and brick. The second thing I noticed was the broad fireplace in the further wall, with charred stumps of wood still in it. I took Fizz's hand and directed her gaze. Without looking at her I knew her excitement.

All the windows were boarded up with untidily hammered planks, the nails splitting the wood wherever they were banged in. You had to navigate by the points of sharp light bursting through them. We followed Stephen into a big living room with another broad fireplace, identical to the one in the dining room. A wooden cross with an icon of long-haired Jesus hung above it, painted in blues, whites and browns. The floor was uneven, rubbly. But here were the central rafters holding up the house – two of them, broad as tree trunks, bolted together with steel belts. Even as a layman, I knew you couldn't get those any more, legally or illegally.

I said, How old is the house, Stephen?

He said, Very old, sir, much too old. Before you were born, before I was born. Believe you me, sir, this is a historical house. You are standing on history. Many great men have been here. Gandhiji stood where you are standing.

Gandhi? Mahatma Gandhi?

Who do you think, sir? Mahatma Gandhi! He sat at that table

and had tea. The lady and him. Full of talk of ahimsa and satya-graha and all those freedom things.

I said, You are joking, Stephen.

He said, Right there, sir, believe you me. In his white dhoti. Sipping tea, with a smile. He came to visit Kamla Nehru at the Bhowali sanatorium.

Was Jawaharlal Nehru with him?

No, no, sir, he was in jail. Believe you me, sir, always country before wife. No offence meant, madam.

Fizz said, Stephen, I want you to say that in front of your wife.

Stephen giggled. Madam, I am not Jawaharlal Nehru, he said.

Against the back wall of the living room was the staircase to the first floor. Fizz followed me as I followed Stephen. One step was perilous and Stephen warned us of it. We came out onto a lobby with doors opening in every wall. Three of them led to bedrooms and one in front to a long balcony that ran the length of the house. Accustomed to hard floors, we stepped gingerly on the planks. There was an ominous creak at every step. Stephen noticed our cautious progress and laughed.

Believe you me, sir, an elephant could do the foxtrot with a rhino on these floors and nothing would happen, he said.

And in a fit of proof he began to jump up and down, loudly humming the tune of Come September. Pah-pah-pah-paan-paan-paanpah-paan-paan. Paanpah-pah-paanpah-pahpah-pahnpah . . .

The floor shook. We almost leapt out of our skins.

Fizz said, Stephen, control yourself. You are wrecking my house.

There was much more light here, filtering in from the front bal-cony and from the gaps in the planks above us. I climbed up the last steep ladder to peep into the attic. It was vast and desolate with two boarded-up windows at either end and the roof all patched up, the wood beneath it rotten with water seepage.

When we reached the bottom of the stairs again, Stephen stopped and began to struggle with a door to his right, which we had missed on our way up. After some pushing and pulling he managed to coax it open.

This is the last room, he said grandly, Actually rooms.

When we stepped in and looked up, the sky was a lovely blue. Just a slim rafter bisected it – the last remnant of the roof. The room above was missing. You could see the stumps of the wooden beams that had once held up the floor in an unbroken line in the stone wall. Some were sawn off neatly, others splintered as if they'd been snapped on a knee. We were in a closed box with no lid. It could have felt like an open-air squash court were it not for the devastation at our feet, which made me imagine I was standing in a bombed-out house in one of those Battle of Britain films.

The floor was covered with rubble, rotting wood, clumps of soggy grass, goat-shit, rusting clamps and nails, dead branches, tattered sacks, empty bottles, dented cans, curling half-sheets of tin. A door and two windows, off their hinges, lay propped against the wall, the glass squares eyeless, the wood mouldering. The immovable walls rose around us two floors high, the mustard-coloured lime plaster peeling, exposing their solid bone of stone.

Even in the brightness of day, the high blue sky, and Stephen's incessant chatter, it was eerie. Like being given a sudden glimpse of how it would all end. The solid house on the far side of the door merely on its way to becoming this ruin here.

The decay embedded at the heart of all creation.

This macabre feeling would come to me recurringly when we began to renovate the house. Each time a line of bricks was laid; each time fresh wood was sawed, shaved and hammered in; each time concrete was poured from the mixer; each time the sheets of tin were straightened and cut; each time all I would see was their eventual distress.

The process of demise set off by the act of creation.

Planting the seeds, I saw not the trees but the firewood they would finally be. And always the image that came to me was of this high double room, with no floor above and no roof above that, and the debris of all that had once been alive dead at my feet.

Stephen said, Believe you me, sir, when these rooms are done you will not want to leave them. These will be the best.

I looked at the rubble, the missing floor, the missing roof, the single rafter holding up the sky.

We all see and hear what we want to.

You hear the sound of doors that close and I of doors that open.

Should I ask him if Abul Kalam Azad ever visited too? Sipped tea with the lady?

When we went out the front door, he stayed inside. I will be with you in a minute, he said. We heard him squeaking home the bolt. We waited on the stone veranda. Above us were the decaying planks of the balcony – grey-black wood, rotting, with large gaps. Stephen appeared from around the house, grinning. He had jumped through the kitchen window, then pulled it shut.

Safest place in the world, he said, The only robbery we had here was five years ago. Eight cabbages from Prem Singh's fields near Gethia padao. The police chowki carried out an inquiry. Caught the thief. Had to work in Prem's fields for a month.

Stephen then led us on a tour of the grounds. There was another ruin on the terrace in front of the house. Only the stone plinth remained. He said it had been a greenhouse. There was a double-storey set of rooms near the front gate. One double-storey set near the rear gate. Both in disrepair, doors and windows damaged, the tin on the roof torn open. Most of the estate was overrun and you could barely make your way through it – lantana, grass, bushes, creepers were everywhere. The trees needed pruning; many had become mere clumps.

When we were back under the deodar, I said, Does the car come with the house?

He said, Believe you me, sir, it may not look it now, but many famous people have travelled in that car.

Yes, I wanted to say, Louis and Edwina Mountbatten.

We shook his hand and said we would get back to him soon.

He looked at Fizz and said, Madam, you buy this house and you will never forget Stephen.

More prophetic words than any we could have imagined.

He left, his yapping dogs dragging him. I noticed the pied one with a broken hind leg was the most aggressive, baring its teeth and snarling at everything. Even the other three dogs backed away from it. We followed the circus slowly, with the lame dog turning to make rushes at us. When we were out the lower gate – well, there was no gate, just broken stone pillars – we crossed the road. Next to the milestone, Bhowali 10 km, was a small stone berm. Sitting on it, you got a bottom-up view of the house. The stone under us – naked, uncloaked in concrete – was warm.

In minutes the sun got to our bones, making us dreamy. Just behind us the valley fell away dark and green. In front rose the hill with the house on top with the chimneys on top. Next to it stood the deodar, its three prongs taller than the house, taller than the chimneys. The sky was big and water blue. There were daubs of cotton clouds on it. Engines could be heard ebbing and accelerating around the mountains. The bushes were busy with the flutter and chatter of tits, chats, finches, nuthatches, little birds impossible to identify. We sat there, smelling, looking, listening, being.

We both knew what we were going to do.

Fizz said, Mr chinchpokli, I could live here forever.

I said, It's the famous car, isn't it?

She said, No, it's Stephen's charm. The dog hair he wears so casually.

We sat there for a very long time till the sun fell behind the opposite peak, in a burst of bleeing red. Villagers strolled past; cars, buses, trucks rolled past; we received curious looks, but no one bothered us. Before the sun fell the air turned cold. I had to roll down my shirt-sleeves, and Fizz wrapped her dupatta around herself. We walked back up to the house, and onto the highest terrace – the water pipe was still gargling – and watched twilight sweep across the valley. All around points of light began to puncture the gathering dark. Beacons shone on inaccessible slopes that looked uninhabited by day. Men truly go everywhere.

The house lay below us in complete darkness, its two chimneys now like the cocked ears of a giant animal. One minute the sky was darkening, the next it was spangled with stars. We had not seen so many since Kasauli many years before. We were holding hands and turning slowly to take in everything.

Fizz said, What do you say – if I count them right, we go for it?

I said, Absolutely. If you get it wrong, we just climb into the Gypsy and leave.

She said, Give me a minute.

She stared up, moving her lips silently. Then she said, I would say three million two hundred and seventy thousand seven hundred and thirty-three.

I said, Bingo! It's yours!

I pulled her into my arms and held her close – and then closer – while the water gargled angrily beside us. She smelt and felt better than anything in the world. Better than anything I had seen all day, all my life.

Later she said, We have found it, haven't we?

I said, I think we have.

The one spot on the planet to which our ankles are shackled and where we have to return, no matter how far and wide we wander.

The one spot that would give us back the wholeness we had slowly lost over the years. The one spot that would set the Brother clattering in ceaseless delirium.

The moment was broken by a furtive scuffing in the bushes at the bottom of the slope. We could see nothing, but we were aware this was big cat country. We picked our way past the lime trees carefully – me holding aside the branches with the juicy green thorns. Starlight and a half moon provided enough illumination to avoid slipping. An occasional dog bark split the fresh night. When we got into the Gypsy the wheel-less Ambassador under the deodar looked like a big sleeping beetle. I expected it to scurry away when I fired the engine.

The deodar itself – the thick trunk splitting from a fork eight feet up into three ramrod-straight branches that spiked the skies: the Trishul as we would later learn – seemed like a sentinel of another, pre-human, age. Shiva's weapon left behind on this hill in Gethia. To guard us and our dreams.

For me, it alone was the price of the house.

When we rolled down the slope and cut sharply into the road, we saw a big dark figure slide back from the verge into the shadows of the crumbling outhouse. It was so sudden and startling we saw almost nothing, and when I slowed down to look back there was nothing to see.

What was that? I said.

Fizz said, Whatever it was, it looked pretty frightening.

And as I took the bend – the Gypsy's headlights bouncing off the stony mountain face – to start climbing the road to Nainital, where we were planning to spend the night, she said, And I think it didn't have any arms.

# On the Road

We bought the house.

It took nearly six months. The process was prolix, and Taphen's wayward conduct drove us ragged. There were two Taphens. One was grand and expansive: It's all yours, all yours, sir! You can take it for free! What is a house? The good lord meant us all to live under the open sky! The other was wildly abusive: This house will never be sold! Never! And certainly never to murgichodhus like you!

Not time of day but ingestion of alcohol governed which Taphen you encountered. Often he was full of sweetness in the evenings and a frothing monster in the morning. It had to do with when he could lay hands on the Bagpiper. We learnt to take our chances. And soon in exasperation I joined battle. If he was offensive, I abused him right back. We traded violent charges.

Stephen, you are the ugliest asshole in all of Kumaon! Your mother drank quinine instead of water while carrying you!

You bastard Dilliwalla! You want a mountain house? You come here and Taphen will give you his hotfat lollu in your prettycity backside!

Stephen, you are the son of a snake!

And you, sir, are the penis of a porcupine!

Taphen compounded matters with his memory lapses. One day the land with the house would be forty naalis; the next day, thirty; the next, thirty-five. One day he would say the price was twenty-two lakhs; the next, it would be twenty-four; the next, twenty. Till the day we went to get the stamp papers prepared for the registration we were not sure what we were paying for the house.

Later I was to discover he was known in these parts as Taphen Juggler. Thanks to knowing English, and being an indiscriminate alcoholic, he straddled two different worlds. He sucked up to and sipped tea with the government officials and the visiting elite from the cities, charming them with his lilting English and his knowledge of the area; and he drank and slept and ate with the villagers and locals, being who he was, a hill-man among hill-men. He was a Juggler because he cut deals with the administration for civil work, repairing roads and embankments; purloined construction material from government sites and medical supplies from sanatoriums and hospitals; bought and sold illegal wood; bought and sold illegal stone; bought and sold legal and illegal land. And scrupulously laid it all at the altar of the Bagpiper.

One day when he was only half drunk he took me to the back of his house, pointed me at a pit nearly ten feet across and said, People ask me, Taphen Juggler, what have you done with your life? And I bring them here and say, This is what I have done! Do you know anybody else who has done this?

In the pit were heaped booze bottles of every size, shape and colour. Tall bottles, squat bottles, round bottles, hexagonal bottles, rectangular bottles, half bottles, quarter bottles, in colours of green and brown and lime and cream and clear transparent glass. Except for a few at the top which had soggy, fraying labels, the bottles were naked of any markings, and ran many layers deep. Most of them were grimy with mud, but there was enough glass glinting there to dazzle the eyes even in the fading light of evening.

Taphen said, When I was young my father's brother told me there are two kinds of men in the world. One kind drinks and lives – like a man. The other kind talks about the one who drinks and lives – like a woman. So he said, Decide, my son, do you want to drink and be a man or talk and be a woman!

He was squatting on his haunches at the edge of the monument he was constructing to his life, holding his head in his hands.

He said, Before I die I have to fill it up.

There was more than two feet to go.

Taphen was an interesting guy, but he infuriated me. Fizz was more ambivalent. She abhorred his constant hustling and his alcoholism, but admired his love for his dogs. He sleeps with them, she would say, He sleeps with them – that's something.

Who else would? I'd say.

It's his appetite for the Bagpiper, she'd say, It's his appetite that undoes him. But appetite undoes everyone, doesn't it?

No matter the explanations, I was deeply relieved to be done with him when I handed him the last of his money in the land registry office in the higher reaches of Nainital, and passing on the envelope containing two per cent of the amount, that was the settled rate for the bribe to the clerk, took my papers and walked out into the mid-morning sun. For six months he had leeched me in driblets and I was sick of his wheedling.

But Taphen was never done. He followed me out and shouted expansively, Believe you me, sir, you will never forget me! I have given you a slice of history and geography in one cheap deal!

He was bathed and shaved for the occasion and was wearing a shiny black suit and a faded red tie. To Fizz's compliment he said, Madam, you have to make sure the menials don't lose their respect for you.

Taphen claimed he was getting only a small part of the money. The rest had to be shared with his host of siblings. And sure enough a decrepit bunch of five – come from Dehradun and Moradabad and Bareilly – clustered under the huge pine tree next to the canteen wait-ing to collect. The three men looked wasted, ravaged by germ and gin, and each had a lit cigarette between his fingers. The two women sat on the edge of the veranda, frumpy in sarees, careworn and glassy-eyed.

Taphen said, They are all drunkards. I drink and work. They drink and beat each other up.

The old colonial building sat several loops above the bus-stand and the lake. I asked Fizz to drive the Gypsy down while I walked.

She asked no questions. I took off at a fairly brisk trot, paying no attention to the sauntering locals and the lazy commercial activity. The road was a patchwork of sun and shadows. By the time I reached the splendid lake with a humming busyness at its head – the shops, the buses, the tourists, the vendors, the ponies – I had soaked in the sweet feeling of ownership and knew I had made the right decision.

When I look back now my antennae must have been stuck deep in mud. History and geography and tearaway demonology.

In one cheap deal.

Cash upfront.

And pay the price later.

We became obsessed with the house.

It was like suddenly acquiring a fully grown child. A baby is an organic process and you tie your life in with it slowly and incrementally, day by day, week by week, year by year. But if you get yourself a grown-up child it demands a complete and immediate engagement. You need to divine, analyse, understand, correct, all at once, because there is not much time. If there are character defects you address them directly. There is no time for subtle suggestion and slow steering.

Armed with the Bibi's money we fell upon the estate, determined to swiftly bend it to our will. The first sweep of clearing the grounds revealed we had got more house than we had paid for. As the four young boys from the village swung their iron scythes – at fifty rupees a day – hacking at the bushes and grass, unexpected paths began to emerge. Under Fizz's supervision, nondescript clumps of undergrowth became neat oaks, and the clearing of the old rubble widened the terraces.

Taphen came by with his yapping quartet, dog hair all over him, and said, Madam, it is beginning to feel like the olden days.

Damyanti, his stocky wife from the plains, from Shahjahanpur, where she had been a schoolteacher, scoffed, Olden days! Madam, he is not Taphen Juggler, he is Sheikh Chilli! If you believe half of what he says, you will go mad. When he was trying to marry me he used to tell me grand stories about Christmas parties and rum cakes and plum wine, about English newspapers that came from Delhi, and a big car in which all the children could fit in one go! And when I came here I found a small ditch full of empty bottles, and now after thirty years I have a big ditch full of empty bottles!

In a falsetto Taphen said, Don't be silly, Sheikh Chilli! Dig a big pit! Quickly fill it!

The wife said, That's it! That's all he can teach! So now my older boy, Brian, drives a roadways bus in Pithoragarh, and makes his own bottle collection. He says he will one day dig a bigger pit than his father.

Dig a big pit! Quickly fill it! sang Taphen.

The wife said, You see! What a fool he is! But Michael, my other boy, is a good son. I protected him from his father. He is my son. He does not drink.

Taphen said, He doesn't drink. He gives injections. Right, left, centre. Thishsh!

The wife said, Shut your liquoring mouth! Madam, he is a nursing attendant in Haldwani. It is true he wants to give everyone injections. When he comes he doesn't bring gifts, he brings his injections. He says health is the greatest gift in the world. Everybody hates poor Michael. He comes with his black bag and walks around pulling down everyone's pants and poking them. Look at me. I have got more than a hundred. In my arms, in my stomach, in my thighs, in my buttocks. He says, Mother, this is for tetanus, this is for rabies, this is for hepatitis, this for A and this for B. He says, Mother, this is the poke of god. But when people want to come to my house they ask, Is Michael there? When they meet each other they ask, You met Michael? He poke you? When the children see him coming they shout, Jectionmichael is here! Jectionmichael is here! And they all run screaming. I want to cry. This scoundrel Taphen and his Brian are drunkards and everyone invites them! And my poor Michael, trying to help – and no one wants him!

Taphen sang, Gawdalmighty, I do not joke! Give me a poke! Give me a poke! Dig a big pit! Quickly fill it!

He tilted the quarter-bottle into his throat.

With disgust the wife said, He even asked Michael if he could get a whiskyjection.

That night I told Fizz, Please keep these idiots out of here! I can't bear them. All the mixed blood has deranged them!

Fizz said, Baby, don't be shameful! What about Michael? You want me to invite him? For a little poke? God's little poke!

I know where to get that! I said.

We were in the room above the dining area. The planks were all black-brown with age here, and some of them had big cracks you could peer through for a full view of the room below. The floor creaked ominously each time you put a foot down and we had still not developed an ease about walking on wood. There was only one window in the room and it overlooked the Jeolikote valley. It was at the window that you got a true sense of the thickness of the stone wall. The sill was two feet wide, and you sat on it with the same sense of security as on a sofa in a living room.

From the window you could see all the way down to Beerbhatti on the right and to Jeolikote on the left. You could also see the point at which the road forked for Nainital and Almora: the Ek Number: Number One. In the armpit of the first terrace below us was the lantana bush with the nightjar. It had not yet begun to toc. It wasn't even ten. We always tended to turn in early here, exhausted by the mopping-up operations. Today the moon was big, pouring into our room and lighting up the valley in a silver glow. The road across was a shining ribbon with glowworms riding on it slowly. On the wavy top of the mountain above was a line of pine trees marching in single file, soldiers with big helmets on night patrol. We were sitting on the sill looking down, our legs scissored into each other, her hands in mine.

In the four months since we had bought the house we had cleared the grounds – hacking, cutting, burning – and collected all the stone from the rubble in neat heaps under Trishul, the deodar. A crane had been summoned from Haldwani and the Mountbatten car had been removed and placed near the village shop a little up the road. In a week the thakur had taken off the last doors, put wooden planks inside and made it his tea cafe. We were also discovering the intricacies of architecture and how it worked in the hills. And making the acquaintance of those who worked it.

Here Taphen initially had his uses and therefore the licence to swing by and bullshit us. Till we discovered the full range of Rakshas's virtues. We needed serious handholding to lick the house into shape, to make it liveable. We needed carpenters, masons, labourers, plumbers, electricians. We needed to know where to buy the materials – wood, stone, sand, bricks, cement, gravel, tin. We needed to know the zoning laws and the weather patterns. When the squalls hit, when the rains, and when the hailstorms. How big should the windows be; how strong the doors; how thick the tin. What was the true threat of monkeys and panthers and wolves. And smaller vermin from mites to moths.

A decent bathroom – that was our challenge in chief. The house didn't have one. There was a cavernous room – absurdly, next to the kitchen – with a hole in the floor. The hole was in a raised slab of concrete, three feet by three feet, in a corner. It had a half-height brick wall around it and a half-door on uneasy hinges. A shabby little enclave in a large room. When you squatted you could look over the wall and door and survey the rest of the bathroom. The brass tap at the far end; the small mirror hung above it; the dirty ventilator above that; and a narrow cement slab with soaps, toothpastes, oils and shampoos queueing up to be used. Occasionally one of us bathed while the other squatted, and we talked. When you stood up you had to lean on the half-wall for a few moments to uncramp your limbs. Then you had to walk across, fill a bucket, and walk back.

Fizz said, It's a balanced morning constitutional – exercises every muscle from sphincter to bicep.

The original inhabitant of the house, it seems, had used thunder-boxes and washing bowls. The later ones had created the hole in the floor. Now we needed to put in a couple of bathrooms next to the bedrooms. Knocking in the plumbing was one obstacle, but the far bigger problem was opening up the two-feet-thick stone walls to attach the bathrooms. And since the bedrooms were upstairs and had wooden floors this was an even greater challenge. We had come up with no solutions so far.

The undergrowth was alive with chirring insects as we sat holding hands. The moon was tracking its way across the starry roof of the valley, and the lights were dying on every slope.

Fizz said, If the mountain will not come to god for the poke, god will have to bring the poke to the mountain.

She took her right hand out of my grasp and put it on my track pants. My hips moved involuntarily.

She said, Why do you think Taphen hates Rakshas?

I said, Yes.

She said, Today he again told me, madam, be careful of that bandicoot. Believe you me, he has one arm but four eyes. Four eyes but eight ears. Eight ears but eighty ideas. They say he talks to spirits. You will think of something and he will know. The good sir will be smiling and his pants will be gone.

I said, Yes.

Her hand was now full. I was floating above the valley. Like the eagles at high noon.

She said, And he said, I am a drunkard, madam, but that man is a druggie. Believe you me, I will go to my grave – and so will we all! – but he will go to jail. Do not pass go. Do not collect two hundred. Go straight to jail.

I said, Yes; yes.

My track pants were on the wooden floor. The world was now no bigger than a small hand. And I was soaring higher than all the eagles in all the world's valleys.

Fizz said, But I don't think we should listen to Stephen. I think Rakshas is an OK chap.

My eyes were closed. But I knew she had moved. Was moving. She was not on the sill. Now she was on the sill.

Rakshas–Taphen; rakshas–taphen; rakshas–taphen; rakshas–taphen. They were steady strokes.

Warm and dry; hot and wet; hotter and wetter.

Rakshas–taphen; rakshas–taphen; rakshas–taphen . . .

Fizz–me; fizz–me; fizz–me . . .

Hindu–Muslim; hindu–muslim; hindu–muslim . . .

Good–bad; good–bad; good–bad . . .

In–out; in–out; in–out . . .

Love–sex; love–sex; love–sex . . .

Rakshas–taphen; rakshas–taphen; rakshas–taphen . . .

Later we sat naked with a blanket around us, she leaning into me. There were very few lights in the valley now, and they were all far apart, veranda and gate lights, guardians of the final night hours. We both felt a sense of relief. Our bodies had become so erratic around each other that each time they ignited we felt we were healing. The cuts closing, the skin growing over them again. Strangely, while the house had made our spirits soar, it had done little to move our bodies. Normally novel situations, new settings, every act of togetherness, electrified us. But we had failed to shake the rafters here, as we had both expected to the first day we stood on the highest terrace looking down at the house and the valley. We were acutely aware of it. We didn't know what to do about it. And without saying it, I think we were both simply putting it down to sheer physical exhaustion.

Since we had bought the house we had become desperate roadies. We had been coming up every weekend. Without a break, every single weekend. Leave Delhi on Saturday pre-dawn; start back for Delhi on Monday pre-dawn. I had worked it out with Shulteri: Saturdays off for working longer hours on weekdays, and the late shift on Mondays. Because I had fallen off the radar it did not matter to him.

In the last year he had lost ground on the pole because King Cupola had been slopping a lot of grease in his direction. He was frantic, agitating to regain his position. If ever there was a book in his head, I was sure it had by now seeped out of his toes.

Every Saturday Fizz and I would wake at four in the morning and be in the Gypsy by four-thirty. Before turning in for the night we would have packed and loaded. The back seat and boot would be full of household bric-a-brac. Nails, bolts, hinges, power-plugs, rolls of electric wire, curtain rods, cutlery, glassware, utensils, lightshades, wrenches, can openers, screwdrivers, corkscrews, buckets, mugs, bedlinen, tablecloths, pillows, quilts, curtains, racks, clothes-pegs, insecticides, mosquito repellents, shampoos, soaps, towels; plastic containers full of tea leaves, biscuits, powdered milk, dals, rice, flour, spices, condiments; tins of condensed milk, baked beans, rasgullas and a few times ghastly sausages from INA market. There would also be bottles of beer, whisky and wine, wedged between the linen.

Jammed in on the floor would be tree saplings – shisham, peepul, banyan, jacaranda, gulmohar, amaltas, silver oak, kachnar, neem, semul, bottlebrush, bamboo. Some would be in dirty plastic casings, straight from the Jor Bagh nursery; some in small pots purloined from Fizz's veritable forest on the terrace. The branches would be carefully adjusted, some curved safely under the roof, and some trained out of the window from where they waved spectrally at passers-by.

Then there would be our books – which had begun to wing their way up in steady handfuls; a box of music cassettes, the weekend's menu; and finally the Brother, which went up and down with us, sitting on the rear seat, cloaked in its black shroud, waiting, like me, to see the light.

It had been months since it had felt a clack rattle its bones. The hill house had become an excuse to avoid its gaze. I kept it in perpetual purdah, and walked in and out of the study without looking at it. The cosmos-in-a-kernel story of the young Sikh had long been lying comatose, the last half-sheet still trapped on the roller, buried in darkness. It was waiting to be mercy-killed and cast irretrievably into the biblioblackhole.

We would leave with a flask of hot tea in Fizz's hands. Delhi would be sleeping, and we would speed along the empty roads and be over the Nizamuddin bridge and into and out of Hapur before the sky began to lighten. And then it would be one town after another, one bottleneck after another, one level crossing after another, as we sped and stuttered our way to the foothills. And then minutes out of Kathgodam, having threaded the misery of Haldwani, we would take the first bend of the first incline and everything would fall away and our spirits would begin to sing like Julie Andrews on amphetamines.

We felt we had become Kerouac and Cassady tearing up and down the great Gangetic plain – hurtling up the mountain, touching 5,438 feet, and then rolling back all the way to Delhi. Like those skateboarding kids on ESPN who go up and down curving walls, not falling, not stopping. In a rhythm that is its own logic and end.

In no time it became the best-known road of my life. I knew where its curves were lean and where voluptuous, where its skin was pitted and where flawless, where danger lurked in the shadows and where it was innocent of all deception.

I learnt the code of the road. How to race for the head of a bottleneck and cut in sharply the moment it began to clear. How to overtake from the left by going off the road – once in Hapur for half a kilometre we actually drove through the frontage of shops, sending men, children, sacks and chickens flying as a monster jam clogged the main road end to end. How to avoid tangling with bullock carts and tractor trolleys – rural juggernauts with nothing to lose. How never to make way for anyone, for no one will ever make way for you. How to take on trucks but never buses – contrary to popular wisdom, bus drivers have a meanness truck drivers can never match. How never to take a road dispute to a police station – we did once near Gajraula, and two hours of infuriating questions later were told we were best off letting it all slide.

We discovered which dhabas were good for tea, which for parathas, and which for sandwiches. In the frenzy of those months I also confirmed a suspicion I had harboured for years, that most dhabas in India are manned by idiots. Not as in the foolish, but the born deficient. I think parents in villages – unaware of the great psychiatric institutions of the cities – look upon dhabas as therapeutic and vocational outlets for their benighted sons. And canny owners teach these boys the names of five dishes and the fundamentals of carrying and washing plates and glasses. I would not be surprised if they are only fed and never paid.

The command structure of most dhabas it seems is: one smart owner, one sane cook, one sane head waiter and a posse of idiots. There was one just before Moradabad, Punjabiyan Di Pasand, where everyone bar the owner was unhinged. Once when I went around the outer wall to take a piss, I ended up looking through the open window into the kitchen. At the height of summer, the cook was sitting in front of the fires wearing a khaki sola topi – stained with sweat and grime – and singing a Hindi film song at the top of his voice. He saw me and started banging the burnt ladle against his cardboard hat, demanding, Dal fry from chirrimirri colony? Dal fry from chirrimirri colony?

Behind him a young ragged boy in torn shorts, washing dishes under a running tap, began to grin and drool and bang two steel plates together. Loudly he warbled, Dalfry-dalfry! Dalfry-dalfry! Chirrimirri-chirrimirri! Chirrimirri-chirrimirri! The lunatic duo fell into a wild jugalbandi, hammering on steel and cardboard, smiling happily, chanting, Dalfry-dalfry! Chirrimirri-chirrimirri! Dalfry-chirrimirri! Dalfry-chirrimirri!

Suddenly there was a roar from outside, Fudhihondayo! Shut your mouths up! Have your mothers been raped?

The two fell silent, as if shot through their heads.

I zipped up and ran.

Forget the cook, this dhaba did not even have a sane head waiter who could collect the bill. After you ate you had to go to the

counter and make your reckoning directly with the burly sardar who
owned the place.

Handing you the change, he would say, It's not their fault. They
are the innocent ones. It is the world that has gone mad.

I was convinced you could trawl through India's dhabas and con-
script an army of the insane to wage war against the armies of the
sane. And in the din of battle you would not know who was which.

Fizz and I had never been on the road like this. Neither of us in our
teens had been part of a bike or car culture, nor had we done touristy
things like haring off to see temples and monuments. The travelling
added a new layer to our relationship. We began to live for the road.
We bought a range of flashlights, a small axe for protection, pop
music that was good for only one trip up and down. Through the
week we talked about things to be bought, things to be taken up, for
the journey, for the house. We acquired comfy tracksuit bottoms and
T-shirts; our toilet bags were never unpacked. We began to drop out
of the lives of our friends.

I loved the driving. The open road, the unfurling landscape, the
world controlled by a steering wheel. Saturday pre-dawn the Gypsy
would roll out of our lane – the yellow street-lights still glowing – and
I would be happy. Happier still would be Fizz, bathed, scrubbed,
glowing; the flask of hot tea in her hand. There was one unforgettable
trip – in the last days of March – when she kept her hand high on my
thigh all the way up, and in a strange trick of memory the entire
journey burnt itself into my mind.

I drove in a daze yet missed nothing.

The early-morning roadside marts with tight-skinned onions and
deep-green watermelons. The big potatoes in tilted carts, shining like
apples. The open fields crowded with wheat stalks turning from green
to golden – often a green patch next to a gold, the slow child ripening in its time while the sibling has moved on. The story in sugar cane
even more disparate. Trolley- and truck-loads of sliced and bound

stalks, blocking traffic, working their way to the mills – sweet spears threatening passers-by as they swayed dangerously outside the confines of their carriers – while squares of tall hairy cane still stood in the fields, hemmed in by a sea of midget wheat. The gobar stooks, smoking fetidly through the day, like bombs from antiquity preparing to explode. The phallic chimneys of endless brick kilns stroking out red bricks to blight the countryside. At Brajghat the sweep of the Ganges shrunk to a stream and preyed upon by god's shanties and fragile boats. The sky an unwashed blue, a dust haze hanging in the air. Large-lettered, garish advertisements on every available wall, of house, dhaba, shop. For colas, cigarettes, bidis, soaps, and often bold offerings for a one-stop solution to all sexual problems. Call Doctor Doctorlola, ABCDEFG (London), HIJKLMNO (America), and find the strength of day in the dead of night! And everywhere the proliferating congress grass, laden with its white-tipped lung missiles, choking plant and man. And as prolific as the congress grass the symbols of a new India, PCO and STD booths, by the dozens, in every village and every shop. Rural India frenetically dialling the world. Hello, good morning, we are all well and not yet dead!

And the tyre shops and the auto-repair shops and the eateries, and the people everywhere, squatting, walking, eating, sleeping, defecating, urinating, riding, watching – every every where, all the way from our house in Delhi to the forest plantation at Rudrapur, without a comma, without a semi-colon, without a pause, a Finnegans Wake of humanity, inscrutable and much too profuse.

And alleviating all this the march of a million trees. In the first stretch the pale-skinned eucalyptus, flanking the road several rows deep, long in limb and low in stature, often marooned in pools of water of their own making. And then the shishams, twisted in the body but glittering in their pearl-drop green leaves. And around every trunk a wash of white paint, declaring it the property of the state and not the people. And then, as you ripped through the heart of India, the ringed-in mango groves now riotously in bloom with the flower that would become the lord of all fruit bursting whitely through the prolific canopy of dirty green leaves, forcing a nation to hold its breath against storm and canker.

Fizz said, This year we shall bathe in mangoes.

I only moaned.

Then, as you turned off from Rampur, ran the messy five miles of truck and shop, and entered the agricultural belt of Bilaspur and Rudrapur, there began to appear the geometric lines of young poplars. The enterprising migrant farmers of the area were testing new commercial frontiers. The poplar as the new cash tree: seven years and you chop and sell. On both sides of the road, amid golden-green wheat fields, young trees were shyly coming into lovely leaf. The poplars had been arranged two ways. As boundary trees, hemming in the crops without casting on them a wilting shadow. Or in Chinese-chequer groves: in squares, precisely eight feet apart, cutting a dead-straight line any which way you looked. Even in infancy they were two-men tall, and it was only the frailness of their torsos that gave away their age.

In total contrast, through the journey, there appeared a variety of old ficus trees that were monumental in their spread and stature. Some banyans, some peepuls, and some that we could not identify. Fittingly, they grew singly and far apart: next to a village school; in front of the local courts; in the middle of the market chowk; in the yard of the police station. Fizz said, her hand hot on my thigh, These are the lions of the plant kingdom. The poplars are the deer.

The most magnificent lion could be seen sprawled at the last bend before the Rampur level crossing. A mammoth banyan in a rise of mud in the middle of a stagnant pond. It would have needed six men to span its girth and a thousand could have slept under its ancient canopy, which was being continually pushed further by its hanging roots. At its thick ankles grew a small stone temple. It had a triangular saffron flag fluttering above it, and saffron paste had been rubbed onto the tree trunk. From a speeding distance it was not clear which god resided there, but it is safe to say the tree could have easily sheltered the entire Hindu trinity.

The last of the great trees before you hit the foothills were the statuesque semuls, the silk cottons. They began to appear in large numbers as you approached Rudrapur, and multiplied as you drove out of the town and headed for the reserved plantation that ran to Haldwani. The semuls were Zulu warriors, straight-backed, stout-limbed, tall. That day in March most of them were without leaf or flower, their many arms and many fingers clutching starkly at the blue sky. They strode grandly by the roadside, and could be seen climbing up the mountains all the way to Jeolikote. On the plantation stretch Fizz put her head in my lap and I became king of the road, and king of life, and king of the world. I was now tall as the semuls, with veins of steel. But my strength was an illusion – that melted when the forest ended and she lifted her head – just as I discovered in later years was the case with the semuls. They were, in fact, weak in the wood, and could easily come to grief.

I remembered other things.

When I stopped to piss after Gajraula – and I had to wait long moments for the blood to ebb – Fizz pointed out the waves of marijuana flowing by the roadside. You could pluck it, rub it assiduously on your palm for hours and create the black plugs of peace and nirvana. Or you could grind it into milk and hallucinate into happiness. Fizz plucked a few juicy stalks and threw them into the back of the Gypsy to dry. After that I smelled green and gravitated into even higher realms.

And finally all along the way, in glorious splashes, were the mustard fields, now coming aggressively into flower, swathes of stunning gold-yellow, as heady to look at as smoking marijuana.

By the time we took the Number One fork after Jeolikote and raced up the steep curves to the house on the hill I was like a hungry man who has been taken to the dinner table and brought back unfed a hundred times. On each trip he has been given a delicious little savoury, but denied the big meal.

Fizz gave me the big meal later that night. It was a feast fit to stun a king.

My voice must have filled the vale profound.

As we sat on the windowsill – past midnight now – it was the only other electric incident of the past few months that I could recall. We were naked; the mountains of the day – men and cars – were asleep; the mountains of the night – animals and trucks – were on the move; and we were aware that what had just happened had not been happening of late. For the most part, so far, our days were just full of the business of life. Interesting, revealing, satisfying, full of new kinds of discovery, but just the business of life.

And Fizz and I had never lived by that.

We had lived by the magic of our skins.

We tended to panic when we missed it.

But to be fair the business of life went well. Full of new kinds of discovery.

Soon enough we found the right workers.

Soon enough we unearthed the infinite virtues of Rakshas.

Soon enough we cracked the problem of creating the bathrooms.

And thereby embarked on the road to unravelling our lives.

The key man who came into our employ was Bideshi Lal. He was the master carpenter and he had with him a team of boys, the youngest of whom was only six. He was called DoInchi, and he lent his tiny hands to the planks of wood when they were being hammered and planed; and later, when everyone else rested, he collected the shavings and stuffed them into sacks for the night fire. Occasionally the older boys chiselled him some weapon of war, a sword, a pistol, a bottle-shaped grenade. When no one was looking he practised for battle, launching frontal attacks on the pear tree near the veranda, and tossing the grenade deep into the enemy of grass.

The tree was attacked to the sound of dhish! dhish! dhish!

The grenade detonated to the sound of dhummm! dhummm!

Later, when DoInchi was resting from the din of battle, Rakshas would ask him, How many Pakistanis did you kill today?

With a grin DoInchi would say, One hundred and ten.

Rakshas would pat him with his good arm and say, Arre,

bahadur! I can do that with one hand! Tomorrow you must kill two hundred and twenty!

Bideshi and his boys were from Baheri in the foothills. Bideshi was thirty-five and had ten children – nine daughters, and the tenth, a son. The oldest worker on his team of eight was twenty-one. They were all short and scrawny and gifted with prehensile hands and feet. They could perch on crumbling sills and sloping roofs for hours and hammer away ceaselessly. Over the months I waited for one of them to take a fall, but they were effortless and precise. The team profile altered every now and then. A familiar face would vanish and a new one appear. But one boy was a constant, and he was not allowed to scale the walls and the roof, though he could saw, shave and hammer a piece of wood as well as anyone else.

He was the strongest, with big muscular arms, and was called Chatur – clever – Lal. He walked with a sideways gait, and always had a brown hen with him. The boys called it his begum. When he came to work he carried the hen under his arm, and while he worked the wood like a piston, smoothing every bump silken, he tethered his begum by a long string tied around her claw. When they sat down to eat lunch – rolling out their rotis and achaar – he held begum in his lap, letting her eat what she chose off his hand. I never heard him talk. But sometimes at twilight or in the early morning I would hear him wandering around the grounds, calling aa aaa, aa aaa, aa aaa, as he looked for his missing begum. Sometimes when he held her close I thought he was whispering to her, but I never could tell what he was saying.

Bideshi Lal said Chatur was his older brother's son. A piece of masonry had fallen on his head when he was five and the concussion had left him slow. He understood little, but was gentle and patient and could talk to animals. I commiserated and Bideshi said, From some god takes away brains and from others bodies. It seemed Bideshi's son, child number ten, after nine daughters, had a polio leg and could barely walk.

Bideshi brought in Dukhi Ram, the chief mason, who was from Bihar, and so gaunt that his cheeks seemed to touch inside his mouth.

It was difficult to tell his age. He could have been anything from forty-five to sixty-five. He spoke in dialect, much of which eluded Fizz and me. While Bideshi loved making conversation, tossing out possibilities and theories, Dukhi Ram hated being asked anything. His attitude was: explain the job and be gone. He wore a small white dhoti and was always squatting on his haunches. I never saw him standing except when he was walking.

His clutch of boys was from his district of Madhuban. There were four of them, all in their twenties. While Bideshi's boys smoked bidis, Dukhi's boys constantly chewed on lime and tobacco. One of them, a dark squat fellow with fat lips and curly hair, had a beautiful voice, and sometimes at night you could hear him singing sonorous folk-songs full of longing. Bideshi's boys were playful – you could hear them ribbing each other and laughing. Dukhi's boys had a doleful air. I felt the Bideshi boys lived with the happy assurance of those whose roots and home are close at hand, whereas the Dukhi boys – many days' journey from their home, in an alien terrain, often numbed senseless by the cold – carried with them the sadness of exile.

Dukhi and his boys worked only with brick and concrete. They could build walls, plaster them with cement and execute the intricate task of casting roofs – weaving the iron fretwork, aligning the shuttering, pouring on the concrete. But they could do nothing with stone, hewn or unhewn.

The stonemason was brought in by Rakshas. He was from Bhumiadhar up the road. He was old and always wore a Gandhi cap – like Pratap, Abhay's father. Unlike Pratap, I discovered it had nothing to do with politics, it was just that he had once worked in the government as a fourth-class employee and had never shed the regime of the cap. Rakshas called him Goli, but in deference to his age we said Goliji.

Rakshas laughed and said, Goliji! We call him Goli because he almost killed half the village handing out random tablets when he worked as a peon in the sanatorium!

It was a treat to watch Goliji work. His forearms were strong, and with sure blows of the hammer and chisel he chipped and dressed the stones. It was slow, tedious work, and laying just three feet of wall could take him and Rakshas several days. The brickmen in contrast went lickety-split. Dab of cement, bang. Dab of cement, bang. Entire walls could be grown in a day.

Part of the army consisted of irregulars. The electrician, the plumber, the painter, the grille-man, the wood and stone polishers – they all came and went, from Haldwani and Nainital, on a summons. Then there were the daily workers from the village, willing to attempt any labour for sixty rupees a day.

The regular army was only the Bideshi boys, the Dukhi boys, Goliji and Rakshas. They lived on the grounds, Rakshas in the out-house by the lower gate, all the rest in the two-storey block by the upper gate. They had a proprietorial air about the estate and were deeply committed to making the house happen. You could hear them in their off-hours arguing intensely about holding walls, angles of the roof, size of windows, width of beams, distance between rafters, placement of septic pits, quality of wood, sal versus tun, New Zealand pine versus Kumaoni pine, hinge windows versus sash windows, ceramic tiles versus white marble, corrugated-iron roof versus Nainital-pattern roof.

The army had one field commander and one generalissimo.

The field commander was the stump-baton-waving Rakshas.

He led the army into battle every morning with waves of his stump, fought with it shoulder to shoulder, and bawled it out relentlessly. In the evening he warmed the troops with his camaraderie and his wit.

The generalissimo was Fizz.

She drew up the plans; presided over the supply chain; and made the daily reckoning.

With her matter-of-fact approach and lack of aggression, Fizz had early made deep inroads into the ranks. Instead of the imperious memsahib, they affectionately called her didi. I, of course, was sahib, immemorially the dickhead with the money. Actually it was Fizz's ingenious reconfiguring of the house – leading to a slew of attached bathrooms – that made them fall to their knees and hail her as supremo.

She cracked the problem one evening, sitting under the deodar and staring up at the house. We were both there, on the red sandstone bench we had built against the boundary wall. It was high summer and we had, a few hours earlier, been given a taste of the ballistic gale that struck every afternoon between two and three and tore past the house. It came roaring in from the direction of Jeolikote and went towards Bhumiadhar. Everything left out in the open – clothes, chairs, books – was swept away and had to be recovered from all parts of the estate. If you stood against it, you were pushed back inch on inch. If you opened your eyes, it threatened to peel back your eyelids like banana skin. The first keening sound, the first warning gust, and the workers put their tools down, took out their bidis and lime and tobacco, and squatted in a line in the lee of the house and listened to the wind howl. Half an hour later it would be gone, its last flapping robes gathered neatly and taken away. A hush would descend. Not a blade of grass would turn.

Then Rakshas would say, admonishing with his stump, All right, it's over. She's gone. Move your withered black asses and get back to work!

Rakshas said the gale was a spirit of the mountain which slept for forty-nine weeks every year and, waking, raged on this route for three weeks. Its purpose was to remind men that they were still inferior to nature. He said sometimes men became so arrogant that they failed to heed the warning. Then the land began to slip. He said the spirits of the mountain were benign, but if they were snubbed too often they rained death and destruction.

Looking up from under Trishul, Fizz said, Veranda. The answer's a veranda. We should have thought of it earlier. The answer is always a veranda!

She kicked me off the bench, picked up a chalky stone and drew out her plan on the red slab. She made one big square – the main house. She then attached two small squares on either side. The right-hand square was the goat shed, currently a big lean-to with a collapsed tin roof and half a door and the smell of goat-shit deep in its stone walls. The square on the left side was the big lean-to against the other wall – our current hole-in-the-floor bathroom. Then with the screeching point of the stone she drew a semicircle that connected the outer wall of the goat shed with the outer wall of the hole-in-the-floor toilet. The line glanced the corners of the front veranda, extending it further out.

Grandly she handed me the stone and said, So what do you say, mr chinchpokli?

I said, That's good. So we use the veranda as a bathroom?

She said, Yes, noble master. You use the veranda in the true spirit of chinchpokli, while I use the bathroom.

Taking the stone back from me, she flattened out the slanting roofs of the goat shed and the hole-in-the-floor bathroom on either side of the main house with screechy-scratchy determination. She then put smaller blocks on top of these flat roofs. And on these she put slanting roofs.

She said, The ground beneath our feet. Ching Chow says no man can shit on a sloping floor.

I said, Oh! That's an idea!

At the bottom of her draughtsmanship she signed Fiza, with a flourish under it. Then she threw the stone over her shoulder.

It was a brilliant plan. Cast a veranda all around the house; give it a concrete roof; on it lay the bathrooms; open the walls of the rooms on the first floor and attach these bathrooms to them. It was organic and simple. It did not fundamentally disturb the old structure; it built around it. In fact the veranda would act as a concrete belt to protect the old wood and stone house. It would also provide large common areas on both floors for use in times of bad weather. And when we began to plan it in detail we realized it would also give us an extra three bedrooms.

Rakshas said, his stump rotating enthusiastically, If all the women in the world had brains like didi all the men in the world would be happy.

Looking at me askance, Bideshi Lal said, Some the gods give brains; others the gods give money.

Squatting on the ground, Dukhi Ram said, Shall we start?

His lugubrious pack glared at him balefully.

In the background DoInchi exploded the pear tree with a grenade attack. Dhummm.

Fizz said, All of you later. First Goliji.

Fizz didn't mind doing the new rooms and the recast kitchen and bathrooms in brick – because they would be plastered over – but she wanted the plinth of the veranda to be cast in stone to cohere with the original look. We were there the morning Goliji, in his Gandhi cap, took a ball of white string, tied it around a big stone and, aligning it with the outer wall of the goat shed, pulled it out twelve feet in a straight line. Then he wrapped it around another big stone, and his coordinates were set. Rakshas tested it by twanging it like a guitar string. The rest of the army stood around and watched.

Rakshas and Goliji, helped by the daily wagers, then dug a shallow trench under the stretched string. The top soil ran out after ten inches, and the pickaxes began to bounce off the rock. Rakshas fished in his pocket and came up with an old coin with a hole in it and a squiggle of snake made of copper. He tied them together with several strands of red mauli, and reverentially buried them at the head of the pit. A dozen Khaaskhushboo agarbattis were lit – their incense strongly sweet even in the open – and everyone bowed in appeasement to the spirits of the house. A box of wet orange laddoos was opened and everyone tossed one into their mouth.

Goliji then selected a big stone from the pile set up next to the site and chipped off the awkward edges with gentle blows of the chisel. Stumbling under its weight, he lifted and dropped it at the goat shed end of the trench. Kneeling, he jostled it around till it settled securely. Then he turned to the pile and like a fastidious buyer of fruit began to feel and turn the stones till he was satisfied with the shape and size of one. He gave it a few loving chips. Then he slopped some of the cement mix – they used a thick gravel mix for stones and a thin gravel mix for the bricks – on the first stone and with tender care placed the second one on it. With gentle taps of his hammer he brought the two into near-perfect alignment.

Rakshas began the same process from the other end; working, with one hand, as fast as Goliji, but not with the same finesse.

Fizz and I sat and watched all day. By evening the wall was over-ground, and we had discovered that irregular stones have as much symmetry inherent in them as assembly-line bricks.

The pattern was set. We would start off a new phase one week-end, and return the next to take stock of it and flag off the next. While Rakshas and Goliji put down the sprawling veranda, the Dukhi boys were busy executing brickwork to remake the outhouse near the upper gate. Stone was a scarce commodity and even if you managed to get some legally it was cripplingly expensive. So we were plucking out stone from the upper outhouse and using it in the main building, and the outhouse was being remade with the lesser material of brick.

Unlike the cavalry of the masons – brick and stone – who had joined battle with minimal preparation, the Bideshi boys were like archers who had to prepare hundreds of fine feather-winged arrows before they entered the fray. Relentlessly from dawn to dusk the young boys sawed, shaved and stacked the planks of chir pine and shisham that had been bought from the teeming timber yards at Haldwani. They had set up their planing board in the living room, and all day it was like a giant insect going shcik-shcik-shcik. In the evening, when it went to sleep, a strange silence came upon the house. DoInchi then, with his tiny hands, stuffed two sacks to bulging with the pale-coloured shavings, and musclemoron Chatur – his hen on a leash – carried them to the outhouse.

In the night they were burnt on the wood fire, and as the army sat around, the Dukhi boy with the fat lips would sometimes sing his

longing into the valley, and sitting far away on the back terrace we
would hear it and be moved.

Some trips we started back on Sunday evenings, but most often we
left before dawn on Monday and were at the outskirts of Delhi by
nine. Getting home – depending on the traffic – could take an hour
to two. It was always a downer to be back, though setting off from
the mountain top was nice.

The hill roads would be empty; the slopes still asleep; the stars
making their final pinpoints; and often a moon was hanging in late,
lighting up the valley magically. At times you could turn off the headlights and cruise for several kilometres in a silvery dark, and forget
for a moment who you were, where you were, and what was the
nature of everything. Once, above the Beerbhatti bridge by the huge
tun with a girth bigger than our deodar, we saw a flash of leopard's
tail disappear into the bushes. It gave us a high for days.

But by the time we hit Delhi's hinterland we were in distress. The
heat was on, the dust was rising in clouds, and the last stretch after
Hapur was tight as a churidar, with several legs trying to get into it.
The buses came at you like bats out of hell and there were always
wrecks from recent accidents – crumpled cans of metal, as if squeezed
by a giant hand – lying by the wayside.

When the road eased soon after the Ghaziabad turn-off, to
become a generous four-laner, then a new kind of dismay took over.
All through the journey the road was flanked by unfinished buildings.
Iron rods sticking out, floors half-finished, walls unplastered, windows and doors missing, terrace balustrades half-done. The road-
scape suggested no one wanted to finish a building any more –
everyone wished to keep open the option of endless addition. As
Hindus know, we live forever: there is no hurry to complete anything.
But what appeared now on the last stretch, on both sides of the highway, was a half-made urban sprawl that was devastating. Harsh,
without a trace of green. Tiny, naked houses, their bricks stitched

together with ugly cement, jostled with each other to gain some air. Most were boxes, two storeys high, with barely a window. The paths between them were unpaved; the sludge clogged the open gutters; garbage heaps grew where they could find purchase; black hairy swine nosed in them for succour; small green-black ponds played host to man and buffalo.

This was the twilight zone. Here lived the clueless bastards of modernity and antiquity.

A life without the dignity of the bucolic, and without the possibilities of the city.

The old talisman of the regenerating land had been left far behind.

The new one of wit and sleight of hand was too far away.

Few would escape this twilight zone and finish the journey.

Very few. Very very few.

And even those who did would arrive in a city of sand.

Sausages in a giant sausage machine of drivers, guards, peons, riders, labourers, waiters, coolies, office-boys, dishwashers, dhobis, sweepers, beggars.

A pilgrim's progress from lesser hell to greater hell.

Abandon all hope ye who venture here.

As we travelled month on month, we saw the dismal sprawl spread like a rash. Towards the city and away from the city, towards the road and away from the road. A landscape without hope. Skin rubbed raw, beyond balm and succour. Even the rains – which rescue everything on the subcontinent – failed to put a shine on it. There was no green to sparkle up. The naked brick boxes, the dust and the sludge, just became more despondent in the damp, and squadrons of mosquitoes set upon everything, completing the hellish aspect. On days the wind blew towards the road, the faecal stench invaded the nostrils and stayed there for hours, resisting all rinsing by water, soap and cologne.

Looking at the sprawl, it was difficult to imagine any avenger of souls pulling off a rescue act.

Even Gandhi would have had to dig deep for an adequate response.

It was better when we left Delhi. The rash was clouded in darkness or fog and we could fix solely on the waiting mountains. The only worries were the railway crossings and the snakes fattening on either side of them.

There is no doubt the mountains sustained us even in Delhi. With my writing haemorrhaging I had become terrible company. As long as we were visiting sanitary and hardware shops in Kotla Mubarakpur and Hauz Khas market, or the stone traders on the Mehrauli road, I was OK. Fizz would take the lead and I would engage.

We would talk up the house for hours: the architecture, the materials, the views, the trees, our plans to leave Delhi in a few years and settle there. The adult-education classes we would start in the outhouse; the monthly health clinics we would hold, bringing up our doctor friends to treat the villagers; an annual art camp for artists; the room over the dark valley to be made a writer's retreat; the terrace with the lantana bush which we would buy for growing herbs. Our girls, who would be born in nearby Nainital and grow up in the house, free spirits who would identify a tree before they would a cartoon character.

Ficus religiosa before Porky Pig.

The green barbet before Yosemite Sam.

At this point Fizz would say, But I will not tutor them at home! They will go to regular school and be given moral instruction by singing nuns!

That's it! We are selling the house!

We were happy in the mountains, sitting out on the terrace at all hours, sipping tea or whisky. We rediscovered Scrabble after fifteen years and soon our skills were sharper than ever and the seven-letter words flowed. We spent a lot of time tending to the saplings which Fizz kept procuring and planting with a ferocious fecundity.

We were happy being there, we were happy talking about it, but the moment the house stepped out of the frame I withdrew into myself and had nothing to offer. In those many months I don't think I once initiated a trip to the cinema, or going out for dinner, or visiting any of our friends. When Fizz did, I sometimes agreed, and sometimes I stonewalled it through sheer silence.

I look back now – when it is all over – and am appalled at my behaviour. The number of times I got up midway through an evening with friends and said I wanted to go home. The number of times I rose in the middle of a film and said it was too awful to endure. The number of times I even insisted we abandon a meal because the food was inedible or the restaurant lacked all grace. When we got home I took refuge on the terrace, under the gulmohar, and she retreated into the embrace of CNN. Occasionally she was asleep by the time I went in, but most often she was awake. Once the lights were off, we reached for each other, and an old rhythm took over, and we pieced together the puzzle of heart and hair and heat and damp and hardness and softness and smell and taste and memory and desire, and there was an enduring pleasure and peace in that.

Fizz took my mood swings mostly on the chin, aware I was struggling with strange demons. But sometimes she snapped – and we lashed at each other with no mercy: I calling her a frivolous bitch; she calling me the great writer chinchpokli; I saying I had nothing more to offer her and I was at my wit's end; she saying I was becoming totally neurotic and needed my wits examined to figure where they began and where they ended.

Then we froze each other out till our bodies built a bridge, or the house on the hill necessitated a discussion.

I did try, a few times, to cloister myself in the study with the Brother, but nothing happened. Absolutely nothing. I read what I had written about the medieval sardar and it was completely phoney – crap-in-a-kernel. I pored over the scribblings in my spiral pad and there wasn't a single idea or image that had a drop of juice in it. I tried to conjure up one new sentence that would remind me I could write, and I couldn't come up with even a phrase. I paced up and down the tiny room, Beethoven's Ninth playing remorselessly in the background. By the time I left the room, hours later, I was invariably in a worse mood than when I entered it. More uncertain of myself; ready for more bad behaviour.

Fizz would cast one glance at me as I emerged from the study and know I was fallow as a eunuch.

I brooded much of the time, but today I cannot even recall what it was I brooded about. What I do know today is that I was not in a unique space. Many – very many – people live there, tormented by the knowledge that they are not in the right place, but unable to discover what, and where, the right place is. Crabs without water, unable to swim, unable to die. Going through life's motions, but floundering in the wilderness within. And most of them have no Fizz to make it all bearable.

I kept going to work, but in that charged place I had made myself so abject that I was a pitiable creature. I knew people mocked me all the time, but I didn't wish to defend myself. I didn't even know what there was to defend. I could have quit, but that was a step I feared. I think I felt the office routine was a rope tethering me to the ground, and if I cut it loose I would float away for good. To where no one could reach me, and from where I could never come back. And in a curious way the salary was important. It made me feel my keep was my own. For despite our many rationalizations, the money still lay between us.

Fifty-seven lakh thirty-two thousand seven hundred and forty rupees. Or what was left of it. Unearned, cheerfully squandered.

Digging into our ribs.

I think for much the same reasons Fizz did not stop her freelance work. She kept accepting idiot manuscripts from Dum Arora and preparing them for swift dispatch to some biblioblackhole, and she kept logging up interviews for ms meanqueen. The passage of time revealed the woman to be as tough as she looked, cutting into life with her hatchet face.

Familiarity did not bring mellowing. Each time Fizz met her she was angry with the world and wore a moralizing sneer. As if she knew some pathetic truth about others that they did not. Fizz could never properly locate the source of her anxiety. Fizz felt it perhaps had to do with the fact that her husband was a rich wastrel – scoping the social scene for edgy liaisons – and she was an intellectual fed on feminist vitamins. Her self-image did not match her location in life. She was a jazz band in a five-star disco. She didn't want to leave the luxurious hotel, but she also knew her music had no takers there. Digging herself in, she had decided the listeners didn't matter; and for the hotel which had imprisoned her she had developed an abiding contempt.

The world is a hard place. Treat everyone like cicadas.

Fizz, with her own particular brand of empathy, did not actively dislike her. She managed to look past the tough carapace and engage with the work. It was the husband Fizz found insufferable, with his oiled charm and his eyes on her ass. She noticed ms meanqueen treated him with a frosty niceness – a kind of nice-being-with-you-you-sad-bastard air. Each time Fizz emerged through the gate, neat envelope in hand, she said, Let's get out of here – the groozy horror show is over for the week.

Fizz's gleanings on onan continued to entertain us. She became an eloquent analyst of the subject. She found men have an imagination no one gives them credit for. What had men not done with themselves? Hugged washing machines while they vibrated. Stroked between the cushions of rexine sofas. Inserted fine wires into their depths and turned them slowly. Received dire fellation from thick-tongued canines. And gentle shocks from low-voltage plug points. Assaulted broad taps gushing with hot water. Rubbed against pillowy flesh in crowded buses. Violated cakes, buns, watermelons, puddings. Peeped, sneaked, tweaked, leaked; used clothes, shoes, handbags, bed-sheets, towels; fantasized about friends, colleagues, teachers, cousins, maids, aunts, neighbours, nurses, children, mothers-in-law, film stars, sport stars, TV stars, toothpaste models, others' wives, others' daughters, others' mothers, even others' brothers, uncles, fathers, friends. One even mentioned a golden Labrador.

The devotees of onan had a fascinating panoply of practices.

And onan rewarded them instantly each time they worshipped at his altar.

Fizz said, Let me tell you, the King of Onan is richer than the King of Oman.

I said, Because pumping your own pleasure beats pumping your own oil?

She said, Don't be crude.

I said, Sorry. So who in your considerable research is the King of Onan?

Fizz said, Actually the King of Onan is the true slave of onan. He who succumbs to onan at every fleeting stimulus is in fact the king. In succumbing he conquers. In surrendering he overcomes fear, prejudice, superstition, lust, avarice.

I said, Jaundice?

She continued, Yes, and jaundice too. In exploring himself he arrives at a profound peace. A non-seeking, even if temporary. In learning to love himself he learns to love others. He is a real sufi king. Complete within himself and full of giving. The great onanists are the true great lovers.

I said, And who, in your considerable research, Doctor Doctorlola, are these?

She said, My hero!

# The Edge of Reason

We were not there when they came upon the cache.

The phone rang after nine-thirty, when the long-distance rates were down to half. It was Bideshi calling from the thakur's shop and I could hear Dukhi in the background trying to prompt him. The line was poor and their voices came and went. I gathered they were asking for permission to open something, but I couldn't understand what. We went back and forth fruitlessly.

Finally I said in irritation, Anyway, we are coming there in two days – we'll figure it out.

Bideshi said, OK, sahib! So you are saying we should open it!

I said, Just wait, we'll be there on Saturday.

Bideshi said, OK, sahib! If you say so, we'll open it!

After I put the phone down I wondered why Bideshi and Dukhi were calling me. Normally when they wanted to check something they routed it through the one-armed field commander. Where was Rakshas? I tried to call back the thakur's shop next morning but I couldn't get through. I forgot about it.

On Saturday when we drove the Gypsy up to the house at ten in the morning and parked it under Trishul, the Bideshi boys were taking a tea break and DoInchi had just finished exploding the pear tree and was reclaiming his grenade. Chatur was sitting in the sun with his begum under his muscular arm, talking to it in whispers. The hen's eyes were alive with interest and enquiry.

Rakshas came around the house, waving a short stick in his hand like a tennis racket, and the moment I saw him I remembered the garbled phone call. What was it? I asked, What did you want to open?

He stared back at me blankly and said, I did not want to. I told them not to. They said they had taken permission from you. The fools.

Dukhi, squatting, looked up sheepishly at Bideshi and said, The less said about it the better. We dug up a mountain and unearthed a mouse.

Bideshi said, Arre, sahib, what a state we were in. We thought the struggles of our life were over. But the infinite one gives only wisdom to the poor. The diamonds he gives to the rich.

It seems when they opened the thick stone wall in the room at the back – the bombed-out room, where I had stood that first day look-ing up at the sky, waves of rubble at my feet – they came upon a wooden chest. It was buried beneath the section of wall under the window. The discovery sent the workers into a frenzy. The chest was large enough – and heavy enough – to seed cinematic fantasies and they trusted Fizz to share the treasures.

They did not need to dig it out with care because it was placed in a neat stone-lined chamber, and the one-inch space between the chest and the lining was packed with strips of wood, which were now black and rotten. It had a large old iron padlock of the kind that needs a hollow key which has to be turned several times. After they called me and dubiously obtained my permission they wrestled with it for hours, and finally one of the Bideshi boys had to go down to Haldwani and bring up a locksmith.

The chest was lying in the lobby on the first floor, and Fizz loved it the moment she saw it. It was made of thick flats of deodar and had iron lashings holding together all its joints. The boys had cleaned it up and the wood shone rich. The big iron lock, rust flaking from it, hung with its mouth open like a panting dog. The locksmith – work-ing outside the zone of his experience – had damaged it permanently. Fizz ran a hand all over the chest, feeling its iron bones – the strips, the rivets, the bolts – and the smoothness of the wood before removing the lock and pushing the lid open. There was no electricity and we had to ask the boys crowding around to move away from the doors to give us some light.

Dukhi, who was back to squatting on the floor, shouted, What do you loafers want to see? You think this time there will be gold bricks in it?

Bideshi said in his high-pitched voice, Give them one each! In school they spent their time running away from them! Not one went past class five! And now they are pushing each other to get to them!

The chest was partitioned into four equal compartments and each was stacked to the top with identical-seeming books. The top four in view were all dressed in tan leather. When I bent down and picked up the one closest to me, an identical one in tan leather was revealed underneath. Before opening the one in my hand, I picked up the second and another identical one bobbed into view, and there was yet another similar one below it.

With his goofy grin Bideshi said, Keep going, sahib, keep going! The fun has just begun.

I told the boys to pick up the chest and put it in our bedroom, off the lobby, near the window overlooking the Jeolikote valley. There was light here, and a chair. Bideshi, Dukhi and the boys were waiting for our reaction. I said, Let's see what comes of this – for some people it may be more valuable than gold.

Bideshi said, Arre, sahib, in our destiny we have only two meals a day. If someone gives us gold it will turn to dust in our hands.

Fizz said, It's a beautiful chest, Bideshi. Can you make me one like this?

With chronic bravura Bideshi said, Arre, didi, I will make you one even better!

The chest had sixty-four identical tan-leather notebooks packed into it, in four stacks of sixteen each. Each notebook was more than two inches thick, and when I cracked open the covers of one the first page was blank and the second was written over from top to bottom in tightly mounted lines in a small looping hand. I flipped to the last page and it too was covered to the very end with the same tight, round hand. I opened pages at random and each was choked with an endless succession of tiny circular alphabets. Tiny wordwheels, rolling on and on. As far as I could see, there were hardly any paragraphs, any obvious beginning or end to the pages. The words had been given no room to breathe, as if the writer was afraid they might come alive and jump out of the notebook.

I picked another and ran a random check on it. There was no difference. The insides of the books were as identical as the outsides. Page after page of tiny rolling words in a faded royal blue ink; the paper thick with a little crumble coming into it, its colour running to cream and deepening. Fizz was doing the same, taking the notebooks out and checking them to see if any were different. It was obvious the boys had gone through the same drill earlier, for the books were dust-free, and the interior of the chest had been wiped clean. If there was any order to them there was no sign of it; and if there was any order in their original placement it had been lost in all the casual handling.

If you examined them carefully, you could identify the ones that had been at the bottom. Their pages were almost stuck to each other and you had to peel them open slowly from the edges. The only other hint as to chronology was the ink: it was faded in many of the books, almost too faint to read. Some pages also seemed smudged – whether in the writing or later it was difficult to tell.

By the time we had haphazardly riffled through them all several hours had passed. When Rakshas came up to call us for lunch we were sitting amid stacks of tan leather. The moment I saw him I knew something was wrong. His usual ebullience was missing and his handsome craggy face was set and unsmiling. The stump lay sullen, unmoving. I also realized he had been absent from the drama of the last few hours.

I said, What's all this, Rakshas?

From the doorway, he said, The past should always be left buried. We can barely deal with the present. But these foolish men of the plains don't know anything.

I repeated, But what is all this, Rakshas?

Without looking at me, he said, I don't know. I don't know anything. All I know is that the past should be left alone. My father used to say the present belongs to doers, the future to thinkers and the past to losers. The past should be left alone.

That evening Taphen came by, knowing we had arrived from Delhi. As ever, he reeked of whisky and was covered in dog hair. But he too was unusually sombre. We sat on the terrace, looking at the sun dying over the valley. An army convoy was winding its way up from Beerbhatti, the olive-green trucks travelling equal distances apart, making the mountain groan.

Taphen said, What have you done with them?

I said, The chest? The notebooks? They are lying in our room.

He said, They should have never dug them out. You burn them now, sahib. Madam, believe you me, the past should be left untouched. Everybody in the mountains knows that. That is why there is peace in the mountains and trouble in the plains. You all dig up temples and mosques and dead people and dead ideas, and bring all the old trouble and mix it with the new trouble and make it all into bigger and bigger trouble. My boy Michael says, Papa, I give you this poke and it keeps all diseases away. But in the plains you say, Let me take the old diseases and injection them into the new diseases so that it creates such an ibnfatuta disease that no one can ever cure. People say the past is important. I say the past is a trap. Let me tell you, madam, there is no man in the world wise enough to learn from the past – they all dig in it for trouble.

I said, What are those books, Stephen?

He said, I don't know anything, sahib. I am just saying bury them, burn them, throw them away. Why play with the past? What is there in it for any of us?

The sun had dropped below the peaks and was now like a glowing lampshade. The valley was in perfect last light, clear and quiet. Some of the convoy was now behind us, climbing on its way to Bhumiadhar, Bhowali and finally the cantonment at Ranikhet. Even the rhythmic sound of the trucks couldn't shrapnel the peace of the waning day.

I said, Stephen, there is something you are not telling me.

He said, Sir, believe you me, I am telling you a lot. I am saying leave what is buried well alone. The world needs living men not ghosts.

I tried hard to get him to tell me more, but he wouldn't budge. He kept saying he knew nothing except that the past should not be stirred. It was dark by the time he rose to leave. The slopes and valley were alive with a thousand lights. The moon was weak, just beginning its journey to fat – in ten days it would floodlight the entire valley.

Taphen wanted someone to walk him around the curve of the road, from where he climbed the dirt-track to his house. He no longer brought his dogs over because they went berserk when they saw the boys, and there was always a fear that Chatur would attack them with an axe if they threatened his hen. Now there was no one to escort him. All the workers had repaired to their quarters and were busy bathing, crapping, washing, cooking. There was no question of asking Rakshas. Taphen was tense. He finally said, Sir, will you walk with me to my house?

On the way he told me he had a deep fear of the dark. He said when he was nineteen – and he was a strapping boy then – he had been jumped at the lower gate of the house by the devil. He said the devil was more than seven feet tall, had glowing embers for eyes and long curving talons for fingers. When it opened its mouth a low, far-away howl emerged, and there were no teeth, just a dark, gaping abyss without end. Taphen said he was in the school boxing team and he tried to defend himself, but the devil picked him up by his neck and effortlessly dangled him above the road. His dog began to mewl like a cat and went and hid under the culvert. Just when he knew he was about to die a truck came around the bend and, as the full glare of its headlights fell on the devil, he dropped Taphen and vanished.

We were at the bottom of the curving path that led to his house.

Up the track, where it bent for the last climb, a bulb hung from a soapnut tree casting a circle of yellow light.

I said, Stephen, do you want me to walk you up?

He said, No, this is safe, sir. It's the outhouse area I am afraid of.

I said, But Rakshas lives there. Alone.

He said, But he's a Hindu, sir. The devil wants only Christian souls.

It had been a long day – we had left Delhi at four in the morning – and we were ready to turn in before it was ten, two whiskies each inside us and dinner eaten. Rakshas had served us on the terrace, and had been silent and hostile as he brought and cleared the dal, gobhi and rice. In the dark the lights on the Nainital slope were like a cascade of glittering diamonds. At the very top, where the cascade began, you could see the shadowy spires of St Joseph's.

Fizz went in before me, and when I followed her a little later she was stacking all the notebooks back into the chest. I pitched in. Four neat stacks of sixteen each. When it was done Fizz closed the lid and hooked the damaged lock back, its mouth panting open. In a bizarre move, she then lifted our suitcase and placed it on the chest, almost pressing it down.

I looked at her. She had done it absently.

When we were under the quilt and it was so dark we could not even see each other, Fizz said, You think it's OK?

I was holding her hand. I squeezed it hard.

I said, Of course it is. Don't let these two jokers spook you.

She said, They were being very strange. And it's the first time I've seen them in agreement over anything.

I said, They are mountain guys. The mountains thrive on hokum tales. That idiot Stephen was telling me he once met the devil. By our gate. The lower one.

Fizz chuckled, And what happened? The devil ran?

No. It picked him up and dangled him above the road. In front of the Bhowali milestone.

OK, stop it now. You are scaring me.

He said it had red embers for eyes and a howling abyss for a mouth.

Stop it!

I pulled her into the crook of my arm and put my mouth on her forehead. She lay there with her head on my chest, her leg and arm flung over me. Her T-shirt had climbed up and her body felt warm. The hair was just beginning to push through her skin and I found its slight bristle exciting. That incipient roughness so much sexier than silky smoothness.

She said, Did you read any of them?

I said, No. I was just flipping through them to see if any were different.

She said, What do you think they are?

I said, Obviously some kind of notebooks. Diaries or some such.

She said, What are we going to do with them?

The first toc of the night rang out dully. I made a note in my mind – for the nth time – to check out the lantana bush. I knew if I went down there and squatted quietly for a few hours I would be able to see the nightjar.

She said again, So what are we going to do with them?

I said, Read them. Figure them out. Sell them for a million dollars to some idiot in London. Give them away if they are boring.

She said, Who do you think wrote them?

I said, Some serious neurotic. That's a frightening amount of writing.

She said, And without a Brother.

True, I said, A true maniac.

She said, Not maniac, mr chinchpokli, just inspired and disciplined. The question is can you do what he did?

I said, The good Doctor Doctorlola, the real question is can he do this?

I rolled on top of her, trapping her face down. My hands covered the back of her palms on either side of her head. My mouth lay by her left ear. The smell of her hair and skin filled me. I began to grow where she was most ripe and she moved to give me room. As my desire grew, it became an animal sensing its way home. It slipped on dampness and surged. I kissed her on the back of her neck, under the hairline, where her sweetspot lay. She moaned and arched. It slipped all the way in, raging against the heat.

Can he do this?

She said in a faraway voice, Anyone can do this.

I lifted myself off the fullness of her and then went back in.

Anyone?

She said, in a voice even further away, No one.

I kissed her from her sweetspot to the corner of her mouth. I could hear her wetness now. Each time I asked her, Anyone? she said, No one.

And each time she was a little further away.

I kicked off the heavy quilt. There was more room for manoeuvre. I said in her ear, No one? And she said, Only you. And I said, No one. And she said, Only you. And by the time I had asked her the question a dozen times she could no longer hear me and I could no longer hear her but we were both as completely in the same place as we would ever be.

Later she said, adjusting the quilt, Mr chinchpokli, do you know something? Your answer is always a question!

Hurtling down the deep chute of sleep, I murmured, Inside all our questions lie all our answers! without having any idea what it meant.

The next day I did not get out of bed till evening.

By the time I rose and went for a bath the workers had packed up for the day and Fizz was sitting on the terrace watching the sun fall. In the morning when I had woken I'd asked Fizz to pass me one of the notebooks to flip through while I sipped my tea. I ended up having breakfast and lunch in bed, and managed to stay with the reading through all the hammering and shaving and jabbering that filled the house.

When Rakshas came to give me lunch, he said, without a smile, My father said the wisest men are those who know the limits of their wisdom.

Fizz was too busy conferring with the masons and carpenters to bother about me. The few times she sauntered in she said, The great lord chinchpokli hard at work!

I saw the day change through the window opposite our bed. The oak leaves come alive with chattering birds in the morning; the oak leaves shine with the polish of the midday sun; the oak leaves dance with the tearing wind in the afternoon; the oak leaves fade and settle with the approach of night. When I threw aside the quilt – rank with sleep smells – to rise and bathe, the day was done and I had read a mere ten pages.

They were enough to have stopped me dead in my tracks.

The wordwheels were difficult to read and the language was con-voluted, with terrible grammar and spellings. Often the sentences didn't seem to follow each other in any logical progression. You had to keep going back to grasp the full essence of what was being said. For someone who wrote so poorly sixty-four notebooks was a dis-play of incredible self-belief.

But the content. But the content . . .

When I walked out onto the terrace, Fizz said, So what does he say?

I said, He does not.

She said, Then?

I said, She does.

Unusually, it took Fizz a moment and then she said, You mean it's a woman?

I said, Yes. We should have figured by the handwriting.

So who is she?

I've only managed to read ten pages. Can't tell from those.

Obviously the one who lived here?

I would imagine so. Where else would a chest full of notebooks come from? Must be the lady they refer to. The one who built the house.

What's her name?

Don't know yet. Taphen just refers to her as the madam. I don't think he knows too much about her either. I have asked him a couple of times and he's always vague. Just says she was very bold, very brave. In his words: believe you me, sir, even the white men were afraid of her.

What did you find?

I told you. Very little. Just managed to read ten pages. It's very difficult. The syntax is bad, the writing illegible – not easy to make sense of it.

Fizz got up and with her feet began to tamp down the soil around the silver oak we had planted on the terrace. A few hard heels on its right side and the sapling straightened up a little. Its leaves had a black discolouration on the edges. Probably the frost. She wiped her sneakers on a tuft of grass and said, So what did you figure out?

I said, From ten pages? Lady Chatterley does the lower Himalayas.

She said, What?

It took me ten minutes to explain what I meant. She made incredulous noises. She wasn't sure whether I was telling the truth or having her on.

Finally she said, So what is it? A kind of novel?

I said, I have no idea. The material is startling, but I don't know whether it's real or dreamt up.

She said, But I must say you haven't lost your ability to instantly unearth the dirty bits in any book! Sixty-four volumes and you find the right ten pages!

In the night, as I was about to get into bed and pick up the notebook again, the fragment of a vague memory floated to the surface. I

immediately laced up my keds, pulled on a jacket and asked Fizz to
do the same.

She said, Where do you want to go?

Let's go and meet Taphen.

Now?

I said, I need to ask him something.

Now?

Now.

Bagheera, whom we had acquired from a retired army officer in
Bhimtal, was still an eight-week-old pup – a black ball of fur who ate
and slept the whole day in a wicker basket in the kitchen. So there
was no dog to accompany us, but I picked up the smooth sandalwood stick we had once bought in Janpath, and Fizz had her small
black Lazerlight. It cut a sharp hole in the darkness and the devil did
not jump us at the lower gate.

When we took the curving path up from the road to Taphen's
house our feet crunched on fallen oak leaves and gravel, setting the
dogs hollering. The naked bulb, slung from the soapnut tree where
the path bent back for the last stretch, cast sinister shadows all
around. By the time we rounded the bend the barking had become
infernal. It had many registers: wild yapping; bass growling; sharp
yipping; and an unbroken howl set to rouse the valley. But we had
been there before – when we were buying the house – and knew that
when the first curtain of dark was drawn, Taphen tied up his dogs
inside two large iron-grilled cages that flanked his front door. The
guldaar – the spotted one – loved dog meat, and four dogs were
merely four swipes of his paw. Some nights the leopard came and sat
in front of the cages, and the dogs lost their bowels and became
mewling wrecks.

Taphen was soaking drunk and slumped in his easy chair. His thin
arms hung at his side, fingertips touching the green linoleum floor.
His half-golden glass sat by his right fingers. Ringlets – hundreds,
overlapping each other – marked the floor around the chair,
commemorating years of golden evenings. A small television set
was making noises in front of him. All you received here was the

national channel, Doordarshan, and you had to rattle the roof antenna every day to coax the link. At the moment you could hear nothing but a crackle and see nothing but blurred figures.

We sat down on a flowery suite with curvy legs and curvy back.

Damyanti said, Come and share him with me! Why should Damyanti alone be the beneficiary of the wisdom of the great Taphen Juggler, the Sheikh Chilli of Kumaon!

And she went inside to get fresh glasses.

I said, Stephen, tell me something.

He said, Why should I tell you anything? Why should I tell anyone anything? Does anyone tell me anything? And who are you?

I said, Stephen, when I came to your house the first time you had a portrait of a woman on your wall. Where is that? And who is she?

He said, She is the Queen of Sheba, and she is sleeping. And she doesn't sleep with blackies like you!

Damyanti had come in with two squat glasses on a plastic tray and was offering them to us with a half-bottle of Bagpiper. But I was in no mood to drink.

I said, Shut the fuck up, Stephen, and answer my question!

Fizz put a hand on my arm and said, I think we should go.

But I was in no mood to back off. Taphen was looking at me with bloodshot eyes. He picked his glass, drained it and parted his wasted thighs.

Damyanti said, Taphen, don't say a word now!

Taphen said, You bastard Dilliwalla have you ever taken a lollu ride? Come, I will give you a hotfat lollu ride. In one shot I will show you all of Kumaon! Two shots all of India! Three shots all of the world! Eiffel Tower to Empire State Building. Come!

Fizz got up and said, I am going.

Damyanti said, Shut up, you wretched fellow! Oh why can't Michael give you a poke that cures you of this disease!

I said, Taphen, you are a dog! And you'll die like a dog!

Fizz said, Stop it! What's wrong with you?

Taphen meantime had removed his belt and was struggling to unbutton his grey trousers.

Fizz was now pulling on my arm and Damyanti said, Please, sir, leave now before he fills us all with shame.

When we walked out the door the dogs began to wail and yowl, throwing themselves against the grille, drooling at the mouth. There were aluminium bowls of water lying in both the cages, dented and cracked, and they rattled and splashed as the dogs banged into them.

Outside Damyanti said, joining her palms, You must forgive us. He is sometimes man sometimes beast. Even I don't know when he will be what.

Before Fizz could soothe her I said, Damyanti, do you know the picture I am talking about? Who is that? And where is the picture?

From inside Taphen exploded at the top of his voice, Bastard blackie, doing khusphus with my wife! Come and talk to Taphen's lollu and then you will know! Who is she? She is your mummy's mummy! And she will sleep with me tonight!

In her firmest voice Fizz said, pulling on my arm, We are leaving now!

Damyanti said, Sir, please . . .

Fizz was furious. She walked ahead of me all the way home, the beam of her Lazerlight bobbing angrily. When we were in bed, she said, What's wrong with you? What was all that about?

I said, I am sorry.

Actually I was quite surprised myself. I thought I had learnt to sidestep Taphen when he was a beast.

Fizz said, And what is this picture you were getting hysterical about?

I said, Nothing. Really nothing.

Fizz curled up into a ball and was asleep in minutes. With all the tramping you had to do up and down supervising the work, it was impossible not to get bone tired. But my muscles were slack with rest and there was no way sleep could seduce them. I wanted to pick up the diaries and read some more, but if there was one thing Fizz could never handle it was an overhead light when she was sleeping. At home I had a shaded lamp next to my bed, but all we had here was a big hundred-watt bulb, stark naked in a white plastic holder, throwing a bright splash on our heads and on the blue-washed walls.

I remembered the portrait. It was a large oil, set deep in a thick wooden frame. The colours were not rich, in fact they were a little faded, a sort of bleached yellow. There was no background, no setting, just the portrait filling the frame. The woman in it had been painted at a slight angle, the right shoulder leading. She was clearly a white woman and you didn't have to look at her wide-necked gown to know it. The features were sharp, but the mouth was wide and full – presenting a curious mix of restraint and recklessness. The hair was caught at the back, covering her ears, disappearing into the back of the canvas. But it was done in layers, full, not plastered to her head.

Though she was painted in slight profile, the painter had made her look straight out of the canvas. His triumph had been the eyes. They were alive and looked back at you with a disconcerting directness. Boldly he had also painted in the hint of a cleavage: a line and, flanking it, the swell. Around her neck was a pendant, a religious symbol, hung on a link chain.

The portrait – twice seen fleetingly amid the plastic bric-a-brac of Taphen's sitting room, including gaudily painted terracotta Jesuses and cute nativity scenes – had snagged in my memory because the religious symbol was not a cross but an om. I had thought then that it was the kind of cheap portraiture billboard painters did in 1960s and 1970s India to hawk to the gentry in the small post-colonial towns – anglicized figures which suggested grace and refinement. I thought the om was an irreverent painter's subversive touch.

In the room in the dark it was utterly quiet. The last dogs had gone to sleep and the nightjar was lying low today. If it had toc-ed, I had missed it. I lay on my back with my eyes open, but I could see nothing, not even the thick rafters right above. My head was full of what I had read, and my mind was beginning to play tricks, casting the woman in the portrait into the words in the tan notebook. I tried to separate what I had read from the image of the woman, but I couldn't. And then, as I watched with sightless eyes, the woman began to do the things she had described. I closed my eyes, and pulled the quilt over my head, and threw an arm around Fizz, and pushed my face into her billowing hair, but I could still see the woman. She was looking directly at me.

I stared back into her eyes and was still doing so when I fell asleep. And then I had a vivid dream unlike any other in years. The lady in the portrait had slipped into bed with me and was doing with me all that was written in the notebook. Her full, wide mouth was excruciating wherever it touched me; her hands probed me in ways I had never known. She moved all over me, going everywhere. I was handled, mastered, consumed till I was whimpering.

When I woke in the morning I felt I was back in school, an adolescent whose body is best unlocked when his mind is asleep. I remembered her nipples were fat, and I remembered there was a big mole under her left breast. Some of the encounter was hazy. I could not recall if she finished me. I don't think she did; I carried over my arousal to Fizz and, turning her over on her back, filled her with an urgency I had not felt in a long time.

Later, resisting the urge to take up the notebook again, I got ready and walked back to Taphen's house. Our own place by then was humming with voices demanding, commanding, reprimanding, and a variety of tools hammering, shaving, plastering. Rakshas was still maintaining a low profile and I overheard him ask Fizz why we had gone to Taphen's the night before. Rakshas's ire was basically directed at me. I don't think he blamed Fizz for anything. Then or later.

Taphen was not at home. Damyanti said he had woken feeling violently ill and had called Michael to come up from Haldwani and take him to the hospital. She looked tired herself. She was sitting on the steps of the porch, between the dog cages, her grey hair loose, oil glistening in it, taking in the sun. All four dogs were splayed out on the concrete patch in front of her doing the same. They opened their eyes and looked at me without stirring. Damyanti said they had had a bad night. The panther had come in the small hours of the morning and convulsed them into a frenzy. She said she had spent all morning cleaning the cages.

I said I wanted to see the portrait.

She was wary. She looked all over – her feet, the sky, the dogs – for help.

An exhausted woman digging daily into her inner resources to cope.

For a while she pretended she was not sure where it had been stacked away. When I refused to budge and insisted we take a look around the house, she capitulated. It was stashed in an enclosed veranda – a kind of storeroom – at the back of their bedroom, beside a set of broken dining chairs. It had been covered with a fraying lime-green sheet with white lilies printed on it. When I picked it up, uncovered it and propped it up on one of the chairs, I realized that in recalling it I had been much too kind to its condition.

The bottom of the frame had split, pushing out splinters; the paint was cracking in tiny wafers at the edges; and the expanse of creamy chest had been tarnished by sharp objects, pencils, pens, abrasions by other furniture. Someone – a child – had even tried to mark the tips of the breasts with barely noticeable points of grey lead. The om around the neck, done in a silvery blue, stood out even more in the general degradation of the canvas.

I pulled up a chair and sat down opposite her. Miraculously the face had survived without a blemish. The skin ran smooth, with rose highlights on the cheeks. The nose had lost none of its sharpness. The mouth was an invitation, the ripe core of the frame. Its promise balanced the hauteur of the nose. Damyanti went away to brew me a cup of tea. The woman assessed me with steady eyes, a slim, prematurely greying man in blue jeans and a maroon pullover, unshaven for two days, a tiny gold stud glinting in his left ear. She looked into his eyes and understood it was easy to haunt him; he was the kind of man who courted demons. She understood men like that. She wondered if he knew where he was headed. It made her smile.

As I looked at the portrait, I felt the eyes had begun to crinkle. I looked away, over to the tree-layered mountain slopes of Bhumiadhar, to clear my head. It was a lovely morning. Blue skies, strong silent sunlight, the eagles beginning to cut air circles. Damyanti came in with the tea, a big ceramic mug with Donald Duck cavorting on it. I looked back at the woman. She had stopped smiling, but was still looking at me.

I said, Damyanti, sit down.

Damyanti had tied up her hair. It was wetly flat with the oil; her scalp shone through. She was wearing her unease plainly. When I made the demand again, she pulled in a cane murra from the bedroom – its twine unravelling – and sat down on it.

I said, Who is she?

She said, I only know what Taphen tells me. He says this is the lady of the house.

Is she the one who built the house? The house we live in now.

Yes. That is what Taphen says.

What else does Taphen say?

Nothing. He refuses to talk about her. In the beginning when I would ask he would shout at me. When he was man he would say, She was one-of-a-kind lady, no one like her, a goddess, full of loving and giving. And when he was beast he would scream, What do you want to know, you crazy bitch? She was a hundred times crazier than you! She was a bloody churail! A white witch! And don't keep asking questions because if she gets between your legs you will be running up and down the hill roads screaming for help!

I said, So what do you know?

She said, Nothing, sahib. This painting used to be in the big house where you now live, but when Taphen began to try and sell the house, he brought it here and put it in our drawing room. When I tried to clean it, he shouted at me and said, Don't touch it, you crazy bitch! Just let it hang there.

You didn't ask him why?

Can you ever ask Taphen anything sensible, sahib? Then some months ago he is sitting there one evening becoming a beast, and he begins to shout, Damyanti! Damyanti! Take her away! Take her away! See how she is looking at me! I am telling you she wants something from me! She is going to punish me for selling the house! And so I took the painting off the wall and put it here in the storeroom. Next morning he says, all man now, You did the right thing, Damyanti. Now cover her face with a sheet. You know what they used to say here: if you look into her eyes then you are lost.

I said, How did Taphen come to have control of the house?

She said, I don't really know. He refuses to talk about any of it. But I think his father worked for her and she left it to him.

What else do you know?

Nothing. Except that Taphen says she hardly ever stepped out of the grounds of the estate. She never went to Nainital or Haldwani or Bhimtal or Saattal or Naukuchiyatal or Ranikhet or Almora. Many people around here never ever saw her. Taphen says she had a rifle and she used to fire at anyone who entered the grounds uninvited. He says she did not even like the white man to visit her. Sometimes English officers who came to meet her were asked to leave from the gate.

Does Taphen remember meeting her?

He doesn't tell. He says he was too small when she died. And he says she refused to be buried in the big graveyard where all the whites are, up on the Nainital road. She wanted to be buried in Gethia.

In Gethia? Where?

On the hill. Behind the house.

Do you have any other picture of her?

No, sahib, nothing. I don't even want this one. It spooks me.

I said, Does Taphen have anything else of hers? Anything.

No, nothing. Nothing that I know of. That day when Dukhi and Bideshi found the box and opened it, Taphen went mad. He began to bark and howl like the dogs when they smell the panther. He went walking up and down the rooms, beating his fists against the walls. He kept shouting, Dig, dig, dig! Everybody wants to dig for trouble!

Dig up each other's pasts, dig up mosques, dig up temples, dig up churches, dig up houses! Is like digging your nose! You dig more you get more dirty! You have to blow it all away! Blow it away and forget it! Blow and go! Blow and go!

I turned to look at her sitting on the chair and she was looking back at me steadily. Her eyes were blue-grey, and I stared into them for so long that my eyelids began to ache. They seemed full of a kind of knowing, and I wanted to know what it was.

As I rose, her eyes held me, challenging me to leave. I stood rooted. Then Damyanti stepped forward and draped the floral sheet over her face, and I was free to move.

I said, Did he discuss what they found in the box with you?

She said, Discuss? Taphen? You know donkeys that give milk?

Outside the sun was blinding, and the lazing dogs did not cock an ear as I walked down the steps and caught the path that ran away from the sun, between the ranks of old oaks, winding down to the main road.

In the afternoon, while the house was being hammered and plastered and caressed and cajoled, I quietly peeled away to take the goat track to the top of the ridge. Though it was right above our house, we had not explored it. But from the house you could see all the way to the top, the big pine trees marching in single file till they reached the peak and gathered in a cluster to survey the valley and take stock of their strategy.

The grass here grew in thick golden clumps and the path was rocky – often to the point of slipperiness – and I had to step with care. When you were not on shrapnelling rock you were on a carpet of pine needles, and that – given the absence of traction in my flat rubber sandals – called for even more sureness of foot. At this hour you could see the occasional goat munching up the hillside, but soon they would all be retrieved by their owners and corralled in.

It took no more than fifteen minutes for me to crest the peak. The view from here was spectacular. Parts of the valley not visible from the house opened up. A large seasonal pond lay right below me like a sheet of glass, not a scratch breaking its surface. Later I learnt it was the cricket field in the winter months and the village swimming pool in the monsoon. Next to it the valley cut one fold deeper and you could see a few small huts studded inside it. Around me were old pine trees, some towering fifty feet and more. There was a lot of thorny undergrowth, alive with insects and flitting birds. When you looked back at the house you only saw the roof – its smooth red skin neatly lined with ridges, the Nainital pattern – and the two chimneys in tight hats.

Despite all my attempts, I failed to find her grave. The brambly undergrowth got in the way, and though the hilltop looked small from a distance it was much too large to scour in a few hours. At one point I caught the dull glint of masonry and thought I had found it. But when I cleared the creepers I realized it was just a small water tank, long abandoned, which had been cracked open by the foliage over the years.

When I got back Fizz said nothing. That was Fizz, always slow to suspicion, inclined to trust. The day's work was over and Bideshi and Dukhi were sitting on the front veranda, drawing out next week's plans with her. Chatur was feeding his hen mustard seeds from his cupped palm. After each peck the begum cocked her head to look into the boy's eyes, and her throat gobbled with food and emotion. When I bent through the barbed wire to enter our property I had noticed Rakshas standing near the kitchen wall, observing my excursion. His handsome face was set and neither of us said anything.

I picked up the tan book and went and settled on the terrace, and when Fizz finished with the workers and went in for a bath I was still there, and when the light faded I was still there, and later I took the book with me to bed, and when Fizz tried to open a conversation about the day I stonewalled her, and when she put her hand on my thigh I ignored it, and when she, exhausted by the day, turned over to go to sleep, I felt a sense of relief.

I turned off the naked bulb and turned up the hurricane lamp I had asked Rakshas to leave by my bedside.

Drowsily, Fizz said, Found more dirty bits?

And then she was gone. I dipped my left shoulder and leaned into the lamplight; by the time I fell asleep, the book crooked in my forearm, several hours had elapsed.

At some point in the night I woke suddenly. The lamp was burning out its last millimetre of wick. It cast no light; it was just a yellow pinprick in the grey night. Some dark instinct had dragged me out of my slumber. I pushed aside the heavy quilt and swung my legs out. It took me a moment to find my rubber slippers. With utmost caution, moving on the lightest of feet, I walked across the room – the floorboards gave, but stopped just short of creaking. I eased the door open and then tiptoed along the edge of the lobby, keeping my feet on the end planks, where they rested solidly on the stone wall. Down the stairs I counted carefully and stepped over the sixth. When I reached the bottom the darkness diffused a bit. There was moonlight swimming in through the windows. I walked through the living room carefully and when I came into the dining room she was sitting on the old easy chair, her fine bones catching the night light.

I saw her and knew she was waiting for me.

She was wearing a maroon silk gown, and though the bodice ran low, the gown had high collars that banked her neck and hair. Those eyes – the painter's triumph – were looking at me with mysterious intent. She gave a slow smile, her full mouth blooming into a reckless promise. When I got close to her she reached out with her hands, put them on my shoulders and pushed me down to my knees. As I watched, kneeling in front of the chair, she pulled up her voluminous gown slowly. Her legs were full – the thighs round and heavy – and her skin was smooth, with a kind of inner glow. When she parted her legs her readiness shone.

She put her hands in my hair and pulled my face into her. She held it there and the only things that were moving were my lips and tongue. There was so much of her it filled my mouth. Her root caught in my teeth; her body opened up on the wide wings of eagles. I began to drown in her abundances and she held the back of my head and steered me like an animal. Then, in a bizarre move, she threw the gown over my head and it rained down my back till I was drenched in it.

I was now in a dark cave of rustling silk. I had no need to find my way; with firm hands she took me where she wished. My arousal was intense. For the first time since I was a boy I feared I would lose myself without even a touch. Soon she deftly gripped me in her toes and began to move me slowly, with the mastery of a practised hand. Enough to set me boiling; not enough to let me spill.

I did not know where my pleasure began and where it ended.

I sucked the eagle wings into my mouth and began to fly.

I went too high. I could not breathe. I began to choke. Suddenly the world bucked and it began to rain. My face was soaked, and the musky water – full of seaweed and sun – ran down the curve of my nose and past my stubbled chin, and I began to fall, and her toes pulled me down faster, and I closed my eyes, and the wet wings caressed my face, and I was dizzy and peaceful, happy to freefall endlessly, aware this was the greatest way to go.

The sweet joy of total surrender.

When I woke in the morning I was drained. In a familiar ritual, Fizz was reaching for me, her hand warm on my stomach, her breath sweet near my mouth. But I was exhausted. I hugged her, kissed her cheek, and trapped her hand where it lay between us. She tried again, kissing me under my ear, working at prising open the door of my desire, but it was firmly bolted and it hurt me to see her struggle with it. All our lives her lightest touch – a mere glance – had swung the door open. In contrition I pushed open her door instead and, putting my hand on her, loved her till she was temporarily free of me.

Then I got off the bed, took the tan book and went into the bathroom.

When we went back to Delhi I took two of the notebooks with me. The rest I carefully packed back into the chest, covered them with a plastic sheet and, getting Bideshi to fix the hinge, put a big Godrej lock on it. The brass key went into the pocket of my jeans. Uncharacteristically, we drove down in near silence. For once I did not notice anything around me. I was now fully inside my head.

Fizz was left to change the music and begin an uneasy journey into an understanding she would never finish.

Nor would I.

We delude ourselves about the neatness of life. The truth is no life is neat. Those we see – and those we read about – seem to possess neatness only because we know so little about them. The hidden sprawl behind the face at the door is always vast. Every life is beset by its unseen demons – avarice, jealousy, deceit, lust, violence, paranoia.

There is no neatness in any life – great or small. It is only an illusion men foolishly pursue. The face at the door is just that – the face at the door.

All lived lives are a mess.

The neatness in my life had begun to crumble some time before, but now it disintegrated completely as I vanished into a world of endlessly opening doors, teasing riddles and lives without boundaries.

For the first time I began to understand how shallow neatness is.

How cramping, how limiting.

For the first time I understood neat lives are comatose lives.

Soon the greatest neatness of my life, Fizz, began to diffuse.

Even now, so many years later, I find it difficult to fully understand how it happened so quickly, but each word read in those tan notebooks became like a stitch pulled out from our relationship. I read and read and read – every spare moment of my day and night – and the stitches snapped loose one by one.

I fell into those books like a frog into a well. I never wanted to get out. My universe became encased by tan leather. The books were a challenge: wordwheels without chronology, without grammar, without punctuation, riddled with archaisms and spelling errors. Sometimes I had to go over a sentence ten times before I made sense of it. In six months I managed to read only eight notebooks, but they ensured my life was in tatters.

To begin with I became erratic about going to work. Then, soon enough, I resigned. No one even noticed. Shulteri took the letter and marked it to King Cupola with a terse recommendation, Please accept. The fat Aggarwal boy from the accounts department came and retrieved my identity card and made me sign many papers. He said my full and final settlement would reach me in a month. I considered going round to make my last goodbyes, till I realized my life might have been pulled inside out but no one was interested and nothing in the office had changed. The activity on the greased pole was as frenetic as ever and, energized by new entrants, the Glansmen were busy giving each other serious boot-on-face.

The laws of testosterone – demanding relentless competition and conquest – were firmly in place. Every man was an erection that would not be denied.

So I disappeared like a shadow in the dark. I had become so insignificant that I did not even merit the ritual farewell cake with pineapple chunks studded in the cream and a faded red cherry stuck on top.

Fizz was worried when I quit. But our conversation had dried to a seasonal river in summer. We kept talking the functional stuff; we kept going up to the house every weekend; the house kept taking shape – roofs were pitched, bathrooms laid, wiring infused, pipes dug; but with every week the last pockets of nourishment in our relationship were sucked dry, and soon we had to struggle to find a single drop in the parched riverbed.

I stopped going out altogether. And when our friends dropped in I locked myself in the study on the pretext of finishing something urgent. Sometimes I agreed to go catch a film, but Fizz could see it was a grudging concession to her. She was right. I couldn't wait to get back to the notebooks. There was life in there that I could taste, drink, seek out. The small talk of our friends was unbearable, as were Fizz's workaday concerns.

Bouts of sullenness began to grip her. Tragically, they left me unaffected.

❦

The fact was I was too busy grappling with my own self. On some days I feared I was losing my mind. I had been a cynic and an atheist all my life. I had railed against the rituals and religiosity that filled my family and clan. Everyone I knew was full of superstition: don't call out at the back of someone who's leaving; don't travel on the ninth day of a trip; if a dead person asks you for something in a dream you are in trouble; if a cat crosses your path do not proceed . . .

Everyone I knew had a personal godman, guru or idiot-savant. As a boy, I had watched with disgust my parents and other clansmen – including my boxwallah suited-booted-tied father and my Manhattany cousins Tarun and Kunwar – genuflect abjectly to scruffy and illiterate seers, sufis, mystics, clairvoyants. Holy men whose wisdom was tested even as they greedily mopped up offerings from their devotees.

The disgust increased as I grew older, discovered the vast archives of Western literature and philosophy and became a child of empiricism and rationality.

I understood Nehru; I did not understand Gandhi.

I understood science and art; I did not understand ritual and religion.

I understood romantic and sexual desire; I did not understand supernatural and extraterrestrial devotion.

We would go somewhere. To Agra to my uncle's, to see the Taj Mahal, the Fort, Fatehpuri Sikri, and someone – my uncle, his brother, someone – in the evening would say, Bhaisahib, have you heard of Baba GoleBole? He never speaks, and he blesses you with a kick to your head. And they say whatever wish – one wish – you have in your head at the precise moment he kicks it, that wish comes true. Some people have got distracted, had the wrong thought in their head at the time and paid a heavy price for it. There's a Mr Pandey, works in the State Bank, lives on Civil Lines, who had a fight with his wife on the way there and was angrily wishing he could be rid of her when the foot struck. The very next day she fell ill with a deep ache in her bones. Every day her situation worsened and the doctors could make no diagnosis. Finally, one day, when Mrs Pandey was almost dead, Pandey remembered his moment of error. He went rushing back to the ashram of Baba GoleBole. The Baba's aides said once the kick had been landed its power could not be recalled. Pandey begged and pleaded. The aides conferred. There was a way. If Pandey got himself another kick and in that very moment reversed the wish, perhaps it would work. So in went Pandey again. The Baba was sitting on a six-foot-high wooden platform, his legs dangling, silver bichchoos adorning every toe. Pandey bowed under him, his hands clasped together, and was kicked in the head. This time his thoughts were in order. Two days later Mrs Pandey began to recover. She was fine and fat now and back to haranguing Pandey.

So next day off would go my whole family to be kicked in the head by Baba GoleBole.

Everyone I knew had a humbug story about how they – or someone they knew – had witnessed a miracle. A miracle cure, a miracle piece of information, a miracle apparition. I had a cousin in our Salimgarh village, who worked the fields, who said he had met Parashurama – the legendary axe-wielding slayer of the kshatriyas – while walking through the babool forest one night. He said the demi-god was striding very fast, ten feet tall, his huge axe in his hand, his hair flowing to his shoulders. My cousin saw him and shrank in terror. But Parashurama broke step and gave him an effulgent smile. So empowering was the smile that my cousin felt the strength in his limbs instantly quadruple. The next day when an ox misbehaved on the plough he brought it to the ground with a single blow of his hand.

There was another aunt of mine, LaddoMassi – my mother's cousin – who lived in a crumbling village house just outside Amritsar. She had once mastered the art of making a cooking stove talk. Many in our clan had been witness to this feat. LaddoMassi – who was class six fail, and had in nine efficient years produced four sons and three daughters – took a brass pump stove with three legs, shined it up till it sparkled, then set it in the middle of a deep brass thaal, also shining with a mustard-oil wash. The area around the thaal was decorated with arcane patterns in golden haldi, red chilli, white salt, black pepper and the green heart-shaped leaves of the peepul. It was the twilight hour and the light was beginning to fade. The Stove-Devta had to be summoned after sunset and before nightfall. LaddoMassi began to chant an invocation urging him to appear. It was a simple request, repeated over and over. Ten minutes into the chanting the stove began to tremble. LaddoMassi then instructed everyone gathered in the courtyard to shut their eyes tightly and not say a word.

She then threw the first question: Stove-Devta, in how many days will my son return from fighting insurgents in Nagaland? He was a captain in the Gurkha Rifles. Amid the straining ears and closed eyes, four distinct tinny taps broke the silence of the crowded courtyard. A gasp ran through everyone.

LaddoMassi then asked, Four days?

No tinny tap came.

She then said, Four weeks?

A clear tinny tap rang out.

After that everyone got a chance to ask their question, and it went on for a long time till the Stove-Devta's limbs were exhausted and he could answer no more.

Family lore maintained that all that was presaged came to pass.

My Manhattany cousins and their swish parents had a Guruji too, on the outskirts of Bombay. They sought his advice in matters of money, property, sorrow and celebration. The young Guruji – he was no more than twenty-five and had announced his extraordinariness by reciting the Gita from inside his mother's womb – the young Guruji wrote mantras with a plastic ballpoint pen on strips of paper torn from a school register, folded them into tight chits and handed them to his devotees. My cousins had studied at Stanford and Harvard and routinely broke the bank nailing multi-million-dollar investment deals. But every night when they returned, high and happy, from nightclubs in London and New York and Bombay, having carelessly blown hundreds of dollars on food and drink and lines of drugs, having carelessly penetrated men and women, each of them put his chit into an empty glass, filled it with water and drained it in a gulp before going to sleep. The wet chits were removed, carefully put out to dry on the side table and returned to their wallets the next morning. With the godtonic inside them they were protected against all harm and primed for every success.

My uncle said and my cousins echoed, The world is full of unknown powers. Why take a chance?

Why take a chance?

When it came down to it, that was everyone's learning. Why take a chance? Every and any godman, seer, guru, baba, astrologer, tantrik, clairvoyant, crank and crackpot might hold the key to your destiny. We all knew true stories of the kind. Why take a chance?

So no one in India was taking a chance. Everyone had their supernatural ticket tucked into their back pocket. Everyone had access to some godtonic.

I had fought it all my life, though admittedly the passing years had made a dent in my profound cynicism. I had long argued that if there was a greater god his principles were sadly out of alignment. What should matter to him was the intrinsic worth of people, their daily decencies and their everyday conduct. Why should half-ass rituals and token obeisances count for anything? Why should he mandate an army of gimcrack middlemen in various guises – each extracting a commission – to lead the faithful to him? Why decree all this bowing and scraping?

This was the behaviour of a second-rate potentate not a greater god.

And if it was a second-rate potentate to whom we were being led then I was not interested. On the other hand, if he was the real McCoy, then I was doing fine in body and spirit.

I would be the agnostic god embraced. If there was one. And if he was worth his calling.

Quod erat demonstrandum.

The answer no one gave me then, and the answer I know today – when it is all over and nothing matters any more – is that the bowing and scraping is not for the mighty King Dong who sits above us all. We do it for ourselves, to train ourselves in humility. Or so it ought to be.

Our daily tutorial in arrogance management.

The power walk of the ego to keep it from fat. Four kilometres in forty minutes four days a week: the heart-watchers' formula. Seven genuflections for seven minutes seven days a week: the ego-watchers' formula.

To remind us that we know that we do not know.

But at the time the algebra of my beliefs was being held up to serious scrutiny. Having been reduced from non-believer to unbeliever, I felt I was now being set up for further humiliations. From Nothing Else Exists to Who Knows, Perhaps to Yes It Does. I was acutely embarrassed by this slide. I could hear the echo of years of strident argument – as I trotted out theories of empiricism, rationality and evolution – boom in my head. I could hear Fizz and me laughing and wondering at the mumbo-jumbo that infected even the sanest of our friends.

And I could hear the sneering voice of my father say, Your kind of knowledge is actually a profound ignorance.

So while I was aware of the crisis I was triggering in Fizz's life, I was even more acutely aware of the growing chaos of my own. There was no way I could talk to anyone about it. What was there to say? That I had drowned deep in some strange notebooks. That decoding their secrets had become the single obsession of my life. That it was not just that. That I was also hallucinating every night. That I felt beset by a presence. That I sensed it at my shoulder when I sat reading. That I sensed it in my bed when I lay sleeping. That some days I woke in the mornings feeling ravished and drained, resentful and desirous. That I had tried to pull myself away from it all, but was simply unable to do so. That I thought I knew who the presence was. Though I did not know what it wanted from me, barring a seduction that was frightening in its intangibility and power.

What was there to say?

That I was having an out-of-body experience? I felt like my cousin who met Parashurama in the forest, ten feet tall with the giant axe on his shoulder, biding his time before launching another global attack on the kshatriyas. I wanted to laugh myself out of the room. I needed a kick in the head from Baba GoleBole. I needed a hundred kicks in the head from everyone I knew.

But there was nothing I could say.

And Fizz could only watch in despair.

Some months after we bought it we had christened our house and put up a marble plaque on the stone pillar that held up the upper gate. In elegant Trajan, all caps, the old Muslim carver in Haldwani had chiselled, First Things; and underneath it, in Times italic, our names. He had copied my printout to perfection, then added something of his own. In a flourish at the bottom he had put a single neem sprig, artfully curved, its five leaves etched with intimate delicacy.

First Things.

What was in the beginning.

Before ambition, before job, before office, before designation, before byline, before car, before house, before marriage, before need.

Before need, before need, before need . . .

Purity of the primary. The wholeness at the start.

Love and desire.

Heart and art. Fizz and me.

First Things.

In elegant Trajan with fine serifs.

It was ironic, for we were now adrift in the country of last things. Where the fruit decays on the branch before it can bloom. Where the falling rain burns all it touches. Where the air sears the lungs with every breath. Where love has no passion and is the mere memory of another time.

Fizz did not know many things. But she did know that my body had turned against her. It had broken a pattern that had been the greatest verity and exhilaration of our life.

It had, it seemed, in a deep act of betrayal, set out in search of another.

# BOOK FOUR

# Kama: Desire

## An Unlikely American

Catherine had first encountered India in her father's store.

John's Oriental Curios was an unlikely store quietly tucked into Chicago's Lake Street. It had a narrow facade, and was set a little deeper in the lane than the other buildings because it had a wide veranda. If you were riding by briskly there was every chance you would miss its ornately carved walnut door, with the image of a springing tiger, and prominent brass studs in the four corners. But if you were sauntering past slowly – which no one in Chicago was doing even in 1897 – then you could not miss the Chinese silk screens shading the windows, the Ceylonese demon mask scowling above the entrance, and the heavy wood-and-iron Rajputana shield with the insignia of the sun at its centre hung next to the carved door with two glinting swords crossed above it. And if the door happened to swing open as you walked past, you would be transfixed by the magnificent curving tusks of an Indian elephant growing out of the far wall, goring the thick and musty air inside the store.

If you stepped in, pushing aside the curtain of tiny carved animals in wood and ivory hung down the doorway, you fell through a geographic warp. The room was lit by shrewdly placed gas jets that created waves of shadows. John understood his clientele and kept the illumination low, enchancing the mood of mystery. But the fact is even a blind customer would have instantly known he had entered somewhere unusual. The first breath would have caught the rich redolence of strange spices, Indian ittars, preserved animal skins, polished sandalwood, opium hookahs and the subtler fragrances of dried fruits, deodar chests, scented silks and Assam tea.

And if you were not blind you would be accosted by an exotic visual feast that could not be worked through in any single visit. More exciting than the curves of white ivory scything the air were the gleaming tiger skins hung on the walls: the black and orange stripes so aesthetic, the snarling maws at head level baring polished canines rich with menace. Each disembodied animal had a plaque nailed next to it. Catherine's favourite was a slim-faced one with a damaged eye. The One-Eyed Princess of Kaladhungi, Kumaon, United Provinces, 1892. Her look was almost benign, as if she were winking. When John sold it one morning, his ten-year-old daughter was deeply upset and, having failed to convince her that a shopkeeper cannot get attached to his goods, he tried to recover it, but the customer was a newly rich realtor from Boston and could not be traced.

As compelling for Catherine were the ranks of big jars with snakes floating in them, chemically frozen. There were kraits, vipers, rat snakes, grass snakes, and the splendid hamadryad, the cobra, with its menacing hood furled in death. There was also an ochre-coloured speckled rock python, but it was too fat and big to put into a jar and had been preserved in a big square aquarium, where it bulged against the glass obscenely. The young girl peered at them all for hours in revulsion. There were other animal pickings, which she found much less interesting: porcupine quills in a glass; pelts of flying foxes, jungle cats and wild dogs; some giant moths, butterflies and beetles in display cases; stuffed owls and the great Indian hornbill; trophies of antelope and shiny skins of spotted deer; showy fans of iridescent peacock feathers; occasionally the skin of a cheetah, so feminine in its silky slimness; and the curved horn of a rhino, grey and leathery, with no trace of appeal.

Her father kept the rhino horn behind the mahogany counter where he made his reckonings, and sometimes when his mates came by they held it in their hands, stroked it slowly and laughed about it.

One of the things Catherine loved doing in the store was opening up the pouches of rare spices and inhaling their aromas. She loved the smell of the deodar chests and would put her smooth cheeks against the cool wood, close her eyes and float in the light fragrance. The scent of the ittars she found too strong, but she quite liked the peculiar pungency of the animal skins, hide and hair, dead yet alive.

She also loved gazing at the prints of ink drawings and watercolours that filled an alcove beneath the tusks. They were mostly scenes from the subcontinent. Armies clashing, one set in caps and coats, the other in turbans and flared tunics. Grand processions, with caparisoned elephants, cheetahs on chains and dark-skinned multitudes cramming the pathways. Maharajas in state at opulent durbars being cooled by giant fans and sporting aggressive whiskers. Bazaar scenes with a bustle and energy – of goods, people and animals – impossible to conjure in all of Chicago. Animated cock fights with cheering throngs, some European, mostly Indian. Riverside ghats with burning pyres and praying natives. Hunting tableaux with the cornered tiger crouching at its last stand while armed white men on elephants close in for the kill. Indian women in half-veils, sharp of feature, rounded in body, with eyes the shape of almonds.

There was another set of prints that lay in a drawer behind the counter where John sat. Catherine discovered them when she was thirteen, and they set her to flames. The palm-sized prints lay trapped in a book called *The Indian Kamasutra: The Play of Love*, and showed men and women doing things to each other she could never have imagined. So graphic, so engorged, so naked, so acrobatic, so ecstatic. So boldly the almond-eyed women seized the moment, so in control did they seem. The girl peered at the pictures when she was alone in the store and felt her body burn and melt.

One in particular transfixed her. A big dark man, without a turban, with a flowering moustache, his torso bare, a servant of some sort: facing him an almond-eyed beauty, voluptuous in the extreme, her breasts swelling out of her bodice, her garments made of rich brocade, a princess of some sort. From the folds of the man's dhoti springs an unnaturally swollen phallus; holding it in her left hand, her skirts pulled up to her waist, the princess wraps her naked right leg around the servant's broad back, and feeds it into her thick-lipped softness. There is no ambiguity to the scene: the woman is the aggressor, the man compliant. Both their faces are radiant with pleasure. Each time Catherine saw the picture she clutched her hands between her thighs and felt clammy and faint.

What bored her the most in her father's store were the counters full of silks and satins, astrakhans and sable-trimmed coats, fancy cashmere shawls and fur-lined gowns. Nor was she beguiled by the intricate jewellery, the necklaces and earrings, nose studs and toe rings, of emerald and ruby and jade. Even the fancy mirrors studded with silver work did nothing for her. She wondered at the women who came to the store and spent their time cooing over these vanities, blind to the other riches stacked around them. If this was all they wanted, she thought with anger, they ought to go to the fancy marble-fronted buildings on State Street, to be served by courteous greeters, and escorted through vaulted rooms full of ornate trinkets and expensive apparel. Catherine decided before she was thirteen that women were blind to the wonders of the world and out of timidity used an obsession with clothes and ornaments to insulate themselves from greater experience.

Her mother was no different.

Even as a young girl Catherine saw her exquisitely pretty if consumptive mother, Emily, exhibit supreme indifference towards her father's wanderlust. She never once heard Emily ask John interested questions about where he had been and what he had seen; she never once saw her animated about his stories or his store.

She never saw her mother any other way but glacial and manicured.

She could not imagine her doing any of what she had seen at the bottom of the drawer. She could not even imagine her without her clothes, admitting to her breasts and her secret places.

John was twice as old as Emily when he first met her. He had turned forty and twenty-four of these years had been spent wandering the

world. He was an unlikely American – he had turned his back on the
safer adventures of the sprawling virgin continent, on the gold rushes and the ranch-grabbing, and had taken to the seas. He had ranged
as far as Japan, Java and Sumatra at one end, and Egypt, Tanganyika
and Zanzibar at the other. But his favourite was south Asia, the
sprawling Indian subcontinent, infested with tigers and other wild
beasts, run deep by an ancient civilization and vast learning, ruled by
a few white men but suffused by a million dark gods.

He had docked at the ports of Calcutta, Bombay and Madras, and
travelled through the heart of the land to Cawnpore, Agra, Delhi,
Lahore and the Frontier, riding the horse, the camel and the elephant,
and sometimes with relays of men bearing him on their shoulders on
bobbing palanquins; he had ridden through desert, forest, rain,
storm, enduring disease and pestilence, marvelling at the great
Mughal monuments, the ancient Hindu temples, the stark Buddhist
monasteries and the greater Himalayas.

In later years when his marriage had taken away his legs and his
travels were done he would say, That place is the good lord's wildest
experiment. There is no land anywhere – and you know I have travelled where the waters will go – that is so strange and wondrous. In
it he has thrown in all manner of things – man, beast, climate, geography, history, disease, wealth, wisdom – and he wishes to see what
will come of it.

And when the listener asked, So what has come of it? John would
become pensive and say, To speak the truth, it is impossible to tell.
Perhaps the knowledge that you can be rich and poor at the same
time, fearless and fearful in the same instant, wise and foolish in the
one breath, great and pathetic in the single moment.

And when pressed for explanation he would continue, The native
is beyond all scrutiny. He arouses deep admiration and deeper contempt. He yields to no understanding. He is full of the body and full
of the occult. He makes dazzling monuments and lives in mud huts.
He grubs for so little and rejects the much. He is stripped of all
dignity and yet fully possessed of it. He has nothing to give, but is

generous with it all. He is ground under the boot of the white man,
but will not be mastered. He is beyond all fathoming.

Of the eight trips John had made to India, twice he had acted as
a musketeering mercenary and six times he had travelled as a trader.
Once he almost died of malaria in the forests of central India near
Gwalior. For three weeks he was racked by bouts of fever and so
wasted did he become that he started to pray for death. The village
apothecary's bitter leaves, which he was forced to chew, failed to turn
the tide; then one day the village headman's wife gave him a wooden
amulet in the holy sign of om, and he put it under the rolled-up shirt
under his head and soon the fever began to recede. He still wore it
around his neck and when he slept it lay under his pillow.

The amulet did not move his wife, nor did his tales. In fact when
John told his stories his wife's eyes glazed over. The leathery adventurer, with kind eyes, hooked nose and hair in a loose ponytail, had
first seen his future wife while passing through New York. On a
whim he had dropped by to visit his aunt on 32nd Street when Emily
walked in to deliver a newly published Bible she had just bought. Her
cheeks were full of rose and she was so vulnerably beautiful that his
heart lurched.

John was a man of profound experience and appetite and had
fornicated vigorously in every land with every colour and slant of
woman. With the adventurer's sense of curiosity and joy he had discovered that – contrary to the myth men propagate – no two women
were the same. And what was most different was what men most
thought was the same. Each time a new land had been sighted from
the deck of his ship he had wondered with excitement about the
women who awaited him.

He was a connoisseur of a woman's secret places. He knew each
smelled different, tasted different, and opened up differently. Before
he began and after he was done, he loved to set a taper artfully so it
lit up the inner thighs. He most loved that last inch where the flesh
was the softest and the thigh flared the final time before melding into
the mysterious ridge where the hair grew. Sometimes he closed his
eyes and felt that final spot with just the tips of his fingers and was

transported. But what he cared for the most was the looking, the careful examination and analysis; and like an outstanding scholar he inspected his material patiently and with love, and with a photographic memory filed it away for future reference.

Many women were shamed by his frank gaze; others moved to exhibit themselves lasciviously. The study of women taught him that the great lord was an artist without limits: with creative flicks of his finger – a twist here, a curl there – he endlessly made the same thing different. A man wishing to plumb women could not do so in a lifetime. John looked and looked and noted the patterns.

There were secret places that were set close to the skin, opening up like a wet cut in a tight tangerine; there were those with softly puffy ridges, lovely as a peach, the unseen image in every schoolboy's imagination; there were those that were hooded like the cobra, flaring at the head, guarding all ingress; there were those that opened on the wings of eagles, ready to soar; there were those that hung low like the wattles of a turkey, demanding a suckling mouth; there were those that were set so far at the back that they were best approached from the rear; and there were those that were set so boldly upfront that they could be entered without the bending of a knee; there were those that were lush and tangled as Amazonian forests; and those that ran smooth as the desert sands of the Sahara; there were those with roots that stood out like flagstaffs, the muscle of their stems thick between the fingers; and those whose root continued to elude even after days of probing; there were those that yawned open in listless anticipation; and those that stayed tightly shut, waiting to be importuned; there were those whose depths could not be fully plumbed with the longest finger; and those that bottomed out at the insertion of the smallest; there were those that wept copiously all day with desire; and those that barely moistened even when laved with love; there were those that were a mere tube, a tunnel of flesh, prosaic in their purpose; and those that were a bazaar of alleys, maddening in their subtleties, capable of endless charm; and then there was the unforgettable one he saw in Calcutta's cobra gullies that was not one but two, set side by side, separated by a single wall of flesh, each capable of penetration, each different in its warm-wet embrace.

For a scholar like John this was the ultimate discovery. When he had loved both of them at length, and gazed at them long, he knew god was a good man and a glorious sensualist who wished the greatest delight for his fumbling creatures.

John's studies taught him that no man could fully know a woman unless he had known her body. And there was nothing about a woman's appearance that gave any clue to the workings of her body. A beautiful woman, bold as a harlot, could at the moment of reckoning turn cold as a fish. Whereas one retiring as a fawn, when ushered to the brink, could become a force of nature, a tigress not to be denied her share of the flesh. You could know a woman all her life, but when you entered into her private spaces you were bereft of all learning. Each time you began from the very beginning.

Each woman was a challenge, and he explored each with the same sense of wonder that he brought to his adventuring in alien lands.

And he never ceased to be surprised.

He had but one rule of thumb. He looked for some kind of allure in the face. A smoothness of skin, a fineness of feature, a fullness of mouth, a seduction of eye. As he told his mates, when his travelling legs were gone and they came to visit his store, The body doesn't matter, only the face does. When you make love to a woman all you see is her face: if it holds you to itself then all is well, and it can never be too bad.

Young Emily was blessed with a surpassing allure in the face. The moment John saw her a deep tremor rocked his soul. It was not as if he had not known love before. All men know love at the moment they pour themselves into the depths of a woman. And so had John, fleetingly, with every woman he had entered, even the most abject of the species. But this was different. It was a surge of longing, and of protectiveness, and possessiveness. A need to gather her in his embrace and make her the centre of his world. To serve and cherish and adore her. It was love – not at the moment of ecstasy, but much before and beyond the carnal.

Men are thus struck, in the strangest of ways, in the passage of a moment, in the most false of impulses, the course of their lives altered forever.

When they were eventually married John discovered his beautiful wife was innocent of her body, and incapable of ardour. With all his great experience he patiently set to mapping her slim frame. He pressed and probed, kissed and licked, caressed and sucked, watched and weighed – painstakingly searching for the buttons that would get her body ticking. He knew each body has a code; it cannot long elude a determined lover. He failed to see that some codes are so snarled they just cannot be untangled.

He went further, trying aphrodisiacs. He had always maintained a cabinet of powders and potions picked from his travels in India and the Far East. Ginseng and tiger bones, monitor lizard oils and potions of cayenne and cloves, pepper and garlic, ginger and liquorice, nutmeg and saffron. He used them on her, slyly and boldly, singly and in combinations, weekly and daily, waiting anxiously for the igniting spark.

But the body of young Emily, even after months of being laboured upon, of being cajoled and fed, remained resolutely inert.

Of course she did not shut him out. She went through the rituals, while remaining completely detached, untouched by any trace of desire.

But something strange and unexpected began to happen to John's body. It started to become addicted to the unresponsive body of his wife. Unwitting Emily had embedded in her the precise code to John's desire. The feel of her skin, the slope of her narrow waist, the musk of her secret places, the upturned nub of her breasts, even the sweetness of her breath, began to drive the crusty traveller into a frenzy. He had dined at the world's most exotic feasts, but this one dish was perfectly flavoured to master his palate.

He woke in the morning raging, and even when he was done the desire lingered. At night he was tumescent long before she came to bed. He had not known such craving since he was a teenager. He found himself peeping at her when she was at her toilet; and he found himself uncovering her gently to his gaze when she slept. Sometimes when she stood against the window to draw the blinds, he fell to his knees, and pushing up her clothes buried his face into the back of her thighs, weak with want.

She tolerated it all, giving herself up to him with neither complaint nor passion. Her Bible-beating mother's strenuous instruction – on morality and responsibility – had made her incapable of both enjoyment and protest.

And John, who had coupled with acrobatic houris and moaning beauties across four continents, struggled to understand the electrifying nature of his wife's passivity. As time passed he ceased even to look for a response in her, engaging with her body as and when he wished, sinking ever deeper into the addictions of her flesh.

His lifelong verities began to die one by one.

He had always claimed desire was a two-way street and it was not possible to desire someone who did not desire you back.

He had always felt the variety in a woman's oeuvre determined her allure.

He had always known that women's secret places and the earth's endless curve would be the leitmotifs of his life till his last day.

He had always believed that every woman you enter leaves a mark on your soul that nothing can erase.

But all that changed.

Till he had married he could recall every woman he had entered as well as the quality of the arousal, but now as young Emily lay inert and he became more and more obsessed with her, the limbs and curves, the moist openings and musks, of a hundred loved women began slowly to fade. And, as inexorably, he lost his need to chase the earth's curve. He could not bear to be away from his maddeningly passive wife for months on end. He needed the high of her body to get through the day.

He had to turn to the store to construct a surrogate world.

And in an attempt to hang on to who he had once been, he began
– like the best men of his time – to write down all he had seen and
known. Since custom at the store was always thin, he sat behind his
mahogany counter writing away in a big stitched accounts register –
putting it all down before it faded away, not knowing who he was
doing it for, not knowing what purpose it would ever serve. He wrote
without any mastery of language, but he wrote from the fullness of
his life. And because he never expected anyone ever to read it, he
wrote without artifice or fear.

Little did he know the words were vindicating themselves even as
they were being written. Little did he know he was being read as
quickly as he wrote.

Catherine, who hated her Mrs Mills Private School for Dancing,
Culture and Deportment; Catherine, who hated the sludgy gutters
and sodden streets of booming Chicago; Catherine, who hated the
itinerant ragwomen on the prowl and the Italian immigrants
aggressively hawking fruits at every corner; Catherine, who hated the
florid-faced drunken Irish policemen and the screaming adolescent
black boys vending endless newspapers; Catherine, who hated the
cold in Chicago that ate into her bones and her spirit; Catherine, who
hated the posh stores on State Street that sold vanity wares from Paris
and London; Catherine, who hated the fancy ladies cavorting on the
boulevards in silk dresses and lace parasols bought at Potter Palmer's
Emporium; Catherine, who hated going out in the family brougham
with her bloodless mother; Catherine, who hated going for picnics to
Lake Michigan with her precious cousins; Catherine, who detested
visiting her maternal uncle on Calumet Avenue with all its affectations; Catherine, who abhorred the attempts of her mother's friends
to get into the *Bon-Ton Directory* of Chicago's most prominent and
fashionable ladies; Catherine, who hated Chicago society where
men were gods and women mere decorative appendages: young
bored-angry-frustrated-contemptuous Catherine found in the words
of her father, John, the nourishment for her soul.

As the ponytailed adventurer wrote, so the young girl read. The
moment he was out the door she was behind the counter. When there

was no more to read, she looked at those hidden pictures. Between the mysterious allurements of John's Oriental Curios, and the magical tug of her father's lived words, and the dark, limb-melting seduction of those erotic drawings, Catherine grew up to be a woman for whom there was simply no place in Chicago.

If there was any Emily in Catherine it was only in her physical beauty. Her soul and her spirit were fully John's. It filled her with grief to see him greying and weakening in that imitation store. By the time she was seventeen and he was sixty, he was dying of alcohol, and his eyes were always rheumy and far away. Sometimes she got him to tell her stories she had heard many times before, but he always broke off mid-sentence, looking back to somewhere he had once been as a young man and would never go again.

Seldom, very seldom, before the first mid-morning drink, he would rouse himself for his lovely daughter and march up and down the store, his scraggly ponytail swinging, orating on the wonders of the artefacts that filled the shop, pointing at them, touching them, raising them above his head in triumph, extolling the glories of a marvellous world. But these attempts to inspire his girl quickly collapsed, and after each desperate exhibition he fell into a loneliness and a silence deeper than before.

It broke Catherine's heart.

She would have given anything to see him alive and virile and full of purpose once more.

She would have given anything to rouse him to set off on one last journey.

Emily – the indifferent object of so much adoration – Emily, a ripe forty now, had turned increasingly to religion. She had a World Saviors' Bible Club with a group of similar women. They met every day and read passages aloud. They made out lists of people who needed help. Some were met with and given unsolicited instructions; others were sent relevant biblical passages that had been hand-copied by members of the club. There was also charity to be done. The Salvation Army had by now gained strong roots in Chicago and Emily's Bible club assisted them in collecting money and materials to help the wretched. The club members maintained long and detailed lists of every act of kindness – spiritual and real – that they ever performed.

Emily and her friends were in a hurry. They needed to heap high the mountain of virtues in the world. They were millennialists, apocalyptics. The end of the world was less than a hundred years away. With their daily acts of charity and faith they were helping, in their own small way, to redeem mankind.

Catherine thought her mother was a dumb crank.

John said, In India they don't worry about the world ending. They believe the world is a playful illusion set up by a playful god. It goes on forever. Lifetimes are like sports matches. You win some, you lose some, but you are never debarred from playing. If you play well you move to a major league, if you play badly you go down to a minor. It's up to you where you want to try and play. God is not a grim judge and executioner; he is a benign referee, establishing the rules and keeping the score. And you can, if you wish, even argue with the referee and disagree with him. The referee himself, by the way, is not above some facetious foul play and rule bending.

Catherine said, And what does the World Saviors' Bible Club have to say about it?

John said, They think it's a very wicked idea of god.

In the time she had from saving the world, Emily looked earnestly for a husband for her daughter. A young man with a Christian heart and a big store, or a young man with a Christian heart and a small store. She might as well have planned a vegetarian dinner for a tiger. Apart from her father, Catherine detested every other man around her – young and old. She hated their arrogance and their vanity, their souls of pure commerce and their fair repulsive skins.

It was the black men she found attractive, with their air of quiet earthiness and oppressed ancestry, the mix of humility and rebellion; their smooth dark skins with virile sinews moving underneath. But they were like shadows: to be seen everywhere, but difficult to engage in a conversation or in an encounter.

There was one, furtive and fleeting, in their kitchen: Jim, the slim young negro who came in twice a week to weed and hoe the garden, and told her stories about his childhood in Alabama, opening up her body with a rasping pain and being done with her before the pain could turn to pleasure. The backyard door was ajar and the sun was blinding bright outside, and young Jim rushed away even before his last spasm had passed. A strong musk remained behind.

It happened one more time in the same kitchen, at mid-morning, with the sun blinding bright outside; and as she bent across the table, her face hot against the smooth cypress wood, Jim again rushed out even before the excruciating tremors in his body had come to rest. The strong musk remained behind, and there were stains on the floor.

She did not ever repeat it, but she did not ever regret it either. The moment had been nothing, but there had been pleasure before and after, in the anticipation and in the memory. She knew – through instinct and reading – that pleasure in the act itself would come, in time, and with a different kind of man.

She knew she would not find such a man in Chicago.

Without stating it, Catherine had been preparing all her life to leave Chicago and had been unconsciously receiving her instruction at John's Oriental Curios. She often felt she knew less about the city she had spent her life in than the fabulous lands whose magic had washed up in her father's small store. She had developed a feeling of kinship even with the floating reptiles trapped like her in stifling jars, and she often found herself stroking the rhino horn and caressing the silk of the hanging tiger skins, her heart full of vague longing. She began to study the dozens of parchment maps John kept in a folder, plotting a route through vast tracts of water. And then, when her mother began to invite young men home for tea, she began to confide in her father, and seek from him ways of escape.

John loved both life and his daughter enough to let her go. As he grew more infirm the thought of leaving Catherine in Emily's custody terrified him. He began to make lists of his friends in the world; he began to tutor the young girl in ports and sea routes, ships and fares, languages and cultures, clothes and habits, morals and mores, cuisines and currencies, religions and rituals.

One morning Emily held the Bible club meeting at her home, and there was a young man she invited who was writing a monograph titled 'The Science of the Apocalypse and the Art of Surviving It'. He was very polite, very pale, and spoke with great eloquence. His wide sideburns quivered with passion as he described the roaring fires that would burn the world when the final judgement was delivered and every man's reckoning made. They would rage forth from the deepest bowels of the earth and scorch the heavens; the stars would be singed and the sun charred black.

The women listened with grim eyes and folded hands.

He said with sincerity, Men who have done violence to men, men who have coveted more than their need, men who have turned their backs on the Lord, and women who have let Beelzebub insinuate their limbs with sinful desire – all will roast in the apocalyptic flames and will not be allowed the respite of demise. Eternally, eternally, eternally. Without mercy or reprieve. Without yesterday or tomorrow.

The few women who as yet hadn't crossed their legs now did so.

In the evening Emily told her husband and daughter the young man was her choice. The next morning, John – without taking his first swig – began to prepare for one last journey. By the time Catherine came to the store in the afternoon everything was ready. Next morning they left for New York. Emily did not know it was the last time she would see her daughter. Catherine did, but it caused her little pain. The only child and the mother had lived under the same roof all their lives, but they were total strangers to each other. One was preparing for life, the other for the apocalypse. The two roads did not cross anywhere. Catherine tried to summon up sorrow for Emily but it would not come; only when Catherine was dying, all those years later, all those thousands of miles away, did she find in herself a tear for her mother. `

But a week later, on the bustling quay in New York choked with hollow-eyed emigrants, she clung to her father and wept like a baby. John's teeth were gone, his hair was thin, his skin was loose and grey and his arms were weak, but he held her with a strength greater than any in his life. Sometimes a parent will pass on a slice of their soul to a child – it is a melancholic bond, the persistence of longing. At the quay, bidding goodbye to his girl, John suddenly felt his life was done. He could think of nothing to return to in Chicago; he could not think of what he would wake for the next day. He took off his talisman – the wooden amulet in the holy sign of om, the conqueror of malaria and every evil eye – and hung it on his daughter.

He needed no more protection; she could not have enough.

And Catherine – weeping like a baby – hoped her father would but once ask her not to go so she could turn her back on the big bobbing ship and gratefully return to the warm embrace of his shadow.

For weeks on the rolling deck she filled the ocean with the salt of her sorrow.

London left Catherine cold.

Her father's friend, Mr Salisbury, was old, with a bad eye over which he wore a black patch. He ran a successful pawn and antique shop on Bond Street which was different from John's Oriental Curios. He sold trinkets – some incredibly expensive – obtained from the fabulous and teeming royal houses of India. Most had been plundered or purloined by adventurers, mercenaries, company men, soldiers and officials of the Raj, aides-de-camp and secretaries, servants of the royal households, as well as wives and mistresses of the maharajas and princes. Others had been hawked by royalty itself, as it struggled to sustain its profligacy between the greedy squeeze of the British and the moral pincer of an awakening nationalist sentiment.

There were silver and gold salvers and glasses, Persian carpets, crystal chandeliers and lamps, marble chess sets, paintings of the Mughal and Kangra miniature schools, tapestries in silk with royal monograms, bird baths engraved in jade, hookahs gilded with gold, daggers studded with diamonds, chairs with tiger feet and serpent arms, marble coffee tables with inlay of lapis, intricately carved jewel boxes, polo mallets bearing famous names, tubs big enough for a man and a woman to turn cartwheels in, tea services so intricate they would have taken craftsmen years to create, hand-tooled pistols and muskets, busts in marble and bronze of long-nosed bewhiskered beturbaned kings and princes, exquisite silver and gold cutlery, and emerald- and ruby-studded bric-a-brac like walking sticks, swords, decanters, cigarette holders, ashtrays, spittoons, mirrors, hairbrushes, temple bells, riding saddles, bidets; and there was a large-sized dildo of polished Ceylonese ebony custom-ordered by the ageing prince of Karimthala to pleasure his Czechoslovakian mistress. She had sold it when she had been finally cast out. It was a work of art, with fine ridges and a perfect frenulum. Mr Salisbury had had it washed and given it a fresh coat of varnish.

Mr Salisbury and John had made a mercenary expedition together to the Frontier, where he had had his left eye taken out by a tribesman's scattershot gun. John had helped rescue and repair him. The bond of battle is stronger than any; he was determined to help his friend's daughter. But she puzzled him. He couldn't fathom why she had come to London and what she wished to do. All she did was ask him endless questions about India and about the Indian things that filled his shop. He concluded she was just like her hook-nosed father, the rare American interested in things beyond her own shores.

Mr Salisbury mandated his youngest daughter, Florrie, to give Catherine a tour of London. The two girls wandered through Madame Tussaud's, the British Museum, Westminster Abbey, the Tower of London, Buckingham Palace, Kew Gardens, Trafalgar Square. Often Florrie's lover, a pale, thin youth studying to be a mechanical engineer, accompanied them. Amid the monuments the two of them found nooks and crannies to practise amour. Soon Catherine was exasperated by their constantly flushed faces, and their continual search for a broad pillar or a dark corner. The tour for them consisted only of lingering, letting the others move on, so a quick lunge and grab could be made. In between the pale boy told them fantastical stories about air machines that would in the near future help men soar into the skies and even fly across the Atlantic. Catherine wondered at what all men will say to get a feel.

As with the skits of passion, the American girl soon became bored with the endless testaments to imperial grandeur and military prowess. Statues, monuments, declarations. Were men the same everywhere? Swinging between arrogance and the apocalypse.

To lift Catherine's darkening mood, Florrie took her to Brighton. It went badly. They arrived with the sun out and revellers on the beach, but soon after it began to rain and for two days it did not cease. At the Metropole noisy families milled about, reading items from the papers aloud and playing word games, while their shrieking children raced up and down the corridors like banshees out of hell.

All three evenings the two young women were approached by young men exploring a dalliance, but Catherine was repelled by their pale skins and smooth advances. Florrie – game for some fun – had to suffer alongside.

Florrie reported Catherine's discontent to her father. Mr Salisbury tried even harder; he was, after all, alive because of John. He scanned *The Times* every day and directed his friend's daughter to whatever was in vogue in the city: plays, opera, lectures, readings. He took her to Ascot to see the races. She was sent off to Oxford and Cambridge, where she walked the cobbled streets and tried to find in herself an empathy for the thick mood of high learning and higher privilege.

In it all Catherine saw not the hub of the civilized world, with all its art and learning, its accomplishment and refinement. What she registered was the snobbery, the class consciousness, the pretension and the affectation. The flesh of exploitation that lay just beneath the skin of enlightenment. The stupid accents and the stupider hats.

Basically it was like Chicago, just stratified more stylishly and with a greater sense of self-assurance. Here it flowed from the India under the heel; back home it sprang from the black shadows in the streets.

Men will be – she concluded – who they can suppress.

In three months she was ready to flee. This was not where she had set out for. John wrote to her; and so did Emily. Her mother's letter was long, running to many pages, and was an unpausing lament of betrayal. It talked of love, loyalty, piety, duty, gratitude, and pronounced Catherine a failure on every count. It said it was clear her father's wayward seed had overridden every noble intention of her mother. It recounted in painstaking detail every effort of hers to edify her daughter from the time she was a baby. It heaped blame on John and his curiosity shop. She should have never allowed Catherine to spend so much time in that infernal store, with all its voodoo stuff, its snakes and skins, its powders and pastes, and its sexual horn. It was her tragic misfortune that her daugher had been bewitched by the base life; and it was clear now that when the apocalypse came, for the daughter's sins the mother would have to roast eternally. The letter was interspersed with chunky passages reproduced verbatim from the Bible.

It ended: Your heartbroken and doomed mother, Emily.

Catherine read it in a rush and put it aside. There was nothing in it for her.

John's letter filled one side of one page. He wrote that the journey back to Chicago had been the longest journey of his life. He said when she learnt the truth of Catherine's departure, Emily had wailed and wept so much and for so long that he had actually, for the first time in his life, slept over at the store for two nights. But the store was no longer a happy place. It seemed to have been suddenly vacated of its soul. But she must not worry; nor must she look back. She must remember that no day is guaranteed to any of us. That each of us has only one moral duty in the world: to live our life to the fullest.

So must every sane god decree, including Emily's.

To find your way in the world you have to look ahead. There is a road for everyone; and a resting place. She must seize her happiness where it came to her; she must take her pleasures where she found them; she must go where her heart took her.

Love and desire.

John wrote, All desire and all love are legitimate. You do not have to desire for a hundred years or love for a hundred for it to be true. The love of a fleeting moment, the desire of an instant, is as legitimate and true as that of three score and ten years. Let no one tell you different. In the moment you are touched by love or desire you are touched by the divine. In my life I have been so blessed, again and again; and there is no greater blessing I would seek for you, my daughter. The apocalypse will not come, or it will, but before that we shall have here itself our paradise. It is only assured to those with the capacity for desire and the gift of love. Your mother had half of one. May you have the full of both. May it be your father's legacy to you.

It ended: Your loving father, whose spirit ever rides by your shoulder.

It was the first letter John had written to her. She suddenly realized he had never even spoken to her in such a fashion. Her knowledge of his free-spirited expansive nature came from the stories of his travels and her surreptitious readings of his diaries. Most of their lives, when John had talked to her, he had either narrated wild anecdotes or horsed around playing the high fool.

She read his letter three times, slowly; sat with it in her lap for hours, looking out of the first-floor window at the drizzling grey London sky; and made up her mind to leave.

There is a road for everyone; and a resting place.

Paris grabbed her.

It had a libertine anarchy that was most appealing. The snobberies here appeared to be less of wealth and station, more of eccentricity and art. And the air – wherever you went – was thick with desire, consumption, a lust for life. It also helped not to have the chaperoning eye and arm of a father's friend. She crossed the Channel light, leaving her heavy luggage, the chests and trunks, behind and arriving with only two large suitcases.

Florrie's beau – who put his hands up her dress while telling her tales of flying machines – Florrie's beau passed Catherine on to a friend who rented a flat near the Boulevard du Montparnasse. The friend was a rich dandy. His father had made a fortune running an aggressive trade in Africa, then choked on a bone in a London restaurant while everyone was boisterously drinking and laughing all around him. When someone finally turned to ask him a question, the exploiter of a hundred tribes had been dead for quite a long time and looked fairly calm. Young Rudyard was left to think of ways to burn a fortune. He went at it with a sense of purpose. After he had trashed London, he moved to Paris. The city was equal to Rudyard's appetite for hedonism. And it was a good base from which to launch dizzying excursions of pleasure to Spain, Italy and the Riviera.

When Catherine arrived at the flat Rudyard was leaving on one such jaunt. He was part of a group of seven, four men and three women, and they were all draped around the living room waiting to leave. They acknowledged her with wry smiles. She felt gauche, uncertain of herself. They looked as if they could fall to drinking and fornicating at a moment's suggestion. Rudyard was warm and full of compliments. He said seeing her made him want to change his plans and stay behind. He held her firmly by her elbow and guided her to her room. And then suddenly they all left in a flurry of bags and cat-calls and the flat was eerily silent.

Her room was large, with satin drapes and oil paintings of nobility on the walls. The bedstead was brass and unnaturally high – she had to take a little hop to the floor when swinging herself out of it. There was a small balcony with cast-iron railings, from where you had a good view of the bustling street below. In the bathroom was the novelty of a bidet and it took her no time to divine its possibilities.

The flat was full of heavy furniture. Big wooden bureaux, weighty suites, ornate chairs, a grand piano and large paintings in gilded frames that must have cost a fortune. It all appeared pre-appointed; nothing seemed to possess a personal touch. Only at the entrance to Rudyard's bedroom was there a sign of individuality – a big African mask, its thick lips bared, the teeth wide and big, the earlobes long as pencils.

Left to herself Catherine did precisely what she had been made to do by her host in London: the tourist sights. The palaces and monuments bored her quickly, but Notre Dame and the Eiffel Tower held her. Both of them for their scale and peculiar ugliness. She sat for hours at the foot of each, trying to understand the neurosis of human grandeur and the shapes it can assume. But it was the Louvre that finished her off, retired her from the sightseeing trail. By the time she had been through four wings it was evening and she was more tired than she had ever been in her life. Everything she had seen was a mash in her head, the Greek and Roman statuary, the Renaissance and Reformation oils, even the crooked smile of La Gioconda, for which she tramped through long corridors to discover a small, forgettable canvas.

When she dragged herself out into the quadrangle, daylight was fading and the space was strewn with people recovering from their aesthetic exertions. Most of them seemed ready to lie down and die. Some children were actually sobbing from exhaustion and hunger. She could not spot a single happy or animated face in the scores around. Catherine thought, What a burden high culture is. What a toll it takes.

That night, after a hot soak, she stood outside on her balcony and watched the crowds milling below. The strange sibilances of French and an array of perfumes wafted up to her, along with a frisson of sexual energy. This was the Paris she ought to be a part of. From her perch above them she felt she could look into the heads of the hurrying couples and see assignations and anticipations unfolding there. She saw them in the words of her father in the accounts register; she saw them in the poses in the prints in the store, full of brazenness and acrobatics; she saw them in the frenzy of young Jim, pounding into her from the back, trembling uncontrollably.

She became so aroused, breathing in the perfumes and the sexuality, straining it through the sieve of her memory, that she had to go inside and sit on the bidet and let the water run and run till she was drained of all tension.

Rudyard and his companions returned the next morning. Catherine was still lazing in bed, letting the ache of the Louvre seep out of her limbs. Their hectoring voices, laced with loud laughter, splintered the silence of the flat. Catherine waited and soon enough there was a drumming on the door. She answered and Rudyard came in. Parted in the middle, his golden hair fell around his face; his jacket was off and his thumbs were hooked into his black braces; his white shirt was crisp and half out of his trousers. He was at his rakish best, leaning stylishly against the wall, heaping on the compliments.

In the evening he took her out to dinner to a restaurant called Le Chat Blanc in the Rue d'Odessa near the Gare Montparnasse. He said it was always full of soon-to-be-famous artists and writers. They sat downstairs in a corner and the room was already electric with conversation and clinking glass. Rudyard asked her to keep an eye on the wooden staircase at the far end – you could often spot a famous name walking down. Catherine could not recognize any famous names; and she couldn't care less. Rudyard ran tongue-twisting labels of wine past her, none of which meant anything. Then they began to drink. First champagne, then wine. In no time she felt better than ever before in her life. Rudyard told her wild stories about his days in

Paris and every few minutes interrupted himself to exclaim how stunningly beautiful she looked.

They never got to ordering or eating dinner. Rudyard held her right hand in a soft caress and leaned close to make himself heard above the growing din. She was swimming sweetly. She could smell the scent he wore and feel his winy breath on her skin. He was so close she could see the black pores on his chin where the hair had been finely shaved. His lips were moist and fleshy. Then suddenly, without preamble, she was kissing him, and it went on for a long time, and she became dizzy as his mouth worked all over hers, sucking at her lips, pushing his tongue onto her teeth.

The wine and his mouth made her lose all sense of where she was and of everyone around her. They just sat there, leaning their mouths into each other, their hands still on the table.

Rudyard had to hold her tight to walk her out of the restaurant. In the hansom going back he cupped her face in his hands and with his skilled mouth teased it all over. She stared at the African mask as he carried her past it, wondering what it would feel like to be kissed by lips that thick. He deposited her on the bed and with a sure touch uncovered all her secrets. She let him rove where he wished. He spent a long time on her nipples, excited by their thickness. When he found the mole beneath her left breast, he told her it was a clear sign her life would be governed by her heart and not her mind.

Through it all she remained in a mixed state of detachment and desire, a keen observer even as she was an enthusiastic participant. It wasn't bad, but the only memorable part – the best part, the memory of which always brought a surge in her – was the first kiss in Le Chat Blanc. The headiness of fine wine and a practised mouth.

In the morning he took her again. In a more perfunctory fashion, pushing into her from the back as she slept curled on her side. She didn't mind: it was something to get out of the way. Rudyard lifted her hair and kissed the back of her neck when he had finished.

The next nine months were a giddy ride on a runaway carousel. She let herself go, becoming an integral part of Rudyard's sensation-hunting entourage. The only question to be answered every day was where and how to test one's pleasures. New restaurants were trashed every night, quantities of wine drunk and spilled, ladies of the night discovered, novel dares thrown and accepted.

Antoine drank a flagon of Cabernet without breaking for breath and had to be revived with a feverish pumping of his chest and stomach; Marie hoicked up her voluminous gown and pissed noisily in the middle of Boulevard St Germain; Count Vladimir tried to ride a horse saddleless with Anne lodged on him and almost broke his organ in the ensuing fall; and in an eatery they would never visit again, while walking out, Catherine lifted her skirts from the back and showed to the gasping room her tight white bloomers. Rudyard's act – and it was a wonder he could conjure it up with all the wine inside him – was, late into the night, to walk nonchalantly through the aisle of a restaurant with his fly open, his stout erection sticking straight out.

It was this, more than his money, that made him the leader of the group.

Sex underlay everything. Every excursion, every exertion, every diversion. And every night ended in it. Rudyard ran the pack with élan and took whom he wished. Catherine did not mind. She liked him immensely. He had all the charm and generosity and warmth and non-fidelity of someone who has been given everything in life and has only to extract good times out of it. Rudyard and she took their pleasure of each other in the unnaturally high bed in her room or in the unnaturally large one in his, but Catherine knew that was where it ended. She knew she was just another charming amusement for him; and he, for her, was a wonderful guide to new frontiers and an engaging pedlar of curiosities.

She enjoyed her time with him, but in fact very often gained her final satisfaction not in bed but on the bidet, playing with memory.

With Rudyard – and in time with Antoine and Count Vladimir – she learnt the workings of her body. What brought it alive, what made it soar, what tripped it to a halt. There were other dalliances too, past midnight, in a haze of alcohol and derring-do; fleeting, experimental, the mining of experience. Her father's accounts book,

and the vivid prints, had prepared her well, given her an attitude. The
Gospel of Fr John was clear: we must take our pleasures where we
find them.

Love and desire. To question them is to question life.

One weekend Florrie's gangly beau arrived in Paris to spend time
with his friend. On the way back from carousing at night, in the
cab, he began to tell her about the flying machines, and she, giddy
with alcohol, and wishing to give him delight, caught his head and
pushed it between her legs. Next morning he woke up sentimental
and attempted to talk romance, but she was bored with him already,
and seeing his thin lips and earnest expression wondered why she had
bothered to indulge him. When she mentioned it to Rudyard later, he
was expansive, declaring, You must always be charitable with it –
everyone has far less of it than they need.

He was disproof of his own saw. He clearly had too much; too
much of everything. And in time Catherine tried it all too, smoking
opium, eating hash, visiting the grand whores of the city. At the Rue
Sainte-Cécile she watched Count Vladimir being consumed by the
Italian sisters Marie and Rachel, black-haired and dark-eyed with
buttocks of polished marble. Rudyard wagered a double fee if the
sisters could finish his friend in ten minutes. The young count – an
émigré from Russia – struggled to hold back but was whimpering
with relief before the clock had struck its time.

At the Boulevard Haussmann she saw the balloon-breasted Lucie
Krauss couple in such a fever with the black as ebony Céline Pearl
that their whole raucous company was stunned into a silence of
sexual tension.

At the time Paris was not to be denied anything. At the Rue
d'Antin she witnessed the city's latest sensation, the fifteen-year-old
brunette Jeanne, come in from Algeria – whose hymen was still in the
auction – display herself with such seasoned abandon that the
onlookers were set to fidgeting. Her clitoris was the size of a small

finger, and when she reached her apogee it waggled in a wild shiver. Each day men went into paroxysms watching her. Rudyard put in his bid for the deflowerment and was told he would be informed when the auction had closed.

But the wildest she saw was the black-eyed diva Marguerite de Barras from Catalonia, at Rue Notre Dame de Lorette. She had breasts that looked up at the sky and haunches that were reputed to milk a man insensible without her moving an inch of her torso. She inhabited a house full of animals and exotic birds – garish macaws and cockatoos, a peacock, a hunting falcon, twittering budgies, a couple of golden orioles, a crested serpent eagle. There were dogs, cats, civets, foxes, monkeys, a porcupine, even a small sloth. Many were kept in cages; others wandered around in barred rooms. The stench filled the house and, when you walked in, there was a moment of recoil. Her room was at the furthest corner on the east wing, and she left the window open in a gesture of accommodation to her clients.

She cost a lot; she had so many mouths to feed. But her act was unique in all of Paris. She was ravishingly beautiful and she did everything a man's wayward imagination could dream up – often throwing in her menagerie for the true perverts. When you went to Marguerite you expected to fulfil the darkest desire that had ever crossed your mind. Sex after a time is only novelty. There could be no greater woman for a man than Marguerite. It was said that she had given so much happiness to an ageing raja from western India that he had showered her with rubies and emeralds, and promised to bring her a trained cheetah.

Catherine saw her do things she would never ever see again.

In a way it was fitting that Marguerite and her extreme acts proved to be the last straw. Months of pushing her senses every night had begun to tell on Catherine. Her curiosities had been sated, the edge of discovery had begun to blunt. The thought of one more long night trawling the bars and whorehouses, of playing one more wild prank which produced more tedium than excitement, of giving herself up one more time to a pale-skinned man in an exercise of rubbing

that produced neither desire nor pleasure – the thought of one more
night pursuing desperate gaiety had begun to depress her.

Catherine had arrived at an important understanding. Without
the lubrications of love, you cannot continually desire the same person. No matter how magnificent the pleasure. Love is the replenish-
ing oil in the machinery of desire. If it does not exist you have to
move on before the unoiled machine comes to a rattling-grinding
halt.

John, the father, had intuitively known this truth. He had kept
moving, from person to person, from fresh desire to fresher desire,
never tarrying long enough with one person to require the oil of love.
Till he found Emily and, in her, both love and desire; and lost the
need to keep moving.

Catherine understood this, as the bidet became more pleasurable
for her than the men she slept with.

Desire is a wonderfully promiscuous thing, but when it is trapped
in monogamy it cannot survive without love.

Through his haze of breakneck pleasuring, Rudyard realized
Catherine was slowly slipping out of his space. She found him often
looking at her intently, studying her for her levels of engagement in
their latest pleasure caper. Her growing disinterest was evident and
soon she began to withdraw from some of the nightly revels. Initially
Rudyard tried to mock her, heaping her with the homilies of hedonism: one life; one youth; make the best of what you have; no one has
seen tomorrow; no one has returned with a report on the afterlife; it
all ends when it ends; the body is the temple, the phallus is the priest,
the cunt is the shrine, the orgasm is god.

Catherine wanted to report that the temple and the priest were
not leading her to god.

But she held her silence, letting him rant. And then suddenly,
revealing an unexpected twist in his character, Rudyard turned. As if
he had been reprimanded, he began to slow down. The insane rush-

ing around whorehouses and bars eased; they found themselves – all of them – settling down to more leisurely dinners. Conversation began to spill beyond the boundaries of posture and concupiscence.

She discovered Count Vladimir – the short runty count who was always forced to make a spectacle of himself with the whores – was a storehouse of learning on art and literature. He spoke with intimate knowledge of Russian and French and English novelists, describing and differentiating them; and he had a fine understanding of how the Impressionists had changed the function of the canvas. One night at Le Chat Blanc he gestured at a slim, serious man eating fastidiously at a corner table alone, and told her the man was a young English novelist struggling early with writer's block. He said he was in Paris to get past it and dined there most nights. His name was Maugham.

Another time he excitedly pointed out a stocky man of radiant face and great energy at the centre of a noisy table of pretty women and aggressive men. The count ordered each of the group to take a good look. He said the man was a brewing storm. He was beginning to kick the pants off the old art world – even the great Impressionists, who were actually still new. He was doing things on canvas no one had ever seen before. His name was Pablo, and the rumours said he could paint and draw in a frenzy all day and make a woman whimper with pleasure all night.

Catherine could believe it. Even across the length of the swirling room the life-force shone out of him. He could have had anyone – man or woman – at his table. He could, with but a gesture, have had Catherine. If only once; if only to test the promiscuity of desire.

In the large group at that table there was only one other person who caught Catherine's eye. He had small and delicate features and seemed to be the calmest one there. The women flanking him were constantly leaning into him with conversation, and he was talking to them with a gentle smile, without urgency or aggression. His hair was parted on the left and smoothly combed down, and his moustache was neatly trimmed and ended at the corners of his mouth. There was the glint of a diamond stud in his left ear. What set him apart was his air of containment and the colour of his skin. She would come to recognize both as peculiarly Indian. The skin was the colour of soil; the calm air came from a civilizational belief in the preordained order of things and one's firm place in it.

The man found Catherine's eye across the room and his gaze was steady and warm. He looked at her without blinking, and for a long time she held his eye. When she looked away and looked back he was still looking at her.

Like her father, John, in New York more than twenty years before she was seized by the false moment of instant love.

She returned by herself to Le Chat Blanc the following night and he was there, waiting, alone, neat and contained. She went and sat by herself and soon he came over and sought to make her acquaintance. He was fascinated by her story and at their very first meeting asked her more about her life than Rudyard and his friends had in twelve months. He felt the amulet with the om; discovered the story of Emily and John; unearthed her love of India; traced the trajectory of her travels and tried to understand her need of them.

They met again the next day. And the next. She was dazzled by the range of his knowledge and his experience. Like her father he had travelled across vast swathes of the globe, but he possessed not only the gleanings of the voyager but also the erudition of the academic. He could talk not only about the sights and sounds and colours of the world but also about its economies, histories and politics. He appeared to know much about art and music and literature, and he asked her questions about these things in America, of which she knew nothing.

His name was Mustafa Syed, and he created an inordinate excitement in her. After pushing her body for twelve months, having her mind stoked was incredibly erotic. She had never imagined the spoken word could carry such a charge, could turn her limbs to water. Each day she rushed back to meet him; and the meetings became longer and longer. He would order the wine – always red –

and before they began drinking he would explain its attributes to her. They would drink slowly, and when the bottle was over he would order another, a different red, and again explain its attributes to her.

He spoke English gently and with a fine sense for its sound – a low, deep timbre, the phrases unfurling without haste like movements in music – and it was mesmeric just to watch him construct his complex sentences. She had never heard English spoken with such richness and style. In comparison, the eloquent young conjuror of the horrors of the apocalypse – the finest speaker she had heard so far – appeared like a tribal drumbeater.

The long hours she was away from Syed she spent rolling and repeating and examining in her head the words they had last shared. She began to see the world in a new way. As a vast dynamic enterprise constantly in flux, ever being moulded and remoulded, shaped by men and their ideas and efforts; not, as she had subconsciously assumed all these years, as a stable entity you could partake of as and when you wished.

John had told her the world was a wonderful place to visit.

Syed suggested it was a wonderful place to be studied.

Each time she met him she felt another window had been opened in her head.

Syed spoke mostly about things outside of himself. Inevitably, having ranged the world, his conversation would turn to India. Like John, he was passionate about India; but, unlike John, he spoke as an insider, and unlike everyone else she had ever heard talk about India he did not hold forth on its exotic magic – the religions, languages, wildlife, cultures, histories and the antiquity.

He spoke mostly about its tragic dereliction; its unrealized people.

Like a true nationalist he spoke not with pride alone but also with a great deal of anguish. Like a true nationalist he wanted the cure, not paeans to the disease. He wanted the patient to heal and be redoubtable, not to lie in torpor and be wasted by delusions. He understood the past was over and it could at best be only a guide, not a template; he worried for the false consolations and fraudulent triumphalism of a time long dead that could infect and corrode the energies of the present.

His quiet anger and passion moved Catherine. The strange pull of a country she had never set eyes on deepened.

Syed was tough on the colonialist British, but he was not as quick to dump all of India's woes at their doorstep. He was far more tough on the ruling elites of India, the feudal lords and the princes. He said the Indian people, the abjectly poor peasantry, had been let down badly by their rulers for a thousand years. Overtaxed, oppressed, never shown the light. Indian royalty might have patronized and helped create – mostly for their own pleasures – great art, literature, monuments and music, but they had done nothing to build in processes, schemes, laws, institutions, to educate and improve the lot of their people.

They had behaved like wanton schoolboys, not wise men.

The great progressive impulses of rationality and universal human dignity that had kicked alive elsewhere had passed India by. While Europe in the last three hundred years had made the triple-jump of science, enlightenment and individual rights, and landed firmly in the happy sandpit of social reforms and rule of law, India's potentates had fed their people a thin gruel of bullshit mysticism and half-assed religion. No schools, no colleges, no courts, no hospitals, no roads, no power, no water, no progress. Just bullshit mysticism and half-assed religion.

The masters of more propagating the virtues of less.

While their own trinkets – of jade and ruby and diamond – multiplied, their palaces became more and more baroque, their cars arrived custom-made from Rolls-Royce, and their harems burgeoned with so many beautiful women that it would need a man to have a hundred phalluses to keep them all satisfied – while their indulgences grew, feeding off new European toys, the Indian people became poorer and poorer. A once great civilization – a crucible of science and astronomy and medicine and literature and philosophy – a once great civilization, India had become an enclave of the ignorant and the wretched, ruled over by the vain and the gimcrack.

But, said Syed, all was not despair. Once again things were happening on the subcontinent – ideas were on the move, people were on the move, new creative forces were being generated. He said there were men in Poona and Bombay and in the Punjab and in Bengal, and there was one who was whispered of in South Africa, who were all speaking a new language with a new confidence. They were emerging – in ones and twos, lawyers and teachers – from the educational pathways the British had begun to lay, and Syed hoped they would soon begin to pose questions that would send both India's feckless royal and the avaricious colonial ducking for cover.

The question that undoes kings.

Who gave you the right to take away my rights?

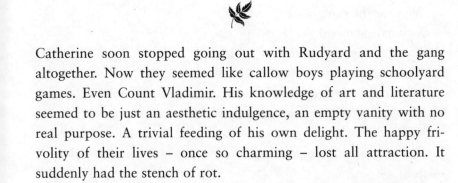

Catherine soon stopped going out with Rudyard and the gang altogether. Now they seemed like callow boys playing schoolyard games. Even Count Vladimir. His knowledge of art and literature seemed to be just an aesthetic indulgence, an empty vanity with no real purpose. A trivial feeding of his own delight. The happy frivolity of their lives – once so charming – lost all attraction. It suddenly had the stench of rot.

She could not bear now to have any of them even touch her. And Mustafa Syed never once attempted to. She would visit him at the Grand Hotel, and he would never presume to invite her up to his room, but would sit with her in the lobby and talk to her for hours. He talked and talked and talked, softly and intensely; and she came back each day damp with desire, his lovely words more sensuous than any caresses she had ever known.

One day, less than two months after they had first met, he told her he loved her. He held her hand when he said it. She came back in a daze.

The next day when she met him again, still in a daze, he said he was leaving for India soon and would she go back with him.

She said yes and when she went home thought about her decision.

She still knew almost nothing about him. The only facts about himself he had let out so far were: he had been up to Oxford and taken a degree in philosophy, and he was a fine player of cricket who could have played for England if he had learnt to keep quiet about his political beliefs. He said he had royal contemporaries who had done so successfully. Syed said, Games are only games for those granted privilege, rich men and rich nations. For the oppressed everything is a weapon of war – the war for life and dignity.

Catherine thought of the black shadows back home in America and understood something of what was said.

The next day she resolved to ask him some direct questions. When they met at lunch and before the wine had arrived, she asked, Where will I stay?

With me, he said.

As what? she said.

As whatever you choose, he said.

Who else stays with you?

My family. My brothers, cousins, uncles, aunts, nephews, nieces, grandparents, great-uncles, great-aunts, my wife.

Wife?

Yes, I have been long married. Since I was fourteen. But it doesn't matter.

It does to me. You said you love me. How shall I stay there?

In whichever way you choose.

But what do you want me there as? What are you taking me there as?

As my wife. As my companion.

But what of your wife?

It doesn't matter. She will say nothing. Nor, I hope, feel it. She will understand.

This is most unexpected. I need to think about it.

Actually, you don't. You read too much into it. But, if you wish to, then you must.

Catherine did not go back home. She went and sat at the foot of the looming Notre Dame and thought about it all. She knew she was going. There was nothing she wanted to do more than to keep listening to his words. But what did it mean to be some kind of add-on wife marooned in a sea of family, in an alien land, amid alien people and an alien religion? She needed to think it all through, make her reckoning seem sound. When she looked up the gargoyles were snarling down at her, challenging her.

After some time she stood up and went inside the cathedral and settled into a pew at the back. It was the hour of vespers and in the half-light of lamps could be seen several heads bowed in supplication and petition. Others moved about soundlessly lighting candles to their hopes.

In that cavernous space, Catherine looked at the big stained-glass windows, seeking a divine cue. A young man with a flowing beard walked through the aisle muttering, The lord moved in faith; in faith should we move. The lord moved in faith; in faith should we move. At that moment she thought: How big must a house of worship be before it can contain god? How many arguments does faith need before it can believe? She had always abhorred her mother's religious hysteria, but now, in Notre Dame, searching for a courage she already possessed, she became totally freed of the terrors of religion, of the terror of the unknown.

She never entered another church, or any other house of worship, again.

When she emerged through the big door it was dark outside, and when she looked up the gargoyles had retreated into the night and were no longer snarling down at her.

They boarded their ship at Marseilles. When Rudyard saw her off at the station in Paris he was melancholic. So were the others. She kissed each of them and each one whispered words of caution, begging for care in food, drink and conduct. She had loved and pleasured with each of them, and they had rushed her through the happy anarchy of youth that ought to be everyone's share. They had helped her discover some of the wonderful paths her father had first intimated. A sense of deep loss came over her.

Anne said, Bring me back a maharaja. With a diamond in each armpit.

Count Vladimir said, Some of that Frontier marijuana would be nice.

Rudyard said, Syed, take good care of her. And we want her back soon.

Syed only smiled gently, his eyes still.

Catherine did not imagine that she would not be coming back ever. That she was crossing the waters for the last time. That a journey that had begun in her head in her father's store so many years ago was about to enter its last phase.

In Marseilles they spent the night at a hotel. Syed had – strangely, decorously – booked two separate rooms. After dinner they talked for a long time about the Rudyard gang – so easy always to talk to Syed – and then he softly kissed her goodnight and left her at the door of her room. She wondered at his extreme restraint and lay awake for a long time, stroking her feverish body into a calm.

On the ship too Syed had booked two separate cabins. With grace and consideration he had given her one that was a notch better than his; only a floor separated them. They spent each day and evening together, on the deck and in the dining halls – he had begun to teach her words of Hindustani – but at night Syed always kissed her warmly at her cabin door and turned away. She scrabbled for answers. Fr John had said nothing about lovers who will not make love. She closed her eyes, put her hands on her body and rolled with the rolling ship.

When three weeks later they docked in Bombay, Syed had still not gone beyond the doorway kiss. He was talking as beautifully as ever and it moved Catherine as much as before, but she had begun to worry.

# The Philosopher Nawab

They journeyed across the burning plains of central India by train and the full blast of the subcontinent blew her off her feet. From the moment she disembarked at Bombay – feeling a rejected virgin – she was caught in a riot of colours, sounds, sights. Every sense was under immediate assault. Right away she noticed the great Indian paradox: a sense simultaneously of great bustle and great torpor.

They stayed at the grand Taj Mahal Hotel by the seafront and again there were two rooms waiting for them. And when, a day later, they took the train from the Victoria Terminus they were in one bogey, but it had two compartments. Catherine was now distraught and were she not so completely absorbed by everything around her, she would have cornered Syed. As the train pulled out of sleepy stations, she saw the endless unfurling of the green and brown fields staked with babool and banyan trees, cattle moving across them in slow motion, and bare-bodied peasants, mostly in turbans, who seemed as if they had been planted there from the beginning of time.

On the train she took an instant liking to the dark servitors who seemed to arrive every few minutes to ply them with copious amounts of food and drink. Not for a moment, then or ever after, did she feel threatened by the native. They were ever-smiling, deferential, yet held themselves apart with a strange dignity.

She remembered her father's words and saw the truth in them. It held good for the rest of her life.

A wonderful people, but totally unknowable.

When they reached Delhi Syed took her to see the wonders of Mughal India, and other relics of history that went back a thousand years further. They rode out through scrub country and kikar forests to see the astonishing twelfth-century minaret, the Qutub Minar, and she became dizzy looking down from its fifth storey.

At the ruined city of Tughlaqabad big rhesus monkeys baited them with jeers. And at the Purana Qila the hucksters told them this was the original site of the kingdom of the Pandavas. But what fascinated and appalled Catherine the most was the walled city, in particular the triangle of wonders: the massive Red Fort, the stately Jama Masjid and the frenzied commercial causeway of Chandni Chowk.

It was a mirror to the teeming madness of India. On the one hand were millions of buzzing flies feeding off the legendary sweetmeat shops, wretched beggars with limbs eaten away by leprosy and faces pitted with smallpox, and mangy dogs getting between everyone's legs, trailing fleas. On the other were opulent shops overflowing with goods from all parts of the world. It was said you could, in Chandni Chowk, buy or trade anything that was buyable and tradeable in the world. From Persian carpets to Chinese silks, Arabian horses to Indian elephants, Brazilian cocoa to Afghani opium, Turkish soaps to English sanitaryware, ayurvedic herbs to homeopathic globules, rubber-bodied whores to cushion-lipped catamites.

More marvellous still were the mendicants she saw. There were naked sadhus, their bodies pierced through with iron rods, their matted locks touching their ankles. One stood on his right leg, his penis hanging to his knees – like an elephant's trunk – weighted down by a big stone. As they walked past, he swung it cheerfully like a pendulum. Syed put a perforated coin into his bowl. There was a seller of potions who pursued them aggressively, offering Catherine a white powder that would help her get rid of all of Syed's concubines and wives, sucking the juice out of them and leaving their loins withered like dry leaves.

She saw a fakir, thin as a blade of grass, with a flowing grey beard and flying hair, walking jauntily with a bamboo pole across his left shoulder, at the ends of which hung two cane baskets. Syed pointed to him excitedly and said his name was Baba Muggermachee, and he crossed the river Jamuna every Monday morning riding a crocodile to collect alms from the traders. The Baba, he said, could at will summon any crocodile from the river to serve as his transport.

Catherine looked at Syed. This was the man from Oxford who always talked of the grand impulses of rationality and progress. Syed broke into a smile and said, There are many things in the world we don't understand – it doesn't pay to be too sceptical.

She loved him dearly at that moment. The flesh of vulnerability beneath the skin of utter calm. In time Catherine would come to recognize this as the salient Indian trait: the tight circle of reason, outside of which lay the great unknown. There was no such thing as a fully rational Indian. You bowed to the god of reason, you bowed to the god of science, you bowed to the god of empiricism, and then you finally bowed to the god of all other things, small and big, known and unknown.

You tracked your life between the god of reason and the god of unreason.

Bowing to both, offending neither.

There was no contradiction there. Only the vain saw any.

In any case a naked fakir riding a crocodile to work appealed to her more than a haranguing young man totting up his good deeds and consigning everyone else to the roaring fires of the apocalypse.

Just before they returned to their hotel, Syed led Catherine through serpentine lanes behind the Jama Masjid till they reached a small island of serenity: a plain whitewashed grave, a tiny pavilion next to it with latticework windows, and a big neem tree arching over all of it. It was the mazaar of a famous pir, and the young man who sat in the pavilion in meditation was his disciple. Syed sat down cross-legged on the cool marble floor and Catherine did the same. Syed said something. The young man – a piece of white cloth tied across his forehead, his beard scraggly – turned and looked at Catherine for a long time. Then he closed his eyes and sat motionless.

When he came out of his trance he spoke rapidly to Syed, putting his hand on Syed's hand.

The moment they stepped out of the pir's oasis into the bustling lane Catherine wanted to know what the young man had said.

Syed said, He is a soothsayer. He says in your life you will know many joys: of wealth, status, children, love, desire. But always they will be flawed. Always shrouded in shifting veils. There will ever be a serpent in the garden. He says in your life you will live the highest and touch the lowest.

Syed could well have fixed that prophecy.

Or rather Prince Syed could have.

Catherine had a lifetime of surprises waiting for her when they arrived at her lover's home. Syed was royalty. His father was the Nawab of Jagdevpur. Their principality spanned eight hundred and twenty-five square kilometres, and lay close to the foothills of the Himalayas, some two hundred kilometres from Delhi. The British had awarded it an eleven-gun salute. The royal enclave of Hukumganj was littered with the ruling family's palaces. The architectural inspirations were varied – Mughal, French, English and ancient Hindu. Syed was the object of much bowing and scraping, but she was relieved to see that for himself he had built a relatively modest English-style cottage – with fifteen rooms – and put in around it wide Indian verandas.

Syed designated a plush suite of rooms as Catherine's and settled her in. All the furniture was Burma teak, mahogany and rattan – heavy colonial with a dark polish. Outside the windows were manicured rose bushes, flowering trees like champa and harsingar, and creepers like chameli and quisqalis. Over time she would become addicted to their shifting perfumery. Syed, on the first day itself, earmarked an old bearer, Maqbool, and a spry young girl, Banno, to look exclusively after her needs. The two of them hovered just outside her rooms and she had only to murmur and they arrived.

The most impressive part of Syed's house was its elegant two-room study – a large room with a plush sofa, and an anteroom. The shelves ran from floor to ceiling, and there were four stools – with one step, two steps, three steps and four steps – to help you retrieve books. There were two writing tables, one in each room, and strategically placed lamps. The luxurious sofa had indigo-coloured silk cushions, and a low coffee table in front of it – perfect for lazy reading. Syed himself had a leather armchair with an ottoman for his feet. In the anteroom the most intriguing thing was a deep, tall wooden cupboard, always kept shut. When she finally opened it one day she found it crammed with notebooks bound in tan leather. There must have been at least two hundred of them.

But where were his family? On the third day she began to make enquiries of the retainers. Very quickly she realized Syed was something of a pariah in the family. She gathered it was bad news that he had come back with a white woman in tow, but no one seemed to expect any better of him. The young girl, Banno, said the family treated him with shame; his conduct was a disgrace, unworthy of rulers; and he brought ill luck on all who chanced on his path.

This made Catherine love Syed even more. That evening – in the library, over a glass of burgundy – she began to draw level with him. When he launched into a disquisition on Lord Curzon and the partition of Bengal, she stopped him, and like a tight-assed but benign schoolmistress neatly laid out all her questions.

Who was his wife?

Where was she?

Why was he not with her?

Who was he?

What was he doing?

Why was he doing whatever he was doing?

Why had he brought her here?

What did he expect her to do?

Why were they not doing what two people in love should continually do?

Syed held his head in his hands for a long time. Then he looked at her for a longer time expressionlessly, weighing something. She waited patiently. Then he stood up and, pacing up and down the study, began to talk.

🌿

Syed was the first-born son of the Nawab of Jagdevpur. He had a wife, Begum Sitara, but he had nothing to do with her. Syed and Sitara had been betrothed by their families when they were eight and five, and married when they were fourteen and eleven. Thirty-one elephants had marched in step to mark the occasion, and over three days ten thousand people had been fed grand meals. Begum Sitara now lived in the main palace with his family; occasionally when he visited his family he met her too. Syed said he had never had anything to say to her, and his two attempts – at the beginning – to fulfil his conjugal vows had turned out to be distasteful affairs.

The failure had to do with him not her. He had always lived with a nagging unease about his station in life, but it was Oxford that undid him completely. There he became obsessed with political philosophy and the evil men do to each other. He read Voltaire and Rousseau, Benjamin Franklin and Thomas Jefferson, John Ruskin and Abraham Lincoln, Karl Marx and Friedrich Engels. He wondered at his family's right to rule, and he blanched at their exercise of that right. He wrote long angry letters to his father, exhorting him to enact more humane taxation rates, build more schools and colleges, and to cease the practice of opulent rituals and ceremonies which drained the state exchequer and helped keep his subjects in thrall. So relentlessly did he lecture the old nawab on the moral duties of kingship that the nawab pronounced him a disgrace and a danger to the dynasty and, disinheriting him, declared his younger brother the heir apparent.

In his book of aphorisms the nawab wrote, Too much education makes common men into kings and kings into common men.

Every few years the aphorisms were collected in a book and published as *The Divine Wisdom of the Nawab, the Father of the Benighted People of Jagdevpur*.

Schoolchildren wrote essays on these sayings.

Disgraced, Syed was given the option of staying away from India, claiming a hefty maintenance and doing what he wished in Europe and England. He contemplated it briefly; but then saw it as a defeat of his beliefs. He realized he needed to return and act, if nothing else, as a listening post for his people and a conscience-keeper for his family.

Zafar, his brother, the nawab-to-be, baulked at the prospect. Syed's presence would undermine his authority. An angry tussle ensued. Finally, Syed gave an undertaking that he would not overtly interfere in the workings of the state; in turn the family would give him the room to live his life as he chose.

Why did he settle thus?

Why was he not with Begum Sitara?

Why were Catherine and he not doing what two people in love should continually do?

All these questions were linked to one answer. When he was thirteen Syed had found deep sexual love with the handsome young tutor who taught him mathematics. His name was Arif and the very thought of him made the boy-nawab ache with excitement. Syed discovered his hands, mouth and romantic soul with Arif. For the benefit of the servants, the tutor and the pupil chanted the multiplication aloud while their hands kept time on each other under the table. There were days when they chanted so loudly and so long that they were painfully sore by the time the tutorial was over.

At night, as Arif had instructed him, Syed massaged perfumed oils into his skin and made it soft and tender.

Syed prepared for his maths lessons by reading romantic poetry.

When time passed and the young nawab refused to make the journey to his adolescent wife's bed, the puzzled father ordered his aides to lead the boy there. Syed was vehemently repelled by the experience. The flab of the breasts, the slimy insides of the thighs, the emptiness at the crotch, the peculiar smell of a woman's skin – he wanted to flee. And he did. Some weeks later he was led back one more time – the royal household was abuzz with the first failure. Begum Sitara had been prepared with even greater diligence: bathed in asses' milk, her body rubbed with scented unguents, her passages oiled and flavoured with aromatic vapours. Syed almost threw up in nausea.

The next day Arif and his ward chanted the tables with unprecedented fervour, and had reached ninety-nine twelves are, when the nawab walked in. The two chanting boys were caught between standing and sitting, deference and disguise, tumescence and terror.

Arif was sacked the next day.

In his book of aphorisms the nawab wrote, The tables of arithmetic must never be learnt in a room, but always in the open, under trees.

For decades after, no children in Jagdevpur ever chanted their multiplication numbers under a roof.

Syed fell into a deep sorrow. He pined for his lover every moment of the day and would lie awake at night aching with want, memories of Arif's musk and mouth, hands and hair, thickness and throb, tormenting him. He would rub himself to gain relief and some sleep. And a little later he would be awake again. Some nights he would run through the cycle six–seven times, and when dawn broke on the palace turrets he would be exhausted from placating the demons of his desire.

The nawab was a man of the world. He understood both boys and desire.

Soon he brought in a new teacher from the nearby town of Dhampur. His name was Iqbal and he had the looks of an Adonis. By the fifth day Syed and Iqbal's hands were keeping time under the table as they chanted aloud. The ache of Arif lessened. Every two months the nawab brought in a new, hand-picked tutor.

The nawab knew that in the young love and desire must never be mixed. It makes for dangerous – often fatal – obsessions.

In his book he wrote, The good cook who loves to eat very swiftly kills himself.

Syed, of course, discovered that the novelty of bodies can banish the pangs of love.

And in eight hundred and twenty-five square kilometres of Jagdevpur every young maths teacher began to wait in hope of a summons from the palace.

The nawab's strategy only succeeded in part. He had calculated that his son would soon discover there were joys to the world beyond men. He had been down that route, as had every other man he knew. Each of them had finally come to the pleasures of a woman and stayed there, keeping men for the occasional diversion. But Syed continued to neglect his wife. The nawab tried to fix him a second marriage. And this time Syed – a ripe nineteen now – revolted.

Over the years Syed had failed to learn any maths, but while waiting for his tutor-lovers had read enough literature, poetry and philosophy – in Urdu, Arabic and English – to have made him his own man and a royal misfit. He had discovered the world of ideas and idealism; against the grain of his lineage he had become sensitized to the rights of others.

Syed was racked with guilt over Begum Sitara, his young wife, but there was nothing he could do about it. He couldn't bear to touch her; and to talk to her was to talk to a child of privilege whose world was so narrow and so gilded as to hold nothing at all. There was no way Syed was going to allow another young woman to be sacrificed at his altar.

The nawab and his son fell into a relationship of grim silences and raging rows. Jagdevpur, like every princely state in India, was not unused to scandal in the palace, but the daily facing down of the nawab was demoralizing to his sense of authority. He resolved to send his son abroad – hoping white women, white education, and white air, would temper and cure him. Syed at least had one thing that would stand him in good stead at Oxford: he was a terrific cricket player, with a front-foot lofted shot that routinely crashed the ball out of the royal grounds.

Oxford did the contrary. It made Syed even more acutely aware of the immense gap between the common man in England and the common man back home. He understood how his people had been cheated and betrayed by those who ruled them. At least with the white man there was loyalty and a duty to his own people, a code of honour and responsibility. Back home it all stopped at the doorsteps of the palaces. The people were fodder to feed the royalty's fantasy lives.

At Oxford Syed read relentlessly, made radical friends and began to travel. He became a communist before the word had any vogue; he concealed his royal past; and by the end of his first year, having dazzled with his batting in university cricket, he gave it up, declaring it a frivolity, an indulgence of the colonial British and India's self-regarding princes. In later years he would say, If this game ever spreads to our masses they will become as lazy and feckless as our royalty. And let's be clear, Indian history cannot possibly turn on a leg glance.

As he had in maths with his tutors, Syed adventured in philosophy with his white mates. He found little joy there. The feel of white flesh, the smell of white flesh, did nothing for him, so different it was from the freshly bathed, soil-skinned, oil-massaged, supple bodies that had filled his teenage years. But he gave himself up to the experiences, mostly through need, partly through curiosity and sometimes through affection.

Syed believed you could love with someone out of pure affection. If you cared enough for someone it was not too much to share your body with him, even if it did nothing for you. All Syed had to do was to close his eyes and think of the handsome tutors in Jagdevpur chanting maths tables.

The first trip he made back from Oxford he ran amok. The driving need of his body overwhelmed all the refinements of books and ideas. He was no longer a boy. He was a man now, much travelled, much experienced, with the self-assurance to seek out what he desired. The men flowed through his chambers with no regard for the hour. Shamelessly he made his aides his procurers. He liked his men a little masculine, a little dominating. He wanted to be mastered. He could not have enough. On some days he went through as many as ten different stallions – men whose names were a blur but whose bodies were burnt into his mind.

By the time he was ready to go back he was exhausted, physically and mentally, and inside him was a hollow feeling that comes from too much indulgence. Crippled – like many good men – with nagging doubts about his own relevance, he needed once again to fill up his emptiness with more substantial matters. So he was glad to leave, but he had barely reached Oxford before the ache and longing for the men of Jagdevpur filled his body again. And he drowned it in the only way he knew, through relentless reading and writing.

The cycle repeated itself again and again. The ideas and books and refinement at Oxford; and then, back at home, the orgy of letting go. Tragically, for the moment Jagdevpur concluded that their fallen prince – like most other nawabs – was only a creature of the flesh. They failed to intuit his innate nobility of ideas and feelings; they failed to read his eloquence of speech and thought; all they saw was the remorseless feasting of the body.

The nawab was eager to keep his son far away. He encouraged Syed to find a life in England or Europe and assured him of lucrative remittances. As it was, the viceroy's Home Office had its eye on Syed's inflammatory views. The India Office mandarins in London had sent in intelligence that the boy was writing up angry pamphlets, and freely making seditious talk. The Home Office's displeasure had been conveyed to the nawab by the political agent, Lieutenant-Colonel Sean Brosnan. Some of the ire had been allayed by the nawab's decision to displace Syed and nominate his younger son as the heir, but he knew official eyes were on his state, and Jagdevpur could be gulped down into the belly of the Raj on the slightest pretext. In the jargon of the bazaar, Without the exertions of a burp.

In his book the nawab wrote, The king who possesses no big cannon must learn to lie low in his castle.

But Syed was not willing to be banished. He wanted to help lift the spirits of his people; and he wanted their bodies. He wanted to spend more and more time in Jagdevpur and less and less in Europe.

The nawab was mortified. Soon every catamite in his state would be lurking around the palace walls, and his people would gossip the royal family into ridicule. Worse, there was no way of knowing how Syed's radical views might antagonize Brosnan and the British. The nawab resisted Syed's attempts to return permanently. The father and son argued, fought, raged, ranted, trashed each other as tyrant and homosexual, and finally arrived at a compromise.

Syed would build and live in a house away from the main palaces.

He would acquire a wife to live with him to contain the public innuendo.

He would exercise discretion in the numbers and choice of his lovers.

He would not publicly berate the nawab or the British.

In turn the nawab would leave him alone to lead his life.

All of Syed's upkeep would be paid for.

What was his due of the family money would be his.

And he would be given possession of the splendid library of Jagdevpur – with its collection of classic Arabic and Persian manu- scripts, and magnificent medieval miniatures of the Mughal, Rajput and Kangra schools.

Syed left in a stern proviso: if the nawab ever committed an act of outrageous tyranny the covenant was off.

The nawab's caveat was: you get into a scandal that threatens the existence of the royal family and you are on your own.

Most of it proved easy. The nawab made the money available and Syed built himself the English cottage. The library he took over immediately and began to reorganize and recatalogue. He brought in a firm of excellent bookbinders from London to help salvage thousands of loose sheets and train local boys in the skill.

The most difficult item of the agreement proved to be the wife. He could not bring in Begum Sitara because, apart from the horrors of her body, she repelled him with her foolishness; and he lacked the callousness to diminish her with his disgust every day. In the orbit of Jagdevpur there was not a woman he knew who engaged him in the least; and if he took a dummy wife from among the common people he was not only condemning an innocent woman to a null life, but also courting the possibility of further scandal.

Thus it was in despair, sojourning in Paris and dining with a group of friends who had invited a libidinous, upcoming, hell-raising artist, that he saw a handsome woman across the room and was surprised by the om she wore around her neck. It clearly had no vogue or value and he wanted to know its provenance. The woman did not seem to belong with the boisterous group she sat amid, and she gazed back at him with an air of such mysterious interest that he became curious.

On an instinct he came back the next evening.

By the time the third consecutive evening had ended and he was back at his room in the Grand Hotel, he knew he was as close to falling in love with a woman as he would ever be. In fact she was the first woman in his life who had interested him at all. She was unlike any woman he had known. She thought differently; she came from even further afar than him; and she had a mind more open than the maw of a preacher.

She never once enquired about his station or his wealth; he never once heard her speak of a jewel or a dress.

And he loved to talk to her. She had a quality of listening that made talking meaningful, that in fact made talking a deep and sensual pleasure.

And so, without calculation or conspiracy, he came to want to take her back to Jagdevpur to live with him, to be his companion. To share his days, if not his bed. To listen to him talk, to understand what drove him. Rebellion needs a witness; idealism needs a witness; sacrifice needs a witness. If only he could take Catherine back . . . she could make it possible for him to do the things for his people – and himself – that he needed to.

And in all this did he think about her needs at all?

Yes, he did. Yes, he did. He would take care of every need of hers that he could; those that he couldn't he hoped they would find ways of satisfying otherwise. Catherine sat motionless, soaking in the monsoon of information breaking over her.

Syed was still pacing up and down the study, looking at the carpeted floor. Night had fallen as he talked, and the retainers had come in on soundless feet and fired the lamps. The unsipped wine in the goblets reflected the light, richly red. You could hear the dogs barking in a welter of registers in their air-cooled kennels at the other end of the seventy-acre palace complex. The nawab was a dog maniac and maintained a pack of nearly three hundred, of every breed, colour, size. The annual dog festival he held in the second week of October brought in all of India's dog lovers, as well as every pimp and pedlar. No gathering is complete without a lashing of illicit sex.

In Chicago her mother would now be waking, readying to save the world, to heap higher the mountain of virtue. Her body would be cold, her heart would be cold – and out of such wretched material would she be making a dubious calculus of good and bad. Her father would be waking too, swimming out of a haze of alcohol, and soon preparing to leave for the store. His body would be weak and wasted, his heart heavy. From such poor material would he be making a nostalgic calculus of wonderful pleasures tasted and wonderful opportunities missed.

One a fearful preparation for the future; the other a rueful celebration of the past.

Life lived versus life calculated.

What was she being asked to do? Live or calculate?

Catherine rose from the sofa, walked up to Syed and embraced him. It was the first time she had done so and it was an act of profound affection. Syed held her close and was overwhelmed with gratitude and love.

Syed married Catherine, and it created its share of gasps and ripples. Jagdevpur's royalty were orthodox Shia Muslims who only married among their own aristocratic ranks. A white American boggled the fevered minds of the mullahs. Pitching in were the India Office and Lieutenant-Colonel Brosnan, who made their own murmurs of discontent: it was British policy to discourage such marriages;

they undermined the foundations of white supremacy. But the nawab knew how to manage ranting mullahs, and the Raj mandarins he placated by pointing repeatedly to the fact of the disinheritance.

Catherine asked Syed if he wanted to give her some guidelines, a rudimentary map of conduct to steer her through the labyrinths of Indian royalty and family.

Syed gave her only one.

Never be too deferential. Indians love masters: they are tough with the weak, and weak with the tough; frightened of the cruel, and cruel with the frightened.

She took Syed's facetious advice in good faith and developed a carapace around herself. She could not bring herself to be masterful and tough, but she could make herself inscrutable. It is the ploy of many who wish neither to practise nor to suffer aggression. Inscrutability.

It served her well. It brought her respect and it kept the trouble-makers at bay. It also allowed her to hold on to her island of privacy. A privacy she sorely needed, given the unusual nature of her household.

All Indian palaces were built on principles of libertine excess, but Catherine and Syed's house had a uniquely egalitarian spirit. As the years rolled by, the two of them – husband and wife – learnt to share the pleasures of the body together, even if not with each other. In a tribute to the harmony that prevailed in their relationship, in a tribute to their mutual trust and love, they gave to each other full voyeuristic privileges. In a dark corner of his bedroom Catherine would sink into an armchair and watch him on his large bed push his body to exquisite frontiers.

He was delicate when naked, with narrow shoulders and narrow hips. And because he had so much sex he was never engorged till someone went to work on him. Once he was, he was relentless. And even though he had no need to, he gave as much pleasure as he got.

She saw scores of men pass through his bedroom and each one left sated.

It was an act of honour: allowing the democracy of the body to flourish. Syed did not control the proceedings. Like a good lover he left the initiative open on the bed, to be seized by either participant in whichever way. He led and he was led. He pushed and he was pushed.

Catherine realized men love other men with the same kind of passion and tenderness that they love women. They are also as inventive and as unexpected. In the accounts register of her father, below the counter in the store, she had read about the endless variety of women's secret places. Now she realized men were no different. In fact the secret of their body was even more enigmatic. What a man revealed when he took off his clothes had no relation to what he looked like otherwise. There was no equation of size, shape, colour, hairiness, that could be applied.

She saw puny men endowed like kings, and mighty men modest in the extreme. She saw thin men fat as wrists, and fat men thin as fingers. She saw beautiful men with gnarled roots, and ugly men with beautiful tree trunks. She saw taut men make soft statements, and flabby men prove hard as bone. She saw large overtures expand into disappointing notes, and small introductions swell to symphonic proportions.

She also realized the hand of the creator was more nervous when shaping men: it was a rare specimen that the great artisan managed to sculpt straight and true.

Most curved and bent, ballooned and sharpened, fell left and right, zigged and zagged, in an anarchy of construction whose principles were difficult to divine.

Many of the men delivered to Syed's doorstep were lovers of women. They came merely to serve a master. Yet each left the room fully spent. There was one who was his lover. His name was Umaid. He was sharp-nosed and broad-shouldered, with big sideburns and thick long hair. He was the keeper of Syed's stables and he could make him whimper as no one else. With Umaid – and only with

Umaid – Syed would linger after it was over, tenderly tracing his muscled body with fingertips, caressing his drained organs with love.

When Catherine asked him how he could love Umaid sexually, and her unsexually, and still want so many other men, Syed said, Only one venom poisons all people – the urge to own. It kills desire, kills love, kills friendship, kills kinship. It shrinks the muchness of the world to a set of walls, a fistful of silver, a pair of limbs. I treat desire as a rite of celebration not a ritual of ownership. Always, desire as celebration. Nothing else. Not ego, not control, not proprietorship. So I celebrate Umaid, and the others life brings to me, for I wish to own none of them.

I desire Umaid because I do not own him.

I do not wish to gain ownership and forfeit desire.

I give myself up to the muchness of life.

It is never richer than in the realms of desire.

Catherine saw the wisdom in what was said. She thought of Fr John and mournful Emily. Fr John made so much lesser than himself by the rites of ownership. And sad Emily with her sad friends, full of calculations about the here and the hereafter, their tight little lives and their jumpy moralities.

Catherine herself was deeply aroused by the voyeurism as she sat in the shadows, her hands slippery between her thighs. She was aware that Syed and his partner gained additional arousal from the knowledge they were being watched – by a woman and a white one at that.

Many times, after it was over, Syed would be in some shame. In an effort to conceal it he would repair with her to the study, open a bottle of red wine and casually discuss the encounter. What he had enjoyed, what he had disliked. He would sketch comparisons. Play at being clinical. She would offer her own observations. Sometimes she would be fulsome, remarking on the beauty of two men loving each other.

Even though he defended it eloquently, Catherine knew Syed felt diminished by his driving homosexuality. He would often say to her, I don't want to die like Wilde – a smart guy who talked a lot but changed nothing. Catherine was aware Syed carried a heavy guilt about all he should be doing for his people. But consumed by his own need he had made a Faustian bargain with his father – suppressed the urgings of his conscience to pursue the demands of the flesh.

Locked inside the walls of his English cottage, the energies he should have poured into public good he ended up pouring into pleasuring the body.

Every now and then he tried to fight it. A week would go by and he would not let his retainers allow a man in. He would hunker down in the study, scanning manuscripts brought in from the library, writing copiously in a refined hand into a tan notebook, holding himself in with a visible effort.

He would write turgid essays like 'The Legitimacy of Pleasure: Desire and Exploitation', in which he would defend his position while trashing the nawab's. Other prolix ruminations had to do with ideas of equality, humanism, the colonial beast, the sins of religion and the virtues of reason.

He was that ironic animal: a highly literate man who wished to identify with the coarse. Once he wrote a curious argument, 'The Rural Phallus: Evolution's Cunning Revenge'. In it he contended that the peasant, unable to develop any overt superiority in the face of a domineering elite, had over millennia gained an edge in a hidden way by being endowed with a greater size and virility.

But Catherine could see the writing was not enough of a safety valve. He would be tight and tense, getting increasingly wound up. Every day the bolt would tighten a few more turns. Slowly he would fall silent, the words would dry up. He would cease to talk, write. Then one day the bolt would get one last twist and the grooves would give and it would break loose and fall clattering out; and when Catherine came looking for him in the study he would be in his bedroom, making geometry with another fine young body, finding his pleasure and his lost voice.

His noble instincts back on the back burner.

Catherine felt less trapped than Syed. She wasn't driven to rut all the time; and she could pick the man she wanted from the ones who ended up in Syed's bed. Sometimes he would commend one. Then the scene would shift to her room – Syed would be in an armchair in a dark corner – and she would take her pleasures as best she could. Wordlessly and with aggression.

Unlike Syed, she felt no need to give as much as she got. She just took and took and took, and when she was done she wanted to be left alone. While they gave, her partners were free to take what they could. But once she reached her unmistakable conclusion, with a great shaking and a single ripping cry, then it was well and truly over. At best there were a few moments for the man to wind up what he could. The man gone, Syed would emerge from the shadows and cradle her head and croon sweet words to her softly.

Strangely this had more meaning for her than the fornication. The act itself was only a release, only a variation on the sensual massages given to her by Banno, and only marginally better than the relief of her own hands. It had none of the insistent wanting before and after – the lingering pleasures – that Catherine would discover in later years are the key rewards of true passion.

Syed's posse of loyal retainers selected, prepared, rewarded and monitored the stable of men. True to his beliefs, Syed was enormously generous towards his retainers, and in their talks with the men afterwards the retainers ensured the virtues of discretion and silence had been fully absorbed. That the master was protected from the excessive din of the rumour mills.

Catherine couldn't care less.

Over the years she had learnt to find her joys without looking over her shoulder. While fully absorbing Syed's lesson of reasonable aloofness, which ensured freedom in the Indian context, she had acquired the confidence to ride out to the fields and forests and revel in the wildlife and countryside that had first, as a child, captured her imagination in John's Oriental Curios. Several times a week she took off on her own to escape the claustrophobia of the cottage.

Sometimes she walked through a ripening wheat field for miles, trailing her fingers over the prickly ears; sometimes she sat by the Banganga for hours throwing small pebbles into its jumping waters; and sometimes she sat under the massive peepul tree just outside the ancient Devi temple, listening to the endless chanting of hymns inside.

Stories of her eccentricity filled the land, her secret powers, her secret practices.

She cared nothing for it. Over the years she had been appalled by the conduct of the royal house. Nothing she and Syed did was a crinkle in comparison.

The hunt for frivolous amusement filled the lives of the rulers of Jagdevpur. The nawab's kitchen had fifty-two cooks, each a specialist in only one dish. Each cook had to cook his dish every day. The nawab pecked at the odd morsel and the rest of the food was directed to the air-cooled dog palace, where it was laid out for the canines on fine crockery.

Every dog had an individual handler and anything that went wrong with a dog could put its handler's work and life in serious jeopardy. The premature death of the nawab's favourite Great Dane, Gulbadan, had seen its handler, Imtiaz, flogged in public till the skin hung off his back in bloody little curls. Gulbadan had been given a state funeral, with a sacrifice of eleven white peacocks, and soldiers in golden braids and red lanyards marching up and down as he was lowered to his grave in a polished teak casket.

The nawab really loved his dogs and each day took one home to sleep in his bed.

In his book he wrote, What a dog can do, a man never can.

It mystified young students for generations.

The zenana was like the dog palace, boasting a myriad specimens and only marginally more plush. The first time Catherine visited it her breath was taken away by the sheer numbers of beautiful women crammed in there, more than a hundred. No man, she thought, has the right to so many. They clustered around her, their skins gleaming with perfumed oils, their ears, noses and fingers glinting with rubies and diamonds, their bodies draped in silks and brocades. But their eyes were empty; even their curiosity about her was dulled. Syed said it came from the knowledge that no amount of information about the outer world would help them change their lives. An air of redundancy crippled their spirits. Some of them had been last taken by the nawab years ago. They had to find outlets for themselves and their bodies within the gilded walls of the zenana.

The nawab had a specially designed thunder-box, capacious enough to hold his fleshy buttocks and with cushions at the back. In a big room it sat atop a large platform, with a sweep of twelve wide steps leading up to it. To its left was a marble-topped table for plates and goblets. To the right were five chairs with writing arms, to seat officials. The nawab sat on his thunder-box for long hours, wrestling with his constipation and meeting petitioners and complainants, who queued up the steps, hands clasped. The business of the state was carried out to lower alimentary rumbles and rectal booms.

The nawab's excesses were staggering. He had four opulent palaces filled with French furniture, Aubusson carpets and rare paintings – landscape and portrait – that had once hung in the finest of French salons. The bathrooms were big as bedrooms and the bedrooms big as ballrooms, and the ballrooms like polo fields. In the royal garage purred six custom-made Rolls-Royces, which Catherine saw drive past but never sat in once. The stables shuffled with a hundred Arabian horses.

The nawab's treasury in the main palace – revealed to her but once – was heaped with jewels: gold ingots, pearl and diamond collars and necklaces, golden breastplates, rings with diamonds the size of rocks, chests of silver coins. In a burnished reinforced frame was a priceless tiara of emeralds, hung with loops of diamonds and pearls, which the family claimed had been given to their ancestors by the Emperor Shahjahan for their help in constructing the Taj Mahal.

Syed said the tax on produce in Jagdevpur ranged between fifty and seventy-five per cent. It was enforced with professional brutality, uncontaminated by any trace of compassion. For most tillers the best outcome in any year was to hang on to their lands, bang in two meals a day, and keep the odd head of cattle from starvation.

All the land in Jagdevpur belonged to the royal family.

The peasants tilled it at their benevolence.

Syed said sometimes his father sat in the treasury naked and wore all the jewellery, the tiara, the breastplate, the earrings, the necklaces, and called in the women from the harem to file past him and be dazzled. His fantasy was to be able to do this with a full erection – as he had heard the Maharaja of Patiala could. But he was so effete, so overpleasured, that everyone knew he had trouble hardening at the best of times.

A dozen apothecaries, vaids and alchemists – on the rolls of the state – mixed and matched herbs and potions all hours of the day in a quest to find the secret of tumescence. Royal flaccidity was a serious matter. The crackpot researchers made each other sick with their concoctions. Burnt holes in their stomachs, sprouted boils and tumours, shed their hair, developed partial blindness, loosened their bowels, rotted their genitals and even lost their minds.

Their declared motto was: Nawab ka loda banayenge hatoda. The nawab's phallus will be made firm as a mallet.

While the nawab was a wastrel, his younger son, the inheritor, Syed's brother, Zafar, was destructive. He was puny – generations of inbreeding leading to bouts of retardation – and was inclined to displays of vengeful power. He had a polio left arm – it hung useless by his side – and his right was always in use punching or slapping someone.

Stung by Syed's conduct, the nawab had protected Zafar from too much learning. He had been tutored in the palace by scholars ordered by the nawab to not dwell at length on literature and aesthetics and philosophy. The liberal arts can be torpedoes for autocracy –

cracking open its hull with humanist and egalitarian ideas, and sinking its grand idea of the divine right to rule.

In any case his older brother's failure to assume the appropriate swagger of a ruler had marked Zafar. He wished to please his father; he wished to please himself. Zafar had been damaged early by his father's indifference and the people's barbs about his bad arm. They called him the aadha nawab, the half-nawab. At the time the handsome Syed had been the cynosure of all; and Zafar the cripple in the background. The neglect had bred in him a lust for approval; and had brought to the surface a dangerous venom that good parenting ought normally to bury.

Given centrestage suddenly, Zafar became a tyrant. He began to maintain armies of retainers and thugs who owed loyalty only to him. They took the cigarettes out of his mouth when he smoked, undressed him when he went for a bath, and even prepared the women for him when he wished to fornicate.

If his father could not get it up, Zafar could not keep it down. He had his own harem in an old haveli that had once belonged to one of his father's dead begums. He filled it with orgies, and there were times when he was buried under so many oiled and naked bodies that his loyal thugs had to dig him out to save him from being smothered to death. He was cruel to the women who displeased him, even unwittingly. He burnt them with cigarettes, flogged their buttocks to shreds, threw them to his thugs, and occasionally even brought in stallions from the royal stables to mount them and tear their thighs apart.

In time he gained the temerity to trawl his father's harem and pick whom he wished. The nawab – straining at his bowels, struggling with his erection – lost the will to cross him. Zafar's gang of hoodlums, wearing a uniform of black salwar suits – and known now as kaale kutte, the black dogs – became more organized, with hierarchies and established roles. Compared to the good how quickly evil organizes itself; how much greater is its clarity of purpose and speed of action.

Zafar's rutting was not confined to women alone. He liked young boys too. In their teens, pretty, without too much hair – basically women with penises. To be picked as the stunted half-nawab's catamite was a dangerous prospect. Succumbing to boys reminded Zafar of his brother's failings and created deep self-loathing in him – he unleashed it on the boys. Within minutes of Zafar finishing – weakly, always weakly, with a sudden grunt – many a boy found himself being dragged into torture and abasement. Some were sodomized with chilli-tipped pestles, others forced to abuse themselves with the royal dogs; the truly luckless had their phalluses chopped into small slices, which were then fed to the vultures.

Eventually Zafar and his black dogs grew so tyrannical that parents learnt to hide their pretty daughters – and sons – from public gaze, and at the intimation of a black shadow even married women took recourse to the burqa.

In his book the nawab wrote, The man with a pretty wife and no musket must learn to make her lie low in his house.

In Zafar's time hundreds of innocent people disappeared into unmarked graves. For a long while Lieutenant-Colonel Brosnan was disinclined to blow the whistle because Zafar did well by him and his superiors. Once, for the governor of the United Provinces and his guests from London, Zafar set up a tiger shoot in the Terai and drove an army of elephants and Jagdevpuris into the forests to drum them up. When the day ended the wheat fields outside Kashipur lay flattened from the commotion and surrounded by exhausted drumbeaters, while in the centre lay six magnificent glassy-eyed big cats, lined up like mahseer after a river run.

Another time the governor of Punjab's nieces wished a partridge hunt. But at the time partridges were scarce in the area. The black dogs swung into action and the bird bazaars of Delhi and Lucknow were toothcombed. Soon large wooden crates packed with birds began to arrive at Jagdevpur's tiny railway station. Several thousand were railroaded in and for weeks their tinny trilling – kaan, kaan,

kaan – filled the town. The dainty nieces and the black dogs shot them all up in three days.

The town collapsed into silence again.

In a mad world even massacres can be harbingers of relief.

Brosnan was kept quiet in other ways too. He didn't care much for fornication, so Zafar's girls and boys were no lure. But he had a secret obsession, for which he was willing to compromise greatly. He was a sultan of onan and a lover of art. He had married his two passions in the pursuit of old erotic Indian miniatures. Of the Mughal school, the Kangra school, the Rajput school, the East Indian school. Among his favourites was the *Variation of Inexhaustible Kindness Position*, a provincial Mughal miniature, circa 1775, where in a sitting position the man's tip can be seen just touching his lover's pouting yoni. Another favourite was the *Gentle Elephant Position* in the Kangra school – the turbaned boy, on his knees, entering his lover from behind, opening her up like a flower, just below the dark bud of her anus.

But his two prized possessions were *The Herd of Cows*, a Rajasthani miniature, in which the moustachioed Lothario stretched out on his back stimulates four women standing on four corners of the bed with his four outstretched limbs – toes and fingers firmly wedged – while a fifth squats on his thick organ; the other was one of Emperor Jahangir in his boudoir, one hand on the head of his pet cheetah, the other on the head of a concubine whose face is buried deep in his lap. *The Afternoon of the Royal Roar*.

From the marvellous Jagdevpur collection – whose true value few understood – Zafar regularly purloined and passed on the miniatures.

Brosnan hid them carefully and made periodic pornography of them.

But then two things happened to throw a spanner in the works. Two things that would eventually sever Catherine's connection with Jagdevpur.

One, in the intoxication of his power, Zafar went berserk. What he and his black dogs used to do by night they began to do by day. Brides were abducted at the hour of their wedding; merchants had

their goods confiscated without reason; the peasants were rounded
up without notice for hunts and construction work; the nawab was
abused roundly in public; anyone uttering a word of protest had his
tongue cut off, his throat slit, his limbs hacked.

The black dogs were all expert users of the Jagdevpuri, the local
switchblade: chakumaars, knifemeisters, who could draw a knife,
flick open the blade and slice the perfect artery – for death or
damage – all in the bat of an eyelid.

Sometimes the bodies were delivered to the family as a warning;
sometimes they were thrown into a big pit, where others lay heaped.
Detractors were walked past it, given the tour of terror, till their
stomachs fell out with fear.

Brosnan of empire was forced to act. No precious miniatures
could hide such behaviour. He summoned Zafar officially and Zafar
had to agree to tone it down. Restraint took the shape of chloro-
form. The deranged young half-nawab was delighted by the discovery of the colourless liquid with the lethal waft. Huge jars of it
were imported from pharmaceutical agents in Delhi's walled city and
stored in his palace. Murder acquired a decorum: it began to be
delivered politely on a handkerchief. Large numbers could now be dispatched without rude violence and telltale signs. Mystified by what
they were being attacked with, the common people named it kaale
kutte ki bu, the stench of the black dog.

Erotic miniatures were quite capable of hiding this.

The second thing that happened was related to the first. Around Syed
there began to coalesce pockets of resistance. For more than ten years
Catherine had seen Syed being nothing more than a generous bene-
factor of his people, not a leader, not an inspiration. But now the men
who began to visit his cottage had less to do with sex or the seeking
of small favours and more to do with matters of state.

They were there to exhort Syed to take the lead in ending Zafar's
reign of terror. Syed's decencies and progressive views were well

known – if anyone could lead them out of this horrible night it was him. Syed felt a thrill: the central moment of his life had arrived. He put in motion a letter-writing campaign, to the viceroy's office in Calcutta and the India Office in London. Using the distant enemy to eliminate the proximate one made tactical sense to him.

But rebels want action not epistles.

They want uniforms, organization, hierarchies, battle.

Syed discussed the matter long and hard with Catherine every day. She was equivocal. She abhorred everything about the Jagdevpur royal family, and would have done much to rid the people of them, but she didn't think Syed was the man for an untidy scrap. He was a savant not a scrapper, a formulator not a fighter, a guide not a general.

Syed was best serving his people the way he had long been doing: meeting petitioners and complainants four times a week on his veranda, holding out a hand to their miseries. He lent a keen ear to the most tedious of stories and was carefully considered in his advice. There was nothing false in his engagement with the people, nothing that was not selfless. And he was staggeringly generous with his money – as if he were going to drop dead the next morning.

Catherine never loved him more than when she saw him on the veranda, giving of his wisdom and his money, with the aura of a sufi.

This was the man, with the intense words, all that time ago in the cafes of Paris, that she had fallen in love with.

But now she feared for him, in this new, strange role. She feared once the action escalated he would be destroyed not just by the enemy – his brother – but also by his own supporters. When she sat in on the nightly meetings and saw the fiery-eyed men orate she also saw the switchblades they held at their sides.

However she also knew if Syed failed to act now the rest of his life would be crushed by regret. She held her counsel and was supportive, allowing him to feel around for the correct path. But Syed was seeking affirmation of his destiny. He wanted Catherine to tell him to seize the moment. When she did not, he began, for the first time in his life, to court every manner of soothsayer, pundit and maulvi. To the last man they told him his hour was at hand – soon the future of Jagdevpur would be shaped by his actions. They ratified this through the position of constellations, the crunching of numbers, the reading of palm lines, the interpretation of dreams.

Syed made his move. He formed a war council. His supporters chose white salwar suits as their uniform and adopted the short-handed sickle as their weapon. One was symbolic of purity; the other of the peasantry. They declared their articles of faith:

God before nawab.

Men before dogs.

White before black.

Sickle before switchblade.

Death before dishonour.

Given the circumstances of their leader, they avoided contentious issues like rich and poor, homo and hetero. As with all men with uniforms and weapons, their testosterone began to pump. They developed a code language in which the third word of every sentence was the operative word. They had a secret salute – touching the nose – its symbolism being they would cut off their nose before betraying another.

In their attempt to fulfil the mandate of men, they swiftly became boys.

Catherine watched in dismay. Even Syed appeared to be enjoying it.

She retreated into the library and began to read. Most of the house became a hive of activity. Men in white came and went all hours of the day and night. Syed was always in counsel, discussing operations and logistics. The leap from parsing books and ideas to second-guessing the motives and behaviour of real people is a mighty one. Syed was not equipped for it. In its understanding of the commoner, the noble elite is far more likely to falter than the venal elite. For base instincts are more universal, more easily tapped into, than the high.

The men around Syed, seizing on his patronage, embarked on their own petty agendas: settling personal property disputes, terrorizing traders for contributions, leaning on the peasants for grain collections, harnessing boys forcibly for their own work, and occasionally raiding the whorehouses for free rutting.

Soon Jagdevpur had another entity to fear: safed kutte, the white dogs.

Both the packs – Syed's and Zafar's – spread out into the streets, the gullies and the mohallas, the temples and the mosques, the fields and the gardens, the schools and the colleges, and war was declared.

Sitting on his pot, rumbling rectally, the nawab wrote in his book, Between white and black we must all struggle to find the peace of our lives.

It all ended badly some months later. For everyone. Particularly Syed. And the denouement was sparked by a gory burlesque. After a few skirmishes between the white and black dogs, which led to some slash and stab wounds, Syed's forces decided to mount a subversive assault behind enemy lines. They chose a target that would hurt the enemy while limiting their own casualties. On a moonless night a swarm of sixty white suits, with sickles in their right hands and fleshy mutton chops in the left, stormed the air-cooled palace of the nawab's dogs.

A mayhem of swinging sickles and leaping teeth erupted.

Syed's white warriors were bitten on their calves, arms, buttocks, crotch. Mungeri Lal, the runty cobbler, was seen riding around wildly on a St Bernard, trying to hack at it hopelessly. Irfan, the wafer-thin tailor, found himself rotating like a top with a Dobermann attached firmly to his penis. Bhola, the sweeper, pushing fifty, was brought to bay by a family of ten yapping dachshunds, all of whom attached themselves to his legs like leeches, while he cursed and kicked and swung his sickle.

When the carnage ended two hours later – with a counter-attack from the nawab's effete guard – four white dogs and one hundred and nine canines lay dead. Labradors, Afghan hounds, dachshunds, retrievers, spaniels, Alsatians, Pomeranians, Great Danes, beagles, Apsos, Dobermanns, boxers, bulldogs, terriers – all lay ripped open on the marble floor, meat pieces still clamped in their jaws. Scores of others lay bleeding and injured against the Corinthian columns, baying in agony.

The retreating strike force, in tattered clothes, melted into the night, limping and leaning on each other, amid moans of pain and peals of laughter.

The nawab went mad with grief.

Brosnan received a bamboo up his ass from the viceroy's office, the discomfort of which no position of the flying tortoise in a Mughal miniature could possibly assuage.

Within days he was replaced by a Yorkshireman, Colonel James Boycott. Boycott was tough, gruff, with little interest in art or onan. He joined hands with the nawab and set about defanging the two sons.

Zafar's black dogs were disbanded. His three key henchmen were exiled from Jagdevpur, on penalty of death if they were spotted again. His powers as a magistrate were taken away, as was his command of the state's ragtag police and its even more pathetic army. Nor could he oversee revenue collection any more. His harem was left untouched, and he was encouraged to spend his days there.

Syed's fate was worse. He was placed under strict house arrest. His visitors were monitored and orders were given that he was never to leave the kingdom. Everyone feared his fiery articulation, his moral force and his potential for directing attention on Jagdevpur. He was allowed to keep his retainers, but his allowance was cut to a fourth since he had no public life left any more.

Boycott had a particular dislike of the native with intellectual pretensions. He hated Syed's refinements and his homosexuality. He took pleasure at the prospect of choking both. He was vengeful in the way he went after the white dogs. Twenty of those involved in the palace massacre were tracked down and arraigned – their fresh scars made them easy suspects. Five were hanged and the others jailed for life. Old Maqbool reported that Umaid screamed out Syed's name in a last plea for mercy when the opaque hood was pulled down over his head.

When he came to see Syed, Boycott did not even acknowledge Catherine – she was white trash, married to brown trash.

He spoke to him as master to slave. Syed said nothing, just looked him in the eye.

But the scholar-prince was totally broken.

He withdrew into the study. He would sit there all day looking out the window at the big-leafed frangipani, hardly ever reading, writing only sometimes. Some of his old lovers still had access to him, but his body had run cold and he no longer craved contact. He appeared to be physically drawing into himself, shrinking. The greatest pleasure of their lives, conversation, died. He barely spoke any more. He and Catherine would both sit there, surrounded by books, letting the day turn, the lamps come on, the silences stack up.

It was around this time that Catherine discovered the therapy of the daily journal. She had seen Syed over the years write regularly in the big tan notebooks, but she had never been curious about what drove the act. Now – sitting years and years away from her childhood in Chicago, stranded on the edge of history, with no prospects in the present and none in the future – she now began to feel the need to make sense of her life.

She asked Syed for the notebooks and for advice.

Syed said, Write without fear and without artifice. Conceal nothing. And do not fret about how you write. Write in the knowledge that what you write is not literature, but the raw material of literature. Out of it someone may make literature one day.

She took out a tan notebook from the cupboard, claimed the table in the anteroom of the study and began to dredge up her life from the very beginning. In a miracle of absorption she could not have imagined, the activity consumed her. At all hours of the day she found herself drawn to the table; and the copious recounting of her life washed over her with a strange peace, the words giving her life a solidity it had suddenly come to lack.

But it could not go on interminably. Words cannot forever supplant living. In time the diary writing shrank to its true role – of part-time therapist – and the large vacancies of her life came rushing back and demanded to be filled.

It was around then that a man came to their cottage seeking an audience. A man who would change their lives again. For the last time.

Boycott had banned Syed's four-times-a-week durbar on the veranda, but visitors were allowed in singly after they had been vetted by the nawab's guard. It was seven o'clock in the evening, but the heat of June was still pulsing in thick waves, and the Indian plains – people, cattle, plants – lay in a stupor, gasping for breath. For weeks a dust haze had hung over Jagdevpur, and even the birds – sparrows, mynahs, crows, parakeets – could be heard for the shortest possible time at the crack of dawn and in the final minutes of dusk. If you ventured along the dust tracks of the countryside, carcasses of dead cattle lay in the cracked fields with sombre vultures snacking on their bones.

Peasants – and anyone else who worked under the sky – woke at four in the morning and were back inside their huts by eight. Those who had to travel moved by night and huddled in the shadows by day. As one giant eye, a million people looked at the horizon, willing it to darken.

Each day the nawab's weathermen hazarded guesses about the onset of the monsoon and were proven wrong. But thanks to Boycott the nawab himself was at peace. Both his sons were out of his hair; wood-and-wire crates with new puppies had begun to arrive at the dog palace; and there were reports from the laboratory of the libido, that the apothecaries had concocted a blue powder which made the organ firmer than an emperor's resolve. It was apparently also leading to headaches, stuffy noses and a misting of the vision, but it was only a matter of time before the apothecaries got around these. So the nawab lay in a pool of rose-petalled water – a rasping hippo draining endless green glasses of khus sherbet, thinking up his next aphorism and dreaming about the blue powder that would swell him to his true station.

Zafar lay naked in another perfumed pool, in his harem in the old haveli, being ministered regular orgasms by his beautiful concubines. But there was no pleasure in them any more. Just a manufactured arousal and an empty release. Without the rush of power there could be no pleasure. He was born to rule, to order, to dominate. He was born to hold the lives of thousands in the palm of his hand. He was born to see fear in men's eyes; and out of that fear, and the power it bestowed on him, rose the juice of his life. What he had been left with now were the hollow pleasures of palace women – clothes, jewels, servants, shallow luxury and tasteless orgasms.

Zafar burned to break free. He chewed opium through the day and broke into flaming rages, thrashing anyone he chanced upon. He wanted to wring Syed's neck and that of his white whore. The stupid bugger – with no control over his ideas or actions – had undone both himself and Zafar. Made them prisoners in their own kingdom. Every minute of the day he plotted ways of getting rid of him. Only if Syed was dead would the balance of punishment shift and allow Zafar to put his hands back on the levers of power.

But his spies reported that at worst Syed was deeply sad. And, while sadness kills, it can take a long time doing so; and Zafar was at the best of times an impatient man.

Catherine and Syed were sitting on the meshed-in veranda when scrawny Ram Aasre – who had married Banno and become part of the household retinue – announced a supplicant. The punkah was moving slowly, ruffling waves of hot air over damp skin. The quisqalis Catherine had planted seven years before now covered the entire wire mesh, keeping out prying eyes. At the moment it was covered with little pink flowers. In the garden beyond, the gulmohars were rapidly losing their startling scarlet blooms. Reclining in a deep rattan armchair, an unread copy of *Madame Bovary* on his lap, Syed almost waved Ram Aasre away but then felt the customary surge of conscience and nodded.

The man who came in was tall and well built with a broad, hand-some face. He wore an unapologetic moustache, bushy and turned upwards, and his lips were unusually full and thick. When he bowed low to Syed he held his head high and still. His name was Gaj Singh. He wanted permission to speak without fear and in confidence.

Gaj Singh had for years worked in the royal kitchens. His appointed speciality was Pudinakorma-ae-Dilbahaar, which was well-beaten mutton done in traditional spices with a final rain of mint juices. The nawab hated it and according to Gaj Singh had eaten it but once in the four years he had been cooking it daily. But it seemed the Dobermanns loved it, and when he was on leave they almost went on a hunger strike.

Gaj Singh said four months earlier he had been transferred to Zafar's palace kitchen. And there he had been hearing things that were evil. Standing erect, hands folded in front of him, looking at Syed but not into his eyes, speaking with a fine mix of deference and dignity, Gaj Singh said pleasure was not evil, luxury was not evil, intoxicants were not evil – the gods had made these to help men taste the gods. But malice was evil, greed was evil, jealousy was evil, murder was evil – these reduced even the gods to men.

These days in the palace of the aadhe nawab, Zafar, the shadows whispered of only one thing: how to get rid of Syed quietly without raising a trace of suspicion. And with him – and here he looked at Catherine in a gentle sidelong glance – and with him, the angrez bibi, the white memsahib.

Syed sat there unmoving, as if he had heard nothing. The violent sun finally died outside and a darkness came over the veranda. Maqbool and Ram Aasre came in with two lamps each, whose grips were shaped like the paws of a tiger.

Gaj Singh said many conspiracies were already afoot. His lordship must meet with care and eat with caution. Every visitor should be frisked before being brought into his presence; every morsel should be tested by another tongue before being passed on to his. His bed must be turned upside-down each night to check for vermin, and the casements in his room must be firmly bolted all hours of day and dark.

In fact it would be best if his honour could leave Jagdevpur at the earliest.

Syed looked on, unspeaking, without alarm or gratitude.

Catherine stepped in and said, We are deeply grateful to you, but why have you chosen to do this? Zafar would have your hide skinned were it to reach his ears.

Gaj Singh looked at the husk of the man slumped in the chair and said, I and my family owe the true nawab our lives. In the mountains we say when we forget our debts, the gods begin to prepare us for slaughter.

It seemed many years ago Gaj Singh's older brother had come with a desperate plea to Syed's veranda durbar. A monster hailstorm had wiped out their crops and cattle – the family was starving. And even though he did not belong to Jagdevpur, Syed had given him money and engineered an appointment for him in the state constabulary. A year later the brother had brought along Gaj Singh and placed him in the royal kitchens, to cook the Pudinakorma-ae-Dilbahaar that the nawab hated and the Dobermanns loved.

Catherine said, And how do we know we can trust you?

Gaj Singh said, It is written on my face. And if I am ever given the opportunity it will be written in my life. From where I come we believe the gods pick and place each of us for a fine purpose. I was sent to the aadhe nawab's kitchens for a reason.

It was true. Though Catherine had asked the question, she had not for a moment found herself distrusting the man. It was the face. Broad, open, clear-eyed, with a peasant's dignity. She realized now that he wasn't actually a very large man, it was his big, handsome face that created the illusion of size.

Catherine said, Where do you come from?

Beerbhatti. About ninety miles from here. Up in the big mountains. Under the divine lake of Naini.

And is there something you have in mind?

Gaj Singh said, I have a suggestion. And I may have a plan.

# Creators and Destroyers

Gethia was just three miles up from Beerbhatti, and the first time Catherine saw it it was shrouded in shifting mists. More than a month had passed since Gaj Singh had showed up at the cottage; in this time Syed had been declared afflicted with galloping tuberculosis and a strong plea to remove him to a hill town had been made to Boycott and the old nawab, and it had been accepted.

But Boycott had made it clear: the first hint of Syed fomenting trouble, even from far away, and he would be recalled and reincarcerated. Meantime Gaj Singh had quit the royal kitchens and come into Syed's employ. It was an exit of no consequence – neither the nawab nor Zafar even knew of his existence. And anyway no one cared for the Pudinakorma-ae-Dilbahaar, except the Dobermanns.

Men like him were in an endless line of servitors. One dropped dead. Next, please.

Unusually Catherine was astride a short hill pony, while Syed was being carried in a wooden palki borne by four wiry coolies. They moved in a beautiful swaying rhythm, feet perfectly coordinated, hips swivelling wide, the breath exhaled in one sibilance of collective encouragement. Haisha. Haisha. Haisha.

The path was a well-worn dirt-track, and the coolies and their burden kept pace with the pony. Gaj Singh walked ahead with the strong strides of a hill-man and at the very rear was another line of coolies – two mules with them – bearing tents, bedding, cooking equipment and provisions. It was early afternoon and they had been on the trail for nine hours. They had left their bivouac at Kathgodam before dawn, and had broken journey a number of times for rest and refreshments.

The monsoon had arrived two weeks before and draped the mountains in a skin of glistening green. Every slope was covered with forests of chir pine and banj oak, and under the oaks the under-growth was thick. Many treetops were festooned with creepers that ran for hundreds of metres. There was the occasional purple splash of a late-blooming jacaranda, and as you went up past DoGaon and Jeolikote puffs of clouds could be seen clinging to the mountainsides. The sound of rushing streams was everywhere, a rich, happy gargle of life.

The bird life was extraordinary, and in the first few hours up the mountain Catherine saw a greater variety of birds than she had seen in more than a decade in Jagdevpur. The most beautiful was a blue pigeon-sized bird with a long flowing tail – three times its size – that hopped from tree to path and back. Sometimes these birds came in a flock shrieking at each other, but mostly they operated in pairs. One would call urgently to its partner and, the moment it appeared, take off and call from a new perch.

Catherine christened them the Tease Birds, and several years later it was Carpetsahib who told her they were red-billed blue magpies.

The path had begun to climb from Kathgodam and it had been wide and comfortable with an easy gradient. The incline was decep-tive, for within no time they had climbed high and the air had cooled dramatically, and as they kept climbing it had taken on the faintest of drizzles – the air itself becoming softly wet – and it had sent the spirits of the convoy soaring and brought on a rash of smiles.

Catherine could not remember feeling lighter or happier in all her life.

At Kathgodam, before dawn, Catherine had pulled on a pair of khaki breeches and a cream muslin shirt. The ease of the clothes, being out in the open under the cool grey sky, the shuffling pony waiting to be mounted, the coolies rushing about in the dark tying and tightening bundles – all of it had brought on a long-lapsed innocent joy.

As she rode upwards and the skies cracked open to fill the mountains with first light, she had shed her sola topi and loosened her shoulder-length hair. Two hours later, before they reached DoGaon, the rose had come to her cheeks. She had removed her brown corduroy jacket and opened the button at her collar. Soon she was humming carelessly.

Later he said he had to struggle to keep his eyes off her. The radiance of her skin, her naked collarbones, the push of her breasts against the muslin, the stretch of khaki against her haunches – he had been inflamed. Later he also said he never saw her look more beautiful than on that first journey up. He said it had to do with the happiness because he also never saw her look so happy again.

By the time they had reached the seven-hut hamlet of Jeolikote, and Gaj Singh had pointed out the peak opposite – across a beautiful, unpeopled valley – where they were headed, Catherine was convinced she was close to the final destination of her life. By the time they had gone past the wedge of Beerbhatti, climbed down to the icy chattering rivulet snaking down from Naini, forded it with great care holding a thick rope, and climbed steeply to Gethia, her sense of belonging had peaked. This was home. This was the one place in the world she was meant to be.

The wet mist was now in play. It was moving constantly, and the mountains and valleys on either side came and went every few minutes. At times she could see all the way across the valley to the dirt-track on the other side, and then when she turned again she could not even see the coolies trailing behind Syed's palanquin. Miraculously Syed too seemed to have woken from his many months of stupor. His eyes were shining and he was talking to his bearers. He wanted to know the names of the places around, the weather patterns, the wildlife in the area.

The places. Bhumiadhar, Beerbhatti, Jeolikote, Naini, and a little further Bhowali and Pangot, and the tals, Bhim and Saat and Naukuchiya, lakes of shimmering beauty laden with trout and carp;

and still further Ramgarh and Nathuakhan and Hartola; and still further Almora and Ranikhet, and then onwards to Gwaldam, Mukteshwar, Bageshwar, Jogeshwar, and the endless dizzy heights of the higher Himalayas.

The weather. The mist, the mist, the mist: Gethia, the peak of swirling mists. Of course there was the sun, beating down directly all year, obstructed by nothing, bringing on high blue skies. And there was the rain, profuse in the monsoon, an endless emptying of the heavens; and sporadic all year around. And there was snow, occasionally, every other year, for a day or two, whitewashing the slopes. And there was the goddess of the gales, who arrived for a sojourn every summer, airing herself in the afternoons, forcing man and beast to scurry for cover. And then, when the gods were angered, there were the storms. They raged as only the gods can and there was nothing to do but kneel and pray. But finally Gethia was the mists, the swirling, dancing, appearing-disappearing mists.

The wildlife. This was a part of the kingdom of the big cats, the striped one, bagh, and the spotted one, guldaar. As kings do, the striped one only came visiting rarely, sauntering up from the forests below to inspect his domains. The guldaar, on the other hand, was a minor chieftain, and with the avarice of the small he skulked in the area, making off with dogs and cattle.

Seldom, very seldom, when a big cat set upon people, a complaint would be made at the government offices in Naini and Kathgodam. When the officers of the government failed, a runner was sent to Kaladhungi, at the foothill of the back road of Naini, where the sprawling bhabbar forests began. There lived there a great white wizard who could move through the forests like a spirit of the night and infiltrate the mind of any big cat. He did not kill for pleasure, only for a higher purpose. And he responded to every call for help. His name was Carpetsahib.

Catherine listened carefully to the springs of information Syed was tapping. This was when she loved him the most. A creature of curiosity and learning and concern; unafraid to glean from the lowliest. When they took a hairpin bend at the end of a long outcrop

– the thin end of a cake piece jutting into the big valley – Gaj Singh signalled they had arrived. Syed tapped the coolies and they gently put him down. Catherine too dismounted. The pony shook itself with a rattle. One of the bearers stepped forward and took its reins. They began to walk, Gaj Singh a few steps ahead but deferentially to the side with his body half-turned towards them.

The air was cutting crisp and Catherine found herself swallowing in lungfuls. Syed smiled and said, It's why we put all our gods on the mountains, and it's why they are all basically nice people. I'd like to see what happens when we start parking them on the plains.

This was vintage Syed. She had not seen him like this in a long time. This alone made the trip a success.

The stretch Gaj Singh wanted to show them ran up and down three small hills, and when they reached the end of the third they were at the bottom of the path that led up to the town of Naini, where the goddess resided, in a lake so large and beautiful that the inhabitants had kept it hidden from the world for centuries.

For exposing her to everyone, the goddess had cursed the foreign intruder and each year the lake waters swallowed one white man as a sacrifice.

Gaj Singh said if you set out to walk now, in two hours you would be sitting by the lake, sipping hot tea. And on the way you would pass the slope where the white man buried his kin – prematurely felled by battle and pestilence, thousands of miles from home – and put a stone over his head, as if the world had time and space to mark all its endlessly dead.

Gaj Singh said, It's all a part of the white man's vanity. Even in death he worries more about the body than the soul.

The entire length of the three small hills was less than a mile – it was truly a wedge of cake sticking into the valley, with three uneven waves on top. When Gaj Singh walked them over it – through barely discernible paths under the oaks and pines – they had breathtaking views of the valley on both sides. The one towards Bhumiadhar was dark and forbidding, with thick forests; the other one overlooking Jeolikote opened up, wide and beautiful, and pulled the eye for miles and miles.

It was a magical day. One minute they were in the caress of gossamer rain, putting a fine film over their hair and skin and clothes; and the next the skies had cleared and the world was high and blue. The mist was ever present, moving steadily, shifting the vista each moment. Sometimes it was so thick and tangible you could almost reach into it and break off a chunk.

The undergrowth was noisy with chirring insects and the trees with flitting feathers, among them the Tease Birds carrying on their charade. Out above the bowl of the valley an eagle was neatly cutting circles.

From where Catherine stood she could see the road curling away like a carelessly thrown string. Every now and then, like a big bead, there was a cluster of tin-roofed huts on the string; and up the slopes, away from the road, there was the occasional settlement sandwiched between narrow terraces, farmed by hand and hoe.

As they stood watching, a thick rainbow took root at the very centre of the Jeolikote valley and began to grow. Without fragmenting, within minutes, it had grown over their heads and dug its teeth somewhere deep inside the Bhumiadhar valley. Speechless they stood under the vibrant arch as it stayed, for a long time, as solid as the mist.

When it finally melted away and the mist again shut out the valleys, Catherine said, Gaj Singh, we are taking it.

A deal was struck. The money was paid.

Boycott was pleased at the prospect of seeing Syed's back. The nawab was happy his son's humiliation would be removed from his gaze. He summoned Catherine and told her, gently, that he hoped Syed would now, up in the mountains, find some peace and happiness. He assured her they would not lack for resources. But Syed refused to meet his father.

The report on Zafar's respönse was, as ever, discouraging. In the misery of his own humiliations, the tormented Zafar thought in his fevered, opium-laced mind that Syed in some cunning way would again get the best of it all, just as he got to the foreign university, and got the white girl, and got the love of the people.

His brother's existential misery broke Syed's heart – they had, after all, been loving playmates once and the empathy of genes does not die easily – but he could not bring himself to meet him either.

Basically Syed had come to life again and was savouring his revival. He wanted nothing to mar it. Catherine and he had rediscovered conversation, rediscovered an animation in their lives. They were spending long hours discussing the siting of their house, its architecture and its embellishments. They made another trip and it was as magical as the first – the mist was still moving, the rain was still falling, and every inch of the mountains was coloured green.

This time they were more fleet of movement. Syed too rode a pony, as did Catherine and Gaj Singh. The coolies were sent ahead with the provisions and equipment.

When they returned Syed wanted to commission drawings and designs by European architects. He was quite taken by the idea of a Swiss chalet, striking pointedly and singularly into the sky. But Catherine shot down the proposal. She was clear. It would be done in the local style, with local materials and by local tradesmen.

It was left to Gaj Singh to conjure it all up.

He left for Kathgodam and came back four days later with a mousy, bow-legged man called Prem Kumar. An impresario of hill constructions. He squatted on the floor and with a chalk drew two long lines in an inverted V, and put a two-storey box structure on top of it. On it he pitched a sloping roof. With four short lines he cast pillars in front of the lower box and pulled out a veranda. Above the veranda he drew a row of tiny little windows – as in a train – and put in an enclosed balcony. Then he leaned forward a little and placed a small rectangle divided into two behind the main building. The cookhouse was ready. Then he shuffled on his haunches a bit and placed two more rectangles at a handspan's length on the two opposite ends

of the main house, and next to them he nailed down criss-cross gates.
Now the servants had a roof over their heads.

He began to enjoy himself. He started planting trees: around the
house, next to the gate, as a shield concealing the servants' quarters
from the main house. He gave some of them branching trunks, others
lush big canopies. He ran amok. He started to contour the inverted
V in the way a real slope would be; then he began to snake a stream
through the valley floor, putting in boulders and tufts of grass. Soon
he had set some birds to flying above the trees and house. Clouds
began to form.

Gaj Singh said, Buss. Enough.

Catherine looked at Syed. Syed said, You decide, this one is your
house.

Catherine pulled a chair close to the drawing on the floor and,
stretching out a finger, began to ask questions.

When Prem Kumar left the house many hours later he had money
in his bag, a smile on his face and a spring in his bow legs. The third
wave – the spur nearest the climbing route to Naini – had been
chosen as the site. It offered the best flat ground and terraces, and it
afforded protection from the violence of the gales which Gaj Singh
said arrived every summer, and occasionally at other times too. There
was a problem about water – there were no natural springs in the
immediate vicinity – but Prem was unperturbed. He said he had
scoped the area and there was a supremely sweet, perennial spring
three miles away, up the slopes of Beerbhatti, just under Naini, and
he would pipe the water from there to the house.

Before he left, Catherine said, We will trust you, but you must
build a house that gives us no complaint.

Gaj Singh said, Oye, Premi, you screw this up and you'll never
build a house in that area again.

Shuffling on his bow legs, Prem said, Sleep in peace, memsahib.
The house will stand for a hundred years, and then it will get a new
roof and stand for another hundred. And in time more people will
drink water from my pipe than made up Akbar's army.

Syed said, Cat, you inspire eloquence even in bricklayers.

Syed kept rejuvenating; and many weeks later in the early evening, struck by the first chill wind of late November, Catherine cut short her daily stroll in the garden, and walked into Syed's huge bedroom, to find him sating himself on Gaj Singh's body. There was only one lamp, next to the massive four-poster with its high canopy, and it was set on low. She walked in through dancing fingers of light and settled in soundlessly in the shadows where her armchair lay.

Gaj Singh was naked in the middle of the bed, his body leanly muscled, the yellow lamplight playing across its dips and curves. Once delicate and refined, Syed now without his clothes appeared small and wasted. At the moment, bent over Gaj Singh's body, he looked like a pathetic mongrel grubbing for satisfaction. Pity and disgust rose in one sharp surge in Catherine, and were then swept away by a driving curiosity.

She could see Syed was greatly aroused and it was the only part of his nakedness that exuded strength. But she could see he was struggling to gain a response from the other man. As Syed loved frantically with hands and mouth, Gaj Singh rose and fell, and when he rose, fleetingly, he was slim and well crowned, a prince in the garb of a peasant.

It was clear the retainer was not in it for love, but for loyalty. He lay with his hands clasped under his head, letting the master take what he wished. Catherine could see his handsome face was blank, looking up at the canopy, neither pleasure nor distaste registering on it.

After some time Catherine put her hands between her legs and they began to slip. Syed was in a frenzy, rubbing Gaj Singh, rubbing himself, twisting and turning on the bed. In the carousel of pleasure, Catherine soon began to ride the first slow turns, the languor taking hold of her body. She was sunk deep in the chair, her feet perched on the edge of the low table in front of her. Syed had started making wet sounds with his mouth. An unstoppable spasm forced itself through

Catherine's body, closing her eyes and making her stretch; and through the blinding sensation she heard the scrape of a table.

When she opened her eyes, Gaj Singh was staring at her. No shadow is so dark or deep as to conceal a beautiful, aroused woman. Catherine stayed the way she was, not closing her legs, not stilling her hands. And as she watched Gaj Singh watch her, she saw him begin to surge and flare like a provoked cobra. Suddenly a prince with the sinews of a peasant. Syed saw the unexpected arousal and fell on it with a moan. Gaj Singh guided him urgently – staring all the while with unblinking eyes into the voluptuous shadows.

The two men now began to push and pull and demand their pleasure of each other.

Catherine's carousel of pleasure was turning faster and faster. The air had been knocked out of her, she could barely breathe. Each time she opened her eyes and saw the lean man on the bed flaring like a cobra, staring at her, the carousel spun faster.

Nothing breeds desire more swiftly than desire. Syed went frantic, bucked wildly and went off in a guttural wail. Gaj Singh caught his master's head and shook it hard till all his desire had been sucked out of him, and the arrogance of the cobra killed.

Through it all his eyes did not waver from the slippery shadows, and he recorded his passage from being to nothingness with a proud, barely discernible grunt. Even after it was over he kept staring into the dark corner; his burning gaze lit the final torch in her body and she went off in a blaze.

She was still shaking when she returned and Syed was asleep, a low snore trembling through the room. Gaj Singh had not moved, nor had his gaze.

That night, as Catherine lay in the dark on her bed – the windows bolted, the moonlight shining through the diaphanous curtains – as she lay propped up against cushions, her core molten, her head full of want, she saw the door open slowly. He stood at the threshold for a long time – as he said later, gathering courage. He was a darker silhouette in the dark room, his strong face unmistakable. She waited and felt her thighs go damp. It seemed like hours before he finally made a move. By then she was so keyed up with anticipation she could have combusted without a touch.

He pulled the door shut behind him softly and left. She spent the most restless night of her life, as Syed the boy had once, lamenting the exile of his beloved first tutor, coercing out relief after relief from the body and failing to find any.

The next day Syed sought him again. This time Gaj Singh made sure Catherine knew he was heading for his master's chamber, and it was only after she had come in and settled into the shadows and he was looking at her look at him that he came alive, an angry cobra, setting Syed to a frenzy.

That night she spent propped up in bed, looking at the door. It did not open. The next day she was again in the armchair and he was on the bed, looking at her. It settled into a bizarre pattern. Both Catherine and he knew he was making love to her while he allowed his master to glut on his body. Across the length of the room they carried out an intense relationship. And every night she stayed awake for him, willing the door to crack open, but he never came.

Syed became besotted by Gaj Singh. He refused to let him out of his sight. Gaj Singh was made to stand inside the study door when Syed was in the study; just outside the veranda door when he was on the veranda; walk right behind him when he strolled in the garden; be inside the bedroom when he was in the bedroom. Syed confessed to Catherine he was in love; it was better than ever; better even than Umaid.

It made Catherine think of Fr John and Emily, and the strangeness of desire. The weird pull of passivity that could infect even the most passionate.

Catherine now began to lock up her diaries. She moved them from the study to her bedroom, placed them in a sturdy wooden chest and ran a lock through it. Now there were thoughts she didn't want Syed to know. She was barely getting any sleep, and her body ached all the time; each day when she left the ritual in Syed's bedroom she felt not relief but an increased fever.

In ordinary sex rubbing brings release; in great passion it ignites a greater frenzy.

Catherine was a bomb whose fuse had been lit.

Prem Kumar had been showing up every three weeks to deliver an update. The terraces had been cleared and levelled; the boundary had been drawn; the holding walls were being constructed; the stone had been ordered for the walls; the lime had been ordered for the plaster; the tin had been ordered for the roof; the wooden rafters and iron girders were on their way to lay the backbone; the pine planks had been sawn and stacked for seasoning. Each time he came he squatted on the floor, did some more drawing, and left with money in his half-jacket and a bounce in his bow legs.

With some cunning, in February, Catherine suggested making a trip to Gethia to check on the construction. Gaj Singh said it was the coldest time of the year and apart from the frost there could also be snow. Syed was persuaded – with difficulty – not to risk it.

The tension, when they set off, could have felled a rhino.

As they began to climb from Kathgodam, Catherine again felt the exhilaration that belonged to the place; this time it was amplified by other anticipations. The site was a hive of activity and miraculously even at this time of year the sun was beating down directly on the spur, making it almost hot out in the open. But out of the sun, under the trees, the chill found the bones.

There were piles of stone, stacks of wood, heaps of gravel, iron girders and sheets of galvanized iron lying everywhere. Prem Kumar sat atop a mound of dressed stone, chewing a leaf of grass, bawling out the workers. He only jumped down to notice Catherine after he was sure she had seen him hard at work. With pride he swept his hand. The stone walls – two feet thick – were all up; and already, even without the roof, there was a solidity and grandeur to the house that radiated out onto the valley and could be seen for miles.

Catherine had spotted it from Jeolikote; and Gaj Singh had said, It sits there like a lion, overseeing his kingdom.

But at the moment the house was not Catherine's dominant concern. She went through the motions of being taken around and shown the progress – she ran her fingers through the veins of the rough-dressed stone, tapped the blond wood – but her mind was full of what lay ahead.

Night fell quickly and the cold descended with the speed of falling rain, soaking through clothes and setting up a shiver. In minutes the entire workforce melted into the dark, and could soon be located only by the small glows of fire in the near distance.

Gaj Singh's men had set up the tents, but Catherine ordered them to make her bed in one of the ground-floor rooms that already had pine planking nailed over it. It was the room at the back, leading off from the living room: it was the first pine floor to be hammered in, and many decades later, at the end of a long and savage century, it would be completely gone and there would only be the debris of rusting tin and rotting wood on the floor, and, looking up through missing planks and missing roof, you would be able to see all the way into a clear blue sky.

The inherent decay in the act of creation.

At the time it had the golden glow of freshly shaven wood and the heady smell of pine sap. Closed like a box, the room was cosy, and Gaj Singh set to warming it up with wood chips burnt in one of the iron trays the masons used for mixing.

Before she turned in she took a walk outside, a thick woollen stole wrapped around her. Low in the sky thin winter clouds were moving slowly, cutting the clarity of the stars. But the moon was thick and in its light, if you stood by the edge of the spur, the Jeolikote valley was a silvery marvel. You could see the road-ribbons, the silhouettes of faraway dwellings, pinpricks of lamplight making holes in the dark, and above the dark mass of the mountains the rows of marching pine trees, clad in big German helmets.

He stood a little away from her and behind her. In one hand was a hurricane lantern, in the other a gandasa, the bamboo smooth as a princess's palm, the curved steel blade at its head catching the moon-light. In the last twenty years too many big cats in these mountains had developed a taste for human flesh, and now there was talk that a leopard had taken up residence in the deep gully under Beerbhatti.

They were standing two terraces above the house. It was where Prem Kumar had dug in the storage tank and, pulling a pipe over hill and valley, set it pulsing with fresh spring water. It was falling now in a steady gargle. Underlying it was the monotone chirring of the undergrowth, broken by the occasional howl of a dog. When Catherine turned to her right, she could see the walls of the house growing just below her, a little naked in the head, lacking a roof. Suddenly she became aware of a toc toc toc sound coming at regular intervals. She asked him if it was an insect; he said no, it was some kind of bird which you could never see. It only spoke at night. It was warning the people that even as they slept time was marching by.

The tension in the cold night air was thicker than the moon.

It could have stopped a herd of charging rhinos.

When they walked down the slippery path – he stepping just ahead and to the side, holding up the lantern – she slipped a little, on loose stone, twisting her ankle. He started, but with both his hands full, could do little. She regained her footing and gingerly made her way down. At the door he hesitated, and the moment yawned between them, full of uncertainty and coiled desire. The timeless puzzle: to know and not know. To find the perfect step that breaks the ice without shattering it to pieces.

When he looked at her she was looking away, and when she looked at him he was looking down. The moment passed.

He withdrew and said he would be sleeping just outside, within shouting distance. She lay on the bed, without pulling on the thick patchwork quilt. Her body was burning, and she was filled with rage and frustration.

To know and not know.

The perfect step that breaks the ice without shattering it to pieces.

She could see him lying on Syed's giant bed, under the scalloped silk canopy, his body beautifully lean and muscular, his nakedness flaring like a cobra. Syed was touching him with his hand, mouth, cheek, nose, and she could only watch. But he was looking at her; and even if you were blind you could see what he really wanted.

Now she lay at five and a half thousand feet, alone in a half-built house, no Syed, no Maqbool, no Banno, no retainers, just him, just outside the door, just waiting for her to call; and it seemed as hopeless as sitting in an armchair in the corner of a room hidden in deep shadows. Desire and rage hammered inside her like a locked child seeking vent and nothing she did with hand or head would silence them.

She floated through a kaleidoscope of dreams – busty Paris whores in gaudy boudoirs putting up surreal shows; massive erections duelling with each other on Syed's big bed; a long-forgotten image from the Chicago store of a fair princess standing in front of a swarthy underling, grabbing his swollen phallus and pushing it inside herself.

He was there everywhere: in Paris; on Syed's bed; in the princess's hand.

But nothing pushed open the door. Time was a torment.

At some point she felt the night had passed and first light was breaking. Inside the room, with its thick stone walls and barred window, it was only a vague sense, some imperceptible lightening of the chinks in the floorboards above her. She was under the thick quilt now and, as she woke, the desire rose in her violently, making her insides coil and cramp. She swung her legs out of the bed and, as she put her right foot on the floor, she felt a stab of pain. She called out to him loudly.

He told her later he had been lying awake all night, waiting for her to call.

He rushed in and she held out her foot. He knelt on the floor, and put his hands on her ankle, and her legs parted involuntarily. He massaged it softly, one hand under the heel, the other receiving the toes. Then he looked up to seek approval. Her eyes held his and it was the moment of the perfect step, the moment when not-knowing passed into complete-knowing; and she reached out with her right hand and caught his head at the back and pushed it into her while her left pulled her dress up, releasing her long-gathering musk into the small room, making his face slip on her shining thighs. She had finished arching in a muted scream even before he found her with his open mouth.

He caught her soaked wings with his lips, wiped them gently with his tongue, and she began to fly; she was still flying an hour later when the sound of workers arriving forced her down.

Instead of two days they stayed for five, and a runner had to be sent back to inform Syed of the delay. In those five days Catherine discovered an intensity of passion she had no idea she possessed. For years she had concluded her desire was a well-regulated need. It could be fulfilled and set aside periodically, and it had no real control over her. In Syed's conversation, in Syed's intellect, in Syed's affections, she thought she had found her peace. The hunger of the body was only about some focused rubbing, and that she could drum up any time she chose. Since her time with Rudyard she had also not been with the same man more than once: for her a hard organ and a hot body were just instruments. She savoured the variety and took her pleasure when she needed it. That was the lesson of Fr John she had lived with for a long time; but now she began to discover his lessons on grand passion.

In those five days they made love twenty-five times. She was awed enough by the ferocity of her need to keep count. They barely slept at night for more than an hour at a stretch; and their planned excursion to the source of the piped water did not materialize because they wanted to stay close to the house so they could retreat into it at every opportunity. They became so wired that just exchanging a covert glance became like having sex. Catherine found herself always damp and each time she reached out Gaj Singh was swollen for love.

She could not stay away from him. Every few minutes she would summon him and take him to a secluded corner of the house and kiss and caress him. Sometimes it would be just clammy hands and mouths; sometimes he would take her standing, with the frenzy of a mad drumbeat, the rolls of her dress gathered and held under her breasts, against the immovable stone walls.

It was a strange position, seemingly impractical, but his flaring head found her with ease, with just a bending of his knees, and the geometry was right, made to design, fully capable of motion, fully made for pleasure.

Sometimes they parted in temporary satiety; sometimes stoked to a greater heat.

The third morning he had to check some pine trunks near Bhumiadhar before they were dispatched to Haldwani for sawing. He was away for two hours. It proved too long a time. She couldn't hold it in and found herself on her bed, seeking with her fingers, staying with the sensations that were rocking her being. When he returned he was fully prepared, and she was on her back, and he was in her without the exchange of a word, and they were both through in no more time than it takes to hammer in a nail.

Three steadying taps. Three firm blows.

At lunch that day he let the workers off, saying the memsahib was unwell and their noise was making matters worse. The men repaired to their shanties on the boundary, and he examined her carefully in the light and realized she was not only white and a memsahib but also voluptuously beautiful. In sheer awe he turned her over, again and again; stroking and kissing her bigness and smallness, her hairness and smoothness, her tautness and softness.

Later he said, again and again, he could not imagine what he had done to deserve this.

On the last night he took her up to the water terrace. The stars were sharp and in such profusion they seemed to be elbowing each other out of the way. This impression grew, for every few minutes a shooting star – pushed out of its place – flamed across the sky and fell off the edge. The last campfires of the labourers were dead, and there were hardly any holes of light left in the grey cloak of the valley. The undergrowth was talking and the water pipe was gargling into the

tank. In five days Gaj Singh had grown into a new assurance and he
was kneeling at her feet, in the wet grass, his head under her dress,
lifting her to the skies.

She held him there with her hands, guiding him; then closing her
eyes, she soared free and light, and became queen of the valley. When
they went inside afterwards their clothes were damp with the frost,
but their blood was hot and pulsing.

Next morning even riding the pony became an erotic enterprise.
She was sore and swollen, but achingly alive. Each time the pony
wrongfooted, and she winced in painpleasure, he, riding beside,
turned his broad face to her in a warmly knowing smile.

Syed was waiting with great anxiety.

He carped bitterly about the delay. He told Catherine he had
suffered in longing for the man while they were away. He said he had
written six poems for him. They celebrated his hands, mouth, thighs,
navel, buttocks and phallus. He said, thinking of him, for the first
time in nearly ten years, he had become so aroused he had to give
himself relief.

Syed said, Cat, I want him desperately, but I don't think he wants
me. I think he only suffers me out of a sense of duty. But the frightening part is I don't care as long as I can have him. He may feel nothing, but I feel enough for both of us.

Catherine held her poise, struggling to make sense of it all.

She knew the anxieties of fresh love would soon shrink the world.

She remembered how, against his nature, Syed had initially been
so possessive of Umaid; how the keeper of the horses had been forbidden any other dalliance. And soon, when Syed's exclusive impulse
had passed, she remembered how the sad-eyed Umaid used to suffer
watching his master's bed fill up with all kinds of men. So often she
would look out her bedroom window and see him sitting on his
haunches under the frangipani, his sweet young face expressionless,

a turban coiled on his head, a big cream-yellow flower from the tree above twirling in his hand slowly.

She recalled how they said he had screamed Syed's name when the noose was adjusted.

Catherine began to feel like Umaid. Sitting in the armchair in the shadows was now like sitting under the frangipani, a lonely and frustrating activity, full of sad and faraway thoughts. Her hands died on her. She no longer wanted to see Syed rutting on him. Her mind raged with different memories. She wanted the heat of his body. His peasant hands, his rubber mouth. His burning ardour.

She had her share of Gaj Singh, every night, but it was never enough. He would come in late, after Syed was asleep, and by then she would have her hands all over herself, stoking and containing her spiralling excitement. When he opened the door the musk of her desire would be wafting in the room; by the time he touched her she would be trembling on the brink.

She loved the moment of his first touch: mouth on her mouth, the very tip of his middle finger, softly, incredibly softly, opening up her flesh. She almost stopped breathing as the fingertip travelled slowly, on the lightest of feet, to the top of the mound where the sentinel had risen. Then the sentinel and the fingertip began to duel, dancing around each other, thrusting and parrying, and she let go of her breath and began to move and moan.

As long as he was there, it wasn't over.

Even when he was done he would continue to kiss and caress her.

When she held his travelling hands, too spent to bear any more stimulation, he would whisper love in her ears.

Catherine had never been worshipped like this. Between the casual libertine chaos of Rudyard's Paris, the warm asexual companionship of Syed, and the clinical intercourse of the catamites, she had known satisfaction, never such adoration. Gaj Singh went at her with continual ecstasy. And till it was time for him to leave – just before dawn – some part of him would continue to love some part of her; and, insanely, within minutes of his departure, drifting in and out of sleep, she would begin to ache for him anew.

She made no confession to Syed, even though it might have made it easier for her to access Gaj Singh. Keeping it a secret was against the grain of their long relationship, but some instinct warned her into silence. She intuited that if Syed saw the two of them making love he would be shattered. The depth of their passion would not be concealed – can oil fail to blaze when a flame is put to it – and she felt Syed, struggling with his own unrequited love for the retainer, would not be able to deal with the knowledge.

Soon she also wanted to stop being a witness to the coupling of the two men. It made her feel wretched. But Gaj Singh would not hear of it. He argued if she were missing he would fail to get aroused, fail to perform, and then Syed might get angry, even go berserk, and undo everything.

And so it came to pass.

So intoxicated did Gaj Singh become with Catherine, so replete and exhausted was he with loving her every night, that it became an unbearable ordeal for him to suffer his master. He complained to Catherine about it; he said he could not go on; he said he was filled with self-loathing. And then suddenly three days running he failed on Syed's bed. Nothing Syed did could bring the bone to the handsome retainer's flesh. Syed stopped and he started, and he stopped and he started, and in the yellow light everything glistened with his efforts, but nothing happened. The glory of his lover stayed hidden in its cowl, drained of all pride, devoid of response.

Gaj Singh tried too, tried as hard. He peered into the shadows to see her voluptuous silhouette and be aroused, as in the past. But now he wanted her, not just a suggestion of her. He tried closing his eyes and reliving his passion. The first trembling moment of holding her foot; the frenzied hammering against the immovable stone walls; the slow scrutiny of her many secrets in the half-light of midday; the journey into her as she stood near the water tank surveying the valley; the nightly unpeeling of every skin of desire.

He thought of how she drove him crazy – not just with her beauty, but with her aggressive abandon, her tabooless pleasuring, her enclosing hand.

But just as the memory began to move him, Syed's exertions would get obtrusive, dragging his mind back to the present, stemming the flow of the blood. On the second day Catherine and Gaj Singh could see a heavy black mood beginning to settle over Syed. His efforts were sullen; his face was set. After more than an hour of rubbing and pulling he dismissed the retainer with a contemptuous wave of the hand.

Later he said, Cat, I think I am losing him. But I am going to make sure I don't.

That night Gaj Singh told Catherine, I should go away; I know if I don't go away quickly this will end badly.

Catherine tried to allay his anxieties. She extolled the charity in Syed's character.

The retainer was not impressed. He said, Listen, you know nothing about royalty. It is true royal blood can become human for some time, even for a long time, but never forget in it resides the devil that never dies. The moment it is questioned, the moment it is snubbed, it springs alive and takes over all that may be good.

The kindness of a king is a strange thing. It resides not in justice or merit or compassion, but in the abjectness of the seeker.

On the third day Gaj Singh tried his hardest to push both mind and body to make it happen, and discovered that there is clearly something else that controls both. Syed was coldly calculating as he kept testing him for a response. Finally giving up, he dispatched Gaj Singh with an ominous warning, Impotence is a virtue only in harem guards. You'd better stop doing whatever you are doing.

Late that night Syed tried to open the door to Catherine's room and found it latched. He sat down in the big foyer outside the bedroom in a beautifully carved Louis IV chair. He was small enough to disappear into its curves. With his old air of containment he kept sitting when the door opened just before first light and Gaj Singh walked out. When the handsome retainer was at the end of the hall-way, about to exit, Syed said softly but loudly in that first silence of daybreak, I knew stallions don't go impotent overnight. They die before they decline. Or they are put to the death.

Gaj Singh's stomach fell out. His legs became water.

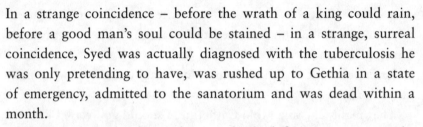

In a strange coincidence – before the wrath of a king could rain, before a good man's soul could be stained – in a strange, surreal coincidence, Syed was actually diagnosed with the tuberculosis he was only pretending to have, was rushed up to Gethia in a state of emergency, admitted to the sanatorium and was dead within a month.

He was brought down the way he had first gone up, on the shoulders of jogging bearers. Disowned while alive, he was now claimed by the clan. Elaborate rituals of royal demise were set into play. Catherine was completely shut out. For his passage into para-dise the long-suffering Begum Sitara – now fat and dumpy, with folds the size of fingers under her eyes – was pulled out of the palace and set to weeping. Even Zafar – already decrepit at thirty-nine, his good limbs withering like his bad, teeth rotting, phallus failing – even Zafar, marred through his life by the luminosity of his brother, shed a tear.

In his book the nawab wrote, In death everyone wins, even the failed and the disloyal.

Instead of suffering on the sidelines, Catherine packed her per-sonal effects, gave away to their retainers vast quantities of all that was being abandoned, and with Gaj Singh as escort and Maqbool, Banno and Ram Aasre as lifelong appendages, left for Gethia. The only thing of weight she carried was a chest full of tan notebooks – many blank, many crammed with wordwheels – and a few miniature paintings.

Perhaps because of her sorrow, and the disregard she suffered at the hands of the royal family, she did not dwell at length on Syed's death and its aftermath. In fewer than three pages of his dying she was firmly ensconced in the house on the hill, amid the redolence of fresh pinewood, under a new roof painted with red oxide and secured down firmly with iron belts against every gale and storm.

After this there was only one more entry about Jagdevpur that could be located. Many months later Gaj Singh visited the town and returned with the information that orders had been passed by the nawab to sanitize all the official records. The existence of Catherine was to be eliminated altogether and Syed was declared long and happily married to Begum Sitara. Portraits of them posed together were painted and put up on the genealogical walls. Any man heard claiming Syed's intimacy, and anyone discovered to be in contact with Catherine, was in line to suffer the nawab's acute displeasure.

Catherine was only too happy to be deprived of the baggage.

She had never in her life craved anything material. Now she cared even less.

She had found her place in the world.

It was inhabited by the demons she had inherited from Fr John.

Love and desire.

In the long years she lived there she saw the hills change and not change. New holes of light appeared in the grey shroud of the valley with every passing season. Once in many years a patch of ancient pines was axed and fresh trees planted. Sometimes an occasional step appeared on the slopes as a terrace was cut to attempt an orchard. And in time brilliant surveyors and tireless road gangs arrived and sketched a road from outside of Jeolikote, around the further mountain, all the way up to Naini.

Standing by her house, Catherine could see, down below, the fork where the new road arced left, while the old one meandered towards her. It took the house in its lazy loop and carried on all the way to

Bhowali and Bhimtal, and Ranikhet and Almora. Gethia was a blip on the journey, an oddity with a tuberculosis sanatorium and a strange white woman on a spur. Catherine was happy about that. There could never be enough privacy.

What changed the least were the hills. Mostly, the pine and oak forests held, and the settlements that appeared came up too slowly to scar the slopes. The Tease Birds continued to decorate the trees, and the big cats kept stalking the ravines, coming up from the Terai, where rampant farming was cutting down the forests.

Gethia remained enveloped in mists and, miraculously, hardly any new habitations grew up around her house. The few that did were out of eyesight, near the sanatorium two spurs away.

The word had spread about her in the mountains. She had a sinister past. It extended not only to palaces in the plains, but across the waters to England and beyond. She had the wealth of a queen and the beauty of a houri. She ate princes for breakfast and peasants for dinner. She had come to the hills fleeing persecution. She had come to the hills to practise secret rites. She was a white woman whom even other whites feared; she worked black magic that even black people feared.

Catherine was aware of these murmurings. As in Jagdevpur, she could not care less and in some ways, in fact, was glad for them. They kept all intruders at a remove. One of the few things she had brought up from Syed's cottage was a bolt-action Winchester. She hardly knew how to fire it, and it just hung at an angle above the fireplace. But people began to say she was inclined to shoot anyone who tres-passed on her property. That at night she glided over her land, cocked rifle in hand.

Many of these tales were first spun out by her own retainers: Maqbool, Banno, Ram Aasre and Gaj Singh. It served their purpose to keep the locals in thrall of the memsahib; and since Catherine was not inclined to correct any misimpression, they took to saying what-ever seized their fancy.

In the weird way these things happen, the rumours created their own fulfilment. Catherine responded to these expectations and fears by living up to them. Initially she didn't mind going up to Naini once every few weeks. It was a busy and beautiful town with the enchanting lake, a mixed bag of locals, plainsmen and British, and lively churches, eateries, shops and schools. It piqued her natural curiosity and she made several acquaintances quickly, but the moment curiosity began to flow back – and there was talk of people coming to visit – she withdrew rapidly.

From her front veranda she could see the lights of the highest point of Naini and she gazed on them every night till the very end. But for the last many years of her life she did not venture there even once. The last time she went there – and it was one of the few firm dates the wordwheels contained – was on 16 May 1924, to attend the funeral service of Mary Corbett, a friend's mother.

She recorded it as a solemn and grand affair – Mary was nearly ninety and one of the founding spirits of the new Naini – and ended it by saying it was the precise opposite of the way she would like to be finally seen off. With just one man by her body, one man who was possessed of the knowledge that she had lived fully and deep. As she would have liked to have been for Syed – just one woman by his grave, the one who knew it all, beyond the deceits and the delusions.

In death, at least, must truth triumph.

Mary's son, Jim, had become an unexpected friend soon after she had moved up. He was visiting Bhumiadhar, seeing off one of his men. He had just come back from the first world war and was disbanding the 70th Kumaon Company he had put together. Five hundred hill-men had followed their hero with total loyalty and had seen little battle but much misery. He had brought them all back but one, who had died of seasickness.

Jim stopped off en route to see the new inhabitant of this part of the mountains, and she took an instant liking to him when she saw the way he spoke to Gaj Singh and Ram Aasre. He was modest and strong, curious without being persistent. Unlike Syed, he lived not in the mind but in the real world and was most eloquent while talking of things outside of himself. A natural teacher, in their long if infrequent association – Gethia fell on a different axis from Kaladhungi–Naini, which was his regular beat – and in the course of their infrequent meetings he managed to gift her three valuable things that completed her absorption into the Kumaon hills.

The first was a rudimentary understanding of the birds and animals she had come to live amidst. A few days after their first chance meeting he sent up a sheet of paper to the house, with a note to say that this was his first self-taught wildlife tutorial and it still stood him in good stead. It was an elementary classification.

### Birds

a) Birds that beautify nature's garden. In this group I put minivets, orioles and sunbirds.
b) Birds that fill the garden with melody: thrushes, robins and shamas.
c) Birds that regenerate the garden: barbets, hornbills and bulbuls.
d) Birds that warn of danger: drongos, red junglefowl and babblers.
e) Birds that maintain the balance of nature: eagles, hawks and owls.
f) Birds that perform the duty of scavengers: vultures, kites and crows.

### Animals

g) Animals that beautify nature's garden. In this group I put deer, antelope and monkeys.
h) Animals that help to regenerate the garden by opening up and aerating the soil: bears, pigs and porcupines.
i) Animals that warn of danger: deer, monkeys and squirrels.
j) Animals that maintain the balance in nature: tigers, leopards and wild dogs.
k) Animals that act as scavengers: hyenas, jackals and pigs.

**Crawling creatures**

l) Poisonous snakes. In this group I put cobras, kraits and vipers.

m) Non-poisonous snakes: python, grass snakes and dhamin.

The chart was based on no science but that of functionality, of natural labour, and was far more useful for the lay seeker than any understanding based on evolution or form. She was to use it as her natural history guide till the very end. It was also Jim who told her that the Tease Bird was actually the red-billed blue magpie.

The second thing Carpetsahib gifted her were three deodar saplings he was bringing down from a trip to Gwaldam. She planted them at three points of the house: near the lower gate, by the upper gate and one in between. Ten years later only one survived, the one in the middle. Twenty-five years later it defined the house: a virile young tree, splitting six feet above the ground into three upheld arms, soaring higher than the house, referred to by the locals as Trishul.

The trident.

Shiva's weapon against all comers.

Seventy-five years later the tree – with a crouching limbless car under it – which clinched a decision.

The third thing Carpetsahib gave her was a sense of the mystery of the Kumaon hills. She received most of it second-hand – from him and her retainers – but it never left her. In a difficult-to-explain way it made her life rich. She had only to sit on her terrace and look at the valley and the slopes and the forever moving mist to know that she was part of something eternal and interconnected, and blessed to be in a special place. At such moments time and distance melted, and she did not feel too far away from Fr John.

Each time Jim dropped by, speaking in his soft, deliberate way, he expanded that sense of specialness. He told her charming stories of ordinary hill folk and incredible stories of hunting down maneaters.

The most fascinating was of the first one he had tracked, more than a decade earlier, the Champawat maneater, a demon that had spread terror in the mountains, claiming more than four hundred lives. The detail that never left Catherine was of the village woman who had been struck speechless for years by a narrow encounter with the monster; when Jim killed it he took the skin to Pali, the woman's village, and the moment she saw it her voice sprang forth from the pit of her fears, and she rushed around shouting for every villager to come and see the pelt.

In the same way, in his long story of the odyssey of hunting down the man-eating leopard of Rudraprayag, the one detail that clung to Catherine was connected to the animal's death. In local folklore there had never been a more rapacious, wily and indestructible creature. Between 1918 and 1926 this leopard had killed one hundred and twenty-five people and kept the religious routes of the area in terror. All attempts to trap it, shoot it, poison it, had for years came to nothing – Jim himself failed on more than one occasion. But when he finally shot it, he discovered the most hated and feared animal in all of India was an old, greying leopard, scarred with wounds, its teeth worn and discoloured and its tongue black with the poisons it had been fed.

Most stories the hunter told her were testaments to faith.

One was about Jim's childhood friend Kunwar Singh, who, shooting in the forest with another friend, Har Singh, unwittingly disturbed a tigress with her cubs. The tigress charged with a furious roar and in wild panic Kunwar shinned up the nearest tree. Har Singh, who was slower, was pinned against the trunk by the tigress standing on her hind legs, her forelegs on either side of him, clawing the bark in a rage. The cacophony of Har Singh screaming and the tigress roaring was broken by Kunwar firing the gun in the air. The tigress bolted, but not before ripping open Har Singh's belly from navel to spine, causing his intestines to fall out.

In terror, fearing the return of the tigress, the men shoved the entrails back inside, along with the humus and twigs and leaves, and tied them in with Kunwar's turban. They rushed to the tin-shed hospital at Kaladhungi, where the young doctor did what he could. Har Singh lived to a ripe old age; the mauled runi tree died first, in a forest fire just before the outbreak of the first world war.

Faith. You had to succumb to faith to find your peace. Everyone Catherine had known in India was in harmony with that knowledge; even Syed, though it had been violently against his temperament.

You tracked your life between the god of reason and the god of unreason.

Bowing to both, offending neither.

There was no contradiction there. Only the vain saw any.

In the hills the god of unreason was dominant. Gaj Singh said it was because all the spirits, good and bad, sought the high ground of the Himalayas. Here, in the abode of the gods, lay both refuge and salvation.

Catherine's retainers were great vessels of superstition and supernatural experiences, but Jim – white man, naturalist, doer, empiricist – was, she discovered over time, no different. He prayed at Hindu shrines and insisted on shooting a snake before embarking on a tiger hunt. And over the years, reluctantly, tersely, he gave her chilling accounts of his encounters with spirits. The one in the forest guest house near Champawat, an encounter he was loath to even articulate; the one in a remote dak bungalow which saw him and his friend being physically thrown out onto the hillside in the middle of the night; the one in Braemar in Naini; the poltergeist in the Ramgarh dak bungalow; and the blood-curdling scream of a banshee – not a churail, which walks on inverted feet and screeches differently – as he sat in a machan above Chuka, stalking the Thak maneater.

In 1929 he told her about his strangest – and uplifting – experience at the sacred hill of Purnagiri, where one night the goddess Bhagwati gave him and his team of hunters a darshan, moving across the precipitous face of the hill in a play of lights. He said it was a gesture of godspeed because they were on the trail of the Talla Des maneater, which had terrorized the area.

On his rare visits Carpetsahib also brought her news of the wider world. Her only other sources were her retainers and their highly unreliable accounts. Jim would bring her copies of the *Illustrated London News*, where she read about the cataclysmic changes overturning Europe. When the second great war began and Paris fell, she thought of her friends, though she had lost contact with them decades before. Jim also brought her news of the Indian nationalist movement, and here his accounts were not that much different from those of Gaj and Maqbool. A great impulse was sweeping the plains and it was driven by great men: it was only a matter of time before India was reconfigured one more time.

All this will change, all of it, said Jim, with a gesture of his hands, taking in the Jeolikote valley, the Naini hills and everything beyond. He himself was making regular trips to Tanganyika and Kenya, a good stalker, reading the lie of the land, staking out the last camp of his life.

Catherine had her own miraculous brush with history one afternoon when two black cars stopped outside the gate and five men walked up the path to the house. One of the car engines needed cooling, and some water for the radiator. Two of the men were in suits, two in white pyjama-kurtas, and the fifth naked on the legs, wearing a small loincloth dhoti and a coarse brown shawl over his shoulders.

This man was thin as a blade of grass; and but for the fact that he was bald and clean-shaven he looked like the striding fakir she had first seen in Chandni Chowk nearly thirty years earlier. Baba Muggermachee. But this fakir, she knew, was riding the biggest crocodile of them all, an antediluvian monster made up of the contradictory and clamorous burden of three hundred million people. It would take all his magical powers to cross the waters. The moment it was done the crocodile would turn and devour him. Then, freed of the spell, it would go back to its chomping-champing wheeling-dealing cunning-running slimy-grimy snivelling-bullying cruel-evil ways.

The fakir's in the belly; and we are running Delhi.

She would not live to hear of his death by bullet. Too much goodness is a dangerous thing. By then the century would have run less than half its course.

That afternoon the great fakir drank two sips of water and none of the offered tea. He smiled gently, asked a few questions; she could think of nothing to ask him and he was quickly gone. Among the three hundred million there was the ailing wife of one he had to visit in Bhowali. As he left, he put his hand on her wrist. It was small and bony, the claw of the poorest.

She thought of Syed and the leap never taken.

The mind receiving the signal from the heart. But the will – the will – never able to receive the signal from the mind.

The circuit of heart–mind–action never closed.

Gaj Singh, Ram Aasre and the rest stood at a distance, their hands folded, their backs bent. He swivelled to them all, leaned into the car and was gone. Gaj Singh said, Can this be him?

So Carpetsahib gifted her knowledge and mystery and the deodar, and the passing fakir touched her with history. And the retainers used it all to embellish her myth. After Carpetsahib stopped by the house a few times they even let it be known that the great hunter was dropping by to swap stories of famous kills. But it was not as simple in the beginning. Gaj Singh was struck by storms of jealousy. He would hover close by when Jim came visiting and be sullen for hours afterwards. Very soon, however, it became apparent there was nothing there.

Jim was a shy man, pursuing other things.

Catherine made mention of it all in her scribblings, remarking that in the great hunter desire seemed to have picked up the wrong spoor and wandered into a territory which had no game and no satisfaction.

The great fakir, Carpetsahib, these were rare – very rare – distractions in the more than two decades she lived in Gethia. The true essence of the story of her long years was singular and unchanging. It had one locus: the house; and one fixation: Gaj Singh. The passion that had first flared in the armchair in Syed's bedroom and then combusted in the hills slowly grew into an obsession. Day after day the tan notebooks of the time were full of initially enthralling, then tediously fascinating, details of their coupling. The discoveries and the excesses. The wanting and the sating.

The descriptions were explicit. Fr John and Paris and Syed had taught her well and given her a candour. She celebrated every part of Gaj Singh's lean brown body. The changing quality of his arousal under different provocations. The way his movable slip of skin moved under her fingertips, satin sliding on marble. How, when she loved him for long, he began to weep with want, putting filaments of stickiness wherever he touched her. How his firm buttocks flexed when he got out of the bed. How his big pouch became a loose offering or a hard statement depending on what she did. The way his full lips drove her into ecstasies, sucking out a trail of unpaining weals everywhere. How he found a maddening spot deep inside her with fingers so creative she thought she would die.

The obsession was complete. Everything about him drove her into a frenzy.

She was eroticized by his armpit smells; his breath on her face; his hands on her forearm. Through it all she maintained the formal decorum of the relationship. In the presence of the others he was another servitor, if a favoured one. He lived in an outhouse like the rest of the retainers. She gave him the one near the lower gate so it was easy to sneak up from there every night, through the oaks, without being seen.

She knew enough to know that if she embraced Gaj Singh openly it would destroy her privilege in the area. It would become impossible for her to command the respect of the other servants and the locals. It would destroy her myth, perhaps even open her up to unknown threats. At another level, and as importantly, she enjoyed her love's clandestine air. It had been born in secrecy and danger, its very provenance couched in the subterfuge of those torrid nights at the cottage: its charge was forever linked to an illegitimacy. To stay with that slightly edgy, urgent feeling made it seem continually fresh.

Intuitively she knew this desire was a lichen, thriving in the damp and the dark. To place it in the glare of light would risk killing it.

When everyone had turned in, and the hills had been taken over by the armies of the night – the moths, the cicadas, the nightjars, the bats, the foxes, the bears and the big cats – Catherine, sitting in the room above the one in which she had first summoned Gaj Singh to hold her foot, would open the door that led out of the house. Weirdly the first-floor door opened not onto a terrace or a balcony, but onto the sloping tin roof of the dining annexe below. Bow-legged Prem Kumar, in a final flurry to finish the house, had blundered. And with all the architectural drawings long ago swept off the cottage floor there was nothing for reference. Instead of putting a room above the dining annexe Prem had, in a rush, pitched a roof and declared the project closed. In a sweet twist, the stonemasons, by then racing to keep their deadlines, had etched a rock-solid staircase along the outer wall, leading to a room that had become a tin roof.

So it hung there surreally, at the back of the house, an unshakeable stairway to a steeply sloping tin roof.

And it was this that Gaj Singh climbed every night as Catherine sat in her rocking chair, a pressure lantern hissing softly in the corner, the door wide open, the valley of Jeolikote spread out below – just beyond the slope of the roof – punctured with a few scattered holes of light and sometimes a sliding coverlet of mist.

He came up the back path on animal feet, and just the faintest crunch of gravel announced he was at the bottom of the stairs, beginning to climb. And even though he came up every night Catherine's thighs immediately went damp.

In no time he had covered the ten steep stone stairs. She first saw his right hand – with a thick iron bangle and a bronze ring – appear around the door jamb, wrist bending backwards, seeking a grip. A featherlight foot on the slanting roof, the sudden murmur of tin, and he had swung himself in. He scraped his leather shoes on the sill; if it had been raining, he shook himself like a dog. Then he closed the door behind him, shutting out the valley and the night. With a little jostling – the pine was forever warping – he managed to push the latch home. Then he went and knelt in front of her, and she caught him and put him inside her clothes.

Sometimes she teased him, played with him.

Sometimes she was in bed under the quilt, pretending to be asleep, when he swung himself in.

Sometimes she was not there and he had to go looking for her in the house, wondering where and in what state he would find her.

Sometimes the lantern was off and she was kneeling on the bed, away from the door, the moonlight shining on her fullness.

Sometimes she was without any clothes.

Sometimes without any hair.

Sometimes in the tedium of waiting she would smear a trail of herself from her wrist to her core, and when he arrived she would give him her hand to kiss and to track his way slowly into her.

Over time, they tried it all. It is remarkable how everything in the world changes except what two people do in desire.

They would endlessly climb peaks and fall off them. Do old things in new ways. And new things in old ways. They became the work of surrealist masters. Any body part could be joined to any body part. And it would result in a masterpiece. Toe and tongue. Nipple and penis. Finger and the bud. Armpit and mouth. Nose and clitoris. Clavicle and gluteus maximus. Mons veneris and phallus indica.

The Last Tango of Labia Majora. Circa 1927, Gethia. By Salvador Dalí.

Draughtsmen: GajnCatherine.

She screamed silently through it all – through gritted teeth, through wide open mouth – and only Gaj Singh knew how loud it was. It ripped through the house and filled the valley. She had the gift of going away completely. Her eyes would glaze over and her body become so tremblingly fine-tuned that it was clear it was stretched to its last limits. A high-tension wire pulled to snapping. Often, later, Gaj Singh would struggle to describe her to herself.

There was nothing they did not do. And it was done not out of a spirit of experimentation, but from an intensity of wanting nothing could stem.

It was inevitable it would lead to annihilation or to new frontiers.

And so one day, in the middle of an unfurling masterpiece while his fingers looked for her essence, there was the sharp hiss of a spitting snake, and when he looked down, the hair on his chest was wet and beginning to drip.

A switch had been thrown. Another door had been opened.

After that Catherine rapidly ascended into a zone that surpassed the understanding of both Gaj Singh and herself. In the beginning she would occasionally squirt in moments of great passion. Short, sharp, clear streams. It would happen when his fingers were seeking in her. In awe he began to probe-press-massage more and more, and slowly she began to erupt like a fountain and flow like a tap. As he loved her, her flesh would swell and contract and swell and contract, almost pushing itself out of her, and then it would gush and gush, and where she sat – the chair, the bed – would be washed wet.

And then, as all restraint fled like a fugitive in the dark, it became so copious it would rain down and there would be small puddles on the floorboards, and he had to bring a mop and soak them out.

For a very long time it was only with the fingers, but then it also began to happen when he was moving in her. He would be on his back and she would be gliding slowly – her eyes closed, her body a high-tension wire about to snap – and then suddenly her flesh would swell impossibly and, as he fought back waves of extinction, she would flow. His abdomen would be drenched, his thighs would be drenched. Then she would start to move again, and soon her flesh would again swell impossibly and she would rain down on him. Now he would be lying in a pool. Sometimes there were as many as half a dozen showers at one time, and by the time it was over, the sheets and mattresses were drenched to the core.

Then they would walk to the other bedroom to sleep.

The missing room – above the debris, below the missing roof – became, for long years, solely an arena of ecstasy. Every night the backward-turned hand would appear in the door jamb, there would be a murmur of tin, a scraping of shoes and the rituals of love would commence.

Very quickly they learnt to put a tarp between the sheet and the mattress.

Each night they would drape the sheets in the living room in front of the fire to allow them to dry. And in a few days of wetting and drying when they went from crisp to stiff, they would be handed to Banno to put in a steamwash.

On days when they finally peeled off the sheet, there would be shallow puddles studding the tarp. You had to hold it from all four corners and drain it onto the sloping roof.

It was beyond understanding.

Her body had shed all limits and evolved into some sexual-spiritual state.

Gaj Singh christened it amrita, the nectar of the gods.

He said he felt blessed to be bathed in it every day.

He said it was like Shiva and Parvati. When they made cosmic love the world was bathed in their libations.

Shiva and Parvati. The primal duo. Creators and destroyers.

In the many years she lived there – more than two decades – she only left Gethia for the plains once. Since the dating in the diaries was so poor it was difficult to tell the year, but it would have been in the early nineteen twenties. She went to Agra. Presumably she saw the Taj Mahal and Fatehpur Sikri and the Fort, but it's not all she could have gone there for because she was away for more than four months. In fact in the wordwheels there was little mention of any sightseeing. Just that she had gone, and the journey had been exhausting, and Gaj Singh had been with her. In later notebooks the Agra trip had an occasional mention, without any light being shed on its purpose.

There were indications that she received letters from Chicago in the early years. There were dismissive references to Emily's apocalyptic rantings, cautioning her daughter not to stray too far from the lord, and to remember that the lord would reach her no matter which forsaken place she was in if she but reached out for him.

John had died while she was still at Jagdevpur. It had taken Syed's immense wisdom to shepherd Catherine through her grief. She had recorded his loss with an almost inarticulate sorrow. She had tried – in her notebook – to write him a letter as an epitaph. It had been a struggle. Four times she had started, My Dearest Father, and then meandered for a few difficult emotional paragraphs and stopped, scored it out and started afresh. Finally the letter had been abandoned for a simple legend, written in small, clear block letters, on perhaps the only uncrammed page in the library of notebooks: John, my father, in the land where I live they say we are born again and again to make good our debts; if it be true, I do pray that I be born your daughter again.

There was no hint she ever wrote to her mother and no reference to when Emily might have died.

At some point – in the early nineteen thirties – the diaries began to become dark, and then darker. A serpent had entered Catherine's garden. Gaj Singh had brought his wife and three children from the village to live with him. The wife's name was Kamla and she was fair, petite and completely unlettered. She did not have the jurisdiction to keep her husband from climbing through the oak trees to the back stairs to the sloping roof every night and he continued to do that. But clearly she had enough in her to distract him.

It seems Gaj Singh began to desire his wife in a big way and his attentions became divided. Kamla had grown from child bride to pretty girl to a maturely beautiful woman and he had finally discovered her enchantments. He would no longer stay the night in the big house, and there were times when he sought to be excused altogether because there were family crises – mostly Kamla or the children, ill or in ache. There were rows, sulks, sudden discoveries of his growing passion for his attractive wife. Once when he did not come Catherine padded down at midnight, on rubber-soled feet, through the oak trees, and stood outside his two-roomed house by the lower gate, hearing him moan. He seemed in a frenzy, speaking gutturally to her in dialect, telling her how lovely she was, asking her if she liked what he was doing. In a flat voice the wife asked him if she was as lovely as the white memsahib and if she felt as good.

Yes yes yes; more more more; better better better: Gaj Singh wailed, hammering out his pleasure.

When Catherine went back into the house her feet and ankles were covered with dew, and she had to dip them in a trough of tobacco water to rid them of any clinging leeches. Then she took her hands to the other places where her body was wet, and smoothing open the wings settled down to fly.

Catherine did not stop raining on Gaj Singh, but now there was an acid in it. The liberations of love and desire, celebrated all her life, began to sour. Something like evil rose in her, marring the great beauty of her free spirit.

She placed the main house out of bounds for Kamla and the children, even the main terraces, two in front and one behind. She did not wish to develop an unwitting bond with any of them. Sometimes from the waterpoint on top she could see the two little girls in tight pigtails and the good-looking boy playing with small flat stones – a kind of skipping game – by the lower gate, but the moment they threatened to look at her, she turned her face away.

Often she would see Gaj Singh on the road below the house, carrying the small boy on his shoulders, making him giggle and squeal. It was clear the boy was his passion. It angered her.

She never gave them anything. They were interlopers, seizing on her love.

She encouraged Gaj Singh to send all of them back to his village. For a long time he resisted, trusting in the nightly ecstasies to balm her resentment. But the balm never went beyond the last shudder and the last shower. The moment he stepped into the doorway to swing onto the tin and leave, the sullenness and the anger came flooding back. While they were at love it was as it had always been, but the rest of the time she simmered in rage.

To cut him to size she shifted her patronage to Banno and Ram Aasre, who were now Mary and Peter. The low-caste couple, once adopted by the generous Syed, had decided to switch loyalty – at least superficially – to a more powerful god. At least one who had more powerful devotees and was less disrespectful of them. The conversion had happened at the feisty Banno's initiative. Now they hung crosses around their neck and went to Naini for mass on Sundays, Banno, ludicrously, wearing a dress, her walk changing, acquiring a sway. At Christmas they were taught to make cakes, light candles and to sing raucous hymns and carols translated into Hindi by the church proselytizers.

The upper-caste Gaj Singh refused to call them Peter and Mary, continuing to bawl them out as Ram Aasre and Banno. He said, They are idiots! If changing a name could change your life I would call myself King George Pancham!

King George the Fifth.

Banno said to Catherine, I know nothing will change for us, but I am sure it will at least for my children.

Gaj Singh said to Catherine, She is foolish. Caste is forever. You can only change it with your deeds, not your name or your religion. The stupid woman thinks if she calls her children annieshannie polliepeter their lives will change!

Catherine let her mind be known by permitting BannoMary's

children access to the main house. BannoMary already had two sons and two daughters and was in the process of adding another. RamAasrePeter and she lived by the upper gate, and their children could come all the way up the front path, up the slope to the house and later even into the house.

BannoMary felt her conversion had already yielded a world.

Now Gaj Singh began to go into fret-and-sulk cycles. He became non-communicative, sullen, his handsome face expressionless and set. It pleased Catherine to know she was getting through to him, hurting him. But with him, too, all the anger and game-playing would collapse the moment their bodies came close to each other. Then the madness took over and it was as good as always. He loved her with an ardour that made him feel his head would explode, and she rained on him like a copious monsoon.

The problem was how to deal with the love when no love was happening.

They fell into an elaborate and corrosive dance of resentment, barbs and constant manipulation. Their driving need of each other – taken out of its purity, crossed with other needs – disfigured their souls.

Finally Catherine ordered Gaj Singh to dispatch his family off to the village and he was forced to comply. She had him to herself now – coming up the moonlit back path under the oaks, the crunch of gravel on the steep steps, the backward curving hand on the door jamb, the murmur of tin, the scraping of feet, the mouth, the hands, the nose, the phallus, the endlessly falling rain, the wet sheets, the puddles of love on the tarp, the dry bed in the other room, the waking in the morning with his love growing in her palm.

The rituals were in place, the pleasure was still surpassing, but she knew something had changed, some crucial part of him was missing. Now when he moved in her and on her, his absent bits distracted her. If you have seen a bottle full all your life, even a little missing can be disconcerting. The eye goes to what is absent, not what is there. She knew the missing bits were with Kamla; she began to worry about when the rest of him would be sucked away by Kamla too.

Catherine could sense his mounting excitement as the cycle – every fifteen days – of visiting his family arrived. She noticed his close shave and crisp clothes, the spring in his step, his high mood on the day he left.

It maddened her.

She took to wandering up and down the estate at all hours of the day and night. Alone, absently. RamAasrePeter and BannoMary protested, fearing she might be attacked by wild animals, beseeching her to summon them each time she wished to take a stroll. Catherine waved them off. After dark she still wanted her private domains out of bounds. She was not yet done with Gaj Singh.

And though she wanted him to want her in the old way, she was sure even if he didn't, she still wanted him.

She could not see it, but she was becoming like Syed at the very end.

Disfigured by driving desire. Failing to make her peace with it.

The writing now became more and more turgid, the wordwheels running into each other, and, like milk that has been stirred over an open flame for too long, gradually became immovably thick. First a deep sense of the torpor of the days – the emptiness, the waiting, the absence of companionship – began to cram the pages. Then the narrative died and the same things began to be repeated again and again, in shriller and shriller tones. A hallucinatory edge entered the prose, and for pages on end it was difficult to make sense of what was being written. Suddenly after all those decades there were garbled references to sin – unsuspected shades of Emily – and mysterious pleas for forgiveness.

She wrote of not giving where it was due.

And of giving where it was not due.

She wrote of sinning against her own blood.

And of redemption and reprieve.

She wrote of her love for Syed and wished his warmth by her side.

And she wrote of visiting church, something she had not done since Notre Dame decades ago.

She wrote of going home to America one last time.

One last time to finish unfinished business.

And she talked of giving to Gethia what was Gethia's.

At some point a fearfulness appeared to swamp her. A mix of hypochondria and paranoia. She began to meander on about ailments, flagging energies, strange nightly visitations. The ramblings became more and more disjointed and dark. She wrote that she felt like Carpetsahib in the dak bungalow, set upon to be flung out. But in her case it was from her own house and not another's.

At one time she wrote of the panther that came every night to sit outside her window by moonlight and taunt her. Sometimes it just stared at her, sometimes it sang a Kumaoni folk-song, in a soft voice, full of warning and presentiment. She said he knew all her secrets, and if she did not satisfy him he would devour her entrails.

And then suddenly the writing stopped.

Death had had its dominion.

# BOOK FIVE

# *Satya: Truth*

# The Hole of History

By the time I swam out of the last eddy of the notebooks I was three years older and the world around me had changed in unexpected ways. The new machismo that had begun to stalk the land at the beginning of the decade was now, in the last years of the millennium, in raging vogue. The great fakir's lingering ghost had been firmly laid to rest. Non-violence, tolerance, compassion, humour – all nailed deep into the ground. The rider of crocodiles had been consumed by dinosaurs.

Mythology had seduced technology and the bastard was among us.

We had taken our high metaphors and made small munitions out of them.

We didn't want to fly on the wings of the Gita; we wanted our fingers on the Brahmastra.

We had become a nuclear weapons state. And now the whole country was a Confederacy of Gleaming Glansmen. There were throbbing erections everywhere. Swollen with the blue pills of propaganda and power; ready to ravage any mouth that dared open in disagreement.

The apothecaries of hate had finally succeeded in making every bigot's phallus firm as a mallet. Har bewakoof ka loda banayenge hatoda.

Even those who were not bigots were busy declaring themselves men, stoking their self-esteem on the size of their organs. The size of their bomb, the size of their history, the size of their people, the size of their gods.

While the fakir was encouraged to die in a corner, his equally great pillion rider on the crocodile, the saint of sanities, Jawahar the Jewel, had become everyone's favourite dartboard. Men who did not qualify to breathe the same air as him – men without courage, nobility, ideas – were spending their days flinging darts at him. We had taken our dreams and were reading them like account books; and our account books had become the journals of thieves.

We had lost grace and found avarice.

We had lost the magic of great struggle and not found the refinements of the mundane.

We were all trapped in an extraordinary burlesque of the petty.

Everyman. Everyday. Everywhere. From our mean homes to the grand edifices of colonial New Delhi.

We had failed to become who we could be.

We were becoming less than who we were.

But the truth was I couldn't care less. Nations and masses of people will go their own perverse way, shining and declining in random cycles of stupidity and valour. I had my own life to contend with and, as anyone who has lived knows, one little life demands as much attention and steering as an entire nation.

Chances were the country would find its way more quickly than I would find mine.

As I struggled to the surface – the tentacles of the notebooks still gripping my ankles – I felt like Rip Van Winkle. In a kind of affectation I had allowed my hair and beard to grow – the hair increasingly washed in grey, the beard black – and I could catch both in rubber bands. It made me look corny – some kind of Far Eastern monk – and I liked that. It was amusing to see the respect the locals gave me, as is due to all who embrace the spiritual. They lowered their voices when they spoke to me and when they passed me on the road they greeted me with a deferential bow. Appearances are truly all. From being the rich city slicker in their midst, I had become the recluse of the big house, the spartan scholar of thick texts.

I was happy with that. I could take a stroll to the dhaba at the padao where the trucks halted, or walk past the tiny grocery shops up the old path that led to Nainital – set beautifully in herringbone bricks – or meander past the tea shacks down towards the crumbling sanatorium, and not feel obliged to talk to any of the groups squatting about pulling on cigarettes and bidis. A raised hand, a polite nod, was enough. Even on days when I went to the padao to eat, I would be served without the customary exchange of conversation, and the voices in the makeshift eatery would lower in recognition of my presence.

I knew the rumour on me was that I had been abandoned by my wife and I was in mourning for her. I knew it was also said I was writing a book to exorcize her memory. All this information came to me from Prakash – who had probably sent it out into the world in the first place. Prakash was the idiot who had succeeded Rakshas in my employ. He was an acne-splattered, gormless fool from Almora, who swung every few minutes from grinning to sulking to grinning. He would have done the moronic ranks of any dhaba proud, but his driving ambition was to enlist in the army. Every year he showed up at the recruitment centre in Ranikhet and was rejected. Any army would be crazy to give a man like him a gun in his hands. But he stayed with hope, even after he had passed the enlisting age. Every morning he peeled off scores of push-ups and sit-ups, and jogged up and down the lower terrace in a high goose-step. He was confident there would soon be a colossal war with Pakistan and reservists would be conscripted. He was keeping himself fit for the moment.

Prakash did everything to keep my life running – the cooking, the washing, the cleaning. Every minute of the rest of his time he spent peering at the small black-and-white television I had put out in the corner of the dining room. It only caught the national network through an antenna lashed to the roof. Each time the reception failed, he would yell for me in panic and go rushing up to the roof and fall upon the antenna, pulling and tugging it every which way, while shouting down at me to confirm that the picture was back. He also whispered to me about the wonders of cable television.

I humoured him because there was no one else in my life to humour. For all his stupidity, he shared my roof and my bread. He was a companion.

Fizz had left me two and a half years earlier and I had grieved for her in passing, but without pulling my head out of the notebooks. Decoding the diaries had been a slow process. Establishing the order, deciphering Catherine's circular handwriting and making sense of her poor prose. As I read, I kept detailed notes and, reading up to fourteen hours a day, it took several weeks to work through each diary. Often I had to go back and forth to check references, align events and their accounts. There was also a lot of dawdling: I can see now how scared I was of finishing with the notebooks: afraid that I did not possess another lifeline; afraid of what lay in wait for me.

The mute Brother and missing Fizz.

Sometimes I would try and imitate something Catherine had done – stand at the waterpoint at a particular hour; sit under Trishul; walk up a certain path – in order to see if I could catch a resonance.

Sometimes there was nothing, and sometimes an eerie sense of other things.

One midnight in the last week of September – the moon semi-ripe, the undergrowth in hectic conversation, the mist moving in slow waves, the nightjar just beginning to toc – I walked down to the lower gate to retrace Gaj Singh's nocturnal path. Prakash was sleeping in the dining room: I insisted on it, not wishing to be alone in the house. I had been reading through a graphic account of a late-night visit, and when I heard the continual crackle of the television stop – at midnight national television died – I decided to live the reading.

I pulled on my old Power keds without socks, put on a jacket, took a flashlight and went down the inner stairs. A zero-watt bulb glimmered in the dining room, and Prakash had hit his first snores. Bagheera, sleeping by Prakash's bed, lifted his head, then put it back on his paws as I unlatched the front door and sidled out. In the blue night I walked down carefully, avoiding trampling the scores of saplings Fizz had planted everywhere. Prakash and I had been poor guardians, but many of the seeds Fizz had nurtured had survived parental neglect, gained some purchase in the indifferent environment and were carrying on. I wove through the waist-high bottle-brushes, silver oaks, tuns and the knee-high neems and shishams, and the grass was damp and slippery under my feet.

The lower gate had been closed off with planks of wood and lengths of barbed wire. I turned and looked up at the house. In the dark it was a crouching animal, the two chimneys cocked ears. Behind me the curving road shone with the moon and was silent, without the kiss of rubber. Just beyond, the Bhumiadhar valley fell away, deep and sinister. I could have been him seventy years earlier, taking a last look around before setting out. The only thing different would have been Trishul. It would have been head high, just beginning to trifurcate. Now the deodar dominated everything, its three trunks holding up the skies, its many branches spreading out, furry and benign.

I climbed up slowly, taking the little-used steep path that went directly to the back of the house. The leaves had a sodden crunch and I had to plant my feet carefully. But I did not turn on the flashlight. As I walked, I felt everything go still around me. The chattering of the undergrowth stopped, the wind held itself in, every toc and tick died, a swoop of clouds swallowed the moon. When I reached the small courtyard behind the house, the high steps were waiting for me. Ten, in solid stone, climbing steeply, clinging to the immovable wall. Naked, unadorned, without a railing.

I looked up in dread. Through the curtains there was a faint yellow glow, like that of a lantern. I could almost hear the hiss of its pressure pump. I wanted to look around, over my shoulder, but I couldn't summon the courage. Do great anticipation and great fear produce the same sensations? His skin too would have been clammy, his heart hammering. I clung to the wall, taking one slow step at a time, holding my left arm behind me to ward off any pursuer. My shoes scrunched grit softly.

When I reached the last step there was no sloping tin roof to swing past deftly. We had laid a concrete slab, creating a modern kitchen underneath. I could now see the dark silhouettes of the Jeolikote valley. And from under the door leaked out the light of the burning lantern. Suddenly I knew she was in there, waiting for me.

I stood there a long time, completely spooked.

Absurdly I even thought of turning around and going back into the house from the front door. Did he hesitate each time he reached this moment? Then, in a rush, I snaked my right arm around the wall, curved my hand backward to grab the door jamb, closed my eyes, and, putting the ball of my right foot on the roof as if it were sloping tin, swung myself into the room. The door creaked back and I opened my eyes, certain she was there.

I had to sit on the bed for nearly an hour before I was calmed.

I kept hallucinating at night. Not every night, but often enough. I would be fine turning in to sleep, if full of what I had been reading, but then at some point the encounter would take place. It always appeared to last for hours and it always seemed very real; most times, when I woke in the morning, I was completely drained. I would drink two cups of tea sitting out on the terrace, looking down at the wakening valley, and then I would go back inside and sleep for a few hours.

Prakash had instructions to wake me up with tea and eggs at around ten.

For a long time it was difficult for me to separate the apprehension from the anticipation. There was a fear of what was happening to my mind and body each night, but a nocturnal fantasy is welcome, even in a grown man. Then in a macabre parallel, as Catherine and Gaj Singh's love soured and the evil rose in them, her nightly incubus began to oppress me. Now when she came her face was twisted with rage and she did not so much caress me as assault me. I struggled to ward her off and she took me as a beast would a man, with violence and without mercy.

In the mornings I woke battered, a deep ache in my limbs.

I also began to lose the ability to go back to sleep. It was most unusual. I had always prided myself on being able to drop off at a minute's notice. Fizz used to joke that I could sleep standing. But now an oppression took hold of me. My head was heavy – with images and queries – all the time, never emptying enough to allow sleep to pour in.

The fractured state of my mind was reflected in the house. It had fallen into a state of steady decay. Its renovation had been abandoned exactly where it was on the rainy night Fizz left me. Not a brick, not a dab of cement, not a plank of wood had been added. Three of the six skylights remained unglazed and had been covered with squares of tin by Prakash and me. Over the months the driving rain had opened them up and carved dark lines of water on the lime walls. The stacks of shaved pine lay in neat rows on the side veranda, no longer crisply golden but discoloured black and grey.

On the lower terrace the sand and gravel piles had slowly dissolved – blades of grass taking root in them – or been carted away by the villagers with Prakash's permission. The three cement bags lying in the upper outhouse had steadily sucked in moisture and become impenetrable rock. Most of the rooms were unfinished, lacking doors, windows, cupboards. When you entered from the main gate the house looked like a grinning skull, the glassless windows of the upper and lower veranda its gaping eyes and nose.

Fizz had put in some fancy taps, but barring the ones in the kitchen and the bathroom upstairs, they were all beginning to jam with disuse. Even the cisterns and pots were grimy and discolouring – Prakash would do everything but take a cleaning hand to the bathrooms; and I couldn't care less.

Similarly the brass bolts and latches she had bought from Delhi were all out of alignment and you had to shake and rattle the doors and windows to persuade them home. In frustration, Prakash and I had acted with crudity, and most of the doors had regressed to being held shut by big bent nails.

On ledges, in corners, in empty rooms all over the house, taps, tiles, elbows, washers, nuts, bolts, nails, hinges, latches, holders, shades, paint tins, all lay in cardboard boxes, gathering dust and irrelevance.

The decay inherent in the act of creation.

The skull beneath the skin.

I could never forget how it had first come to me: standing in the debris of the back room looking up from the missing floor through the missing roof all the way to the big blue sky.

Now it struck me each time I sat on the ledge of the unfinished study looking down the Jeolikote valley, the fork at Number One and the winding hill roads. I felt like a Mughal emperor, melancholically aware that every fantasy monument is dying even as it is being commissioned.

There is nothing so grand that will not soon perish.

Of course I couldn't care less.

The only things that gave me an occasional pang were the plants. I knew how much they meant to Fizz and how distraught their neglect would have made her.

Mercifully many had held their ground and grown: the shishams, jacaranda and peepul in front of the house; the silver oaks along the boundary wall; the sprig of a weeping willow she had plucked by the lake in Naukuchiyatal and jabbed in by the tap on the lower terrace; the bottlebrushes everywhere; the jamun and tun on the back path behind the kitchen; some of the mangoes on the Jeolikote slope; and miraculously, a struggling but refusing to die laburnum on the upper terrace, and a similarly soldiering gulmohar by the front gate. There was also the banyan right between the gate and the house, which after four years was barely six inches above the ground: it would look dead, and then every spring unfurl a single green leaf of hope.

Fizz had not come back once after she left that stormy, rainy evening.

In the beginning I had called a few times, but the conversation had collapsed in the first few words.

Is everything OK?

Yes.

I am sorry for all this.

Yes.

Just pull the money out of the bank whenever you need it.

Yes.

I hope you'll come up soon.

Let's see.

Will you call me if you need anything?

Yes.

You know how I feel about you.

Yes.

Toc. Toc. Toc.

Then, sucked in by the diaries, irritated by her sullenness, I stopped making the effort, and soon the pain began to ease. Some weeks later there was a call from the thakur's shop for Rakshas, and when he came back he glowered at me and said, Didi has left the house and the keys are with your landlord.

I let him walk out of eyeshot before rushing to the thakur's all-purpose store. I rang and rang and rang, but she did not pick up the phone. The call to Rakshas must have been the last thing she did before clearing out.

I was in that instant swept by panic. Where was she? Who was she with? What was she up to? Was she OK? I wanted to jump into the Gypsy and rush off to Delhi. For a time everything else was forgotten. I actually went up to my room, brought down the keys and was near the jeep when I saw Rakshas standing by the goat shed, his good hand holding the stump of his bad, looking at me with a sneer.

Something triumphant in his eyes stopped me cold, and I wrestled myself in, walked up the stairs slowly – past him – onto the water-point at the back. I sat there on the bench, hearing Prem Kumar's eighty-year-old pipe gargle, looking down at the valley, watching the trucks moan through the loops, till the light had died and every flying bird had settled. When I finally got up some hours later, the sky was suffocating with stars and the moon had risen, and the undergrowth was rustling with nocturnal scramblings. As I went in, I saw the one-armed shadow standing by the kitchen, watching me, motionless as a meditation.

By the time the night ended she had consumed me so completely that nothing remained, not even panic.

Two days later Rakshas left me. He said, Go back to Delhi, sahib, and find her. Men must know the difference between gold and brass, or be forever doomed.

I just handed him his money and told him to be on his way.

Four days later the thakur brought along Prakash. Those four lonely nights I slept in the goat shed, bolting myself in, a bottle of water and the long-handled axe by my side. I slept badly, but strangely I was bothered not by salacious hallucinations but by menacing one-armed presences.

Indifferently after that, while out for a walk, to satisfy some strange tic – of duty, curiosity – I would call the house. The unanswered ringing of the phone was almost cinematic. Soon it began to seem like a conversation of its own. The gnarled thakur, the skin of his face wrinkled like testicles, looked at me curiously: the man who dialled and dialled and never said a word. The man who mistook his phone for a wife.

I am sure I would have jumped clear out of my skin if someone had one day actually answered at the other end.

Then one evening there was only a low whine on the line. The next day it was still there. The phone was comatose. Unpaid bills, or perhaps dysfunction. So one afternoon, some six months after I had first learnt of her departure, I got into the Gypsy and drove down to Delhi. It was a strange journey. I drove slowly, K. L. Saigal wailing exquisitely on the car stereo – Fizz would never let me listen to him

– not stopping anywhere, to eat, or drink or piss, avoiding every place that bore our footprints. Even the railway crossings at Moradabad were flowing and I stretched my legs only when I stopped in our lane in Green Park.

The landlord and landlady were watching a serial on television and its domestic din floated out when he opened the door. He looked at me blankly for a moment, then rushed in to fetch the key and hand it over. I said I would see him in the morning. He shut the door gratefully. My advance cheques were with him. He withdrew his money on the first of every month. I was never there. I was a dream tenant.

The house was unstirring as a tomb and covered with dust. At first it seemed Fizz had taken nothing. And so it turned out. Apart from her own clothes and the little trinkets she loved collecting – tiny ceramic animals, ashtrays in different stones, boxes of coloured beads, glass bangles – apart from the totally personal and trivial she had left everything behind. Even the books, the music, the videos.

The rites of departure were complete. Plugs pulled out, windows double-bolted, refrigerator scrubbed, its door left ajar; curtains and chairs aligned; everything washed, cleaned, folded, put away.

On the refrigerator was a yellow post-it. All bills cleared. Nobody owed anything.

I found the rum and sat on the terrace and drank. Rum in the tum is better than shit in the bum. Untrimmed, the gulmohar branches were washing onto the terrace floor. I plucked a branch and caressed my arms with it. At midnight, hungry, woozy, I drove to Yusuf Sarai and ate two egg parathas with several cups of tea.

There was a group of trendy young men, drinking out of plastic cups, eating parathas, talking loudly, and taking turns to kick the dogs that came scrounging for food. It made for some kind of sport. Like a video game: a kick, one loud yelp, a scurrying, many more yelps in diminuendo, and a gale of laughter. Time out for a few bites; then a repeat. I thought of intervening, then just turned my head away.

It was strange to sleep in that bed without Fizz and I made a bad job of it. There were dreams of raining thighs and one-armed shadows, and when I woke it was stranger still to not breathe the sharp cold air of the mountains and see the wakening valley spread out below.

I went to the bank in the morning, and from the little I could gauge she appeared to have withdrawn no more than twenty thousand rupees. That crushed me. I wished she had taken a sub-stantial amount, in fact the whole lot. In Hauz Khas market I found a PCO – a glass cubicle inside another glass cubicle containing fax machines and copiers – and called up several of her friends. They were all frosty and unforthcoming. No one gave me a hint of her whereabouts. I was reduced to asking if she was well.

Yes, she was. Thank you.

And sorry, master chinchpokli, we do not have an address to which you can post more pain.

I did not call any of my friends. Concern, enquiry, explanation. I was not up to any of it. In front of me on the glass of the partition I saw a small card in garish purple. It read: The Music of Moksha. And below it: The Centre of the Circle of Life. The world was in constant flux, but it had a design. You could glimpse the past, the present, the future by dialling any of three given numbers. There was a line draw-ing of a young man in a suit and tie, sitting cross-legged like the Buddha, radiating peace and understanding.

The numbers were in the area. I called the first. Someone who sounded like a servant picked up. He asked if I was calling for moksha.

Yes, a quick dose.

In fact, make it a double.

A woman came on the line. Her voice was soft and caressing and full of concern. She gave me a time in the afternoon. The moksha par-lour was in the annexe of a house in Panchsheel Park. A frothing bougainvillea with white and pink blooms framed the door. Inside, the low table was polished teak with brass trim. Behind it the woman was serene and attractive, with auburn hair that framed her face in a neat oval. She was dressed in a blue Western-style suit. Her white shirt underneath was crisp and pure, and it showed the promise of fair breasts.

This was godtonic with a style. No kick in the head from Baba GoleBole.

She said, You look troubled.

I said, No, I am not.

She smiled sweetly, waiting.

I said, Yes, I am.

She said with a gentle smile, Tell me everything.

Sometimes the best way to play the game is to put it all upfront. Be deceptive through excess. I spoke solemnly. She listened with equanimity as if I were giving her my academic résumé. When I finished she asked a few questions. I juiced up the answers. More hallucinations, more sex. She came and stood behind me, held my head between her palms and told me to shut my eyes.

Her hands were fragrant of vanilla, and smooth and warm. I began to drift.

She intoned softly, Know what you see and see what you know.

I nodded off.

A little later she took her hands away, and said, What did you see?

I don't remember.

Nothing?

Nothing.

Good, good. That's very good.

Then she went and sat down on her chair, steepled her fingers and began to tell me about the energies of the universe. Good and bad. Positive and negative. The pacts we make with the universe when we are born, the scripts we choose. How we settle debts of past lives, square up ancient reckonings. There are no accidents. All whom we know now we have known before. And will know again.

I watched her lips move. The diligently applied lipstick had made her mouth bigger.

I said, Am I Gaj Singh?

She said, It's not so simplistic. But there is some deep connect.

I said, Syed?

She said, It's not so easy to tell. It could be with an earlier life of hers. Some unfinished business from another time. Something she is trying to tell you.

I said, Carpetsahib?

She said, What?

I said, Sorry, never mind.

She took eight hundred rupees from me – the first instalment for moksha – and said I would have to come back for past-life regression therapy. It would take at least four hours. It would give me all my answers. She said she saw a lot of negativity in me. She might even need to perform a psychic operation and excise it. Scoop it out, neutralize it in a bowl of salt water and pour it down the drain. It was a tricky thing. If not handled properly the negative energy could spill out and damage other things in the world, even sometimes corrode the surgeon.

She shook my hand when I left and smiled serenely, full of under-standing and concern.

She said, You must not be anxious. Anxiety blocks the energies of the universe. All the answers are within you. You are living the script you have chosen.

Yes, ma'am. Will do. Will be. Will see.

The world has logic. You have to develop the eyes to see it.

A hundred years after Syed railed against cant I had discovered it.

The great writer chinchpokli. The new tracker of the path between reason and unreason.

I returned to Gethia next morning, and did not come down for another six months. And so the years turned. I kept the barsati, unable to summon the initiative to sort out its contents, and it remained marmoreally still, putting on layers of dust, a memorial of mundanity to our love. Romance in a runcible spoon.

The only person I met on one of the fleeting trips to Delhi was Philip and it was a disappointment. He was with a new television channel, producing talk shows where three people fell upon each other with smart and angry lines and the moderator egged them on. He was dressed in washed and ironed clothes, wore leather shoes, had run a close shave, and did not stick his mouth into the food like a dog. He was married; his wife was a prospering lawyer; and he did not once talk about the epics he had planned to film.

When we parted he asked for my contact number in Gethia and I gave him a wrong one. I did not wish to meet him again.

Throughout the time I remained sunk in the diaries I heard not a word from or about Fizz. And my few feeble attempts to locate her yielded nothing. There was never another withdrawal from the bank. Her militant friends, who would have known, continued to block me out. I called her mother in Jorhat in faraway Assam. The connection was terrible and when she recognized my voice she began to cry. I put the receiver down. The next time I called she put the phone down. For all the information I was gathering I might as well have been living in a prehistoric age.

But more than the riddle of Fizz – as I broke surface from the whirlpool of the diaries at the very end of the millennium – I was still consumed by the riddle of Catherine. Several million words later, having read and reread my notes, I was left with a nagging sense of an unfinished story. Without voicing it I had begun to feel I was the latest player – the last? – in this saga. But what my role was, what I had to do, I had no idea.

I felt the notebooks had brought me to the edge of something, but now I was on my own.

Accentuating my unease was the fact that the nightly incubus had now become a torment. I no longer felt consumed, but hunted. I went to sleep with dread, and my dread proved mostly well founded.

Her face was now always twisted, and there was an insistent venom to her needs.

I woke each morning feeling violated.

I slept badly in the nights and was not sleeping at all during the day.

A wild panic began to take hold of me. The diaries were over, but I was failing to move on. I needed some closure: but what? And how? All lives are an untidy sprawl and it is futile and limiting to try and tie them into neat knots, but mine had become so uncontained, so full of ghosts, that all life was being driven out of it.

More than a month later, after I had read the last word of the last page, as I sat on the window ledge in the unfinished study one morning staring down absently at the moving mist, head heavy with lack of sleep, a thought struck me. Immediately I threw some clothes into a bag, got into my Gypsy and drove down to Rudrapur, and taking the right road from there to Kashipur, began to ask around for directions. In less than two hours of leaving Gethia I was racing through green paddy, officious egrets, and lines of erect poplars, headed out for Jagdevpur.

The speed of oblivion is always underestimated.

The town of nawabs, palaces, pomp and ceremony, of hunts, parades, harems and hangings, the town of Jagdevpur was a crumbling nightmare. The road broke into clumps of tar well before I reached it, and the skyline was dotted with minarets and scalloped walls in the Saracenic style. The first things I noticed when I entered the town were the open gutters, thick with sludge, with coarse-haired black swine inspecting them with their snouts. Old men pedalled cycle rickshaws slowly, transporting burqa-clad women. Lurid posters of Hindi films were everywhere.

At a ramshackle tea shack next to the ramshackle bus depot – flies and refuse all around – I asked for directions. The gathered men – many of them Muslim, some wearing moustacheless beards, others skullcaps – looked at me in direct curiosity. One pointed out the way; another said, Are you a professor?

You drove in through the high crumbling gateway and there were no gates to hold you back, nor were there any guards. The vast palace grounds were barren scrub, apart from an old banyan with hundreds of hanging aerial roots, and a couple of peepuls. The old trees had died and new ones had not been planted. Heads bent low, bony cattle worked the scrub.

The palaces were echoing shells, devoid of furniture, their walls stripped of every adornment, the doors and windows missing. There were three of them, a very large one and two smaller ones. I parked the Gypsy in the front yard of the biggest and walked through each of them, my footfalls resounding amid the gurgling of doves and pigeons. Every high ventilator was an aviary, and the floors were layered with droppings.

Some of the smaller rooms had makeshift doors – clearly slapped on later – with crude bolts to fasten them shut. When you entered them they had the musty aroma of animal skin mixed with the dull odour of cow dung and goat-shit. There were straw and fodder piles in the corners, and iron stakes were hammered through the old mosaic floors for tethering chains.

Many of the rooms were cavernous, with fifty-foot-high ceilings, fit to hold a thousand people. You looked at them and wondered what vanity in man needed such opulent endorsement. The plaster on the walls was peeling like scabs; the columns were all chipped; the flutings broken; the wood on the balustrades plucked and removed. Solid iron hooks in the ceiling spoke of missing chandeliers, and the bathrooms had been stripped of their purpose, the sanitaryware removed, the marble slabs dug out. Plants had wedged themselves in cracks in the walls – many of them peepuls – and would in the coming years tear the palaces apart.

The inherent decay in the act of creation.

The palaces were set on high plinths – plants were already prising them open – and I had to walk up a wide flight of stairs to the main doors. They had large inner courtyards with roomy inner verandas set in lines of engraved pillars. Once the courtyards would have sported ornamental trees next to the broken-down marble fountains.

Now they had been dug up as vegetable beds to grow aubergines and green peppers.

Some of the tiny rooms in the outermost wings were inhabited. I saw women washing and cleaning, and small children playing – expertly spinning wooden tops with a flick of their wrists. Their movements only amplified the desolation all around. Incuriously they turned away the moment they saw me, and I thought it wise to not seek an engagement. One of the small palaces had scores of same-sized rooms all with their front walls missing. This was probably the dog palace. It too had the relic of a fountain in the courtyard.

Soon I was exhausted by the emptiness and the ruins. I had been through barely a fraction of the palaces and had avoided all the dark inner wings and the upper storeys. I went out and the sun was a block of heat pressing down hard.

The banyan tree had a concrete platform around it and a ghurra with a long-handled aluminium cup. I poured the cool, clay-flavoured water from the pot into my mouth, holding the cup high, allowing it to splash over my face and chest. Then I sat and waited. I did not know for what. I could not see any trace of a cottage anywhere. Perhaps it had been somewhere else. The entire place looked so con-summately dead it was difficult to imagine it as it had been in Catherine's diaries.

I curled up on the smooth concrete and fell asleep and dreamt of her riding a horse, pulling me behind it. She was wearing a flowing white gown and a floppy hat. The more I protested the faster she galloped, all the while looking back at me with an enigmatic smile. I was sprinting in sheer desperation now, my legs pumping, about to give under me; my heart ready to burst. Just when I thought I would die, she cut the rope holding me and I collapsed under a banyan tree and passed out.

When I came to I was still there and the shadows in the palace grounds had begun to lengthen. Formations of parakeets were heading for base in green streaks, testing the sound barrier with their screeches. Crows were searching for night lodgings with raucous enquiries. The last pigeons and doves in the palace eaves were fluttering down to rest. I poured another stream of cool water into my mouth and on my face, and walked out to the Gypsy.

The bonnet was too hot to sit on, so I went up the wide staircase and sat down in the shadow of the high palace walls. The sun was a weakening red glow when a cyclist appeared at the main gates. It took him almost ten minutes to reach the huge bitumen-covered front yard, where a hundred cars and carriages would have parked once. He was riding an old Atlas bicycle with a rhythmic click – some missing ball bearings – and a small headlight strung on the handle with a dynamo on the back wheel. I stood up and waved, and he veered over.

He wore a trouser and a bush shirt with a bandanna across his face to protect him from the dust. When he took it off his mouth was stained crimson with paan juice. Before he could say a word he expectorated a thick bloody stream into a corner of the stairs, its splatter almost catching my trainers. I told him I wanted to see someone who remembered the days of the nawab.

He guffawed theatrically and then said from the corner of his mouth, Which nawabs? The ones who became paupers or the ones who made others paupers?

I threw a few names at him. Syed. Zafar. Boycott. The nawab's book of aphorisms.

The speed of oblivion is grossly underestimated.

He knew nothing. The royalty he knew were of recent years. One Abbas, who had gone in the sixties to Bombay to become a film star and had even appeared in a couple of films, in which he had a credit as a villain. He was famous as a rapist, said the man. Another called Abid, who lived in Lucknow, running the family haveli there as a heritage hotel. And one called Murad in Delhi, who had become a fashion designer.

Spitting out another stream of juice, the man said, They are all worse off than us. They have to behave like nawabs but they have nothing. You see these palaces – they have been pillaged of everything that could be taken away. They came here and did it. Tore apart the work of their own fathers. Stood here and said, Take this out, take this away, how much for this, how much for that. Sahib, this town is dead. It died the day the government banned the mining of the iron ore and made trees more precious than men. And these palaces are dead. No one wants these ruins now – not for free. You spend a night here and you can hear the ghosts of men, women and dogs screaming through the empty corridors. I stay here because my father left me here twenty years ago and the ghosts know me and leave me alone.

Dusk was on us and a couple of other men had arrived. They were now all pulling on unfiltered cigarettes and talking expansively of time, fate, wealth and wisdom. But I wanted facts; and I did not wish to spend the night in this godforsaken town. In the fading light the bulk and silence of the palaces was eerie. Seven families lived where once thousands had moved in pomp and passion.

I asked about Syed's cottage. None of them had a clue.

Only when I began to move away in impatience did they focus again on my enquiries. They said, There is only one man who can perhaps tell you what you want to know. His name is Rommel Mian.

I said, Take me to him.

But it wasn't possible. He lived well away from the town on his grandson's patch of fields. First thing in the morning, they said, and proceeded to fix me up for the night. They put out a bed for me in one of the rooms that had a makeshift door, next to one of the animal quarters, and fed me well. After dinner I tried to take a walk in the moonlit grounds but got spooked near the banyan tree and hurried back to the lightless palace.

I slept terribly. I felt beset with presences, and each time the cattle in the next room shuffled or snorted I sat bolt upright, my heart hammering. I only fell asleep when I saw the night lighten through the cracks in the door. I was woken by my father calling for me in the sweet way he had before we became sworn enemies. It was my host bringing me a hot tumbler of tea that almost took the skin off my fingers.

So many years after Bibi Lahori's farm in Salimgarh I took an old mineral water bottle and wandered off into the shrubbery of the palace grounds. I could see it was a wasteland reserved not for the palace inmates alone but also for other townsmen, who sat dotting the boundary wall like ducks waiting to be shot. The pleasure gardens of the nawabs now the crapping fields of the poor. Squatting there, I had an unreal moment. I almost went into a time warp, forgetting for a bit who I was, where I was, what I was doing there: crouched behind a yellow oleander bush, in a medieval dying town, in the middle of nowhere, in the lee of palace ruins, a dented plastic bottle in my hand.

Later my host worked the hand pump while I sat under it, the cold water washing over me in wonderful gusts.

🌿

All four men decided to go to work late and piled into the Gypsy with me. We bounced over rutted dirt-tracks – between green fields, thorny babools, mango groves, and farmers just finishing their morning labours – for nearly an hour, the paths getting worse and worse, narrower and narrower. At one point the mud embankments became so high the jeep was in danger of keeling over. Through it all the dust stayed with us in a cloud, occasionally becoming so dense we had to halt to let it settle before we could see the way ahead.

The set of three rooms was made from mud, dung and thatch, and attached to it – obviously later – were two big squarish rooms in naked bricks. A bulky television antenna was hoisted on the flat roof of the new rooms at the end of a long GI pipe. We had to leave the jeep and walk the last two hundred yards through the fields in a single file. Two frisky mongrels barked us into the homestead, circling us with wagging tails. The yard – smooth as a bald head thanks to many layers of mud plaster – was full of bobbing, clucking hens.

Rommel Mian was a gnarled piece of ginger. He was on a string charpoy in the first mud room. Not sitting, not lying down, a mere fistful of man. He had a full head of grey hair, but his mouth had collapsed without teeth. He lifted a clawlike hand to bless all the men who touched his feet. A wooden chair was brought for me to sit on. From a round beam above Rommel Mian's head there dangled a long string with a tight ragball at its end. At the doorless doorstep where the sun stopped there was a buzz of flies.

He was reasonably alert, but it was difficult for me to understand him because he spoke without teeth and mostly in the local dialect. I talked through my companions. I tried to soften him up with niceties. He told me that he had joined the army during the second world war. They were all lined up in the Jagdevpur parade ground, young and old. Then the white officer barked something he didn't understand. Many men took a step forward. So did he. After weeks of marching up and down, and training with guns and grenades, they were loaded onto a ship. He was sick for days at sea. Then they were in the desert in north Africa. There he began to dig trenches and graves, trenches and graves, and he dug and he dug and he dug, from morning to night, every single day, dug and dug and dug, till Rommel had been vanquished. He defeated Rommel without firing a shot. Then they came back. He took to his bed and never again did a day's physical work. Yet his arms had not ceased aching since then. And each time he slept he dreamt he was digging holes and lying down in each one of them.

Those who tried to mock him were told the name of the man he had bested.

From Shakoor his name became Rommel Mian.

The ball hanging in front of his face was used by him to hit out at intruding birds and hornets without needing to rise from his bed.

Enough niceties, great warrior. Now to the purpose. Unveil the secrets I seek.

Rommel Mian's sibilant lisp was so pronounced that even my companions had trouble following him. They had to make him repeat everything several times.

His father had been a lifelong retainer in the nawab's household and he had grown up with stories about the royal circus. No, you didn't want to know the details. Made you question what the omniscient one was thinking when distributing wealth and station.

Yes, he knew of the white woman the chhote nawab had brought home from England.

Yes, she was very beautiful and she rode a horse as hard as a man.

Yes, she was a sorceress practising secret rites.

Yes, they lived in a separate cottage and not in any of the palaces.

Yes, there was another wife whom the chhote nawab never touched. She died in 1971 – the year Indira Gandhi took away the pensions of royalty – still barren as the desert.

Yes, it is true the chhote nawab was a strange man, strong of mind and weak of body.

Yes, his people loved him and they despaired of him.

Yes, he was disinherited by the bade nawab.

Yes, it was said there weren't enough men in Jagdevpur to fill his needs.

Yes, it appears she was no less than a nawab in her needs too.

Yes, there was also an aadhe nawab. A half-nawab with a bad arm. Zafar.

Yes, he was pitied and he was feared. A good man distorted by his handicap.

Yes, the two brothers fought. And they both lost.

Yes, there was another man. Strong and smart. From the mountains.

Yes, he had both the chhote nawab and the white woman like puppets on a string.

Yes, the chhote nawab was murdered. Poisoned with Pudinakorma-ae-Dilbahaar, beaten meat with a rain of mint. And a drizzle of dhatura.

Yes, she did it.

Yes, the bade nawab did not make a fuss about it, because the chhote nawab had been an embarrassment for simply too long.

Yes, the cottage was pulled down. All traces of her removed.

Yes, the mountain-man took her up to the mountains, where the mists hide the truth.

Yes, she was never again seen in Jagdevpur.

Yes, when he came back after defeating Rommel he heard she was dead.

Yes, he heard it from the mountain-man, who came to visit his father. He held his father's hand and he wept. He said he had lost everything. The all-knowing one had taught him too grim a lesson. He did not deserve it. He had lost love, property, reputation and, worst of all, his child.

Yes, worst of all, his beloved son, who had been made like Zafar an aadhe nawab.

And picking up the ragball that hung in front of his face Rommel Mian flung it at a sparrow that had entered the room. The bird flew out twittering, and in the mud hut the ragball swung back and forth slowly like the pendulum of time.

Rakshas.

A week later, having carefully reread several portions of the diaries, I decided to walk to Bhumiadhar. It was an overcast day and Gethia was thick with shifting mists. But by the time I reached the padao the mist was gone and it was cool and clear. I walked on the wrong side of the road so I could look down the valley, broken briefly by terraces and then running into a carpet of oaks. If I turned around I could see the house, in the shadow of Trishul, a crouching animal waiting to spring.

At the padao dhaba the two helpers were chopping onions and potatoes for the evening dinner, while the wrestler brothers who owned the eatery were on the wooden bench outside shining up their legs with mustard oil. A few truckers sat next to them, chatting idly, sipping tea. Mangy dogs seemed to be under every chair and bench.

The wrestlers raised their hands in salutation. I did the same.

I had never walked to Bhumiadhar before and it proved much easier than I had imagined. Above me the slopes were full of pines, and from below too the pines soared above the road, old and stately.

The road dipped and climbed, and it had a comfortable grassy verge which allowed you to step aside to let vehicles pass. For a time I almost felt light and airy.

It did not take me very long to find the directions to his house. Everyone knew him. Characteristically, he lived away from the main cluster of the village. I had to walk down the slope a little through a series of terraced fields, to his boxy stone house – like a barn – with small windows and old patched tin on the roof. A dog was barking from inside the house in cycles. Stop, start, stop. In the silences in between I called out to him a few times, and then waited.

After some time I went round the house and walked between the rows of cabbages to the end of the terrace where it narrowed to a point, which was nailed in place by a big soapnut tree. The dog in the house stopped barking. Soon another one started off somewhere down below, moving up towards me.

He came up through the oak trees smoking marijuana in a chillum, the yapping dog frisking a few steps ahead of him. He saw me and tucked the chillum into his left armpit, raising his right hand in a salaam. I did the same. He had a wonderful talent for being deferential without being servile.

With a grin he said, I had heard of your new hairstyle.

The dog ran ahead of us to the house and we followed it silently. He unlatched the door, went in and brought out a chair for me. The dog inside had come rushing out. It sniffed around me then ran off, pursued by the other. I sat down and put my feet up on the low stone wall at the edge of his front yard. The sun had begun to dip on the other side of Gethia. We were well down the slope so the light would fade more quickly here.

He came back with two mugs of tea on a chipped wooden tray. Giving me one he took the other and went and squatted on his haunches on the low wall. The tea was strongly flavoured with crushed ginger.

I said, I have read all the books.

He said, What can I say?

I said, I went to Jagdevpur.

He looked at me long and expressionlessly and said nothing.

I said, I went to the nawab's palace. I also met Rommel Mian.

He put his mug down and began to rub his left shoulder with his right hand.

I said, Rommel Mian told me many things.

He said, What did he tell you?

I said, Everything.

He said, So you know everything?

I said, Yes, I know everything.

He said, Then why have you come here?

I said, Because I also want to know it from you.

He said, What do you want to know?

I said, Everything.

He said, Just believe me: my father didn't kill him. He never wanted to. It haunted him to his last day. I don't think he ever slept well again.

I said, Yes.

He said, She went crazy. She kept haranguing my father that the chhote nawab had gone mad. She said the chhote nawab was going to get them both killed. She said he was spying on them every moment of the day. That he was crazed with jealousy and opium. That he was no longer the man they had all known. She said the chhote nawab knew that the royal family would be only too happy to be rid of her and of him. She said that if they wanted to be together, if they wanted to save their lives, they would have to act first, act immediately. She said the great thing was that if they acted first then the royal family would be happy too – happy to be rid of him because he was an embarrassment to them. So it was either them or him. It is true my father was besotted with her – it was, they say, impossible not to be. She was white and very beautiful and my father said she could do things to a man that most men cannot even dream of. My father admitted he was in a trance – he would have slit his own throat if she had asked him to. But he never wanted to kill him. He loved him. He had saved our family's life once; and my father had gone to him to save him from Zafar nawab's evil intentions. Then he had met her, and instead of his saviour he became his killer. But in a real sense he did not kill him. When the time came he told her it was she who would have to do it. He made the dish but she did the deed; he said he could not even bear to look. That night she took him with greater fervour than ever, as if trying to rub the guilt out of her skin. She went through the next few days calm as a saint, daring anyone to cast even an accusatory look at her. As it turned out, everyone was relieved. Then she gave away everything to all those who had worked for her, took along Maqbool, Banno and Ram Aasre, turned her back on Jagdevpur and never returned again.

I waited, not saying anything, letting him open any new path he chose.

He pulled on the chillum with a strong sound, his handsome, craggy face expressionless. He offered it to me. I cupped my hands under the pipe, sucked hard twice without letting my mouth touch the clay, and held the smoke in. He took it back and pulled on it hard again. His eyes, I noticed, were rheumy. His years were beginning to tell.

He said, It was a strange relationship. It was like the great sagar manthan, an epic churning. Like the manthan it produced equal amounts of nectar and venom. My father said he tasted paradise with her again and again and again, but in the end there came the poison. But believe me, sahib, he loved her. He loved her very deeply. He lived for her, did everything for her. He called her the fountain of joy. He said she was like a glorious spring and it was madly heady to be bathed in her. And she loved him too. My father said he could have got her to do anything, to give him anything. But he never wanted it. He never wanted anything but her love. It is true that in the last years of her life they moved apart, but it's mostly because she began to change. Her desire got infected with jealousy and she began to see shadows everywhere. My poor mother, who had never once complained about her, who had lived within herself, happy to take what my father could spare, my mother became a demon for her. How many years we lived without the presence of my father! How we used to wait for him to come and visit us! Sometimes he would come

secretively in the morning and hurry back in the evening. My
mother would actually encourage him to leave, knowing there would
be hell to pay if he was not back in time. We also knew she was taking a lot of ganja – those two low-caste cheats were plying her with
it – and it was altering the balance of her mind.

The word he used was santulan – equilibrium. She was losing her
santulan.

He said, And, sahib, you know no love can survive once it starts
fighting ghosts that do not exist. And desire dies the day it is policed.

Night had fallen. The dogs were back and lying in front of the
doorway, chins on forelegs. He went in and threw a switch and a
yellow bulb sprang alive above the house. All around the slopes were
now punctured with holes of light. In differing voices car and truck
engines were grinding the road above us. Below us it was mostly
dark, the oaks running endlessly, packed together like clutches of
long-distance runners.

When he came back out and squatted on the wall, I said, So what
happened to her?

He said, What happened to her?

I said, Yes, what?

He said, What happens to everybody? She died.

I said, I am asking how.

He said, I thought you knew everything.

I said, I do, but I want to hear what you have to say about it.

He said, What else? Those two got rid of her. That's what
happened. They got what they wanted and then they did away with
her. They gave up their gods to get her crumbs. And she was so
crazed and angry with my father she could not see what she was
doing. You give low-lifes a higher idea of themselves you pay a price.
She tried to be good to them, they did her in. But I suppose she was
paying for her own earlier deeds too. Isn't it true that, as you do, so
shall be done unto you? The chhote nawab's soul must have felt a
balm. But my father was heartbroken. He cried for weeks; for
months after he would go and sit by her grave. And those two? They
didn't take a week to move into the house. With their children and

all their cheap chattel. Start wearing her clothes. Start sleeping in her bed. Start shitting in her thunder-box. Start selling off pieces of her estate. But my father never cared. He treated them like he had always treated them, as low-castes. He always said he had had her, body and soul – he didn't care who got all her silly possessions.

I said, How did they get rid of her?

He pulled deep on his chillum and said, Dhatura.

I had Fizz's slim black Lazerlight in my pocket and I carefully tracked my way back to the road, watchful of the rustling in the lantana bushes. The walk back home was magical. The moon was up early and the sky was clear and crammed with stars. You could see the road shining all the way to the next bend. Every now and then the spell was broken by a vehicle grinding past, but then minutes later, the clamour gone, the enchantment was back. At the padao there were several trucks parked by the roadside, their doors open; and the wrestlers were now hard at work, supervising dinner with their big arms and squeaky voices.

Near the thakur's shop, where the herringbone path climbed to Nainital, I slowed down and became more alert. Six times in the last fortnight the panther had been spotted here between seven and eight in the evening, crossing over from the Jeolikote valley to the Bhumiadhar valley. Three dogs had been killed in the vicinity and we were corralling Bagheera in earlier than usual. But no big cat came padding by and within minutes I was inside the estate, and I could hear the scratchy noise of the television, and see its glow inside the dining room, and in its glow the pasty, pop-eyed face of Prakash.

I picked up the bottle of whisky, a glass and a bottle of water, and went up to the back terrace. Jeolikote was a spangle of lights, and traffic around Number One was heavy, headlights criss-crossing steadily, one out of four veering away towards us. To my right lights were cascading untidily down the Nainital slope, a dangerous sign of the town's growing sprawl. It lived in fear of the day the mountain gods were roused to a fury and let the land slip. On my left was the dark, hairy hump of the Gethia spur, and somewhere among its oaks and pines was a grave.

I suddenly shivered. The weather was turning. Even with the whisky inside me, and a light cardigan on me, I was cold. It was four months to the new millennium. Year 2000. Occasionally when Prakash brought me a newspaper from Bhowali, I could see the armies of commerce stoking up the world for a giant orgasm of celebration and spending. It bored me. But sometimes my head would fill with the things Fizz and I used to say to each other fifteen years ago, when we talked of the future.

Where do you think we'll be?

That was the favourite one. Where do you think we'll be?

Yes, where? In a fucking hallucination, taking notes.

I quickly drained my second glass, put the bottles inside, picked up the short sandalwood stick, and without telling Prakash – who sat unblinking – I went down to the lower gate, picked my way through the barbed wire and walked towards the sanatorium.

When I got off the road and began to climb through the oaks, I turned on the Lazerlight. There was no light shining from the soapnut at the bend in the path. Taphen's dogs had already set up a hollering. At the bend I could see the yellow bulb hanging under a tin shade outside Taphen's veranda. By the time I reached the house the dogs were going berserk. They were inside their cages, flanking the front door. I called out to him. Damyanti came out and she was immediately fearful.

He was in his armchair, bottle on the floor, glass in hand, a rolled-up grey balaclava on his head. I was seeing him after several months and he looked older, more decrepit. His unshaven skin was loose and pouchy, his eyes bloodshot.

I said, Stephen, I know everything about you.

He said, without raising his head, Even the good lord doesn't.

I said, Stephen, I want you to tell me everything.

He said, I know nothing.

I said, I know everything.

He said, Good. Then go away. Remember I told you, Don't read those devilish books.

He wasn't even looking at me. He was staring into his lap. Damyanti gave me a glass and I poured myself a big drink. I was not leaving till I had my answers.

I said, Stephen, I met Rommel Mian.

He said, Who the bugger is that?

I said, Stephen, I went to Jagdevpur.

He suddenly looked up and was still.

I said, Stephen, I went to the Ambedkar colony and met Banno's niece.

He didn't move a hair.

I said, Sorry, BannoMary's niece. She was very kind. She sent you her love, though she said she had never met you. I am sure you didn't know you had a cousin there.

I was lying. But I didn't care.

I said, She said your mother and father had stopped associating with all of them after they changed their religion. But she knew all about you. She said the family had kept track of everything that had happened to you all – all the good fortune and riches, and how it had all happened. She said money alone ought not change anything. Nor ought religion. But together they can corrupt even an angel.

He began to cry. Just like that. Sitting there, without moving, big tears rolling down his wasted cheeks. I kept quiet. Damyanti came and stood in the doorway and watched him.

After some time he said, My mother was a good woman. A very good woman. And my mother loved her. She loved her dearly. More than her own children, more than us. She served her her whole life like a slave. She cooked for her, cleaned for her; and when she was unwell she washed her, bathed her, changed her. Every minute of her life she lived for her, day and night. Sometimes she would call and we would be crying for milk or food, but my mother, she would just leave us and rush away. All these buggers lie if they say my mother changed her religion because of her. She changed it because all these bastards used to treat her like an animal, and treat my father like an animal, and treat us like the litter of animals. That arrogant maader-chod Gaj Singh wouldn't even let his children play with us. We were insects, cockroaches, scum. She went to Jesus not because of the memsahib but to get respect. And Jesus gave her respect. Jesus gave all of us respect. I sit and talk to you like this because Jesus gave me respect. Bugger all those sons of bastards, Jesus gave me respect.

He had worked himself into a rage and a grief. He was moved by his own story.

I waited for some time, then said, Stephen, how did she die?

He said, his tears under control now, He killed her. The maader-chod killed her. He thought he was the big Romeo in her life. Big bloody Romeo. He was the devil, he used to control her. He used to put strange things in her food that cast an evil spell on her. After all, it was he who poisoned the chhote nawab and brought her up here. My mother used to say the chhote nawab was a great man, a rare man, a mahatma. Always doing things for the poor and the needy. He was the one when he came back from England who gave my mother and father jobs inside his house. Nobody else in the palace would have let them come near. And Catherine memsahib loved my mother. Always kept her close to her. When my mother went to Jesus, she is the one who gave her the name Mary. Is the name of the mother of Jesus, she said, now no one can ever dare spit on you.

I said, Stephen, I understand. But why did he kill her?

He said, Because she didn't want him any more. She was sick of him, tired of him. He was using her, cheating her, and after so many years she finally saw the truth. She understood who really cared for her. You know she didn't even allow his children into the house because they used to steal things. And us? We could come and go when we wanted. She loved us. She used to say, This Stephen, he will become a fine priest when he grows up! I can see it. He has caring in his eyes.

I looked at Damyanti. She was impassive, leaning against the door jamb.

I said, Stephen, that's not enough reason to kill anyone. He had nothing to gain.

Taphen became angry. He threw his glass back into his throat, filled it up again, and drained it too in one long draught. Then looking at me directly, he shouted, You think we killed her. Is that what you think? Is that what that one-armed bastard is trying to tell you? Let me tell you, we did not even know she had left the estate to us. But his father the big Romeo did. Because she had told him. To put him in his place. To tell him that the old order had changed. That she had seen through his wicked games. And he couldn't bear it. He thought he owned her. She would be his slave always. He was always giving her hashish to confuse her mind. And he was evil – he was also mixing dhatura into it, a few seeds every time. Sometimes he would give her so much she would not know for days what she was doing or saying. Who looked after her then? Who? My mother. My mother. Mary! BannoMary! The mother of Jesus!

He filled his glass again. I waited. He wasn't done yet.

He said, And that is how she ended up cutting the bandicoot's arm. The maaderchod filled her with hashish, and then he sent the boy to pick up things from the house, and she saw him and hit him with her steel-tipped walking stick, and it slashed his arm open, and in three weeks it had become as rotten as their intentions, and they had to take him to the mission hospital and have it cut off. What a scoundrel he is with just one arm! With two he would have become Sultana daku!

I said, She left them – him – nothing?

He began to shout now, They had sucked her enough. Sucked her body and her soul and taken all her things. What more could she give them? You know Catherine memsahib – she didn't care for any goods and riches. She left everything when she came from the nawab's palace. She cared for love. True love. She gave up everything for it. But that bastard Romeo betrayed her. He broke her heart. He made her suffer. He threw away her daughter. Yes, sir, threw away her daughter. Told her it was either him or her. In her last years she used to weep for her girl. From morning to night she used to weep. Rivers of tears. They created grooves in her face. But it was all too late. He behaved like the devil. And Jesus punished him for it. He took away his son's arm. And then the bastard Romeo became so mad with her he poisoned her. Poisoned her with his bastard pudinakorma! Just like he had done the chhote nawab, with a good seasoning of dhatura! Every day ten seeds. Every day ten seeds. Make her mad little by little. Then one day hundred seeds. Khallas! Over! Finish! The end!

And then he ran amok.

He stood up unsteadily and began to scream, And you come here with your bloody ponytail hair and prettycity backside and accuse me! We suffered! She suffered and we suffered! And just because we became poor and had to sell you our house – her house – you think you have the right to come and ask us stupid questions! Get out of here before I take out my hotfat lollu and put it in your ear! Get out, you bastard!

His eyeballs were swimming in a sea of red. He was swaying like a bamboo in high wind. If I stayed another few minutes he would keel over onto the floor.

But I was done. He was past telling me anything more.

I said, Stephen you are a dog, and walked out.

Outside, Damyanti said, He has suffered. He is not a good fellow. But he is not a bad fellow too. We are all like that. Sometimes man, sometimes beast.

I said, What was it about the daughter? Who killed her?

She said, No, I know nothing about it. But you know he just babbles.

I said, Have they always hated each other?

She said, Like all hate it is touched by some strange love. They never talk, but they will help each other. Many years ago Taphen had a fight with a grocer in Bhowali and Taphen abused his mother and sister till he lost his voice. In the evening they came in a group to get Taphen, but the one-armed one stood between them, his axe in his hand, and asked them to leave if they didn't want his enmity. And when you gave us the money for the house, Taphen wrapped a ten-thousand-rupee bundle in a piece of newspaper and left it on Rakshas's bed. I kept quiet. It is between the two of them. They have known each other since they were children. Taphen can curse him all day, but he shouts at me if I ever say anything.

From inside, Taphen hollered, Damyanti! Is he trying to get inside your salwar? Tell the bastard my gollulollu will make such a big hole in his ear birds will fly in and out of it singing Christmas carols!

The dogs didn't bark me down. There was no scent of panther in the air and they had settled for the night. In the insect-filled silence the short walk through the oaks had an eerie feel to it. For a moment there was a lull on the road – not a sound of an engine – and I could have been a hundred years ago, wandering through a dark drama I did not understand. The moon was on high now and the hills were luminous. It took me mere minutes to make it to the bend in the road where our property began.

The house lay above me, silent and dark, its many windows watchful eyes. Some nightbirds were rustling in the upper branches of Trishul. I stood at the lower gate by the outhouse. It was locked, since Prakash slept upstairs. This was where Stephen had been confronted by the devil many years before and just saved by the headlights of a truck. This was where Gaj Singh had set out from every night, up the back path, up the stone steps, across a murmur of tin, to a woman soaked in love and desire.

I didn't bend through the barbed wire. Instead I kept walking along the road, preferring to go in through the main upper gate. The marble plaque on the pillar caught the moonshine. First Things. And below it our names. And below them the beautifully etched neem sprig. I unlatched the gate, then dropped the latch back, and began to walk once again up the road towards Bhumiadhar.

At the padao there was a small pool of yellow light and the dinner activity was at an ebb. A few late truckers were eating, but only one wrestler and one helper were visible. I hugged the further side of the road and walked behind the parked trucks, not wishing to be noticed. The road shone all the way and there was a mild wind in the pines and the continual buzz of insects in the undergrowth. Occasionally a dog howled, but it was impossible to tell whether the sound was coming from behind me or in front of me, from below or above.

A few times I was spooked, the hair stirring on my neck, and I had to turn around in panic to check if I was being followed. I was grateful each time the sound of a vehicle came to me, reassured by its approach, its blinding lights, and its grating passage as I stepped aside onto the verge. Then, as the sound died, some bends further on, I fell again to looking nervously over my shoulder.

The path that led down to Rakshas's house was easy to spot. The landmark was a cigarette kiosk with an advertisement for white vest and white jockey underpants painted on it. I walked down carefully, and before I had descended three terraces I had set dozens of dogs barking. His barn-like house was dark – even the roof light was off – but his dogs were yapping away inside. I hoped they would wake him. Shouting his name at this hour seemed obscene. I waited. Soon the dogs went quiet. The oak forest below was an indistinguishable mass – the moonlight didn't penetrate that deep.

Finally I called out his name, not too loud. When I called the third time, louder now, the dogs set up a howl again and he bellowed in response. Hill dwellers know spirits come calling for you at night; if you answer they suck up your energies and leave. But spirits only call twice before moving on, so hill people wait for the third call before answering. He came out holding his long-handled axe, a mud-coloured scarf tied around his head, a thick shawl on his shoulders. He looked even more unshaven than a few hours earlier, the grey bristle on his chin heavy.

We sat in the low-roofed front room. It was choked with clunky chairs and tables: unpolished, the nailheads showing, quite likely hammered together by local carpenters. The rafters and planks above us were old and discoloured. The floor was flagstoned. On the wall was a religious calendar – Lord Krishna as a cherubic blue-skinned baby, a peacock feather in his hair, eating a big ball of white butter.

There was another calendar of a saucy Bollywood starlet with bouncy breasts and inviting eyes.

He said, You went and met that drunken scoundrel, Taphen?

I said, Yes.

He said, And how many new lies did he tell you?

I said, He said that she slashed your arm while you were picking up things from her house. And that's how you lost it.

Contempt filled his eyes. He said, What is the truth for people who can change their gods for a few rupees? They have built their lives on lies. How can you believe anything they say?

I said, So how did you?

He said, It is true that I did not lose it to a panther. And it is true that she slashed me and then it began to rot. But she slashed me because I was crying loudly and pulling at my father's sweater while she was trying to talk to him. I think she was high on the ganja that the low-caste woman was giving her. She just swung out in irritation. My father almost jumped on her in anger. But it was only a small cut – just a finger's length. Then one week later my arm began to turn green and hurt till I was screaming the mountain down. Then it became a soggy vegetable. We went to the mission hospital and the white doctor said, Gajraj, you want to give up the arm or the boy?

I said, So in anger your father gave her the dhatura?

He said, No, sahib. He loved her too much. He could not stay away from her. He would try. Then he would rush back after a few days. Before he died he told me he was addicted to her. As some are to ganja. He said, If you taste paradise you never forget it. It was only towards the end that he began to resist her. Those two were poisoning her mind – she was a simple woman, a great woman. They were forcing her to test my father's soul. Forcing her to wring it out of him. He had given her everything. There was nothing more to give. I think he began to withdraw because he thought it might bring both her and him some peace.

He was quiet for some time. Then he said, I don't think it did.

I said, So who killed her?

He said, I told you, those two ungrateful low-castes. They had been eyeing her property. They were scared she would leave it all to my father. Towards the end the padre used to come from Naini to see her because she had begun to have strange dreams – she used to wake in the night screaming. They got the padre to get her to will them everything. Then they began sprinkling on the dhatura.

I said, Was she screaming for her daughter?

He said quietly, What?

I said, Was she screaming for her daughter?

He said, Who told you about her?

I said, I know.

He said, Did she write about that too in the books? She had promised my father she would never speak a word of it. Never.

I lied. I said, Yes.

He said, Then you know.

I said, I only know her side of it. And, as I am discovering, it is not always true. I want you to tell me what you know.

The two dogs had padded down the wooden stairs and curled up on the divan next to him. They had blue nylon ropes knotted around their necks as collars. Rakshas was sitting with both his feet tucked under him and stroking his eyelids. He looked like an old man. The yellow bulb above us somehow seemed dimmer than when I had come in.

He said, Both of them went to Agra for that. She didn't want a scandal, and he had my mother to think about. They were there for four months, staying in the mission. My father was willing to bring the baby back, but she was adamant. She felt it would destroy her position here, and she was afraid of losing my father to any controversy. They were so obsessed with each other I think they didn't want anything to come between them.

I said, You mean she lived.

He looked up sharply. Why? What has she written?

I said, Sorry. Carry on.

He said, They left her with the mission, with a lot of money. My father said she was swarthy like him but had her mother's light eyes. She was one month old when they came away. The sisters said they had nothing to worry about. She would be well taken care of. A home would be found for her. Yes, if possible, in England or America. I don't think they ever spoke about her again. They were both consumed with guilt. They knew they had done a terrible thing.

He stopped and stared past me at the wall. It was easy to see how handsome his father would have been. The big face, strong nose, firm chin. As a child, I had seen peasants like that in Salimgarh. It was not just the features. Something about the carriage, the expression, had great dignity. I was convinced that kind of nobility was available only to those who worked the land. I felt it had to do with hard toiling, having to give yourself up to the vagaries of the weather gods, having to find harmony with animal, plant and soil, living with the knowledge that when it all went wrong you had simply to go back and dig, plough and sow all over again.

There are no short-cuts for those who work the land. No machines that can be speeded up, no deals that can be cut quickly, no salary hikes that can be commandeered, no state goods that can be pilfered. With great effort you give to the land, and in time it gives back to you. You take that as the central principle for life. First to give, before expecting. And to receive stoically whatever comes back. There is no ministry of weather to process your complaints. No boss to petition for a higher yield. There is only the next morning, the waiting plough, the waiting soil.

Farmers are fatalists who work hard every day.

Few things are more noble than that.

Rakshas seemed to be in a reverie. His eyes rheumy. I waited.

Without turning to look at me, he said, speaking softly, My father used to have horrible dreams about her. In them she was a child and she had fallen into a raging river and she was crying to him for help, holding out her little hand, and he was leaning out of the boat, trying desperately to reach her, and he could get only to her fingertips, and they too were slipping away, and he could see her big eyes pleading with him to be saved; he was shouting to her that he was coming, that he was going to save her; in desperation, he would finally jump into the water, looking for her frantically, but she would be gone by then, sunk without a trace, and no matter how deep he dived or how hard he tried she was nowhere to be found. He used to say, If I can just save her once in the dream I am sure I will find her again in real life too.

I said, Did he ever really try to?

He said, Only towards the very end. They had an understanding never to talk of it. They knew it had the potential to tear them apart. He blamed her for it, and maybe she blamed him. But in the last years she began to go crazy for her. She sent my father to Agra to find out. But it was too late. Everything had changed. All the old nuns were dead or gone. And the new ones said it was against the rules to give them any information. He came back after a week. She fell into a deep depression.

I said, So who killed her?

He said, They did. I told you they did. The bloody low-castes slow-poisoned the poor, trusting woman. For her house, for her dresses, for her money. Ten seeds every day.

Ten seeds every day till she went slowly mad. And then one day a hundred seeds.

By the time I reached home it was past two in the morning and the moon had died. The dhaba was closed and there wasn't a prick of light anywhere all the way back. Even the humming-murmuring undergrowth had fallen to slumber. I unlatched the front door by rattling it slowly – the way Stephen had first taught me – and walked up the stairs on the balls of my feet. Not that anything short of a brutal shove could wake Prakash. Bagheera padded after me and lay down under my bed.

In the night I dreamt a girl I knew – I couldn't tell who – had fallen into the river while we were rafting, and was drowning. Desperate, I did everything to save her, even jumping into the water, but I lost her. I was holding on to the edge of the raft screaming her name – Fizzzz – when Prakash woke me and said I had a visitor.

I thought it must be late, but it wasn't. It was only six in the morning – bright and cool – and the sun had still not crested the first peaks. I went down to the front veranda, and Rakshas was sitting on the step chewing a leaf. White-cheeked bulbuls were darting about in the bushes. A whistling thrush was sipping from a puddle near the tap, fluffing its feathers in satisfaction. Rakshas had cut himself a close shave, showcasing his big bushy moustache. He didn't look any younger than a few hours before, but he looked less haunted.

He put his right hand into his pocket and took out a slip of paper. It was old and discoloured, an irregular tear out of some jotting book. I opened the deep-creased folds. It had just three fading words written on it. Gramercy. New York.

He said, That's it. That's all the nuns gave him.

From the crook of his stump he pulled out a tight roll of parchment, tied with a mustard ribbon. I opened it out. There were four beautifully coloured miniatures, the lines so fine, the colours so iridescent.

He said, She left these for her.

Theoneandtruegodbemerciful. Bemerciful.

The position of the flying tortoise in reverse.

The phallus of chance in the hole of history.

Less than two months later I was sitting on the second floor of a hotel on Seventh Avenue at 55th Street in Manhattan, looking down on the most powerful people in the world shopping themselves to death.

I left for Delhi two hours after unrolling the miniatures. I asked Rakshas if he would care to live and work on the estate again, and left him in charge of Prakash and the house. It took me six weeks to get my visa. I had never travelled abroad, but Fizz and I had once, in a fit of enthusiasm for global adventure, got ourselves passports. It had been easy – fixer Mishraji at the newspaper conjuring them up without us having to set foot in any government offices. But now there was no Mishraji, no journalist tag, only forms, travel agents and bribes.

While the visa was obtained I took to the cyber cafe in the lane behind the Green Park market. Connectivity was poor and you had to struggle to stay online. The young man – with sharp braces – who ran it had four computers and I took full possession of one. I would stay there all day, leaving only to eat; at night I would wait for him to tell me he needed to close before I picked up my sheaf of printouts and left.

I tried every search engine. Each time I keyed in Gramercy thousands of entries leapt out. Gramercy parks, Gramercy taverns, Gramercy galleries, hotels, apartments, carpets, printing presses, museums, realtors, insurance companies, rental cars, posters, books, a brass orchestra, an elementary school, venture advisers, attorneys, flower shops, surgery centres, lamps, studios, a grill, pictures, music, plantations. Gramercy, gramercy, gramercy. It was endless. Hundreds could be dispensed with easily, but I still had to run through them.

I also went looking through alumni lists, telephone directories, family trees. I cross-matched Gramercy with India, Agra, orphan, guardian. Each day I printed hundreds of pages from the Internet and, going back home, sat on the terrace, my feet on the stone bench, parsing them. The weather was easing with every day and past midnight the breeze coming in from the Deer Park was cool, making the gulmohar swish against the walls. In the morning I took back the shortlisted ones and sent off dozens of emails.

I used all kinds of elimination criteria to narrow the field. Gender, age, family histories. Many emails earned replies eliminating themselves. By the time the visa arrived and I boarded the British Airways flight, I had a satchel full of printouts, leads pulled from the ever-widening maw of the amoebic web.

Technology hotfoot on the trail of spooks.

Often late at night Master Ullukapillu hooted.

The first time he did I almost leapt up to beat Fizz to the interpretation.

The master says we are all here to solve our own riddles.

But as Master Ukp kept hooting I realized the message was more prosaic.

From the greatest nut tightener in the world to the greatest nut-case.

❦

My nights were a greater mess than ever. She was still there, twisted and raging, taking me as a beast would a man, demanding things, making me fearful; but now there was also always the drowning girl whose hands I could not grasp and a one-armed spectre who surprised me in dark corners. I do not remember a single morning I woke up feeling rested. Yet always I was glad to be awake – away from the creatures of my nights, faced with a day of tangibles.

I visited the bank and was distressed to see there had been no withdrawals, no transactions. Fizz was not going to make it easy for me. The landlord told me she had not been back even once. I kept myself from calling her friends. Their loyalty was unquestionable, and I was afraid I would get provoked and say something hurtful.

When I landed at JFK I was without curiosity for the mecca of the free world. I knew enough about it, had ingested enough of it, without ever having set foot on it. I'd always told Fizz we all got more of America – unasked – than we needed. The world required an americofilter, a valve to regulate how much Mickey Mouse, mac-burger, Schwarzenegger and CNN would flow through.

Two orders of soaring freedom please. Make them large. But no toppings of hype and spiel and schmooze. And, no. No cherry of sanctimony either. Please.

There was a Sikh cabbie outside and he wanted to talk about the Khalistani separatist movement of Punjab. He had arrived illegally fifteen years earlier and not been back since. In a few years he had the papers. His wife and sons had followed him in time. His accent was still unmistakably Amritsar. He had a picture of Guru Gobind Singh on his dashboard. He was grey-bearded, wise and convinced that the Sikhs needed a separate state. I looked at him and wondered at what images of his land he carried inside his head, what affections, what guilts.

The memories of men can be as dangerous as their fantasies.

The drive to my hotel was drab – zipping cars, bifurcating roads, ongoing construction activity, huge billboards, grey skyline – and I was glad New York was not as spectacular as I had feared it would be. Then I hit Manhattan, and when I got off in front of my hotel the breath had been pulled out of me.

This had to be the grand canyon of human vanities.

Medieval churches steepled themselves impossibly to induce awe of god; these buildings of chrome and stone and steel and glass climbed past each other to induce awe of men. Very very rich men, whose kingdoms were brands, whose generals ranged through the world, whose slaves cut across race, region, gender and religion. Whose neon signs were big as ships and probably guzzled more electricity in a day than most villages in a month.

Drop your jaw in the face of the neon as you would genuflect in the presence of the lord.

I was glad to gain my hotel and retreat into my room. Its size was real, its adornments modest. And wonderfully it had a kuveen bed like our room in the hills. It was a refuge from the religious frenzy of commerce in the canyon outside. For the next few weeks I only ventured out when absolutely necessary. And that was mostly to pick up muffins, sandwiches, biscuits and bottles of milk – all so beautifully packaged as to demand reverence. Half the kuveen bed soon became heaped with printouts, papers, directories, maps, and I burned the phone lines all hours of the day and night.

I slept even worse than before.

The bed was too soft, the pillows too high, my head too crowded. Randomly, people were jumping into it from all over: Prakash, Philip, Stephen, my friends from college, Bibi Lahori – like a magician pulling out an endless roll of notes from her vagina, my parents dancing the foxtrot in the nawab's palace, Fizz's mother weeping with one eye and staring me down with the other, Fizz's friends goose-stepping through our barsati in jackboots and helmets,

Syed seducing me with sonorous words and supple fingers, the two Sikhs who first drove us into Delhi drinking uproariously on the hillhouse veranda with Jim Corbett, Shulteri kissing Haile Selassie, Rakshas conducting the Berlin Philharmonic with his stump, Taphen scaling a mountain of bottles to plant a flag at the peak, the moksha woman caressing my body with vanilla hands, ms meanqueen moaning of Kierkegaard under a smoothly stroking Gaj Singh, King Cupola riding Catherine while wearing a Stetson like Abhay.

Tishooon!

In the moments before I woke I was always choking on something, desperately, fatally. Everyone would be standing around, the entire oddball brigade, at a remove, watching silently. Even Fizz. I would be clawing the air for help, unable to speak, but no one would come forward. Then Fizz would say, OK, guys, the show's over! And turn away, and the other side of her would be the demanding face of Catherine, and I would let out a final scream of silent terror.

Each time I woke it took me long minutes to understand where I was.

The quest went badly. Most people were polite, but dumbfounded by my enquiries and eventually irritated. No, there were no adoptions in their family. No, they had no connections with India. No, there was no seventy-five-year-old woman in their house with swarthy skin and light eyes. In fact, would you mind fucking off and calling another day when no one's at home.

Day on day, week on week, the lists and names died on me, and soon along with the muffins and milk I began to pick up bottles of Jack Daniel's. The bourbon helped with my back tooth too, which had begun to throb and was following some kind of twelve by thirty-six pattern. Twelve hours of ache, then thirty-six of quiet.

I would drink and call and drink and call, and when I looked down from the second floor of the Wellington Hotel the street would be crammed to milling with shoppers and gawkers. Japs, East

Europeans, South Asians – everyone elated to be at the centre of the world briefly. Even at midnight the buzz would be ceaseless – like the chirring of the undergrowth back home – and sometimes when I was awake at three in the morning there was still activity afoot. Voices calling out to each other, the street being delittered, last revellers weaving their way back home.

On Sunday mornings the street became a bazaar. The master playing at slave. The rich man's poor-boy fantasy. It was straight out of my childhood in the towns of Uttar Pradesh, with a lot more swank thrown in. Shacks and kiosks were put up on the street. The smell of hot kebabs and cool sherbets filled the air. Bargain sales of throwaway clothes, bags, undergarments, zen pottery, Oriental curios, soul music and, of course, technogadgets lined the road. I walked through it once, the first Sunday; thereafter I would sit on the ledge of my window and watch it unfurl below.

It was only in the fifth week that the magic word came to me. Floating up gently through a sea of bourbon.

I was sitting by the window at night, watching the people flowing from and towards Times Square – in the middle of my ache cycle – when I looked at the bed, not double not single, my kuveen bed from the hills, and I had it.

I actually whooped and punched the air.

In a few minutes I was down on the street, eddying with the crowds, feeling light. I sat down in an open diner and gave myself a large Laphroaig and a bowl of hot pasta. Everything around was neon signs and moving people. I realized after years I was noticing women, packed and full, dominating the street, dressed in tight small clothes, flaunting the only female flesh I had seen in a long time outside of my hallucinatory nights.

I woke early the next morning, full of excitement. I dialled and said the magic word; dialled and said the magic word; it was suddenly so much easier. Three days later a low, faltering voice responded. I tried hard to tell my story and why I wished to come over. But the voice was slow to comprehend and too cautious to invite me. I called back three hours later, with my hanky on the receiver and, affecting an accent, declared I had an important delivery to make.

❧

I checked the address with the front desk and in the early evening, eschewing the subway, jumped into a cab and headed for Harlem. I had imagined slums, rape on the sidewalk, throats being slit in broad daylight. The heat is on. But there was no Chester Himes stuff happening here. Sure, it wasn't the grand canyon of vanities but I thought it looked as smart as the colonies back home in Delhi. Big department stores flanked the roads and the buildings had a solidity. At one point we passed a battalion of billowing djellabas, and had the men in them not been uniformly black it was possible to imagine you were in an Arab city.

The apartment block we stopped in front of had a weathered facade of exposed bricks in a burnt brown. It was a big square box, with rickety iron balconies and iron stairs strung all over its face. It seemed in greater disrepair than other buildings in the area. Inside, the lobby was poorly lit and there was a reek of grime. The air was fusty and there were knotted-up garbage bags along the wall. I decided against the elevator; it was a closed-door one and looked unreliable.

Up the first flight of stairs someone had scrawled: Jesus will come, and so will we! Below it another hand had written: All for the pleasure of the jolly white folk! The jolly white folk!

The stairs were broad but damaged. The matting was torn; the banisters missing pieces. At places even the steel-holding strips hung loose. I had to walk up to the third storey, and on the landing of each floor I looked down the corridor at the numbers of apartment doors lining each side. There were knotted garbage bags everywhere. Either the collection mechanism had gone awry or residents just put their refuse out any time it suited them. I was looking for 314, and when I walked down the corridor I could hear sounds and voices coming through the thin walls.

It was the second to last door on the left, and there was nothing on the outside to suggest the identity of its occupants. I knocked softly. Then harder. Someone scraped aside the cover of the surveillance eye. I tried to look as inoffensive as possible.

A wavering voice said, Josh not home, come later.

I said, I have a package for you. I held up the roll.

The voice said, For who?

I said, For Gethia. For Gethia Gramercy.

The door opened a few inches, a security chain holding it in. She was old and silver-haired and swarthy and light-eyed. She was in a nondescript cream-coloured dress marked with food stains; and she had a confused air about her.

I said, Can I please come in for a minute?

She deliberated in a befuddled way, scanning me up and down; then she struggled noisily with the chain and opened the door. In a glance I knew she had nothing there that was at risk. You would have to be wretched beyond description to assault such a house.

I sat down on the first chair I came across.

I said, I have come from India.

She looked completely blank.

I said, I have to deliver something to you.

She just nodded, looking vague.

I said, Do you know where you were born?

She said, Philadelphia.

I looked around. The room was decrepit. A sofa against the wall had its stuffing oozing out. It clearly doubled as a bed; there was a pillow against one end. A television set in the far corner was hissing softly, some talk-show man working up a studio audience with wild sweeps of his arms. There was a fake fireplace – no pretences, flat and fake – and on the mantel above it a bowl of dirty-red cloth roses. On the wall above it was an icon of Christ on the cross, the terracotta chipped. Just beyond the room I could spy a small alcove, whose walls were hung with worn clothes. The wallpaper everywhere – of tiny purple flowers – was tearing. A rancid smell hung in the air.

I said, What did your father do?

She said, Was a preacher – he travelled with the message.

I said, Did he ever go to India?

She said, He went everywhere. Ma name's from an India flower, he told me.

I said, What else did he tell you about India?

She said, He told me never to go there. It warnt a place for a civil man. He said they have five millun gawds there cos they need to protect themselves against five millun evil things.

I felt I was in the middle of some half-assed Hollywood film. Mr chinchpokli goes to Harlem.

I said, And your mother?

She had blanked out. I repeated the question. I could see her struggling to focus.

After some time she said vaguely, Who sent you here?

I didn't need to answer because her mind had wandered off, her eyes glazing over.

I tried several times to ask after her life and her children, but she just wasn't there. At one point I thought she had nodded off to sleep. I waited. She suddenly woke with a jerk and asked me if I had got the money. Before I could reply she started on a confused account of her daughter's destitution.

As she spoke, a huge wave of despair washed over me. I stopped hearing her and began to wonder what I was doing here. In this rank-smelling room in a strange city, probing a life that had nothing to do with me.

I was exhausted.

There was no more I wished to know. All stories must end at the right moment before they drown in inanities. And if anyone tells you every inanity has value, you can be sure they have never known the exhilaration of the unordinary moment.

The wonders of Fr John had in a hundred years come down to this squalor. The spirit of adventure had shrunk itself to the size of this airless box. Wonderful curiosity had become cheap contempt. The awe of a million gods had dwindled to a one-line dismissal. Emily was winning. Just that the world would end not in a splendid bang, but in a weak leaking away.

Desire, from a distance, has magic. Up close it's only prosaic coupling. Without the plinth of a narrative, a story, it cannot be a glorious monument. It's only the bits and pieces, only a rubbing-rubbing. I had picked something grand and followed it till I had arrived at its mundanities. Just the rubbing-rubbing.

I had taken apart the Taj Mahal and was left with a pile of marble slabs.

I wanted to rush out. Out of the building, into the open air, back to my own country. I unfurled the roll and gave it to her. I explained its value and told her it was a gift from a friend of her father who owed him a good turn. I said it would make her rich for the rest of her life.

She looked uncertain, peering through her thick glasses at the miniatures.

Just then a black man walked in, fine-looking, clearly younger than her.

She said, Josh.

Before he could say anything, I said, I am from India. A friend of Gethia's father left her a valuable legacy. I am just delivering it. Take good care of it. Sotheby's, Christie's, take it somewhere. You'll be OK for life.

As he looked at the paintings, I wrote a name and an address on a piece of paper and, handing it over, opened the door and said, And if you will, send him some of what you get. He preserved them for her. Many thanks and bye.

Josh began to speak, but I was already down the corridor and down the stairs and out the building, and the air was cold and bracing, and the lights were blazing in the shops and the streets, and the early evening bustle was gathering energy, and there was a weedy black man in a floppy hat banging a mandolin and following me for a dollar, and I walked swiftly down the pavement, without looking back, putting as much distance as I could between the building and me.

When I reached the hotel I went not to my room but directly to the front desk, weaving through a lobby full of freshly arrived ruddy-faced tourists muttering in some East European language – many of them collapsed on the floor – and asked the blonde there to help me get on to the first plane back to India.

When I entered the room I thought of one-armed Rakshas and the one miniature I should have kept back.

The position of the flying tortoise in reverse.

The phallus of chance in the hole of history.

The phone rang. The blonde said, You can leave in two hours, or you can leave tomorrow afternoon.

In two hours, I said, I will leave in less than two hours.

# A Teller of Stories

The first time I saw her was in the summer of 1979 when she opened the door of her house. After the solid wood door, there was one of mesh, but she flung that open too without hesitation. It was an innocent time, before terrorism, before assassinations, before AK-47s and gelatine sticks; nobody would do that now without asking enough questions to rattle your confidence. And in this innocence she was a child of her time, slow to suspicion, as I would come to recognize.

It was midday and the white heat began in a line from the overhang of the veranda and scorched the world. Not a leaf stirred in the city's green avenues and the bottlebrush on the patch of grass outside the house drooped low in punishment.

Out in the sun you had to squint to see; and if you forgot to park your bicycle in the shade the hot metal took the skin off your fingers when you returned. Even the rexine saddle burned, as did the plastic grips. I had wheeled my black Atlas inside the driveway and caressed it up against the brick wall, whose feeble shadow created a six-inch oasis.

There was nothing about the day, my mental state, or my physical, that suggested my life was about to change. If fate had tried to pick a more innocuous day to bend the direction of my life it could not have done better.

Later I always insisted I'd fallen in love with her before the mesh door swung shut. She never believed it. The girl who opened the door had the kind of fresh-faced beauty that becalms you, makes you want to linger in its glow. I had grown unused to girls for the many years I had been out of primary school, and as real people girls were distant objects. I was speechless. Then years of missionary school etiquette asserted itself. I said, Good afternoon, ma'am.

For the rest of our years she flung that formality at me. Good afternoon, ma'am. Just as, many years later, she nailed me with that ludicrous mr chinchpokli the moment she heard the urchin boy's chant on the bus. To her credit, she didn't giggle then. It would have destroyed me.

She just widened her eyes and said, You must be . . .

I nodded. She flashed a smile – the world lit up: her perfect teeth I would notice only years later, the details coming into focus slowly – and said, Come in. Miler should be here any minute. He's taken my aunt to the market.

When I stepped inside the first thing I noticed was that the terrazzo floor was polished liked a mirror and she was wearing nothing on her feet. The furniture – straight sturdy chairs with thick arms and a bare, armless sofa – was without elegance, and in the vast drawing-dining hall so spare as to look stranded. I sat down on the edge of the sofa and took off my blue rubber chappals. The floor was cool and smooth.

While I felt no embarrassment about my dusty feet and weathered slippers, I lacked the skills to open a conversation. I had no idea what you said to any girl, leave alone a beautiful one. As a schoolboy, I had grasped the basics of social discourse, but in two years at college I had lost the knack completely, mostly on purpose.

In contrast she wasn't awkward at all. She asked me if I wanted water, tea. I said no to everything, not looking at her, looking all around. She said she knew of me from Miler. He spoke of me often. That cranked up my confidence somewhat.

I wanted to ask her name but I didn't know how.

It's an enquiry I've never managed to master. What's your name? There's something so vulgar about it. A name is something that should be offered up. It cannot be demanded. I couldn't remember if she had offered it up when she opened the door and I had lost it in my bewilderment.

It was simpler to ask her what she was studying. Geography and psychology, at the Government College for Girls. I wanted to know if she was from Chandigarh, or like most of us, a student in transit in a city with no past and no obvious future. But I did not know how to ask without seeming crudely inquisitive. I was scared of saying anything that would blight me in her books. And I had no idea what a girl's book consisted of.

I sat silently, pondering the ugly grey carpet with two fire-tongued dragons edging its sides. Eventually she excused herself and left the room. That's the first time I looked at her, her receding figure, the navy blue corduroy jeans, the white top, the alive hair. Then she turned right at the end of the hall and was gone.

I looked around. In the far wall a service hatch opened into the kitchen, and I could see through to the sink and the crockery stacked next to it. Under the service hatch a wood and glass cabinet ran the length of the wall. Amid the chattel of empty flower vases and crowded photo frames, a Grundig reel-to-reel player squatted grimly. In the many years I was to visit that room, till it became one of the most intimate landmarks of my life, I would never once hear it open its mouth.

Next to the cabinet, tethered to the wall with a thick black cord, was a small white refrigerator, shuddering away at me. It had a big Dennis the Menace sticker stuck onto it. I craned my neck to read the brand and was disappointed to see it was an Allwyn. In a stupid sentimental way I was partial to Kelvinator. When I was six my father brought one home and my mother maintained it with such scrupulous care – no servant was allowed to open it, nothing in it was left uncovered, it was defrosted and washed every weekend – that after ten years of use it was resold for the price it had been originally bought at. A new one was purchased. Bigger. But again Kelvinator.

My parents were the foolish victims of fidelity, repetition. Paid-up artists of the safe world. In everything from clothes to foodstuffs to gadgets, the first brand they used satisfactorily became their only brand for life. In our home Philips replaced Philips, Binaca tooth-paste Binaca toothpaste, Bombay Dyeing Bombay Dyeing, Kissan jam Kissan jam, Bournvita Bournvita, Bata Bata.

On the wall to my right was hung an ugly mountainscape, its holding wire visible above the frame. It was an amateurish oil of a house on a hill, with green-blue mountains ringing the background, and a girl in a long skirt sitting on the veranda gazing at a redly setting sun. The house was a two-storey structure with a sloping roof and thick stone pillars on the veranda. Rashes of green ivy broke on the walls. There was a bank of glass windows on the upper floor and out of one, right above the girl, a man was leaning out looking down at her. On the right-hand side of the frame grew a large tree, thick of trunk, with sweeping branches.

When she returned, padding on bare feet, she asked me if I'd have some bel juice.

She said, It's awful. Ghastly taste. I can't bear to drink it alone.

I said, Yes, it looks bad too.

She said, Miler is the only one I know who loves this crap.

I said, Miler will eat and drink anything.

And that is how I told her my first story.

The story of how I met Miler.

I first met him in the college cafe where, amid the debris of dosas and coffee, there was a noisy coin-glassing game developing. The idea was to flip a fifty-paisa coin from the edge of the table with a flick of your fingers into a glass placed in the centre. Miler, a tall thin sardar with a wispy beard, a big beak of a nose and an oversized turban, was cleaning out the competition, and like filings to a magnet the adjoining tables had been sucked into the game. Sobers, Shit and I, sharing two dosas and planning our next film, were also drawn in. Sobers was eliminated in two turns and Shit flicked the coin so hard it landed in a bowl of sambhar two tables away.

I glassed my second flip. So did Miler. He had an expression of utter calm which I would come to love. He had a bunch of hangers-on – cheering – of the kind who wandered around the hostel corridors looking for someone to acknowledge their existence. If you as much as smiled at them, they'd show up at your room in the evening, ready to strike up a friendship. I glassed my fourth try; so did Miler.

Typically Shit decided this had to be settled differently.

He said, Flip it with your noses.

Miler pushed his armless aluminium chair away. He knelt on the floor and perched the fifty-paisa coin on the edge of the table, the aluminium piping on the Sunmica inclining it like a diving board. Carefully he pulled it out over the edge as far as it would go. His eyes were now flush with the table, his turban spiralling above.

He did a trial run, snapping his head down and up. He then slowly pushed his head forward till his long nose was under the edge of the coin. No one drew a breath. He brought his right hand up and gave his thick glasses an adjusting shake. And then, his eyes on the coin, his nose under it, he snapped his head down.

His turban crashed into the light aluminium table, which reared up on two front legs like a bucking horse. The plates and glasses heaped on the side somersaulted to the floor and detonated like a bomb.

Shit shouted, Run.

The weaselly manager with a pencil moustache shouted, Catch the buggers!

The waiters, in fan turbans and white tunics with green-and-yellow-striped cummerbunds, rushed towards us unenthusiastically, their rubber slippers slapping on the tiled floor.

In a flash we were – more than fifteen of us – out the wide door, rushing towards the playgrounds, laughing and cursing loudly. Looking back to see if anyone was following, I saw Miler was on the floor, fishing blindly for his spectacles, surrounded by a posse of green-and-yellow cummerbunds.

The manager ordered him over to the cash table. Miler loped behind him wordlessly and sat down on a chair opposite. The manager began to scribble calculations on a piece of paper. Miler looked at him with the equanimity of a teacher testing a student.

I decided to go back in.

The manager said, Twenty-one rupees.

Miler looked at me, then at the manager. He was holding the front and back of his turban – which looked like a boat being rocked on choppy seas – and was trying to bring it back on keel on his forehead. He had stood it up straight when it crashed sideways.

The manager said, Nine rupees for three plates, three rupees for three bowls, four rupees fifty paisa for three glasses and four rupees fifty paisa for three dosas. Twenty-one rupees, no sales tax.

I said, We didn't break everything. And I didn't even eat those dosas.

The manager said, He did.

I said, He ate one.

The manager said, He ate three.

I looked at Miler.

He nodded. With every nod, the loosened turban slipped lower.

I said, But we aren't responsible for all the breakages.

The manager said, Then who is?

I said, There were more than fifteen boys here.

The manager said, But whose pagad crashed the table?

I found a five-rupee note in my pocket, opened it out and put it on the table.

I said, OK?

The manager said, Sixteen more.

I looked at Miler. Impassively he put his hand in his shirt pocket, pulled out one five-rupee note, and one one-rupee note, and put them on the table.

Flexing his fingers, the manager placed them flat on the glasstop and with a dirty nail began lovingly to iron out the creases.

Something snapped in me. I stood up and said, Let's go.

He said, Ten rupees more.

I began to walk out. Miler followed, still grappling with his turban.

The manager shouted, Sardarji, I will go and complain in the principal's office!

Sardarji said, He is my uncle.

The manager said, Yes, yes, and Indira Gandhi is your aunty!

By then we were out the door and we could see scores of boys playing soccer and basketball and hockey in colourful shirts, their urgent cries for timely passes and sharp abuse for bungled moves filling the air. Keeping time was the periodic thud of leather on wood as the bowlers kept running in in an endless relay at the cricket nets.

Miler looked at me and for the first time an expression cracked his face. A slow, quiet, deeply knowing smile. He said, Thanks.

I said, The guy's really your uncle?

He said, And Indira Gandhi's my aunt.

We sat down on the concrete steps next to the basketball court and began a conversation that would go on for more than a year without pause, with an intensity we could not have imagined on that sun-drenched afternoon with the sporting cries of students hanging in the air, like the kites skating the thermals higher above.

With the first story I became for her a teller of stories.

The need for the story became the basis of our love.

Curiously – and perhaps aptly – her life already had a story. Her name was Fiza and she came from an unusual home. Her mother was Sikh and her father a Muslim. Falling in love and marrying in the years after the carnage of Partition, they ran into a wall of ostracism from both their families. In despair they abandoned the jagged nerves of the north and migrated far to the east, to Assam, in the 1950s, boarding a train that took more than three days to make the journey.

They went as far as they could and ended up in an obscure town, Jorhat, which – from Fizz's account – was famous for a few things: an air-force base, a gymkhana club for snobbish tea-planters, annual pony races, a big department store and a fine missionary school. The last she claimed was extraordinary: coeducational, free-spirited, sparked by a nun from Europe into a culture of socials, fetes, picnics and infatuations.

Rizwan, her father, struggled with a garment store, then opened a cinema. Her mother, Jaspreet, chipped in, teaching Hindi at the missionary school. They both abandoned obvious religion, and Fiza grew up genuflecting to nothing but the vague father-in-heaven-holy-be-thy-name belted out tirelessly by the bustling-beaming nuns. As escalating ethnic politics in Assam began to derail life and education, her parents decided to send her to the artificial oasis of Chandigarh, increasingly a kind of university town. A widowed aunt of Jaspreet had stood by her through the years and to her house in Chandigarh Fiza was dispatched. Miler was the aunt's great-nephew, notionally a cousin of Fiza's, but discovering her too for the first time.

She was not yet sixteen when she arrived in the squared city and was instantly concussed by its unrelenting priapism: its aggression, its crudity, the daily propositioning by every boy or man who crossed her path. In her home town laid-back commerce and splendid passivity were the established way. That, the missionary school and the endless films she saw – Hindi in her father's hall and English every weekend at the sleepy Gymkhana Club – had shaped her sensibility. The world was benign, it had a moral order and life was a charming story with unfortunate twists that always worked out fine in the end. She had to only look at her father and mother to be assured of that.

Happy marriages can truly wreck children with false hope.

In the north she found there were no rules. From the moment she wheeled her small blue bicycle out of the house she was set upon. Boys escorted her to and from college; they moved in clumps behind her when she went to Sector 17; they followed her into cinemas, restaurants, parks; they threw stones of adoration at her; they exposed themselves from behind trees and hedges, grinning as they moved inside their fists; they left flowers and gifts in her mailbox, one placing a fresh egg there every morning for an entire month. No one attempted a conversation. They were happy to offer instant sex from a distance and be ignored endlessly.

As one of the college boys who did this sort of thing daily – it was called the pehelwani geda, the macho jaunt – said to me, We keep asking – one day we'll get.

By the time I met her she had been in the city almost a year and had learnt to move inside her own cocoon. It had kept the priapic onslaught from scarring her spirit. She remained amused and did not lose her incredible freshness, treating the daily spectacle like one of the films she saw in her father's hall. The boys were all playing a role and no real malice was meant. It boggled me because I knew the boys and how virulent they could be in their unknowing. I tried to tell her. But she was right and I was wrong. To change yourself out of fear is to lose the game.

Life must be risked. Always on your own terms.

Innocently I began to accompany Miler to her house every week. By then Miler and I had spent nearly a year in deep friendship. After the fracas at the cafe we had discovered a furious empathy. We were not about silent communion. We were an orgy of conversation. For me it was like birdsong at dawn after the silence of a long night. We had taken a room together, stopped attending classes, become wanderers in the city, and spent our days talking up books, films, cricket, boxing, philosophy, politics, pornography, people.

Contrary to what people say, the essence of any great relationship is the absence of disagreement. There is no such thing as a healthy difference: every difference is a termite in a relationship's rafters, hollowing it, preparing it for collapse, while every agreement, even false, is one more beam shoring up the structure. So Miler and I never disagreed; and even if we felt differently, we buried the sentiment in the general exhilaration of our togetherness.

Miler confirmed me in my ambition. He prepared me for her. Growing up in Delhi, Miler had done many things, cosmopolitan things: flown in planes, eaten in swanky hotels, danced in discos, attended jam sessions of acid rock, gone to the Osibisa concert. He had the measure of things, he was a man of the world. I had done none of this, but I had done one thing he had not. I had read. Scores and scores of classics.

I had done this unselfconsciously, without any sense of edification, filling in the emptiness of long soporific days in those dusty towns of Uttar Pradesh. The books had come from crumbling school and club libraries. Old mud-coloured hardbacks with a black patch on the spine for the title, purple ink stamps declaring ownership details on ten different pages, and paper that was yellowing and fragile, climate and insects having excavated tiny perforations into the edges. Your fingers became powdery as you turned the pages.

I consumed the entire English literary canon, all the way back to the sixteenth century, even attempting to plough through a massive volume of Shakespeare's collected plays. The paper was so thin you could see through it; and you had to set it on a table to read it.

I understood little and retained less. Their worth only came home to me when I saw it shining in Miler's eyes. He seemed to think it extraordinary that I had read all these books. That I knew so many unusual words. Like skin growing on freshly boiled milk, his admiration settled slowly on me, propelling me with a new ardour between the covers of more books and giving me a sense of esteem I had never had.

This, then, is the person I took to her and this is the person she fell in love with; and later, when the fractures began to show, she was hurt and bewildered as someone who, in a stupid and innocent haze, has bought the mask for the man.

❦

Two story rituals became the warp and woof of my love.

Telling her stories and taking her to watch stories.

Watching was easy. It was what everyone was doing. Cinema-going was an epidemic in Chandigarh. Film tickets were ludicrously cheap – three rupees ten paisa for the balcony, and less than half that for the stalls. You did all the five halls every week and hoped for new releases on Friday. It was fairly common to repeat a film several times.

As with everything else in the city, here too there was a hierarchy.

The really cool crowd saw – and was seen at – the English films.

The grand ritual was the morning show on Sundays at the weird, hangar-shaped KC. The films were an oddball mix of recent and old Hollywood films. *The Great Escape, Jaws, The Duchess and the Dirtwater Fox, Saturday Night Fever, Close Encounters of the Third Kind, Kramer vs. Kramer.* It didn't matter what the film was, the show was always packed.

Perfumes and colognes rent the air and hours of careful grooming were on display. Virile young men in high buff boots, the flares of their jeans fitted perfectly around their ankles, leaned against gleaming Yezdi motorcycles, sardonic smiles curling their lips. Attractive young Punjabi women, their skins glowing with excitement, their bodies already ripe for fantasy – women who at nineteen were peerless sexual sirens, but who would be over the hill by thirty, their appeal drained by children and fat – these women, immaculately clad in finely ironed jeans and clinging kurtas, swayed in huddles, casting sidelong glances, and exciting the boys unbearably.

It was all too much. Everyone seemed on the verge of a weeping orgasm.

In my first month in the city I was given a perfect measure of its affectations by a reed-thin sardar wearing a tight turban and baggy trousers. He was standing on the bonnet of a Fiat car in front of KC, hawking tickets. He had a wispy beard, and his thin shoulders were flung back, bending him like a bow, as he hollered into the air in a high-pitched whine, Paaappeeleeon! Oh, Paaaappeeeleeeonn! Oh, meri Paaaapppeeeleeon!

A sheaf of tickets was waving in his right hand, and *Papillon* aspirants were crowding the car.

I almost never went for the morning show. I felt inadequate amid the display of good looks and confidence. And then there was the crush and the queues. Boys would line up three hours in advance to buy extra tickets to sell to girls, who would then end up sitting next to them. I preferred to be part of the lower orders.

The lower orders lived by the Hindi film. They consisted mostly of students from the small towns and villages of Punjab, Haryana and Himachal Pradesh. Coming to the metropolis had been a huge leap; absorbing it – its sartorial swishness, its behavioural flair, its gender-bending codes, its rituals of restaurants and coffee shops, smoking and drinking, motorbikes and girls – absorbing it all was a fraught affair. You could see it in their eyes. The uncertainty and the desire.

They could be spotted all over. Always moving in small groups, shoring each other's confidence with desperate, often crude, humour; lingering at the mouth of discovery in Sector 17 – outside a restaurant, a swank music store, a trendy clothes shop. In the hostel you would come upon them smoking a Dunhill, caressing the red pack by turns, the lid ripped carefully to preserve the cellophane. Or struggling with the strange fit of a pair of blue jeans they had courageously picked up.

But it was the women who really undid them. They fed their small-town stereotype of big-city-fast-woman into the girls they saw around, and had no means of dealing with it. They would ogle every woman, often following them for hours around markets and along the road, their heads full of fantasy and fear.

Wearing their nerves like epaulettes, most of these boys clung to Hindi films as the only charted island in a shoreless sea. They returned again and again to Hindi cinema's dark womb to make themselves whole. With its particular mythology, it provided the one overwhelming continuity of their lives. Once the lights were turned down they were in familiar territory and not under anyone's scrutiny.

Fizz, typically, patronized both orders. When I first came to know her, she did not – unlike the rest of us – have nerves. She moved inside her own cocoon of certitudes and innocence and made things simple by dealing with them simply.

She went for the films – English and Hindi – and did not let any of the surrounding drama cast a shadow on her temper.

I began to go with her to the Hindi – once a week – but I continued to avoid the Sunday morning production. The Hindi film too began as a group thing, and it was many months before we managed to insulate ourselves enough to go on our own. But it remained an innocent activity, without even the holding of hands, or the uttering of an intimate word, though it all hung about us, acquiring definition and screaming to be said.

But it was the stories she heard, not the ones she saw, that finally created us.

She was a real sucker for stories. A truly gifted listener, she evoked an articulation in me I had never imagined I possessed. When I read the notebooks – twenty years on – I knew why Syed spoke so beautifully. Catherine made him, by listening beautifully. I knew because Fizz had done it for me.

She wanted to hear everything I had to say. About books, films, politics, art, sports, people, life, ideas. She wanted to hear about the capers I had been in during the week, the absurdities that filled my life. She was sold on the offbeat, the irregular, the eccentric. I think she was marked by her father and his wilfulness. And by the drama of the films that had always filled her life.

She was captivated by absurdity and intensity the way most people are by money and power.

I would philosophize, psychologize, agonize, dramatize, rhapsodize, and she would bathe in it all rapturously, as if it were a midsummer shower transforming a season of oppressive heat into sudden magic.

I would show up at her house – her aunt's house – every Saturday evening. In the beginning with Miler, but when he left six months later to go off to his uncle's orchards in California, I would go alone, leaning the Atlas up against the grey wall, pretending to the aunt I was just keeping up a ritual for a friend. I would sit with my feet on the dragon carpet, the voiceless Grundig in my face, the Allwyn shuddering at me, the crude mountainscape looking down from the right, and I would begin to talk.

She would be in jeans, her hair pulled back tight and caught in a ponytail, her classic face attentive, her smile lighting up the world.

I found it difficult to even look at her. It was heady just to be in the same space.

I don't think she had any idea how much she shaped me by her listening.

I became who I thought she wanted to hear.

I began to live my life to tell her the stories.

I filled every week of my life with a story I could tell her: my friends and I shedding our drenched clothes in Neelam theatre after walking through driving rain to see a film, and then being forced out of the hall naked as an earthquake rocked the city; Miler and I drumming up a bovine phobia among our friends, forcing everyone to hide behind trees and bushes each time a cow was spotted; surviving on bananas and milk for an entire week – resulting in terminal constipation – because we had spent all our money on books; five of us walking straight down the hillside from Kasauli – again, no money – to arrive in Chandigarh fourteen hours later with torn skin and tattered clothes.

I narrated and narrated – living, embellishing, conjuring – and they became like the tales of Scheherazade, stories to keep me alive in her life. The way my mother's father had stayed alive in my life by telling me stories from the Mahabharata: when his stories dried up he faded away and I was only next aware of him when he died, an insubstantial husk of the once mesmeric narrator of thrilling tales.

That was my first intimation that the story was always more important than the teller. It was not the teller who breathed life into the story, but the story that kept the teller alive.

For a long time my stories were about escapades and blunders – absurdities that appealed to her, and made her laugh. Then, as Miler's presence slowly vanished, they became about other things, more intimate things, more intense things. Scripts that score out the trajectory of our lives.

Two decades later as I sat in a tight hotel room on Seventh Avenue in Manhattan, sifting through the debris of my life, waiting to catch the plane back home, I knew that more than anyone else it is lovers who need the gift of the story. They need to tell stories to each other continually to keep themselves from disappearing.

Passionate love has nothing to do with any obvious attributes of the lover – class, intellect, looks, character. It has everything to do with the stories the lover can tell. When the stories are stirring, complex, profound – like great fiction they need never be crudely true – then so is the love.

When the stories are thin – their grammar sloppy, their life-force weak, their plot tawdry – then so is the love.

The stories lovers tell each other are tales about themselves, their past, their future, their uniqueness, their inevitability, their invincibility. Stories about their dreams, fantasies, the nooks and crannies of their fears and perversions. Those who can tell their stories with power create powerful love. Those who can't never know the emotion.

Love is the story, the wine in the bottle. The teller is merely the bottle, of some significance only till the wine is tasted. Grand bottles die on the shelf if the wine fails, if the stories flounder.

We all know beautiful people who have never known love.

Like great fiction, the stories lovers tell each other can be about anything and can be told in any tone. They can have the exuberance of Dickens or be spare like Hemingway; they can teem as Joyce or confound as Kafka; they can be mad as Lewis Carroll or sad as Thomas Hardy. They can be anything – grim, comic, philosophic, loony.

But they must be true.

In the peculiarly false way great fictions are true.

In the peculiarly false way great love is true.

> Kissing causes germs.
> Germs we know are hated.
> But kiss me quickly, baby;
> Kiss me, I am vaccinated.

She had learnt this ditty as a schoolgirl in Jorhat. One afternoon in my room she used it on me as a goad. It was like firing a missile into a dam. The waters of my desire crashed through, flooding over everything till nothing was visible but want.

It was strange because for nearly a year I had been content just to hold her hand. In the months after Miler left Chandigarh the arena of our lives had slowly extended beyond the cinemas and that drab living room. I had lost my Atlas, stolen from outside the eatery Prima in Sector 10, and had taken to walking. She had fallen in step with me. She would pedal briskly on her small blue cycle to our rendezvous; we would leave the bicycle in a parking lot, and we would begin to walk.

We would walk for hours every day, from sector to sector, from my room in Sector 9 to the university in Sector 14 to the bookshops in Sector 17 to the cinemas all over the city to her house in Sector 35. Chandigarh was then a great city for walking, with wide roads and lovely trees lining them, arjun, amaltas, gulmohar, neem, semul. Every evening, when it was time for her to go, clinging desperately to one last minute, I would wheel her small bicycle along as I walked her, across the city, to her gate.

There is no greater code for courtship than walking. Learning to keep in step; the opportunity to express little concerns – alarm, caution, the touch on the elbow; the blood running in the veins; the sense of movement and a shared goal; the sense of being just two amid the swirl; and above all the ability to talk expansively in the open air without the anxiety of each other's gaze and close scrutiny.

Those who wish to find love should learn to walk.

As we walked, she made me talk: beautifully and without pause. What Miler had sparked she brought to fruition. Without saying a word, she decreed who I was, who I was going to be. I was reading more than ever before because she wanted to hear about it. I was talking of writing more than ever before because she wanted to hear about it. Every minute I was not with her I was in my room trapped between pages, preparing myself for her, preparing myself for my future.

With Miler leaving I had withdrawn from all our other friendships and had stopped going to college altogether. I had taken a small
room in the annexe of a big decrepit bungalow in Sector 9, and told
no one its location. The room lay above the garage and had dirty
green mango leaves pressing against the window. There was no
furniture bar an old cane chair on the narrow balcony. There was
rush matting on the floor and my mattress was on it, becalmed in
a sea of books. Endless, irregular stacks of them. They made the
room look like a settlement of different-sized multi-storey buildings
designed by architects who could not draw a straight line. I was
spending every rupee my father sent me on buying books, and she
was doing the same, bringing them for me in paper bags, books she
had bought and kept for a few days in her cupboard amid her perfumes and clothes so they smelled of her for days and drove me crazy.

My relationship with my father had collapsed completely. He was
writing long harangues to me about career planning, management
institutes, law schools and civil service preparatories. I thought him
stupider than ever before. I had stopped writing to him and almost
expected him to cut off my money supply. But the two hundred and
fifty rupees cheque kept coming every month, and I kept burning it
on new books.

Once a week I would go to the market and call my mother when
he was at the office and let her know I was well, but the moment she
began to coerce me towards a rapprochement, I would disconnect the
line. Sometimes, after speaking to her, I would sit on the edge of the
market veranda outside Guptaji's grocery store, and be convulsed by
a crazy sadness. Then I would desperately need to be with Fizz, and
if I couldn't be I would begin to walk. And I would walk and walk
and walk – seeing nothing, hands in pockets – till the sorrow had
drained out of me.

For more than a year I did not go home during a single break, not
even during Chandigarh's killer summer, choosing to lie naked in the

torpor, coated in a thick film of sweat under a slow fan, reading slowly, waiting for Fizz to come back from remote Jorhat, waiting for the postman to bring me her daily letter, many many pages, folded over neatly, pressed bamboo leaves in their creases, her perfume, sweet sweet Madame Rochas, wafting through them. I read each letter several times, ferreting out the hidden meaning of every syllable; and sometimes I just lay back on the bed and spread them on my face, filling my head with her smells.

It is strange, given the way it went later, that for so long I was content to just hold her hand and to talk. But I was. There was a surreal, pristine air to it all. I was happy just to be in her space. It turned my sullenness into talk; it made me feel worthy. The time I was not with her I lived only for the time I would be with her. And when the moment came I basked in the glow of well-being.

Two decades on, with effort, I can still inhabit that feeling and know it to be true.

As I failed to progress beyond her hand, with her typical lack of artifice she decided to act. We were sitting on the mattress, surrounded by the high-rise books, and I was reading her some Preludes by Conrad Aiken, when she interrupted me and recited the rhyme. I had my mouth on her before she had finished, and I did not take it off for many hours, till night had fallen and she had to go home.

From that day, 9 January 1981, desire drowned out everything.
Walking, talking, literature.

From early morning I would wait for her, sitting just inside the balcony door, looking down the broken asphalt driveway, trying to read, but failing. There would be *Mr and Mrs 55* or *Barsaat* or *Aar Paar* playing on the flat Philips cassette recorder. I would have the door open as she climbed the concrete spiral staircase. My mouth would be on her face before she had fully entered the room. She always looked and smelled as if right out of her bath, even though she had pedalled halfway across the town.

I discovered how gaudily pink a young woman's nipples are.

And how her face turns the same colour as you suck on them.

I discovered how boundless a woman's body is.

And how you keep finding more the more you seek.

I discovered in love how easy it is to put your mouth everywhere.

I discovered you never love a woman more than when you are deep inside her.

I discovered in me a desire I had never imagined. I could not have enough of her. She would arrive and I would begin to love her, and till I walked her back – always just after dusk – my caressing hands would be on her forearm, and I would force her to linger at the gate till it became suspicious.

When she was not around I was tormented by her smells and tastes – a restlessness that often reduced me to reading barely a page in an hour. We lost the ability to see films or go to restaurants or linger in markets because my need of her was so great it could not be slaked in public.

It is true the first time I lasted not a stroke, and the second time just one, but as the weeks passed we settled into loving for hours on end, till the room only smelled of her, and her silent moans had filled it to bursting. I wished to see no one, I wished to go nowhere, I only wanted to be with her in that tiny room, marooned amid books, drowned in her body.

What a world I discovered, what a world of aliveness and gratification.

I have never lived more keenly. One woman can be a universe.

She was full in a way that is always poorly represented in photographs. She was made for love. Her body was as much about giving as about receiving. I found arousal in its every dip and curve, in its every dampness and musk; and this was a voyage of discovery that would go on for years. Every bit of her worked me into a state, even her Renoir legs, which she hated; and often I would ration myself my pleasures – cutting down on the oeuvre – to restore some sanity to my rutting.

And her face, her face. Her face was an ecstasy, a luminous oil by a Renaissance master; and with her lack of guile it mirrored all she was feeling. I read her love in it and was driven to more craziness. Fr

John was right: all that matters is allure in the face, for that is all you see as you perish in a woman.

I lived in a frenzy. Sometimes I would finish loving her and minutes later, breathing her lingering musk on my face, I would be aroused again. And so it would go on hour after hour. Soon I began to keep back bits of her clothing for when I woke in discomfort in the night, straining with desire.

My vocabulary shrank at an alarming rate. She ceased to listen beautifully. I began to talk poorly. I became a lumbering herd of clichés. Baby talk and clichés. Babble. But nothing else could convey what I was feeling. I had been distilled down to pure and simple fundamentals.

I was now nothing but a beast of wanting, and even when I spoke to her about books and ideas and dreams and fantasies it was only to pull out from her an extra lick of passion.

Over the years she would listen less and less beautifully and I would talk more and more poorly, but the want would only grow. And we would cleave to each other, blessed by the miracle of desire.

I married her in July 1982.

I was twenty-two and she not yet twenty.

By then I could not bear to be parted from her at the end of every day. My need of her was much too great and growing all the time. My mother sulked. My father said he had never had any expectations of me. Bibi Lahori kicked me in the balls.

Musalman! Over my dead body!

Her parents weren't ecstatic either.

Their dismay had less to do with religion and more to do with my poor qualifications as a groom. I had a plain degree in economics and history and a modest career profile. I had begun to work as a trainee subeditor on a Delhi paper, and after six months signed up as a trainee reporter with a local Chandigarh daily earning rupees six hundred a month, plus four rupees for every night shift. To anyone's eyes I had no prospects. The young man as novelist was not a category on the Indian marriage landscape. Fizz, on the other hand, was radiantly beautiful, and intelligent. She could end up anywhere.

I didn't care. I wanted no one's approval.

Those six months in Delhi had been the most unhappy of my life. Every Saturday I would catch the night bus to Chandigarh, spend the day with her and take the night bus back. Sometimes, desperate just to see her, I would travel all night, arrive at the crack of dawn, spend two hours with her and start back to be in time for my afternoon shift. I lived in a daze, aching for the next letter, the next phone call, the next bus journey. The stale smell of night buses invaded my nostrils and did not go for years. In Delhi I made only one friend, Philip; and to him too I could say nothing because it was too densely knotted inside me to try to express.

Well before six months were over I knew if I was not soon with her I would waste away completely and become nothing.

So the moment I had a job in Chandigarh I made my move. I announced a date, randomly; and said we were going ahead. Looking back through the telescope of twenty years, it was a remarkable thing to do.

Her father dug in his heels. Fiza, who had never crossed her parents, now looked him in the eye and became immovable. Her mother had to step in. She reminded her husband of their forgotten history. Rizwan assented most reluctantly. The rebellions of your own youth are no insulation against concern for a pretty daughter.

Just to cut the clamour, I agreed to a perfunctory procedure.

We didn't marry in court because I couldn't be bothered with the paperwork. And we didn't marry Hindu or Islamic. Fiza and I chose the Anand Karaj, the Sikh ceremony, which could be reeled off in the morning, very quickly and very simply, while retaining a sonorous gravitas befitting such a rite of passage.

Her parents showed up and so did mine, as well as some oddball relations, friends and colleagues from the paper. It was a dismal affair and everyone seemed disgruntled with the proceedings. Afterwards there was a lunch with rubbery naans and masala chicken. My father wore his maroon tie and black three-piece suit in the sweltering heat and looked sceptically at everyone. Robust Rizwan in a floral bush shirt had the look of a man who has been mugged in broad daylight. The two mothers struggled with niceties, but it was tough going with the sweat running their pasty make-up into their bright lipstick.

The waiters, in white jackets with green trim and gold lapels, had big patches under their armpits. The smell of sweat filled the room. Big pedestal fans whipped up noise and air. It was all depressingly shabby.

I was awkward in a cream pyjama-kurta, and getting angrier by the moment. Why the fuck had I acquiesced to even this minimal charade?

Fiza, from across the room, could see it building up in me.

She walked across slowly, looking unbelievably beautiful in a maroon salwar-kameez, stood in front of me, smiled to light up the world and said, I am in desperate need of some legal intercourse.

That evening when we got to our room in the hotel – the bed canopy hung with strings of marigolds and tuberoses – we were the happiest we had ever been.

We didn't need anything. We didn't need anyone.

The thought that she would not have to go away any more filled me with a surpassing sense of security and contentment.

She lay on her back, her face glowing, her hair loose in dark coils around her, and said with that smile, Sorry for putting you through all that.

I said, For you, baby, I'd do it again. For you I'd do anything.

She said, Would you dance in the streets?

Anything.

Shell a thousand peas?

Anything.

Take me to Greece?

Anything.

Write a masterpiece?

Anything.

Just kiss me please?

Anything. And again.
And again.

I'd do anything. For you dear anything. For you dear everything.
For you.

# First Things

On the flight back I dreamt I had become light as a feather.

I was on the second leg, from Heathrow to Delhi, and the plane, big as a building, was only half occupied. I had annexed five seats at the very back and was lying hard on my left cheek, in the middle of my twelve-hour throb. With my third Jack Daniels the ageing stewardess's sweet smile had become a warning snarl. Not up to a race spat, I was attempting oblivion.

We were all on the college ground, playing soccer. Sobers, Miler, Shit, faces from my schooldays, my cousins. But I was having trouble staying with the ball. Each time I took a step I rose six feet in the air and went over everyone. I was moving faster and further than all the other players but failing to make any contact with the ball. My team-mates were shouting at me to stay on the ground, to get to the ball.

I was trying very hard but I just couldn't stay down. In fact I was getting lighter and lighter; and the buoyancy felt wonderful. From six feet I was beginning to rise twelve feet each time I took a step. Everyone had begun to gasp in awe. Now I could see the tops of the neems and the gulmohars, the gymnasium and the bicycle stand, the hostels and the auditorium, the tennis stadium and Leisure Valley.

I would come down slowly, hit the ground and float straight back up again, higher and higher.

But soon the feeling of freedom and joy gave way to panic. I was going too high. I was out of control, threatening to float away. The game had stopped and everybody was clustered together in the middle of the field, looking up, screaming. Other players had arrived there too, the basketballers, the jumpers, the wrestlers, the boxers, the athletes, the hockey players and the cricketers in their blinding white flannels. Everyone was looking up, waving and screaming.

Now I was beating my limbs desperately to push myself down, somehow to slow my ascent. I was shouting to everyone below to help me, to pull me down. But nothing was helping. I was hysterical with panic, swamped with terror. Soon I couldn't recognize the faces. Then the voices too began to fade. The group below became a speck. The college became a speck. All of Chandigarh became a speck. All of everything became a speck.

Then the panic passed.

And I kept rising and rising till there was nothing below me and nothing above.

The first thing I did when I got back to our barsati in Green Park in the middle of the night was recklessly to ring the landlord's bell and ask if there had been any news of Fizz. There was none.

When I went up to the terrace, Master Ullukapillu hooted.

Jaan bachi so lakhon paye; laut ke buddhu ghar ko aaye.

Praise the lord, the fool is back, his life intact.

The next morning I went to the bank. Not one transaction.

I called every single friend of hers. Jaya, Mini, Chaya. They were all surprised, polite and completely unhelpful. They claimed to know nothing about her whereabouts, declaring she had been out of touch for years. I could believe that. She was not one to hide behind rocks, but it was as unlikely she would flaunt her wounds.

I telephoned her home in Jorhat. Her mother said she was not coming there in the holidays, then she recognized my voice and began to sob. I waited. She was sniffling uncontrollably. Her father came on the line. He was cold and melodramatic. He said he knew it was a mistake from the moment he set eyes on me.

The world is a hard place. Treat everyone like cicadas.

I said, This is urgent. I really need to reach her.

In the voice of the films he screened in his hall, he said in Hindi, Once a bullet leaves its barrel it never comes back.

I said, Please help me, sir.

He said, Nothing can help you now, son. Not even god.

He put the phone down.

I wanted to say, What about a kick in the head from Baba GoleBole? Would that help? What of a thousand kicks in the head from Baba GoleBole, O Sir Rizwan of the beauteous daughter?

I dialled again.

He said, Wrong number – it was always the wrong number. I knew from the moment I saw you it was the wrong number.

This time I put the phone down.

There were two days to Christmas and it was dark at six in the evening. I pulled the love seat onto the terrace, took my whisky, wrapped the thick grey shawl we had once bought from the Kasauli flea market tightly around me and sat outside. While I was away the landlord had hacked the gulmohar to gain the winter sun. I felt a little naked without the profusion of branches.

The noise of traffic was everywhere. Even our lane, which was an enclave of peace when we first moved to Delhi twelve years before, was bustling with cars and voices. Most were men's voices, preparing for fun. This was festive time in Delhi. Days to party, get drunk and ride the roads. The newspapers were full of advertisements drumming up millennium-eve revelry. All over the city music was blaring out of shops, cars, houses.

I remembered the time, over all those years, when in the last two weeks of December we would be out every night with friends and come home to urgent loving. Then we would lie in bed and relive every year, recounting all the triumphs and disasters. 1981, 82, 83, 84, 85, 86, 87, 88, 89, 90, 91, 92, 93, 94 . . .

She would say, This year will be perfect – one baby, one book, two holidays.

I'd say, First the book. Then baby. Then holidays.

She'd say, You say that every year – then nothing. Suppose I write the book!

I'd say, Perfect. Then I'll make the baby.

She'd say, But don't worry, I won't tell anyone. I'll let you take all the credit.

I'd say, That's it. That's all I want.

With the gulmohar shorn, I could look into the dark shadows of the Deer Park, and already there were fingers of mist beginning to caress the trees. I almost longed for Master Ukp to speak the voice of wisdom, but it was too early for him to give a hoot. I had spent the morning tearing and trashing the hundreds of pages of printouts I had taken from the cyber cafe. I had also called in the maid from downstairs and paid her to clean and mop the house. The quest was over, but it didn't seem like it.

Suddenly a thought seized me. I went inside and called the thakur's shop. Then I put the phone down, waited ten minutes and dialled again. Rakshas was breathless. Did you find her? What was she like? Did she remember anything? What did she say? You told her about us? I said, Hang on, hang on. I'll tell you everything the moment I get there. But first tell me has there been any . . .

No, there hadn't been any. For a moment I had imagined, as in films, there would be a neat coming around. I must have sat there absently for a few hours because Master Ukp finally hooted.

You fool, she's not coming home for the holidays.

And in a flash I knew where she was.

I rushed in, pulled on my thick army parka, stuck my toothbrush into its inside pocket, turned off the lights and was out the door in less than fifteen minutes. By the time I put my Gypsy into the car park at the bus terminus it was past ten o'clock. The terminus had been smartened up since I had last seen it, but the Chandigarh bay was exactly where it had been eighteen years earlier. There was a Haryana Roadways bus leaving as I arrived. I got a seat in the second to last row, propped my knees against the plywood and iron back and slumped into travel mode.

In a few minutes my legs were cramped and the rancid bus smell had filled my nostrils. All the windows rattled and many did not close, and the chill wind blasted in, forcing everyone to hood their faces. Most had blankets and shawls; I had my parka. We were like a bunch of saboteurs on a mission. Fifteen years before, with Sikh terrorism raging, such a bus would have been nauseous with fear. Now everyone snored, collapsed loosely like rag dolls.

Past midnight the driver veered into a dhaba near Murthal for dinner. As I pissed into the pale eucalyptus trees standing in dank water, as I ate my dal-roti off the steel plates, as I worked the hand pump to splash cool water on my grimy face, as I walked along the road just outside the pools of light from the dhaba, I was once again a young man of twenty with an ache in my heart so deep it had no bottom.

When I reached Chandigarh I brushed my teeth without tooth-paste, ate a buttered bun with several cups of steaming tea, and walked up and down to get the blood going in my limbs; then the connecting Himachal Roadways bus was ready. By nine o'clock with a last moaning effort the old bus had scaled the final steep stretch and parked below the shopping block. It was cold, bitterly cold. The sun had not yet penetrated the morning chill, and the normally busy plaza and parking lot were virtually empty. Just beyond, the cobble-stone bazaar seemed to be getting off to a slow start too. The one time I had come with her to Kasauli in the winter we had not got out of bed even once before noon in four days.

Walking down, away from the Upper and Lower Malls, it took me less than ten minutes to get to the school. As I shuffled up the flagged path towards the convent, my spirits plummeted. There was not a sound in the playgrounds; not a footfall in the pillared corridors; not the murmur of a child in the stone-walled classrooms. Schools with-out students have no teachers.

The benign nun in a brown habit and a coarse black shawl said Fiza had left with everyone else when the school closed in the first week of December. No, she did not know where she had gone. Yes, she would be back with the rest in the last week of January. And I was her . . .

I was her avenging angel from hell . . .

The great writer chinchpokli. Chaser of dreams. Fornicator of phantoms. New tracker of the path between reason and unreason. From the land of first things.

I wrote a note, put it in an envelope borrowed from the nun and sealed it.

Sister Graca, so fair of skin and kind of eye, deliver my hopes gently unto her, and may your lord adrift on the cross keep her in good stead.

By late afternoon I was back in Chandigarh. My rotten back tooth – wide open like a crater – had set up such an ache that I could barely open my eyes or speak. There was a dentist across from the bus-stand and he poured in some anaesthetic and fixed me a semi-permanent plug. I had to sit in his anteroom for half an hour for the throb to abate. Then I swallowed a Combiflam and took a rickshaw to that old grey house in Sector 35. The city appeared to have shrunk dramatically since we had loved here nearly twenty years before. Those distances we had walked endlessly seemed quite short now; the lines of trees had been pushed into the background by the bustle of traffic; the cycles driven out by motorbikes and cars.

My memory of the roads was of silence and conversation. Now there was a continual clamour of engines and horns. I thought: no longer can you walk and find love here.

The short-cuts to her house – through vacant lots – which Miler and I had rattled over every week were all gone. The sector had been built up from corner to corner. But the house was unchanged. Same slatted black-iron gate, low grey wall and the bottlebrush drooping low in punishment. The hanky garden – where we would sometimes sit – was in good shape, freshy mown, and the hibiscus bush in the further corner was in trim. I had no bicycle to lean against the wall, and some instinct told me to make the rickshaw wait.

A young woman opened the wooden door, but left the mesh one closed. This was not 1979. It was 1999 and fear was our dominant emotion. India had uncorked all its ghosts – so many of them once cunningly bottled up by the great fakir – and they were running around scaring us witless. Rule by lunacy was our fate, and we were hurtling towards it, with just a mesh door in between.

It took me several minutes to tell her who I was. The aunt was dead. She was her granddaughter-in-law and had heard of me. It was clear she would have liked to see a certificate of identification, but I suppose you don't ask that even of weird relatives who chase the dead in the middle of the night on high mountains.

Inside the Grundig was gone; a big red fridge had eaten up the small white one; the furniture was all plush sofas and glass tables; and instead of the mountainscape there now hung big blown-up pictures of a drooling baby.

Standing uncertainly near the dining table, she offered me tea, but I wanted to go to the bathroom. The one with two doors. It was no longer the white refuge we had so often sought. The tiles, the pot, the sink had all been changed to various shades of green. The mirror above the sink had grown to six times its size.

I looked into it and I could not see the boy I had once been.

I had grown old.

My flowing beard had uneven splashes of grey, and my ponytail hung on lines of silver. In the big army parka I looked like a weary soldier returning home from battle. I looked into my own eyes and I began to cry.

I had not done so since my childhood, and I cried and cried and cried till there was nothing left inside of me.

No love, no longing, no memory, no desire.

🌿

Delhi, Hapur, Garhmukteshwar, Gajraula, Moradabad, Rampur, Bilaspur, Rudrapur, Haldwani, Kathgodam, Jeolikote, Gethia. The magic mantra of our lives. I drove slowly, in a daze, and was glad to gain the mountains. Even though the Nainital road was busy with holiday traffic, I felt a wave of peace break over me the moment the Gypsy began to climb. As I took the fork at Number One, I was seized by the sudden conviction that I would find her up there waiting for me. A crazy happiness filled me and I raced over the old Beerbhatti bridge, past the iron udders of the concrete cow outside the ashram, past the bank of ageing silver oaks at the foot of the sanatorium, took the bend in the road and was home.

Is she here? I asked Prakash, who was shutting the gate behind me.

Who? he said.

Behind him stood Rakshas, the keeper of dark secrets.

I had been away only for a few months, but it seemed to me as if I was returning after a long time. Fizz's saplings seemed to have grown bigger; the house appeared in a worse state of decay than before; the diminishing heaps of sand and gravel had vanished altogether. I gave Rakshas the blue suede jacket I had bought for him and told him it had been sent by his half-sister.

He said, Does she have her parents' good looks?

I said, Yes, she does.

That night I sat out on the terrace way past midnight, drinking whisky and watching the road. It was a clear night and you could see the lights sharp across the entire valley. There were more stars in the sky than ever before.

Can you count them, sir?

Yes, three million two hundred and seventy thousand seven hundred and thirty-three.

Bingo! She's yours. Delivered home, as last seen and chosen.

I played a game, guessing at every vehicle moving up towards us from Jeolikote. Was she in this one? Or this one? The engine roar would peak under me, then vanish around the spur, to reappear a few minutes later behind me, then die in the distance of the padao. My tooth had begun to throb again and I was determined to kill the pain with whisky.

The nightjar began speaking to the night in its Morse code. As the hours wore on and the whisky bottle was drained, its voice grew louder and louder, becoming like the beat of the drum of the universe.

Toc. Toc. Toc.

Soon it was hammering my head open, and I wanted to jump

down into the armpit of the terrace below, reach under the lantana bush and wring its toc-ing neck.

Prakash woke me in the morning late, with eggs and tea. I was a little groggy from the whisky and had no memory of when I had come in. I pulled my hair into a rubber band and went out. The sun was blinding. I had to step back into the doorway in a wave of nausea. The sky was high and pale blue.

My tooth was still throbbing.

After a hot bath I went down to the lower terrace and sat on the redstone bench under Trishul. It was cold there in the shade. Bagheera sat just outside the line of the shadows, drinking in the sun. I noticed Shiva's grand sentinel – Carpetsahib's sapling – was ageing too. Several branches on its windward side had fallen, others were looking fragile, and its skin was acquiring the scaly pallor of the decrepit. From below, the house too looked old, its glassless windows the sightless eyes of the infirm, its fading red roof the tacky bonnet of a crone.

Jectionmichael came up from the lower gate, carrying a small pink plastic box. He was a good-looking man, with neatly cut hair and moustache, the spry step of an army officer, the warm smile of a peasant. I could see his patients being grateful for him. BannoMary–RamAasrePeter's seed had flowered well. He was bringing me Christmas rum cake.

He said, How do you do, sir? If I may say so, you don't look too good.

I said, I am OK, Michael. Just too many late nights. How's Stephen?

He said, Recovering from Christmas, sir. My father, you know, sir, is always recovering from Christmas.

He picked up my wrist and began to take my pulse. Then he put the back of his hand against my throat.

I said, Michael, I have a toothache.

He said, Sir, you are not well. You need an injection.

I said, Michael, do you have one for profound misery?

He said, Excuse me, sir?

I said, Michael, just do it. But after that you have to show me the grave of the madam.

I had failed to find it among the pines and oaks on the spur because it was hidden in a collapsing tin shed behind Taphen's house, next to the booze pit he was steadily filling up. When Jectionmichael pushed open the rotting door, there was a panic of scurrying inside. The only light came from tears in the tin. There was no window. We lifted the sagging door and opened it fully, letting in a big square of sun. We moved the chopped and plucked firewood aside, and there was only one flat marble slab left. The son said his father had vandalized the rest of the gravestones and sold them. I went outside, filled up an old can with water several times, and poured it over the slab till all the dust and dirt had been washed away.

In a thick black Gothic type, busy with curlicues, was engraved:

> Who can ever hold the essence of fire?
> Who can ever know the alchemy of desire?

Below it was written:

> Catherine of Gethia, wife of Syed, daughter of John.
> Died 1942.

Its flower has the shape of a bell, a beautiful purple or white bell, and like all great plants it is akin to men: blessed of many moods, capable in equal measure of good and evil.

It gives of its leaves and it gives of its seeds.

You can smoke it in a chillum; you can mix it in a dish; you can stir it in tea.

When it smiles on men, it mends ulcers of skin, peeping haemorrhoids, bouts of rheumatism, gasps of asthma, nasty bruises and wounds, and anaesthetizes the setting of broken bones.

When it scowls on men, it makes their pulses race, parches their throats, dilates their pupils, twitches their muscles, flushes their faces, turns their stomachs to water, and casts them into depression and nervousness. It makes them 'dry as a bone, red as a beet, mad as a wet hen and hot as a hare'.

When it plays games with men, it makes them hallucinate and dream, it makes them forget and forgive, it makes them sway and smile, it makes them transcend and foretell, it makes them engorge and fornicate.

Robbers use it.

Killers use it.

Doctors use it.

Witches use it.

Lovers use it.

Its heady smoke fuelled the Oracle of Delphi.

Avicenna attested to its Janus face in the eleventh century.

It was worshipped in China as a favoured of the Buddha.

In the East Indies it was the precipitate arouser.

In India it was known before the recording of history.

It is all things to all men, and it grows all the year around.

Merrily by the roadside, to be plucked for free.

It comes from the deadly nightshade clan of Solanaceae. Its bloodline is scopolamine.

Some call it Jimson weed. Some call it thorn apple. Some call it the devil's trumpet. Some call it mad apple.

But in India, in the mountains, everyone calls it dhatura.

It grows by the roadside. Merrily.

To be plucked for free.

The next few days the throb in my tooth became a sonic boom. I gobbled Combiflams and drank dark glasses of whisky but failed to drown it. At night I would sit out on the terrace till the alcohol had wiped me out, all pain, all thoughts, everything. Each night I counted the stars, precise to the last, but she didn't come.

Rakshas hovered in the background, and carried me back in the hours before dawn, slumped in his one arm.

Wonderfully I was no longer plagued by dreams. No one came to seduce me, claim me, threaten me. Each morning I woke weak with whisky and toothache, Prakash bringing me eggs and tea.

By the fourth day I could not bear the pain any more. I took Rakshas in the Gypsy and drove down to Haldwani, taking the curves slowly, dizzy with the throb. Haldwani was in a chaos with everyone on the road driving and walking in every direction. Rakshas had to lean out the window and shout continual abuse to help us make our way. On the first floor of a new but crumbling shopping complex, in the middle of a spare, cavernous room, sat a rusty dental chair. The dentist wore rubber slippers under his loose Terrycot trousers, but took less than a moment to dig in his harpoon and fish out the plug from my back tooth. Almost immediately a wave of relief poured over me. It was the bottled-up pressure he said that had been creating the trouble, inflaming the nerve. He washed the crater with antiseptic and put in a small cotton ball.

He said, At times you need to leave wounds open.

Going back, all the way up, we passed cars speeding towards Nainital, blaring celebratory music. In some places they were parked on the verge and young men – and sometimes women too – were drinking from beer bottles, their faces alive with excitement and happiness, their voices loud.

The air was cold, pricking the skin.

Halfway up I saw Fizz's huge rock with the peepul tree growing out of it, the roots clamped around it like a leg spinner's fingers.

Love moves mountains. Can I move this one for you?

Take it up to our garden, ma'am. Plant it there as a monument.

By the time we reached home the ache in my tooth was completely gone. But by nightfall I was not entirely happy about that. Now I had to think of other things and there was nothing for me to think about.

I went up to the terrace early and began to drink. It was the hour of last light and the road ribbons were humming with traffic. Engine sounds, waxing and waning, filled the valley. As I sat there, the day died and the lights began to come on in Jeolikote below me and in Nainital above. Soon the mountain slopes were advertising the spread of their occupants. The sky was high and full of stars and I knew their number.

In a while the nightjar would start its argument with me, and I would wonder what was keeping me from going down and strangling it.

For some unknown reason I thought of my mother, as the young girl in the school photograph, pigtails flying, bangles flashing, and was filled with sorrow. As I kept thinking of it, the girl in the picture became Fizz.

I drank and counted the stars some more.

First things.

Before love, before desire, before Fizz.

At nine Prakash came up to take Bagheera in and to ask me about dinner. I had been drinking for more than four hours already. I told him to make three rotis and leave them in the hot case.

Just then the nightjar made its opening pitch. Toc.

An hour later Rakshas came up the back stairs – the same ones his father had climbed every night seventy years before to a murmur of tin and his waiting lover – and said to me, There was a call at the thakur's shop just now. She said she is fine and she'll be here in a few days.

I woke early next morning, before the sun was out, and I was light as a feather.

The valley lay at my feet, painted with dew and completely silent.

A few grey lines of smoke were beginning to climb the air.

It was the last day of the millennium, 31 December 1999.

Emily's apocalypse would not come. We would have to keep looking for gentler salvations.

I took the Brother out of the wooden cupboard, peeled off its hard black carapace and wiped its red body. I took it down to the unfinished study and set it on the window ledge of golden Jaisalmer stone. When I sat in front of it, its floating black keys were reaching out for my fingers.

I knew now there was no such thing as a biblioblackhole.

Everything written truly lived forever.

Every real word. Every real story.

You had to find your words. You had to find your story.

Not the Pandit's story, not Pratap's story, not Abhay's story.

Not the story of the young Sikh and his beloved horse.

Your story.

And you had to live it. And when you had lived it, you wrote it.

No better or worse than you could write it.

As the keys reached out for my trembling fingers, I felt myself stir. After a very long time I felt desire fill my root and make it big.

The white-cheeked bulbuls began to move the oaks.

The first eagle of the day launched itself across the vastness of the valley, floating on nothing but self-belief.

I rolled a sheet of paper through the smooth platen of the Brother, put the quivering tips of my fingers on the shining black keys, and began to hammer. The clacks rang out like rifle shots.

Sex is not the greatest glue between two people. Love . . .

# *Acknowledgements*

A small army of people helped us survive the years in which this book was written, as we faced a savage and relentless assault by the government for *Tehelka*'s exposés of corruption. Many of these were friends and family, others complete strangers, a legion of lawyers among them. None of them had anything to do with the writing of this book; but all of them, in different ways, kept the writer going.

Neena and Minty, before anyone else, a reminder of first things.

Tiya and Cara, above everyone else, the promise of all things.

The intimates, who doled out emotion, money, laughter: Sanjoy and Puneeta, Shoma and Aditya, Nicku and Mike, Amit and Peali; Manika, Gayatri and Yamini; Satya Sheel, Rajdeep and Sagarika, Shobha and Govind, Patrick and Abe, Bilu and Roma, Rajeev, Smita, Bindu, Geena, Rahul, Annu, Padma, Farrukh, Sunil Khilnani, Marina, Anoop, Sudhir, Bish, Aniruddha, Charu, Philip George, Kabir Chawla, Mala and Tejbir, Renu and Pavan, Nandini and Sumir, Bani and Niki, Amrit, Ashok, Bina, Shankar and Devina; Karan, Kabir; Gunjan, Chottu, Deepak; Adarsh and Krishan.

Vidia and Nadira, deep inspiration and deeper reassurance.

The public warriors, who stood up to be counted: Ram Jethmalani, Kapil Sibal, Prashant and Shanti Bhushan, Arundhati Roy and Pradip Krishen, Mahesh Bhatt, Alyque Padamsee, Tony and Rani Jethmalani, Vikram Lal, Anu Aga, Khushwant Singh, Vir Sanghvi, Shobhaa De, Manish Tewari, Meet

Malhotra, Uma Shankar, Kavin Gulati, Siddharth Luthra, Rajeev Dhawan, K.T.S. Tulsi, Madhu Kishwar; Rajiv, Ranjan, Porus and Prabha of Erewhon; Mark Tully, Rajeev Sethi, Kuldip Nayar, Madanjeet Singh, Shireen Paul, Niranjan Tolia, H.S. Vedi, Shahnaz and Carl Pope, Dushyant Dave, Malvika Sanghhvi, Dilip Cherian, Seema Mustafa, Nari Hira, Swami Agnivesh.

The thousands of Indians, eminent and ordinary, who wrote up cheques to advance subscribe to a will-o'-the-wisp paper, an unprecedented act of collective media idealism; and Raj-Priyanka and Taizoon-Fatima who then picked up the baton.

My outstanding colleagues at *Tehelka* who against all odds produce a paper we can be continually proud of: Sankarshan, Shoma, Shammy, Amit, Shobhan, and all the others, including Rajnish, Neena and the business boys. Also Brij, Prawal, Arnab, Kumar, Shashi, Mathew and Anand, who survived the devastation of our first battles.

And finally, the book people: Nandita Aggarwal and Andrew Kidd for their brilliant editorial eye; Gillon Aitken and Ashok Chopra for their sharp steering instinct; Liz Cowen and Vatsala Kaul for the fine proofing hand; Winnie Bedi for a roof under which it could be done.